Ab

Aliette de Bodard

This special
signed edition
is limited to
1250
numbered copies.

This is copy __701__.

Of
Wars,
and
Memories,
and
Starlight

Of
Wars,
and
Memories,
and
Starlight

Aliette de Bodard

Subterranean Press 2019

First Edition

ISBN
978-1-59606-952-7

See page 381 for individual story credits.

Subterranean Press
PO Box 190106
Burton, MI 48519

subterraneanpress.com

Manufactured in the United States of America.

Table of Contents

Introduction

I GREW UP IN THE WAKE OF A WAR.

As a child, I always assumed that everyone had one of these in their background. Not the ones I saw in movies, but an emptiness that adults danced around: no battles or stirring feats of heroism, but simply topics that weren't discussed—things that trailed off with a gaze in the direction of us children.

I grew up with loss, and a sense of the world that was and that would never be again: with my mother painstakingly keeping the shell combs she'd taken out of Saigon, using them as pieces of them wore off—first the handle, then the teeth—running the thin iridescent remnants of them through her hair long after they stopped being useful to untangle much of anything. I grew up with the stories of that faraway city—with markets and swimming pools and papaya trees, with people who had made it out and people who hadn't. It seemed to be as natural as breathing.

I can't remember exactly when I realised that my experience wasn't everyone else's. I can remember growing up non-white in a neighbourhood that was majority white and conservative—other children mocking me for being mixed or being Asian, that elusive sense of not fitting in that would chase me my entire childhood, a nagging feeling of not being right I mistakenly attributed to being good in class.

I remember I used to sit in front of the teacher's desk—and that one day I saw someone had carved "alien" at eye level—and that I knew instinctively, with no possibility of doubt, that this had been meant for me. I remember a priest who, when he saw me, said "where in creation have you come from?" in a tone that made it clear people like me shouldn't be here, shouldn't occupy such spaces.

When I found science fiction, it was like coming up for air. It was worlds that were not this one; the wonders of space and faraway history, where a farmboy could rise to become king; where ordinary people could stop evil in its track; and where science was a force for good, and the future had everyone equal without questions of creed and race. It was entire universes where I could hope to finally fit in.

There were a few...wrong notes, though. I couldn't help but notice that Tolkien's heroes were basically Europeans; and that the Easterlings—yellow-skinned or swarthy—seemed to be mostly fighting on the side of evil. I couldn't help but notice that most of the cool things in the future seemed to be happening to men; and that, for all the talk about appearances not mattering, most women seemed to need to be blonde, and young, and beautiful; the dark-haired, yellow-skinned ones mostly seemed to be left by the wayside or to be antagonists.

Most books had silent women, or women who used their looks as a weapon. There were no female friendships. There were no mothers, no families. People drank coffee and spoke English, and most of them were blond and pale-skinned. When someone who did look or sound familiar appeared; when someone seemed like they were going to respect their ancestors and value their families—they were the aliens. They were the funny guys with odd customs colonists met, the ones they tried to commerce with or understand or (in the worst cases) subjugate. They were the invaders that had to be fought back for the sake of civilisation.

I couldn't help but notice that, for all the talk of escapism, the universes depicted by science fiction and fantasy were exactly the same as the one I'd hoped to leave behind—the one where I didn't fit in, where people reminded me in a thousand different ways that I was the wrong skin colour, the wrong gender, the wrong person altogether.

There were a lot of books in my reading that featured China, or some representation of the Far East—I read them all like I read invented worlds, because the China they depicted was so out of touch with my family stories (which are convoluted and complicated, like the relationship Vietnam has with China)—surely they had to be about some kind of fictional China/ Far East that didn't exist. They spoke of martial arts and inscrutable, passive people awaiting to be saved; of some fount of mystical wisdom that awaited the traveller. I thought fake!China must be some kind of faraway land invented by writers, because it could not possibly be the real thing.

As I read, voraciously, it seemed natural to fall into writing: first as a game and then as something more serious. Not writing soon felt like not breathing. I learnt the bases of a story, of a novel, of character and plot. But, as I produced story after story, I still shied away from Vietnam, or from my experience of war. Neither of these seemed appropriate for stories, I told myself. Science Fiction and Fantasy must surely be about other, worthier things. There is nothing about loss, or grief, of emptiness, worth telling. I circled Vietnam from afar: "The Shipmaker" is set in a Chinese galactic empire, and it's only its two main characters that are of Vietnamese descent. I made up elaborate non-western universes, or retold the Chinese fairytales I'd obsessively read as a child—because these were all the ones I could find access to. I wrote about Aztec/Mexica people in space, drew from Ancient India and Ancient China, retold the French myths I'd been taught at school.

Long after I've penned my first published story, I'm speaking with a good friend, talking about our own cultures and how others can get them profoundly wrong—I think how the last story set in Vietnam I read was set during the Vietnamese/American war and featured a dryad captured by soldiers, glibly erasing the rich Vietnamese myths to replace them by bowdlerized Classical Western myths. I tell my friend that she has to write what rings true to her, and that if she doesn't do it—if she doesn't write the stories of her own people, then who will?

I hang up the phone, and stare at the wall for a while, wondering why I'm not doing this. Wondering what I'm afraid of. I say it aloud: I'm terrified that I'll get it wrong. That my family will see it—that I will be judged for it just as I've been judged all my childhood. I think of the heroes in the books I read—the ones who go down in the dark to face monsters, because it's the right thing to do. I think of stories and who gets to tell them, and of what gets written into history—of how tired I am to not see myself in the stories I read.

I write a story about war, and language, and loss—about people fleeing a space station at war, and their descendants painfully meeting the descendants of those who remained behind—about the gap between generations, and how stories will always be incomplete and fragmentary. My husband reads it while I fight the urge to dive under the bed. "Send it somewhere prestigious," he says, finally. "The top of the list. It's worth it." The story is "Scattered Along the River of Heaven": it's my first sale to *Clarkesworld Magazine*, followed by "Immersion", which goes on to be nominated for most of the major awards, and to win a Nebula and a Locus.

I go to conventions and I meet other writers, other readers. As I leave the white-dominated world of my childhood and early adult years behind, I gradually realise that I'm not the only one of Asian descent, not the only non-white person. I hear the word "person of colour." I hear the word "diaspora" and understand that not only does it encompass my own experiences, but also that its very existence means that I'm not alone in those experiences. That there are enough of us to make the word worth uttering. To give it meaning and heft. I understand that it matters all the more that I write my own stories. This is not only for the sake of my child self, but it is for the sake of others. Every story I write is one more quiet statement that our own stories are worth telling, my own contribution to make space at the table for people like me—those who so seldom had a chance to see themselves in stories.

The fourteen stories in this collection are the result of this. Some of them are the 19th Century classics I grew up with, rewritten to include the queer people and people of colour that were absent from their originals. Some of them are set in Xuya, a galactic empire that draws from Vietnamese culture and my own knowledge of science and artificial intelligence—where simulations of ancestors and their attendant knowledge are passed down as prized heirlooms, where sentient starships are family rather than things—where war is a large maw of emptiness and loss that resonates down generations. Some are about magic and loss and sacrifice, and what it means to rebuild; some are about history and memory and who gets passed down to children.

These are my stories, and they matter.

With many thanks to Kate Elliott and Likhain for comments on this

The Shipmaker

SHIPS WERE LIVING, BREATHING BEINGS. DAC KIEN HAD KNOWN THIS, even before she'd reached the engineering habitat—even before she'd seen the great mass in orbit outside, being slowly assembled by the bots.

Her ancestors had once carved jade, in the bygone days of the Le dynasty on Old Earth: not hacking the green blocks into the shape they wanted, but rather whittling down the stone until its true nature was revealed. And as with jade, so with ships. The sections outside couldn't be forced together. They had to flow into a seamless whole—to be, in the end, inhabited by a Mind who was as much a part of the ship as every rivet and every seal.

The Easterners or the Mexica didn't understand. They spoke of recycling, of design efficiency: they saw only the parts taken from previous ships, and assumed it was done to save money and time. They didn't understand why Dac Kien's work as Grand Master of Design Harmony was the most important on the habitat: the ship, once made, would be one entity, and not a patchwork of ten thousand others. To Dac Kien—and to the one who would come after her, the Mind-bearer—fell the honour of helping the ship into being, of transforming metal and cables and solar cells into an entity that would sail the void between the stars.

The door slid open. Dac Kien barely looked up. The light tread of the feet told her this was one of the lead designers, either Miahua or Feng.

Neither would have disturbed her without cause. With a sigh, she disconnected from the system with a flick of her hands, and waited for the design's overlay on her vision to disappear.

"Your Excellency." Miahua's voice was quiet: the Xuyan held herself upright, her skin as pale as yellowed wax. "The shuttle has come back. There's someone on board you should see."

DAC KIEN had expected many things: a classmate from the examinations on a courtesy visit; an Imperial Censor from Dongjing, calling her to some other posting, even further away from the capital; or perhaps even someone from her family, mother or sister or uncle's wife, here to remind her of the unsuitability of her life choices.

She hadn't expected a stranger: a woman with brown skin, almost dark enough to be Viet herself—her lips thin and white, her eyes as round as the moon.

A Mexica. A foreigner—Dac Kien stopped the thought before it could go far. For the woman wore no cotton, no feathers, but the silk robes of a Xuyan housewife, and the five wedding gifts (all pure gold, from necklace to bracelets) shone like stars on the darkness of her skin.

Dac Kien's gaze travelled down to the curve of the woman's belly: a protruding bulge so voluminous that it threw her whole silhouette out of balance. "I greet you, younger sister. I am Dac Kien, Grand Master of Design Harmony for this habitat." She used the formal tone, suitable for addressing a stranger.

"Elder sister." The Mexica's eyes were bloodshot, set deep within the heavy face. "I am—" She grimaced, one hand going to her belly as if to tear it out. "Zoquitl," she whispered at last, the accents of her voice slipping back to the harsh patterns of her native tongue. "My name is Zoquitl." Her eyes started to roll upwards; she went on, taking on the cadences of something learnt by rote. "I am the womb and the resting place, the quickener and the Mind-bearer."

Dac Kien's stomach roiled, as if an icy fist were squeezing it. "You're early. The ship—"

"The ship has to be ready."

The interjection surprised her. All her attention had been focused on the Mexica—Zoquitl—and what her coming here meant. Now she forced herself to look at the other passenger of the shuttle: a Xuyan man in his mid-thirties. His accent was that of Anjiu province, on the Fifth Planet; his robes, with the partridge badge and the button of gold, were those of a minor official of the seventh rank—but they were marked with the yin-yang symbol, showing stark black-and white against the silk.

"You're the birth-master," she said.

He bowed. "I have that honour." His face was harsh, all angles and planes on which the light caught—highlighting, here and there, the thin lips, the high cheekbones. "Forgive me my abruptness, but there is no time to lose."

"I don't understand—" Dac Kien looked again at the woman, whose eyes bore a glazed look of pain. "She's early," she said, flatly, and she wasn't speaking of their arrival time.

The birth-master nodded.

"How long?"

"A week, at most." The birth-master grimaced. "The ship has to be ready."

Dac Kien tasted bile in her mouth. The ship was all but made—and, like a jade statue, it would brook no corrections nor oversights. Dac Kien and her team had designed it specifically for the Mind within Zoquitl's womb: starting out from the specifications the imperial alchemists had given them, the delicate balance of humours, optics and flesh that made up the being Zoquitl carried. The ship would answer to nothing else: only Zoquitl's Mind would be able to seize the heartroom, to quicken the ship, and take it into deep planes, where fast star-travel was possible.

"I can't—" Dac Kien started, but the birth-master shook his head, and she didn't need to hear his answer to know what he would say.

She had to. This had been the posting she'd argued for, after she came in second at the state examinations—this, not a magistrate's tribunal and district, not a high-placed situation in the palace's administration, not the prestigious Courtyard of Writing Brushes, as would have been her right. This was what the imperial court would judge her on.

She wouldn't get another chance.

"A WEEK." Hanh shook her head. "What do they think you are, a Mexica factory overseer?"

"Hanh." It had been a long day, and Dac Kien had come back to their quarters looking for comfort. In hindsight, she should have known how Hanh would take the news: her partner was an artist, a poet, always seeking the right word and the right allusion—ideally suited to understanding the delicacy that went into the design of a ship, less than ideal to acknowledge any need for urgency.

"I have to do this," Dac Kien said.

Hanh grimaced. "Because they're pressuring you into it? You know what it will look like." She gestured towards the low mahogany table in the centre of the room. The ship's design hung inside a translucent cube, gently rotating—the glimpses of its interior interspersed with views of other ships, the ones from which it had taken its inspiration: all the greats from *The Red Carp* to *The Golden Mountain* and *The Snow-White Blossom*. Their hulls gleamed in the darkness, slowly and subtly bending out of shape to become the final structure of the ship hanging outside the habitat. "It's a whole, lil' sis. You can't butcher it and hope to keep your reputation intact."

"She could die of it," Dac Kien said, at last. "Of the birth, and it would be worse if she did it for nothing."

"The girl? She's *gui*. Foreign."

Meaning she shouldn't matter. "So were we, once upon a time." Dac Kien said. "You have short memories."

Hanh opened her mouth, closed it. She could have pointed out that they weren't quite outsiders—that China, Xuya's motherland, had once held Dai Viet for centuries; but Hanh was proud of being Viet, and certainly not about to mention such shameful details. "It's the girl that's bothering you, then?"

"She does what she wants," Dac Kien said.

"For the prize." Hanh's voice was faintly contemptuous. Most of the girls who bore Minds were young and desperate, willing to face the dangers of the pregnancy in exchange for a marriage to a respected official. For a status of their own, a family that would welcome them in; and a chance to bear children of good birth.

Both Hanh and Dac Kien had made the opposite choice, long ago. For them, as for every Xuyan who engaged in same-gender relationships, there would be no children: no one to light incense at the ancestral altars, no voices to chant and honour their names after they were gone. Through life, they would be second-class citizens, consistently failing to accomplish their duties to their ancestors; in death, they would be spurned, forgotten—gone as if they had never been.

"I don't know," Dac Kien said. "She's Mexica. They see things differently, where she comes from."

"From what you're telling me, she's doing this for Xuyan reasons."

For fame, and for children; all that Hanh despised—what she called their shackles, their overwhelming need to produce children, generation after generation.

Dac Kien bit her lip, wishing she could have Hanh's unwavering certainties. "It's not as if I have much choice in the matter."

Hanh was silent for a while. At length, she moved, came to rest behind Dac Kien, her hair falling down over Dac Kien's shoulders, her hands trailing at Dac Kien's nape. "You're the one who keeps telling me we always have a choice, lil' sis."

Dac Kien shook her head. She said that—when weary of her family's repeated reminders that she should marry and have children; when they lay in the darkness side by side after making love and she saw the future stretching in front of her, childless and ringed by old prejudices.

Hanh, much as she tried, didn't understand. She'd always wanted to be a scholar, had always known that she'd grow up to love another woman. She'd always got what she wanted—and she was convinced she only had to wish for something hard enough for it to happen.

And Hanh had never wished, and would never wish for children.

"It's not the same," Dac Kien said at last, cautiously submitting to Hanh's caresses. It was something else entirely; and even Hanh had to see that. "I chose to come here. I chose to make my name that way. And we always have to see our choices through."

Hanh's hands on her shoulders tightened. "You're one to talk. I can see you wasting yourself in regrets, wondering if there's still time to turn back to respectability. But you chose me. This life, these consequences. We both chose."

"Hanh—" It's not that, Dac Kien wanted to say. She loved Hanh, she truly did; but… She was a stone thrown in the darkness; a ship adrift without nav—lost, without family or husband to approve of her actions, and without the comfort of a child destined to survive her.

"Grow up, lil' sis." Hanh's voice was harsh; her face turned away, towards the paintings of landscapes on the wall. "You're no one's toy or slave—and especially not your family's."

Because they had all but disowned her. But words, as usual, failed Dac Kien; and they went to bed with the shadow of the old argument still between them, like the blade of a sword.

THE NEXT day, Dac Kien pored over the design of the ship with Feng and Miahua, wondering how she could modify it. The parts were complete, and assembling them would take a few days at most; but the resulting structure would never be a ship. That much was clear to all of them. Even excepting the tests, there was at least a month's work ahead of them—slow and subtle touches laid by the bots over the overall system to align it with its destined Mind.

Dac Kien had taken the cube from her quarters, and brought it into her office under Hanh's glowering gaze. Now, they all crowded around it voicing ideas, the cups of tea forgotten in the intensity of the moment.

Feng's wrinkled face was creased in thought as he tapped one side of the cube. "We could modify the shape of this corridor, here. Wood would run through the whole ship, and—"

Miahua shook her head. She was their Master of Wind and Water, the one who could best read the lines of influence, the one Dac Kien turned to when she herself had a doubt over the layout. Feng was Commissioner of Supplies, managing the systems and safety—in many ways Miahua's opposite, given to small adjustments rather than large ones, pragmatic where she verged on the mystical.

"The humours of water and wood would stagnate here, in the control room." Miahua pursed her lips, pointed to the slender aft of the ship. "The shape of this section should be modified."

Feng sucked in a breath. "That's not trivial. For my team to rewrite the electronics—"

Dac Kien listened to them arguing, distantly—intervening with a question from time to time, to keep the conversation from dying down. In her mind, she held the shape of the ship, felt it breathe through the glass of the cube, through the layers of fibres and metal that separated her from the structure outside. She held the shape of the Mind—the essences and emotions that made it, the layout of its sockets and cables, of its muscles and flesh—and slid them together gently, softly until they seemed made for one another.

She looked up. Both Feng and Miahua had fallen silent, waiting for her to speak.

"This way," she said. "Remove this section altogether, and shift the rest of the layout." As she spoke, she reached into the glass matrix, and carefully excised the offending section—rerouting corridors and lengths of cables, burning new decorative calligraphy onto the curved walls.

"I don't think—" Feng said; and stopped. "Miahua?"

Miahua was watching the new design, carefully. "I need to think about it, Your Excellency. Let me discuss it with my subordinates."

Dac Kien made a gesture of approval. "Remember that we don't have much time."

They both took a copy of the design with them, snug in their long sleeves. Left alone, Dac Kien stared at the ship again. It was squat, its proportions out of kilter—not even close to what she had imagined, not even true to the spirit of her work: a mockery of the original design, like a flower without petals, or a poem that didn't quite gel, hovering on the edge of poignant allusions but never expressing them properly.

"We don't always have a choice," she whispered. She'd have prayed to her ancestors, had she thought they were still listening. Perhaps they were. Perhaps the shame of having a daughter who would have no descendants was erased by the exalted heights of her position. Or perhaps not. Her mother and grandmother were unforgiving; what made her think that those more removed ancestors would understand her decision?

"Elder sister?"

Zoquitl stood at the door, hovering uncertainly. Dac Kien's face must have revealed more than she thought. She forced herself to breathe, relaxing all her muscles until it was once more the blank mask required by protocol. "Younger sister," she said. "You honour me by your presence."

Zoquitl shook her head. She slid carefully into the room—one foot after the other, careful never to lose her balance. "I wanted to see the ship."

The birth-master was nowhere to be seen. Dac Kien hoped that he had been right about the birth—that it wasn't about to happen now, in her office, with no destination and no assistance. "It's here." She shifted positions on her chair, invited Zoquitl to sit.

Zoquitl wedged herself in one of the seats, her movements fragile, measured—as if any wrong gesture would shatter her. Behind her loomed one of Dac Kien's favourite paintings, an image from the Third Planet: a delicate, peaceful landscape of waterfalls and ochre cliffs, with the distant light of stars reflected in the water.

Zoquitl didn't move as Dac Kien showed her the design; her eyes were the only thing which seemed alive in the whole of her face.

When Dac Kien was finished, the burning gaze was transferred to her—looking straight into her eyes, a clear breach of protocol. "You're just like the others. You don't approve," Zoquitl said.

It took Dac Kien a moment to process the words, but they still meant nothing to her. "I don't understand."

Zoquitl's lips pursed. "Where I come from, it's an honour. To bear Minds for the glory of the Mexica Dominion."

"But you're here," Dac Kien said. In Xuya, among Xuyans, where to bear Minds was a sacrifice—necessary and paid for, but ill-considered. For who would want to endure a pregnancy, yet produce no human child? Only the desperate or the greedy.

"You're here as well." Zoquitl's voice was almost an accusation.

For an endless, agonising moment, Dac Kien thought Zoquitl was referring to her life choices—how did she know about Hanh, about her family's stance? Then she understood that Zoquitl had been talking about her place onboard the habitat. "I like being in space," Dac Kien said, at last, and it wasn't a lie. "Being here almost alone, away from everyone else."

And this wasn't paperwork, or the slow drain of catching and prosecuting law-breakers, of keeping Heaven's order on some remote planet. This—this was everything scholarship was meant to be: taking all that the past had given them, and reshaping it into greatness—every part throwing its neighbours into sharper relief, an eternal reminder of how history had brought them here and how it would carry them forward, again and again.

At last, Zoquitl said, not looking at the ship anymore, "Xuya is a harsh place, for foreigners. The language isn't so bad, but when you have no money, and no sponsor..." She breathed in, quick and sharp. "I do what needs doing." Her hand went, unconsciously, to the mound of her belly, and stroked it. "And I give him life. How can you not value this?"

She used the animate pronoun, without a second thought.

Dac Kien shivered. "He's—" she paused, groping for words. "He has no father. A mother, perhaps, but there isn't much of you inside him. He won't be counted among your descendants. He won't burn incense on your altar, or chant your name among the stars."

"But he won't die." Zoquitl's voice was soft, and cutting. "Not for centuries."

The ships made by the Mexica Dominion lived long, but their Minds slowly went insane from repeated journeys into deep planes. This Mind, with a proper anchor, a properly aligned ship—Zoquitl was right: he would remain as he was, long after she and Zoquitl were both dead. He—no, it—it was a machine—a sophisticated intelligence, an assembly of flesh and metal and Heaven knew what else. Borne like a child, but still...

"I think I'm the one who doesn't understand." Zoquitl pulled herself to her feet, slowly. Dac Kien could hear her laboured breath, could smell the sour, sharp sweat rolling off her. "Thank you, elder sister."

And then she was gone; but her words remained.

DAC KIEN threw herself into her work—as she had done before, when preparing for the state examinations. Hahn pointedly ignored her when she came home, making only the barest attempts at courtesy. She was working again on her calligraphy, mingling Xuyan characters with the letters of the Viet alphabet to create a work that spoke both as a poem and as a painting. It wasn't unusual: Dac Kien had come to be accepted for her talent, but her partner was another matter. Hanh wasn't welcome in the banquet room, where the families of the other engineers would congregate in the evenings—she preferred to remain alone in their quarters, rather than endure the barely concealed snubs or the pitying looks of the others.

What gave the air its leaden weight, though, was her silence. Dac Kien tried at first—keeping up a chatter, as if nothing were wrong. Hanh raised bleary eyes from her manuscript, and said, simply, "You know what you're doing, lil' sis. Live with it, for once."

So it was silence, in the end. It suited her better than she'd thought it would. It was her and the design, with no one to blame or interfere.

Miahua's team and Feng's team were rewiring the structure and re-arranging the parts. Outside the window, the mass of the hull shifted and twisted, to align itself with the cube on her table—bi-hour after bi-hour, as the bots gently slid sections into place and sealed them.

The last section was being put into place when Miahua and the birth-master came to see her, both looking equally pre-occupied.

Her heart sank. "Don't tell me," Dac Kien said. "She's due now."

"She's lost the waters," the birth-master said, without preamble. He spat on the floor to ward off evil spirits, who always crowded around the mother in the hour of a birth. "You have a few bi-hours, at most."

"Miahua?" Dac Kien wasn't looking at either of them, but rather at the ship outside, the huge bulk that dwarfed them all in its shadow.

Her Master of Wind and Water was silent for a while—usually a sign that she was arranging problems in the most suitable order. Not good. "The structure will be finished before this bi-hour is over."

"But?" Dac Kien said.

"But it's a mess. The lines of wood cross those of metal, and there are humours mingling with each other and stagnating everywhere. The qi won't flow."

The qi, the breath of the universe—of the dragon that lay at the heart of every planet, of every star. As Master of Wind and Water, it was Miahua's role to tell Dac Kien what had gone wrong, but as Grand Master of Design Harmony, it fell to Dac Kien to correct this. Miahua could only point out the results she saw: only Dac Kien could send the bots in, to make the necessary adjustments to the structure. "I see," Dac Kien said. "Prepare a shuttle for her. Have it wait outside, close to the ship's docking bay."

"Your Excellency—" the birth-master started, but Dac Kien cut him off.

"I have told you before. The ship will be ready."

Miahua's stance as she left was tense, all pent-up fears. Dac Kien thought of Hanh—alone in their room, stubbornly bent over her poem, her face as harsh as that of the birth-master, its customary roundness sharpened by anger and resentment. She'd say, again, that you couldn't hurry things, that there were always possibilities. She'd say that—but she'd never understood there was always a price; and that, if you didn't pay it, others did.

The ship would be ready; and Dac Kien would pay its price in full.

ALONE AGAIN, Dac Kien connected to the system, letting the familiar overlay of the design take over her surroundings. She adjusted the contrast until the design was all she could see; and then she set to work.

Miahua was right: the ship was a mess. They had envisioned having a few days to tidy things up, to soften the angles of the corridors, to spread the wall-lanterns so there were no dark corners or spots shining with blinding light. The heartroom alone—the pentacle-shaped centre of the ship, where the Mind would settle—had strands of four humours coming to an abrupt, painful stop within, and a sharp line just outside its entrance, marking the bots' hasty sealing.

The killing breath, it was called; and it was everywhere.

Ancestors, watch over me.

A living, breathing thing—jade, whittled down to its essence. Dac Kien slid into the trance, her consciousness expanding to encompass the bots around the structure—sending them, one by one, inside the metal hull, scuttling down the curved corridors and passageways—gently merging with the walls, starting the slow and painful work of coaxing the metal into its proper shape—going up into the knot of cables, straightening them out, regulating the current in the larger ones. In her mind's view, the ship seemed to flicker and fold back upon itself; she hung suspended outside, watching the bots crawl over it like ants, injecting commands into the different sections, in order to modify their balance of humours and inner structure.

She cut to the shuttle, where Zoquitl lay on her back, her face distorted into a grimace. The birth-master's face was grim, turned upwards as if he could guess at Dac Kien's presence.

Hurry. You don't have time left. Hurry.

And still she worked—walls turned into mirrors, flowers were carved into the passageways, softening those hard angles and lines she couldn't disguise. She opened up a fountain—all light projections, of course, there could be no real water aboard—let the recreated sound of a stream fill the structure. Inside the heartroom, the four tangled humours became three, then one; then she brought in other lines until the tangle twisted back upon itself, forming a complicated knot pattern that allowed strands of all five humours to flow around the room. Water, wood, fire, earth, metal, all circling the ship's core, a stabilising influence for the Mind, when it came to anchor itself there.

She flicked back the display to the shuttle, saw Zoquitl's face, and the unbearable lines of tension in the other's face.

Hurry.

It was not ready. But life didn't wait until you were ready. Dac Kien turned off the display—but not the connection to the bots, leaving them time to finish their last tasks.

"Now," she whispered, into the com system.

The shuttle launched itself towards the docking bay. Dac Kien dimmed the overlay, letting the familiar sight of the room re-assert itself—with the cube, and the design that should have been, the perfect one, the one that called to mind *The Red Carp* and *The Turtle Over the Waves* and *The Dragon's Twin Dreams*, all the days of Xuya from the Exodus to the Pearl Wars, and the fall of the Shan Dynasty; and older things, too, Le Loi's sword that had established a Viet dynasty; the dragon with spread wings flying over Hanoi, the Old Earth capital; the face of Huyen Tran, the Viet princess traded to foreigners in return for two provinces.

The bots were turning themselves off, one by one, and a faint breeze ran through the ship, carrying the smell of sea-laden water and of incense.

It could have been, that ship, that masterpiece. If she'd had time. Hanh was right, she could have made it work: it would have been hers, perfect, praised—remembered in the centuries to come, used as inspiration by hundreds of other Grand Masters.

If—

She didn't know how long she stayed there, staring at the design—but an agonised cry tore her from her thoughts. Startled, she turned up the ship's feed again, and selected a view into the birthing room.

The lights had been dimmed, leaving shadows everywhere, like a prelude to mourning. Dac Kien could see the bowl of tea given at the beginning of labour—it had rolled into a corner of the room, a few drops scattering across the floor.

Zoquitl crouched against a high-backed chair, framed by holos of two goddesses who watched over childbirth: the Princess of the Blue and Purple Clouds, and the Bodhisattva of Mercy. In the shadows, her face seemed to be that of a demon, the alienness of her features distorted by pain.

"Push," the birth-master was saying, his hands on the quivering mound of her belly.

Push.

Blood ran down Zoquitl's thighs, staining the metal surfaces until they reflected everything in shades of red. But her eyes were proud—those of an old warrior race, who'd never bent or bowed to anybody else. Her child of flesh, when it came, would be delivered the same way.

Dac Kien thought of Hanh, and of sleepless nights, of the shadow stretched over their lives, distorting everything.

"Push," the birth-master said again, and more blood ran out. Push push push—and Zoquitl's eyes were open, looking straight at her, and Dac Kien knew—she knew that the rhythm that racked Zoquitl, the pain that came in waves, it was all part of the same immutable law, the same thread that bound them more surely than the red one between lovers—what lay in the womb, under the skin, in their hearts and in their minds; a kinship of gender that wouldn't ever be altered or extinguished. Her hand slid to her own flat, empty belly, pressed hard. She knew what that pain was, she could hold every layer of it in her mind as she'd held the ship's design—and she knew that Zoquitl, like her, had been made to bear it.

Push.

With a final heart-wrenching scream, Zoquitl expelled the last of the Mind from her womb. It slid to the floor, a red, glistening mass of flesh and electronics: muscles and metal implants, veins and pins and cables.

It lay there, still and spent—and several heartbeats passed before Dac Kien realised it wouldn't ever move.

DAC KIEN put off visiting Zoquitl for days, still reeling from the shock of the birth. Every time she closed her eyes, she saw blood: the great mass sliding out of the womb, flopping on the floor like a dead fish, the lights of the birthing room glinting on metal wafers and grey matter, and everything dead, gone as if it had never been.

It had no name, of course—neither it nor the ship, both gone too soon to be graced with one.

Push. Push, and everything will be fine. Push.

Hanh tried her best: showing her poems with exquisite calligraphy; speaking of the future and of her next posting; fiercely making love to her as if nothing had ever happened, as if Dac Kien could just forget the enormity of the loss. But it wasn't enough.

Just as the ship hadn't been enough.

In the end, remorse drove Dac Kien, as surely as a barbed whip; and she boarded the shuttle to come over to the ship.

Zoquitl was in the birthing room, sitting wedged against the wall, with a bowl of pungent tea in her veined hands. The two holos framed her, their white-painted faces stark in the dim light, unforgiving. The birth-master hovered nearby, but was persuaded to leave them both alone—though he made it clear Dac Kien was responsible for anything that happened to Zoquitl.

"Elder sister." Zoquitl smiled, a little bitterly. "It was a good fight."

"Yes." One Zoquitl could have won, if she had been given better weapons.

"Don't look so sad," Zoquitl said.

"I failed," Dac Kien said, simply. She knew Zoquitl's future was still assured; that she'd make her good marriage, and bear children, and be worshipped in her turn. But she also knew, now, that it wasn't the only reason Zoquitl had borne the Mind.

Zoquitl's lips twisted, into what might have been a smile. "Help me."

"What?" Dac Kien looked at her, but Zoquitl was already pushing herself up, shaking, shivering, as carefully as she had done when pregnant. "The birth-master—"

"He's fussing like an old woman," Zoquitl said; and for a moment, her voice was as sharp and as cutting as a blade. "Come. Let's walk."

She was smaller than Dac Kien had thought: her shoulders barely came up to her own. She wedged herself awkwardly, leaning on Dac Kien for support—a weight that grew increasingly hard to bear as they walked through the ship.

There was light, and the sound of water, and the familiar feel of qi flowing through the corridors in lazy circles, breathing life into everything. There were shadows barely seen in mirrors, and the glint of other ships, too: the soft, curving patterns of *The Golden Mountain*; the carved calligraphy incised in the doors that had been the hallmark of *The Tiger Who Leapt Over the Stream*; the slowly curving succession of ever-growing doors of *Baoyu's Red Fan*—bits and pieces salvaged from her design and put together into—into this, which unfolded its marvels all around her, from layout to electronics to decoration, until her head spun and her eyes blurred, taking it all in.

In the heartroom, Dac Kien stood unmoving, while the five humours washed over them, an endless cycle of destruction and renewal. The centre was pristine, untouched, with a peculiar sadness hanging around it, like an empty crib. And yet...

"It's beautiful," Zoquitl said, her voice catching and quivering in her throat.

Beautiful as a poem declaimed in drunken games, as a flower bud ringed by frost—beautiful and fragile as a newborn child struggling to breathe.

And, standing there at the centre of things, with Zoquitl's frail body leaning against her, she thought of Hanh again; of shadows and darkness, and of life choices.

It's beautiful.

It would be gone in a few days. Destroyed, recycled; forgotten and uncommemorated. But somehow, Dac Kien couldn't bring herself to voice the thought.

Instead she said, softly, into the silence—knowing it to be true of more than the ship—"It was worth it."

All of it—now and in the years to come, and she wouldn't look back, or regret.

The Jaguar House, in Shadow

*T*HE *MIND WANDERS, WHEN ONE TAKES* TEONANÁCATL.

 If she allowed herself to think, she'd smell bleach, mingling with the faint, rank smell of blood; she'd see the grooves of the cell, smeared with what might be blood or faeces.

 She'd remember—the pain insinuating itself into the marrow of her bones, until it, too, becomes a dull thing, a matter of habit—she'd remember dragging herself upwards when dawn filters through the slit-windows: too tired and wan to offer her blood to Tonatiuh the sun, whispering a prayer that ends up sounding more and more like an apology.

 The god, of course, will insist that she live until the end, for life and blood are too precious to be wasted—no matter how broken or useless she's become, wasting away in the darkness.

 Here's the thing: she's not sure how long she can last.

 It was Jaguar Captain Palli who gave her the teonanácatl*—opening his hand to reveal the two black, crushed mushrooms, the food of the gods, the drugs of the lost, of the doomed—she couldn't tell if it was because he pitied her, or if it's yet another trap, another ambush they hope she'll fall into.*

 But still... She took them. She held them, wrapped tight in the palm of her hands, as the guards walked her back. And when she was alone once more, she stared at them for a long while, feeling the tremor start in her fingers—the hunger, the craving for normality—for oblivion.

 The mind wanders—backwards, into the only time worth remembering.

THE PICTURE lay on the table, beside Onalli's bloodied worship-thorns. It showed a girl standing by a stall in the marketplace, holding out a cloak of emerald-green quetzal feathers with an uncertain air, as if it would leap and bite at any moment. Two other girls stood silhouetted in the shadows behind her, as if already fading into insignificance.

It wasn't the best one Onalli had of Xochitl, by a large margin—but she'd been thinking about it a lot, those days—about the fundamental irony of it, like a god's ultimate joke on her.

"Having second thoughts?" Atcoatl asked, behind her.

Onalli's hand reached out, to turn the picture over—and stopped when his tone finally sank in.

She turned to look at him: his broad, tanned face was impassive—a true Knight's, showing none of what he felt.

"No," she said, slowly, carefully. "I'm not having second thoughts. But you are, aren't you?"

Atcoatl grimaced. "Onalli—"

He was the one who'd helped her, from the start—getting her the encrypted radio sets, the illicit nanos to lower her body temperatures, the small syringes containing everything from *teonanácatl* inhibitors to endurance nanos. More than that: he had believed her—that her desperate gamble would work, that they'd retrieve Xochitl alive, out of the madness the Jaguar House had become...

"This is too big," Atcoatl said. He shook his head, and Onalli heard the rest, the words he wasn't saying.

What if we get caught?

Onalli chose the easiest way to dispel fear: anger. "So you intend to sit by and do nothing?"

Atcoatl's eyes flashed with a burning hatred—and no wonder. He had seen the fall of his own House; his fellow Eagle Knights, bound and abandoned in the burning wreckage of their own dormitories; the Otter and the

Skulls Knights, killed, maimed, or scattered to breathe dust in the silver mines. "I'm no coward. One day, the Revered Speaker and his ilk will pay for what they've done. But this—this is just courting death."

Onalli's gaze strayed again to the picture—to Xochitl's face, frozen in that moment of dubious innocence. "I can't leave her there."

"The resistance—" Atcoatl started.

Onalli snorted. "By the time the resistance can pull the House down, it will be too late. You know it." There had been attacks: two maglev stations bombed; political dissidents mysteriously vanishing before their arrest. She didn't deny the existence of an underground movement, but she recognised the signs: it was still weak, still trying to organise itself.

Atcoatl said nothing; but Onalli was Jaguar Knight, and her training enabled her to read the hint of disapproval in his stance.

"Look," she said, finally. "I'm the one taking the biggest risk. You'll be outside the House, with plenty of time to leave if anything goes wrong."

"If you're caught—"

"You think I'd turn on you?" Onalli asked. "After all they've done to Xochitl, you think I'd help them?"

Atcoatl's face was dark. "You know what they're doing, inside the House."

She didn't—but she could imagine it, all too well. Which was why she needed to pull Xochitl out. Her friend hadn't deserved this; any of this. "I'm Jaguar Knight," she said, softly. "And I give you my word that I'd rather end my own life than let them worm anything out of me."

Atcoatl looked at her. "You're sincere, but what you believe doesn't change anything."

"Doesn't it? I believe the Revered Speaker's rule is unlawful. I believe the Jaguar House had no right to betray its own dissidents, or interrogate them. Isn't that what we all believe in?"

Atcoatl shifted, and wouldn't answer.

"Tell me what you believe in, then," Onalli said.

He was silent for a while. "Black One take you," he said, savagely. "Just this once, Onalli. Just this once."

Onalli nodded. "Promise." Afterwards, they'd go north—into the United States or Xuya, into countries where freedom was more than a word on paper. They'd be safe.

She finished tying her hair in a neat bun—a habit she'd taken on her missions abroad—and slid her worship thorns into her belt, smearing the blood over her skinsuit. A prayer, for whoever among the gods might be listening tonight; for Fate, the Black One, the god of the Smoking Mirror, who could always be swayed or turned away, if you had the heart and guts to seize your chance when it came.

Atcoatl waited for her at the door, holding it open with ill-grace.

"Let's go," Onalli said.

She left the picture on the table—knowing, all the while, why she'd done so: not because it would burden her, but because of one simple thing. Fear. Fear that she'd find Xochitl and stare into her face, and see the broken mind behind the eyes—nothing like the shy, courageous girl she remembered.

Outside, the air was clear and cold, and a hundred stars shone upon the city of Tenochtitlan: a hundred demons, waiting in the darkness to descend and rend all life from limb to limb. Onalli rubbed her worship thorns, trying to remember the assurance she'd always felt on her missions—why couldn't she remember anything, now that she was home—now that she was breaking into her own House?

Six months ago

THE PRIEST of the Black One sits cross-legged across the mat—facing Xochitl and pursing his lips as if contemplating a particular problem. His hair is greasy and tangled, matted with the blood of his devotions; and the smell that emanates from him is the rank one of charnel houses—with the slight tang of bleach. He's attempted to wash his hands before coming, and hasn't succeeded.

Amusing, how the mind sharpens, when everything else is restrained.

Xochitl would laugh, but she's never been much of one for laughter: that was Onalli, or perhaps Tecipiani.

No, she musn't think of Tecipiani, not now—must remain calm and composed, her only chance at surviving this.

Mustn't ask herself the question "for what?"

"I'm told," the priest says, "that you started a ring of dissidents within this House."

Xochitl remains seated against the wall, very straight. The straps cut into her arms and ankles, and the tightest one holds her at the neck. She'll only exhaust herself trying to break them: she's tried a dozen times already, with only bruises to show for it.

The priest goes on, as if she had answered, "I'm told you worked to undermine the loyalty of the Jaguar Knights, with the aim to topple the Revered Speaker."

Xochitl shakes her head, grimly amused. Toppling him—as if that would work... The burgeoning resistance movement is small and insignificant; and they have no reach within the House, not even to Xochitl's pathetic, shattered splinter group.

But there's right and wrong, and when Xolotl comes to take her soul, she'll face Him with a whole face and heart, knowing which side she chose.

The priest goes on, smug, self-satisfied, "You must have known it was doomed. This House is loyal; your commander is loyal. She has given you up, rather than suffer your betrayal."

Tecipiani—no, mustn't think of that, mustn't—it's no surprise, has never been, not after everything Tecipiani has done...

"Of course she has given me up," Xochitl says, keeping her voice steady. "Jaguar Knights aren't interrogators. We leave that to you."

The priest shifts, unhurriedly—and, without warning, cuffs her, his obsidian rings cutting deep into her skin. She tastes blood, an acrid tingle in her mouth—raises her head again, daring him to strike again.

He does—again and again, each blow sending her head reeling back, a white flash of pain resonating in the bones of her cheek, the warmth of blood running down her face.

When he stops at last, Xochitl hangs limp, staring at the floor through a growing haze—the strap digging into her windpipe, an unpleasant reminder of how close asphyxiation is.

"Let's start again, shall we?" His voice is calm, composed. "You'll show me proper respect, as is owed an agent of the Revered Speaker."

He's—not that—he's nothing, a man of no religion, who dares use pain as a weapon, tainting it for mundane things like interrogation. But pain isn't that, was never that. Xochitl struggles to remember the proper words; to lay them at the feet of the Black One, her song of devotion in this godless place.

"I fall before you, I throw myself before you
Offer up the precious water of my blood, offer up my pain like fire
I cast myself into the place from where none rise, from where none leave,
O lord of the near and nigh, O master of the Smoking Mirror,
O night, O wind…"

She must have spoken the words aloud, because he cuffs her again—a quick, violent blow she only feels when her head knocks against the wall—ringing in her mind, the whole world contracting and expanding, the colours too light and brash—

And again, and again, and everything slowly merges, folding inwards like crinkling paper—pain spreading along her muscles like fire.

"With icy water I make my penance
With nettles and thorns I bare out my face, my heart
Through the land of the anguished, the land of the dying…"

She thinks, but she's not sure, that he's gone, when the door opens again, and footsteps echo under the ceiling—slow and measured, deliberate.

She'd raise her head, but she can't muster the energy. Even focusing on the ground is almost too tiring, when all she wants is to lean back, to close her eyes and dream of a world where Tonatiuh the sun bathes her in His light, where the smell of cooking oil and chilies wafts from the stalls of food-vendors, where feather-cloaks are soft and silky against her hands…

The feet stop: leather mocassins, and emerald-green feathers, and the tantalising smell of pine-cones and copal incense.

Tecipiani. No, not the girl she knew anymore, but Commander Tecipiani, the one who sold them all to the priests—who threw Xochitl herself to the star-demons, to be torn apart and made as nothing.

"Come to gloat?" Xochitl asks; or tries to, because it won't come out as more than a whisper. She can't even tell if Tecipiani hears her, because the world is pressing against her, a throbbing pain in her forehead that spreads to her field of vision—until everything dissolves into feverish darkness.

ONALLI TOOK the ball-court at a run, descending from the stands into the I-shape of the ground. On either side of her loomed the walls, with the vertical stone-hoops teams would fight to send a ball through—but it was the season of the Lifting of the Banners, and the teams were enjoying a well-earned rest.

It did mean, though, that only one imperial warrior guarded the cordoned-off entrance: it had been child's play to take him down.

One thing people frequently forgot about the ball-court was that it was built with its back against the Jaguar House, and that the dignitaries' boxes at the far end shared a wall with the House's furthest courtyard.

That courtyard would be guarded, but it was nothing insurmountable. She'd left Atcoatl at the entrance, disguised as an imperial warrior: from afar, he'd present a sufficient illusion to discourage investigation; and he'd warn her by radio if anything went wrong outside.

The boxes were deserted; Onalli made her way in the darkness to that of the Revered Speaker, decorated with old-fashioned carvings depicting the feats of gods: the Feathered Serpent coming back from the underworld with the bones of mankind, the Black One bringing down the Second Sun in a welter of flames and wind.

The tribune was the highest one in the court; but still lacking a good measure or so to get her over the wall—after all, if there was the remotest possibility that anyone could leap through there, they'd have guarded it to the teeth.

Onalli stood for a while, breathing quietly. She rubbed her torn ears, feeling a trickle of blood seep into her skin. For the Black One, should He decide to watch over her. For Tonatiuh the Sun, who would tumble from the sky without His nourishment.

For Xochitl, who'd deserved better than the fate Tecipiani had dealt her.

She extended, in one fluid, thoughtless gesture: her nails were diamond-sharp, courtesy of Atcoatl's nanos, and it was easy to find purchases on the carvings—not thinking of the sacrilege, of what the Black One might think about fingers clawing their way through His effigies, no time for that anymore...

Onalli hoisted herself up on the roof of the box, breathing hard. The wall in front of her was much smoother, but still offered some purchase as long as she was careful. It was, really, no worse than the last ascension she'd done, clinging to the outside of the largest building in Jiajin Tech's compound, on her way to steal blueprints from a safe. It was no worse than endless hours of training, when her tutors had berated her about carelessness...

But her tutors were dead, or gone to ground—and it was the House on the other side of that wall, the only home she'd ever known—the place that had raised her from childhood, the place where she could be safe, and not play a game of endless pretence—where she could start a joke and have a dozen persons voicing the punch-line, where they sang the hymns on the winter solstice, letting their blood pool into the same vessel.

Her hands, slick with sweat, slid out of a crack. For one impossibly long moment she felt herself fall into the darkness—caught herself with a gasp, even as chunks of rock fell downwards in a clatter of noise.

Had anyone heard that? The other side of the wall seemed silent—

There was only darkness, enclosing her like the embrace of Grandmother Earth. Onalli gritted her teeth, and pushed upwards, groping for further handholds.

Two years ago

COMMANDER TECIPIANI'S investiture speech is subdued, and uncharacteristically bleak. Her predecessor, Commander Malinalli, had delivered grandiloquent boasts about the House and its place in the world, as if everything was due to them, in this Age and the next.

But Tecipiani says none of that. Instead, she speaks of dark times ahead, and the need to be strong, and the need to endure.

She doesn't say the words "civil war", but everyone can hear them, all the same.

Xochitl and Onalli stand near the back. Because Onalli arrived late and Xochitl waited for her, the only place they could find was near the novices: callow boys and girls, uneasily settling into their cotton uniforms and fur cloaks, still too young to feel their childhood locks as burdens—still so young and innocent it almost hurts, to think of them in the times ahead.

After the ceremony, everyone drifts back to their companies, or to the mess-halls. The mistress of the novices has organised a mock battle in the courtyard, and Onalli is watching with the same rapt fascination she might have for a formal ball-game.

Xochitl is watching Tecipiani: the Commander has finished shaking hands with her company leaders, and, dismissing her bodyguards, is heading straight towards them. Her gaze catches Xochitl's—holds it for a while, almost pleading.

"Onalli," Xochitl says, urgently.

Onalli barely looks up. "I know. It had to happen at some point, anyway."

Tecipiani catches up with them, greets them both with a curt nod. She's still wearing the full regalia of the Commander: a cloak of jaguar-fur, and breeches of emerald-green quetzal feathers. Her helmet is in the shape of a jaguar's head, and her face pokes out from between the jaws of the animal, as if she were being consumed alive.

"Walk with me, will you?" she asks. Except that she's not asking, not anymore, because she speaks with the voice of the Black One, and even her slightest suggestion is a command.

They don't speak, for a while—walking through courtyards where Knights haggle over *patolli* gameboards, where novices dare each other to leap over the fountains: the familiar, comforting hubbub of life within the House.

"I wasn't expecting you so soon, Onalli—though I'm glad to see you have returned," Tecipiani says. Her words are warm; her voice isn't. "I trust everything went well?"

Onalli spreads her hands in a gesture of uncertainty. "I have the documents," she says. "Williamsburg Tech were making a new prototype of computer, with more complexity. A step away from consciousness, perhaps."

Xochitl wonders what kind of intelligence computers will develop, when they finally breach the gap between automated tasks and genuine sentience—all that research done in military units north of the border, eyeing the enemy to the south.

They'll be like us, she thinks. They'll reach for their equivalent of clubs or knives, claiming it's just to protect themselves; and it won't be long until they sink it into somebody's chest.

Just like us.

"The Americans have advanced their technology, then," Tecipiani says, gravely. It's the House's job, after all: watching science in the other countries of the Fifth World, and making sure that none of them ever equals Greater Mexico's lead in electronics—using whatever it takes, theft, bribery, assassination.

Onalli shakes her head impatiently. "This isn't something we should worry about."

"Perhaps more than you think." Tecipiani's voice is slightly annoyed. "The war won't always last, and we must look ahead to the future."

Onalli says, "The war, yes. You made an interesting speech."

Tecipiani's smile doesn't stretch all the way to her eyes. "Appropriate, I felt. Sometimes, we have to be reminded of what happens out there."

Onalli says, "I've seen what's out there. It's getting ugly."

"Ugly?" Xochitl asks.

Onalli's eyes drift away. "I saw him at court, Xochitl. Revered Speaker Ixtli. He's—" her hands clench. "—a maddened dog. It's in his eyes, and in his bearing. It won't be long before the power goes to his head. It's already started. The war—"

Tecipiani shakes her head. "Don't you dare make such a statement." Her voice is curt, as cutting as an obsidian blade. "We are Jaguar Knights. We serve the Mexica Empire and its Revered Speaker. We're nothing more than that. Never."

"But—" Xochitl starts.

"We're nothing more than that," Tecipiani says, again.

No, that's not true. They're Jaguar Knights; they've learnt to judge people on a word or a gesture—because, when you're out on a mission, it marks the line between life and death. They know...

"You're mad," Onalli says. "Back when Commander Malinalli was still alive, all the Houses, all the Knights spoke against Ixtli—including ours. What do you think the Revered Speaker will do to us, once he's asserted his power?"

"I'm your Commander," Tecipiani says, her voice slightly rising. "That, too, is something you must remember, Jaguar Lieutenant. I speak for the House."

"I'll remember." Onalli's voice is low and dangerous. And Xochitl knows that here, now, they've reached the real parting of the ways—not when Tecipiani was appointed company leader or commander, not when she was the one who started assigning missions to her old friends—but this, here, now, this ultimate profession of cowardice.

"Good," Tecipiani says. She seems oblivious to the undercurrents, the gazes passing between Onalli and Xochitl. But, then, she's never been good with details. "You'll come to my office later, Onalli. I'll have another mission for you."

And that, too, is cowardice: what she cannot control, Tecipiani will get rid of. Xochitl looks at Onalli—and back at her Commander, who still hasn't moved—and she feels the first stirrings of defiance flutter in her belly.

ONALLI DROPPED the last few hand-spans into the courtyard, and immediately flattened herself against the wall—a bad reflex. There was a security camera not a few handspans from her, but all it would see in the darkness was another blur: her skin-suit was made of non-reflective materials, which wouldn't show up on infrared, and she'd taken nanos to lower her skin temperature. There'd be fire and blood to pay later, but she didn't really care anymore.

Everything was silent, too much so. Where were the guards and the security—where was Tecipiani's iron handhold on the House? She'd felt the fear from outside—the wide, empty space in front of the entrance; the haunted eyes of the Jaguar Captain she'd pumped for information on the maglev; all the horror stories she'd heard on her way into Tenochtitlan.

And yet...

The back of her scalp prickled. A trap. They'd known she was coming. They were expecting her.

But she'd gone too far to give up; and the wall was a bitch to climb, anyway.

She drew the first of her throwing knives, and, warily, progressed deeper into the House. Still nothing—the hungry silence of the stars—the warm breath of Grandmother Earth underfoot—the numinous presence of Xolotl, god of Death, walking in her footsteps...

A shadow moved across the entrance to the courtyard, under the vague shapes of the pillars. Onalli's hand tightened around the haft of the knife. Staying motionless would be her demise. She had to move fast, to silence them before they could raise the alarm.

She uncoiled—leapt, with the speed of a rattlesnake, straight towards the waiting shadow. Her knife was meant to catch the shadow in the chest, but it parried with surprising speed. All she could see of the shadow was a smear in the darkness, a larger silhouette that seemed to move in time with her. The shadow wasn't screaming; all its energy was focused into the fight, pure, incandescent, the dance that gave the gods their due, that kept Tonatiuh the sun in the sky and Grandmother Earth sated, the one they'd both trained for, all their lives.

There was something wrong, very wrong with the way the shadow moved... She parried a slash at her legs, and pressed it again, trying to disarm him.

In the starlight, she barely saw the sweeping arc of its knife, moving diagonally across her weak side—she raised her own blade to parry, caught the knife and sent it clattering to the ground, and moved in for the kill.

Too late, she saw the second blade. She threw herself backwards, but not before it had drawn a fiery slash across her skin-suit.

They stood, facing one another, in silence.

"You—you move like us." the shadow said. The voice was high-pitched, shaking, and suddenly she realised what had been wrong with its moves: the eagerness, the abandon of the unblooded novices.

"You're a boy," she breathed. "A child."

Black One, no.

"I'm no child." He shifted, in the starlight, letting her catch a glimpse of his gangly awkwardness. "Don't make that mistake."

"I apologise." Onalli put all the contriteness she could in her voice; she softened the muscles of her back to hunch over in a submissive position: he might not be able to see her very well, but he'd still see enough to get the subconscious primers.

The boy didn't move. Finally he said, as if this were an everyday conversation. "If I called, they would be here in a heartbeat."

"You haven't called." Onalli kept her voice steady, trying to encourage him not to remedy this oversight.

In the starlight, she saw him shake his head. "I'd be dead before they came."

"No," Onalli said, the word torn out of her before she could plan for it. "I'm not here to kill you."

"I believe you." A pause, then, "You've come for the House. To avenge your own."

Her own? And then she understood. He thought her a Knight; but not of the Jaguar. An Eagle, perhaps, or an Otter: any of the former elite of Greater Mexica, the ones Revered Speaker Ixtli had obliterated from the Fifth World.

She'd forgotten that this was no mere boy, but a novice of her order, who would one day become a Knight, like her, like Tecipiani, like Xochitl. He'd heard and seen enough to know that she hated the House's heart and guts; but he hadn't yet connected it with who she was.

"I'm just here for a friend," Onalli said. "She—she needs help."

"Help." His voice was steadier, almost thoughtful. "The kind of help that requires infiltration, and a knife."

She had more than knives: all the paraphernalia of Knights on a mission, stun-guns, syringes filled with endurance and pain nanos. But she hadn't got them out. She wasn't sure why. Tecipiani had turned the House into something dark that needed to be put down, and she'd do whatever it took. And yet...

It was still her House. "She's in the cells," Onalli said.

"In trouble," the boy repeated, flatly. "I'm sure they wouldn't arrest her without good reason."

Black One take him, he was so innocent, so trusting in the rightness of whatever the House did; like her or Xochitl, ages before their eyes opened. She wanted to shake him. "I have no time to argue with you. Will you let me pass?"

The boy said nothing for a while. She could feel him wavering in the starlight—and, because she was Jaguar Knight, she also knew that it wouldn't be enough, that he'd call for the guards, rather than entrusting himself to some vague stranger who had tried to kill him.

No choice, then.

She moved before he could react—shifting her whole weight towards him and bearing him to the ground, even as her hand moved to cover his mouth. As they landed, there was a crunch like bones breaking—for a moment, she thought she'd killed him, but he was still looking at her in disbelief, trying to bite her—with her other hand, she reached into her skin-suit, and withdrew a syringe.

He gasped when she injected him, his eyes rolling up, the cornea an eerie white in the starlight. Now that her eyes were accustomed to the darkness, she could see him clearly: his skin smooth and dark, his hands clenching, then relaxing as the *teonanácatl* inhibitor took hold.

She could only hope that she'd got the doses right: he was wirier than most adults, and his metabolism was still that of a child.

As she left the courtyard, he was twitching, in the grip of the hallucinations that came as a side-effect. With luck, he'd wake up with a headache, and a vague memory of everything not being quite right—but not remember the vivid nightmares the drug gave. She thought of beseeching the gods for small or large mercies; but the only two in her wake were the Black One and Xolotl, the Taker of the Dead.

"I'm sorry," she whispered, knowing he couldn't hear her; knowing he would hate and fear her for the rest of his days. "But I can't trust the justice of this House—I just can't."

Nine years ago

XOCHITL STANDS by the stall, dubiously holding the cloak of quetzal-feathers against her chest. "It's a little too much, don't you think?"

"No way," Onalli says.

"If your idea of clothing is tawdry, sure," Tecipiani says, with an amused shake of her head. "This is stuff for almond-eyed tourists."

And, indeed, there's more Asians at the stall than trueblood Mexica—though Onalli, who's half and half, could almost pass for Asian herself. "Aw, come on," Onalli says. "It's perfect. Think of all the boys queuing for a kiss. You'd have to start selling tickets."

Xochitl makes a mock stab at Onalli, as if withdrawing a knife from under her tunic. But her friend is too quick, and steps aside, leaving her pushing at empty air.

"What's the matter? Eagles ate your muscles?" Onalli says—always belabouring the obvious.

Xochitl looks again at the cloak—bright and garish, but not quite in the right way. "No," she says, finally. "But Tecipiani's right. It's not worth the money." Not even for a glance from Palli—who's much too mature, anyway, to get caught by such base tricks.

Tecipiani, who seldom brags about her triumphs, simply nods. "There's another stall further down," she says. "Maybe there'll be something—"

There's a scream, on the edge of the market: not that of someone being robbed, but that of a madman.

What in the Fifth World—

Xochitl puts back the cloak, and shifts, feeling the reassuring heaviness of the obsidian blades at her waist. Onalli has already withdrawn hers; but Tecipiani has moved before them all, striding towards the source. Her hands are empty.

Ahead, at the entrance to the marketplace, is a grounded aircar, its door gaping empty. The rest of the procession that was following it is slowly coming to a stop—though with difficulty, as there is little place among the closely-crammed stalls for fifteen aircars.

The sea of muttering faces disembarking from the aircars is a hodge-podge of colours, from European to Asian, and even a few Mexica. They wear banners proudly tacked to their backs, in a deliberately old-fashioned style: coyotes and rabbits drawn in featherwork spread out like fans behind their heads.

It's all oddly familiar and repulsive at the same time, a living remnant of another time. "Revivalists," Xochitl says, aloud.

Which means—

She turns, scanning the marketplace for a running man: the unwilling sacrifice victim, the only one who had a reason to break and run.

What Xochitl sees, instead, is Tecipiani, walking determinately into a side aisle of the marketplace as if she were looking for a specific stall.

The revivalists are gathering, harangued by a blue-clad priest who is organising search parties.

"Idiots," Onalli curses under her breath. She's always believed more in penance than in human sacrifice; and the Revivalists have always rubbed her the wrong way. Xochitl isn't particularly religious, and has no opinion either way.

"Come on," she says.

They find Tecipiani near the back of the animals section—and, kneeling before her, is a hunched man, still wearing the remnants of the elaborate costume that marked him as the sacrifice victim. He's shivering; his face contorts as he speaks words that Xochitl can't make out amidst the noises of the chattering parrots and screaming monkeys in their metal cages.

As they come closer, Tecipiani makes a dismissive gesture; and the man springs to life, running away deeper into the marketplace.

"The search party is coming this way," Onalli says.

Tecipiani doesn't answer for a while: she's looking at the man—and, as she turns back towards her friends, Xochitl sees burning hope and pity in her gaze.

"They won't catch him," she says. "He's strong, and fast. He'll make it."

Onalli looks as though she might protest, but doesn't say anything.

"We should head back," Tecipiani says, finally. Her voice is toneless again; her eyes dry and emotionless.

On their way back, they meet the main body of the search party: the fevered eyes of the priest rest on them for a while, as if judging their fitness as replacements.

Tecipiani moves, slightly, to stand in the priest's way, her smile dazzling and threatening. She shakes her head, once, twice. "We're not easy prey," she says, aloud.

The priest focuses on her; and, after a long, long while, his gaze moves away. Too much to chew. Tecipiani is right: they won't be bested so easily.

They walk on, through the back streets by the marketplace, heading back to the House to find some shade.

Nevertheless, Xochitl feels as though the sunlight has been blotted out. She shivers. "They're sick people."

"Just mad," Onalli says. "Don't think about them anymore. They're not worth your time."

She'd like to—but she knows that the priest's eyes will haunt her nightmares for the months to come. And it's not so much the madness; it's just that it doesn't make sense at all, this frenzy to spread unwilling, tainted blood.

Tecipiani waits until they're almost back to the House to speak. "They're not mad, you know."

"Yeah, sure," Onalli says.

Tecipiani's gaze is distant. "There's a logic to it. Spreading unwilling blood is a sin, but Tonatiuh needs blood to continue shining down on us. Grandmother Earth needs blood to put forth maize and cotton and nanomachines."

"It's still a fucking sin, no matter which way you take it." Onalli seems to take the argument as a challenge.

Tecipiani says nothing for a while. "I suppose so. But still, they're only doing what they think is good."

"And they're wrong," Xochitl says, with a vehemence that surprises her.

"Perhaps," Tecipiani says. "And perhaps not. Would you rather take the risk of the world ending?" She looks up, into the sky. "Of all the stars falling down upon us, monsters eager to tear us apart?"

There's silence, then. Xochitl tries to think of something, of anything to counter Tecipiani, but she can't. She's been too crafty. She always is.

"If you believe that," Onalli says, with a scowl, "why did you let him go?"

Tecipiani shakes her head, and in her eyes is a shadow of what Xochitl saw, back in the marketplace—pity and hope. "I said I understood. Not that I approved. I wouldn't do anything I didn't believe in whole-heartedly. I never do."

And that's the problem, Xochitl thinks. It will always be the problem. Tecipiani does what she believes in; but you're never sure what she's truly thinking.

THE CELL was worryingly easy to enter: once Onalli had dealt with the two guards at the entrance—who, even though they were Jaguar Specialists barely a step above novices, really should have known better. She had gone for the windpipe of the first, and left a syringe stuck in the shoulder of the second, who was out in less time than it took her to open the door.

Inside, it was dark, and stifling. A rank smell, like the mortuary of a hospital, rose as she walked.

"Xochitl?" she whispered.

There was no noise. But against the furthest wall was a dark lump—and, as she walked closer, it resolved into a slumped human shape.

Black One, no. Please watch over her, watch over us all...

Straps and chains held Xochitl against the wall, and thin tubes snaked upwards, into a machine that thrummed like a beating heart.

Teonanácatl, and *peyotl*, and truth-serum, and the gods knew what else...

It was only instinct that kept her going forward: a horrified, debased part of her that wouldn't stop, that had to analyse the situation no matter what. She found the IVs by touch—feeling the hard skin where the syringes had rubbed—the bruises on the face, the broken nose—the eyes that opened, not seeing her.

"Xochitl. Xochitl. It's all right. I'm here. Everything is going to be all right. I promise."

But the body was limp; the face distorted in a grimace of terror; and there was, indeed, nothing left of the picture she'd held on to for so long.

"Come on, come on," she whispered, fiddling with the straps—her sharpened nails catching on the leather, fumbling around the knots.

The cold, detached part of her finally took control; and, forcing herself not to think of what she was doing, she cut through the straps, one by one—pulled out the IVs, and gently disengaged the body, catching its full weight on her arms.

Xochitl shuddered, a spasm like that of a dying woman. "Tecipiani," she whispered. "No…"

"She's not here," Onalli said. Gently, carefully, she rose with Xochitl in her arms, cradling her close, like a hurt child.

Black One take you, Tecipiani. Oblivion's too good for the likes of you. I hope you burn in the Christian Hell, with the sinners and the blasphemers and the traitors. I hope you burn…

She was halfway out of the House, trudging through the last courtyard before the novices' quarters, when she became aware she wasn't alone.

Too late.

The lights came on, blinding, unforgiving.

"I always knew you'd come back, Onalli," a voice said. "No matter how hard I tried to send you away."

Black One take her for a fool. Too easy. It had been too easy, from beginning to end: just another of her sick games.

"Black One screw you," Onalli spat into the brightness. "That's all you deserve, isn't it, Tecipiani?"

The commander was just a silhouette—standing, by the sound of her, only a few paces away. But Xochitl lay in Onalli's arms, a limp weight she couldn't toss aside, even to strike.

Tecipiani didn't speak; but of course she'd remain silent, talking only when it suited her.

"You sold us all," Onalli whispered. To the yellow-livered dogs and their master, to the cudgels and the syringes… "Did she mean so little to you?"

"As little or as much as the rest," Tecipiani said.

Onalli's eyes were slowly accustoming themselves to the light, enough to see that Tecipiani's arms were down, as if holding something. A new weapon—or just a means to call on her troops?

And then, with a feeling like a blade of ice slid through her ribs, Onalli saw that it wasn't the case. She saw what Tecipiani was carrying: a body, just like her: the limp shape of the boy she'd downed in the courtyard.

"You—" she whispered.

Tecipiani shifted. Her face, slowly coming into focus, could have been that of an Asian statue—the eyes dry and unreadable, the mouth thinned to a darker line against her skin. "Ezpetlatl, of the Atempan *calpulli* clan. Given into our keeping fifteen years ago."

Shame warred with rage, and lost. "I don't care. You think it's going to atone for everything else you did?"

"Perhaps," Tecipiani said. "Perhaps not." Her voice shook, slightly—a bare hint of emotion, not enough, never enough. "And you think rescuing Xochitl was worth his life?"

Onalli scanned the darkness, trying to see how many guards were there—how many of Tecipiani's bloodless sycophants. She couldn't take them all—fire and blood, she wasn't even sure she could take Tecipiani. But the lights were set all around the courtyard—on the roofs of the buildings, no doubt—and she couldn't make out anything but the commander herself.

As, no doubt, Tecipiani had meant all along. Bitch.

"You're stalling, aren't you?" Onalli asked. "This isn't about me. It has never been about me." About you, Tecipiani; about the House and the priests and Xochitl...

"No," Tecipiani agreed, gravely. "Finally, something we can agree on."

"Then why Xochitl?" A cold certainty was coalescing in her belly, like a snake of ice. "You wanted us both, didn't you?"

"Oh, Onalli." Tecipiani's voice was sad. "I though you'd understood. This isn't about you, or Xochitl. It's about the House."

How could she say this? "You've killed the House," Onalli spat.

"You never could see into the future," Tecipiani said. "Even two years ago, when you came back."

"When you warned us about betrayal? You're the one who couldn't see the Revered Speaker was insane, you're the one who—"

"Onalli." Tecipiani's voice held the edge of a knife. "The House is still standing."

"Because you sold it."

"Because I compromised," Tecipiani said.

"You—" Onalli choked on all the words she was trying to say. "You poisoned it to the guts and the brain, and you're telling me about compromise?"

"Yes. Something neither you or Xochitl ever understood, unfortunately."

That was too much—irreparable. Without thought, Onalli shifted Xochitl onto her shoulder, and moved, her knife swinging free of its sheath—going for Tecipiani's throat. If she wouldn't move, wouldn't release her so-called precious life, too bad—it would be the last mistake she'd ever make—

She'd half-expected Tecipiani to parry by raising the body in her arms—to sacrifice him, as she'd sacrificed so many of them—but the commander, as quick as a snake, knelt on the ground, laying the unconscious boy at her feet—and Onalli's first swing went wide, cutting only through air. By the time she'd recovered, Tecipiani was up on her feet again, a blade in her left hand.

Onalli shifted, and pressed her again. Tecipiani parried; and again, and again.

None of them should have the upper hand. They were both Jaguar Knights; Tecipiani might have been a little less fit, away from the field for so long—but Onalli was hampered by Xochitl's body, whom she had to keep cradled against her.

Still—

Still, Tecipiani's gestures were not as fast as they should have been. Another one of her games?

Onalli didn't care, not anymore. In one of Tecipiani's over-wide gestures, she saw her opening—and took it. Her blade snaked through; connected, sinking deep above the wrist.

Tecipiani jumped backward—her left hand dangled uselessly, but she'd shifted her knife to the right—and, like many left-handers, she was ambidextrous.

"You're still good," Tecipiani admitted, grudgingly.

Onalli looked around once more—the lights were still on—and said, "You haven't brought anyone else, have you? It's just you and me."

Tecipiani made a curt nod; but, when she answered, it had nothing to do with the question. "The House still stands." There was such desperate intensity in her voice that it stopped Onalli, for a few seconds. "The Eagle Knights were burnt alive; the Otters dispersed into the silver mines to breathe dust until it killed them. The Coyotes died to a man, defending their House against the imperial guards."

"They died with honour," Onalli said.

"Honour is a word without meaning," Tecipiani said. Her voice was steady once more. "There are five hundred Knights in this House, out of which one hundred unblooded children and novices. I had to think of the future."

Onalli's hands clenched. "And Xochitl wasn't part of the future?"

Tecipiani didn't move. "Sacrifices were necessary. Who would turn on their own, except men loyal to the Revered Speaker?"

The cold was back in her guts, and in her heart. "You're sick," Onalli said. "This wasn't worth the price of our survival—this wasn't—"

"Perhaps," Tecipiani said. "Perhaps it was the wrong thing to do. But we won't know until long after this, will we?"

That gave her pause—so unlike Tecipiani, to admit she'd been wrong, to put her acts into question. But still—still, it changed nothing.

"And now what?" Onalli asked. "You've had your game, Tecipiani. Because that's all we two ever were to you, weren't we?"

Tecipiani didn't move. At last, she made a dismissive gesture. "It could have gone both ways. Two Knights, killed in an escape attempt tragically gone wrong..." She spoke as if nothing mattered anymore; her voice cool, emotionless—and that, in many ways, was the most terrifying. "Or a success, perhaps, from your point of view."

"I could kill you," Onalli said, and knew it was the truth. No one was perfectly ambidextrous, and, were Onalli to drop Xochitl as Tecipiani had dropped the boy, she'd have the full range of her abilities to call upon.

"Yes," Tecipiani said. A statement of fact, nothing more. "Or you could escape."

"Fuck you," Onalli said. She wanted to say something else—that, when the Revered Speaker was finally dead, she and Xochitl would come back and level the House, but she realised, then, that it was only thanks to Tecipiani that there would still be a House to tear down.

But it still wasn't worth it. It couldn't have been.

Gently, she shifted Xochitl, catching her in her arms once more, like a hurt child. "I didn't come here to kill you," she said, finally. "But I still hope you burn, Tecipiani, for all you've done. Whether it was worth it or not."

She walked to the end of the courtyard, into the blinding light—to the wall and the ball-court and the exit. Tecipiani made no attempt to stop her; she still stood next to the unconscious body of the boy, looking at some point in the distance.

And, all the way out—into the suburbs of Tenochtitlan, in the aircar Atcoatl was driving—she couldn't get Tecipiani's answer out of her mind, nor the burning despair she'd heard in her friend's voice.

What makes you think I don't already burn?

She'd always been too good an actress. "Black One take you," she said, aloud. And she wasn't really sure anymore if she was asking for suffering, or for mercy.

ALONE IN her office once more, her hands—her thin, skeletal hands—reach for the shrivelled mushrooms of the teonanácatl—and everything slowly dissolves into coloured patterns, into meaningless dreams.

Even in the dreams, though, she knows what she's done. The gods have turned Their faces away from her; and every night she wakes up with the memories of the torture chambers—the consequences of what she's ordered, the consequences she has forced herself to face, like a true warrior.

Here's the thing: she's not sure how long she can last.

She burns—every day of her life, wondering if what she did was worth it—if she preserved the House, or corrupted it beyond recognition.

No. No.

Only this is worth remembering: that, like the escaped prisoner, Onalli and Xochitl will survive—going north, into the desert, into some other, more welcoming country, keeping alive the memories of their days together.

And, over Greater Mexica, Tonatiuh the sun will rise again and again, marking all the days of the Revered Speaker's reign—the rising tide of fear and discontent that will one day topple him. And when it's finally over, the House that she has saved will go on, into the future of a new Age: a pure and glorious Age, where people like her will have no place.

This is a thought the mind can hold.

Scattered Along the River of Heaven

I grieve to think of the stars
Our ancestors our gods
Scattered like hairpin wounds
Along the River of Heaven
So tell me
Is it fitting that I spend my days here
A guest in those dark, forlorn halls?

THIS IS THE FIRST POEM XU ANSHI GAVE TO US; THE FIRST MEMORY she shared with us for safekeeping. It is the first one that she composed in High Mheng—which had been and remains a debased language, a blend between that of the San-Tay foreigners, and that of the Mheng, Anshi's own people.

She composed it on Shattered Pine Prison, sitting in the darkness of her cell, listening to the faint whine of the bots that crawled on the walls—melded to the metal and the crisscrossing wires, clinging to her skin—monitoring every minute movement she made—the voices of her heart, the beat of her thoughts in her brain, the sweat on her body.

Anshi had once been a passable poet in San-Tay, thoughtlessly fluent in the language of upper classes, the language of bot-handlers; but the medical facility had burnt that away from her, leaving an oddly-shaped hole in her mind, a gap that ached like a wound. When she tried to speak, no words would come out—not in San-Tay, not in High Mheng—only a raw croak, like the cry of a dying bird. Bots had once flowed to do her bidding; but now they only followed the will of the San-Tay.

There were no stars in Shattered Pine, where everything was dark with no windows; and where the faint yellow light soon leeched the prisoners' skin of all colors. But, once a week, the prisoners would be allowed onto the deck of the prison station—heavily escorted by San-Tay guards. Bots latched onto their faces and eyes, forcing them to stare into the darkness— into the event horizon of the black hole, where all light spiraled inwards and vanished, where everything was crushed into insignificance. There were bodies outside—prisoners who had attempted to escape, put in lifesuits and jettisoned, slowly drifting into a place where time and space ceased to have any meaning. If they were lucky, they were already dead.

From time to time, there would be a jerk as the bots stung someone back into wakefulness; or low moans and cries, from those whose minds had snapped. Shattered Pine bowed and broke everyone; and the prisoners that were released back to Felicity Station came back diminished and bent, waking up every night weeping and shaking with the memory of the black hole.

Anshi—who had been a scholar, a low-level magistrate, before she'd made the mistake of speaking up against the San-Tay—sat very still, and stared at the black hole—seeing into its heart, and knowing the truth: she was of no significance, easily broken, easily crushed—but she had known that since the start. All men were as nothing to the vast universe.

It was on the deck that Anshi met Zhiying—a small, diminutive woman who always sat next to her. She couldn't glance at Zhiying; but she felt her presence, nevertheless; the strength and hatred that emanated from her, that sustained her where other people failed.

Day after day they sat side by side, and Anshi formed poems in her mind, haltingly piecing them together in High Mheng—San-Tay was denied to her, and, like many of the Mheng upper class, she spoke no Low

Mheng. Day after day, with the bots clinging to her skin like overripe fruit, and Zhiying's presence, burning like fire at her side; and, as the verses became stronger and stronger in her mind, Anshi whispered words, out of the guards' hearing, out of the bots' discrimination capacities—haltingly at first, and then over and over, like a mantra on the prayer beads. Day after day; and, as the words sank deeper into her mind, Anshi slowly came to realize that the bots on her skin were not unmoving, but held themselves trembling, struggling against their inclination to move—and that the bots clinging to Zhiying were different, made of stronger materials to resist the fire of Zhiying's anger. She heard the fast, frantic beat of their thought processes, which had its own rhythm, like poetry spoken in secret—and felt the hard shimmer that connected the bots to the San-Tay guards, keeping everything together.

And, in the dim light of Shattered Pine, Anshi subvocalised words in High Mheng, reaching out with her mind as she had done, back when she had been free. She hadn't expected anything to happen; but the bots on her skin stiffened one after the other, and turned to the sound of her voice, awaiting orders.

BEFORE SHE left Felicity, Xu Wen expected security at San-Tay Prime's spaceport to be awful—they would take one glance at her travel documents, and bots would rise up from the ground and crawl up to search every inch of skin, every body cavity. Mother has warned her often enough that the San-Tay have never forgiven Felicity for waging war against them; that they will always remember the shame of losing their space colonies. She expects a personal interview with a Censor, or perhaps even to be turned back at the boundary, sent back in shame to Felicity.

But it doesn't turn out that way at all.

Security is over in a breeze, the bots giving her nothing but a cursory body check before the guards wave her through. She has no trouble getting a cab either; things must have changed on San-Tay Prime, and the San-Tay driver waves her on without paying attention to the color of her skin.

"Here on holiday?" the driver asks her in Galactic, as she slides into the floater—her body sinking as the chair adapts itself to her morphology. Bots climb onto her hands, showing her ads for nearby hotels and restaurants: an odd, disturbing sight, for there are no bots on Felicity Station.

"You could say that," Wen says, with a shrug she wills to be careless. "I used to live here."

A long, long time ago, when she was still a baby; before Mother had that frightful fight with Grandmother, and left San-Tay Prime for Felicity.

"Oh?" the driver swerves, expertly, amidst the traffic; taking one wide, tree-lined avenue after another. "You don't sound like it."

Wen shakes her head. "I was born here, but I didn't remain here long."

"Gone back to the old country, eh?" The driver smiles. "Can't say I blame you."

"Of course," Wen says, though she's unsure what to tell him. That she doesn't really know—that she never really lived here, not for more than a few years, and that she has a few confused memories of a bright-lit kitchen, and bots dancing for her on the carpet of Grandmother's apartment? But she's not here for such confidences. She's here—well, she's not sure why she's here. Mother was adamant Wen didn't have to come; but then, Mother has never forgiven Grandmother for the exile on San-Tay Prime.

Everything goes fine; until they reach the boundary district, where a group of large bots crawl onto the floater, and the driver's eyes roll up as their thought-threads meld with his. At length, the bots scatter, and he turns back to Wen. "Sorry, m'am," he says. "I have to leave you here."

"Oh?" Wen asked, struggling to hide her fear.

"No floaters allowed into the Mheng districts currently," the man said. "Some kind of funeral for a tribal leader—the brass is afraid there will be unrest." He shrugs again. "Still, you're local, right? You'll find someone to help you."

She's never been here; and she doesn't know anyone, anymore. Still, she forces a smile—always be graceful, Mother said—and puts her hand on one of the bots, feeling the warmth as it transfers money from her account on Felicity Station. After he's left her on the paved sidewalk of a street she barely recognizes, she stands, still feeling the touch of the bots against her skin—on Felicity they call them a degradation, a way for the San-Tay government to control everything and everyone; and she just couldn't bring herself to get a few locator-bots at the airport.

Wen looks up, at the signs—they're in both languages, San-Tay and what she assumes is High Mheng, the language of the exiles. San-Tay is all but banned on Felicity, only found on a few derelict signs on the Outer Rings, the ones the National Restructuring Committee hasn't gone around to retooling yet. Likewise, High Mheng isn't taught, or encouraged. What little she can remember is that it's always been a puzzle—the words look like Mheng; but when she tries to put everything together, their true meaning seems to slip away from her.

Feeling lost already, she wends her way deeper into the streets—those few shops that she bypasses are closed, with a white cloth spread over the door. White for grief, white for a funeral.

It all seems so—so wide, so open. Felicity doesn't have streets lined with trees, doesn't have such clean sidewalks—space on the station is at a ruthless premium, and every corridor is packed with stalls and shops—people eat at tables on the streets, and conduct their transactions in recessed doorways, or rooms half as large as the width of the sidewalk. She feels in another world; though, every now and then, she'll see a word that she recognizes on a sign, and follow it, in the forlorn hope that it will lead her closer to the funeral hall.

Street after street after street—under unfamiliar trees that sway in the breeze, listening to the distant music broadcast from every doorway, from every lamp. The air is warm and clammy, a far cry from Felicity's controlled temperature; and over her head are dark clouds. She almost hopes it rains, to see what it is like—in real life, and not in some simulation that seems like a longer, wetter version of a shower in the communal baths.

At length, as she reaches a smaller intersection, where four streets with unfamiliar signs branch off—some residential area, though all she can read are the numbers on the buildings—Wen stops, staring up at the sky. Might as well admit it: it's useless. She's lost, thoroughly lost in the middle of nowhere, and she'll never be on time for the funeral.

She'd weep; but weeping is a caprice, and she's never been capricious in her life. Instead, she turns back and attempts to retrace her steps, towards one of the largest streets—where, surely, she can hammer on a door, or find someone who will help her?

She can't find any of the streets; but at length, she bypasses a group of old men playing Encirclement on the street—watching the shimmering holo-board as if their lives depended on it.

"Excuse me?" she asks, in Mheng.

As one, the men turn towards her—their gazes puzzled. "I'm looking for White Horse Hall," Wen says. "For the funeral?"

The men still watch her, their faces impassive—dark with expressions she can't read. They're laden with smaller bots—on their eyes, on their hands and wrists, hanging black like obscene fruit: they look like the San-Tay in the reconstitution movies, except that their skins are darker, their eyes narrower.

At length, the eldest of the men steps forwards, and speaks up—his voice rerouted to his bots, coming out in halting Mheng. "You're not from here."

"No," Wen says in the same language. "I'm from Felicity."

An odd expression crosses their faces: longing, and hatred, and something else Wen cannot place. One of the men points to her, jabbers in High Mheng—Wen catches just one word she understands.

Xu Anshi.

"You're Anshi's daughter," the man says. The bots' approximation of his voice is slow, metallic, unlike the fast jabbering of High Mheng.

Wen shakes her head; and one of the other men laughs, saying something else in High Mheng.

That she's too young, no doubt—that Mother, Anshi's daughter, would be well into middle age by now, instead of being Wen's age. "Daughter of daughter," the man says, with a slight, amused smile. "Don't worry, we'll take you to the hall, to see your grandmother."

He walks by her side, with the other man, the one who laughed. Neither of them speaks—too hard to attempt small talk in a language they don't master, Wen guesses. They go down a succession of smaller and smaller streets, under banners emblazoned with the image of the *phuong*, Felicity's old symbol, before the Honored Leader made the new banner, the one that showed the station blazing among the stars—something more suitable for their new status.

Everything feels…odd, slightly twisted out of shape—the words not quite what they ought to be, the symbols just shy of familiar; the language a frightening meld of words she can barely recognize.

Everything is wrong, Wen thinks, shivering—and yet how can it be wrong, walking among Grandmother's own people?

Summoning bots I washed away
Ten thousand thousand years of poison
Awakening a thousand flower-flames, a thousand phoenix birds
Floating on a sea of blood like cresting waves
The weeping of the massacred millions rising from the darkness

WE RECEIVED this poem and its memories for safekeeping at a time when Xu Anshi was still on Felicity Station: on an evening before the Feast of Hungry Ghosts, when she sat in a room lit by trembling lights, thinking of Lao, her husband who had died in the uprisings—and wondering how much of it had been of any worth.

It refers to a time when Anshi was older, wiser—she and Zhiying had escaped from Shattered Pine, and spent three years moving from hiding place to hiding place, composing the pamphlets that, broadcast into every household, heralded the end of the San-Tay governance over Felicity.

On the night that would become known as the Second Ring Riots, Anshi stood in one of the inner rings of Felicity Station, her bots spread around her, hacked into the network—half of them on her legs, pumping modifiers into her blood; half of them linked to the other Mheng bot-handlers, retransmitting scenes of carnage, of the Mheng mob running wild in the San-Tay districts of the inner rings, the High Tribunal and Spaceport Authority lasered, and the fashionable districts trashed.

"This one," Zhiying said, pointing to a taller door, adorned with what appeared to be a Mheng traditional blessing—until one realized that the characters had been chosen for aesthetic reasons only, and that they meant nothing.

Anshi sent a subvocalised command to her bots, asking them to take the house. The feed to the rioting districts cut off abruptly, as her bots turned their attention towards the door and the house beyond: their sensors analyzing the bots on the walls, the pattern of the aerations, the cables running behind the door, and submitting hypotheses about possible architectures of the security system—before the swarm reached a consensus, and made a decision.

The bots flowed towards the door—the house's bots sought to stop them, but Anshi's bots split into two squads, and rushed past, heading for the head—the central control panel, which housed the bots' communication system. Anshi had a brief glimpse of red-painted walls, and blinking holos; before her bots rushed back, job completed, and fell on the now disorganized bots at the door.

Everything went dark, the Mheng characters slowly fading away from the door's panels.

"All yours," Anshi said to Zhiying, struggling to remain standing—all her bots were jabbering in her mind, putting forward suggestions as to what to do next; and, in her state of extreme fatigue, ignoring them was harder. She'd seen enough handlers burnt beyond recovery, their brains overloaded with external stimuli until they collapsed—she should have known better. But they needed her—the most gifted bot-handler they had, their strategist—needed her while the San-Tay were still reeling from their latest interplanetary war, while they were still weak. She'd rest later—after the San-Tay were gone, after the Mheng were free. There would be time, then, plenty of it.

Bao and Nhu were hitting the door with soldering knives—each blow weakening the metal until the door finally gave way with a groan. The crowd behind Anshi roared; and rushed through—pushing Anshi ahead of them, the world shrinking to a swirling, confused mass of details— gouged-out consoles, ornaments ripped from shelves, pale men thrown down and beaten against the rush of the crowd, a whirlwind of chaos, as if demons had risen up from the underworld.

The crowd spread as they moved inwards; and Anshi found herself at the center of a widening circle in what had once been a guest room. Beside her, Bao was hacking at a nondescript bed, while others in the crowd beat down on the huge screen showing a sunset with odd, distorted trees—some San-Tay planet that Anshi did not recognize, maybe even Prime. Anshi breathed, hard, struggling to steady herself in the midst of the devastation. Particles of down and dust drifted past her; she saw a bot on the further end, desperately trying to contain the devastation, scuttling to repair the gashes in the screen. Nhu downed it with a well-placed kick; her face distorted in a wide, disturbing grin.

"Look at that!" Bao held up a mirror-necklace, which shimmered and shifted, displaying a myriad configurations for its owner's pleasure.

Nhu's laughter was harsh. "They won't need it anymore." She held out a hand; but Bao threw the necklace to the ground; and ran it through with his knife.

Anshi did not move—as if in a trance she saw all of it: the screen, the bed, the pillows that sought to mould themselves to a pleasing shape, even as hands tore them apart; the jewellery scattered on the ground; and the image of the forest, fading away to be replaced by a dull, split-open wall—every single mark of San-Tay privilege, torn away and broken, never to come back. Her bots were relaying similar images from all over the station. The San-Tay would retaliate, but they would have understood, now, how fragile the foundation of their power was. How easily the downtrodden Mheng could become their downfall; and how much it would cost them to hold Felicity.

Good.

Anshi wandered through the house, seeking out the San-Tay bots—those she could hack and reprogram, she added to her swarm; the others she destroyed, as ruthlessly as the guards had culled the prisoners on Shattered Pine.

Anshi. Anshi.

Something was blinking, insistently, in the corner of her eyes—the swarm, bringing something to her attention. The kitchens—Zhiying, overseeing the executions. Bits and pieces, distorted through the bots' feed: the San-Tay governor, begging and pleading to be spared; his wife, dying silently, watching them all with hatred in her eyes. They'd had no children; for which Anshi was glad. She wasn't Zhiying, and she wasn't sure she'd have borne the guilt.

Guilt? There were children dying all over the station; men and women killed, if not by her, by those who followed her. She spared a bitter laugh. There was no choice. Children could die; or be raised to despise the inferior breed of the Mheng; be raised to take slaves and servants, and send dissenters like Anshi to be broken in Shattered Pine with a negligent wave of their hands. No choice.

Come, the bots whispered in her mind, but she did not know why.

Zhiying was down to the Grand Master of Security when Anshi walked into the kitchens—she barely nodded at Anshi, and turned her attention back to the man aligned in the weapons' sights.

She did not ask for any last words; though she did him the honor of using a bio-silencer on him, rather than the rifles they'd used on the family—his body crumpled inwards and fell, still intact; and he entered the world of the ancestors with the honor of a whole body. "He fought well," Zhiying said, curtly. "What of the house?"

"Not a soul left living," Anshi said, flicking through the bots' channels. "Not much left whole, either."

"Good," Zhiying said. She gestured; and the men dragged the next victim—a Mheng girl, dressed in the clothes of an indentured servant.

This—this was what the bots had wanted her to see. Anshi looked to the prisoners huddled against the wall: there was one San-Tay left, an elderly man who gazed back at her, steadily and without fear. The rest—all the rest—were Mheng, dressed in San-Tay clothes, their skin pale and washed-out in the flickering lights—stained with what looked like rice flour from one of the burst bags on the floor. Mheng. Their own people.

"Elder sister," Anshi said, horrified.

Zhiying's face was dark with anger. "You delude yourself. They're not Mheng anymore."

"Because they were indentured into servitude? Is that your idea of justice? They had no choice," Anshi said. The girl against the wall said nothing; her gaze slid away from Zhiying, to the rifle; finally resting on the body of her dead mistress.

"They had a choice. We had a choice," Zhiying said. Her gaze—dark and intense—rested, for a moment, on the girl. "If we spare them, they'll just run to the militia, and denounce us to find themselves a better household. Won't you?" she asked.

Anshi, startled, realized Zhiying had addressed the girl—whose gaze still would not meet theirs, as if they'd been foreigners themselves.

At length, the girl threw her head back, and spoke in High Mheng. "They were always kind with me, and you butchered them like pigs." She was shivering now. "What will you achieve? You can't hide on Felicity. The San-Tay will come here and kill you all, and when they're done, they'll put us in the dark forever. It won't be cushy jobs like this—they'll consign us to the scavenge heaps, to the ducts-cleaning and the bots-scraping, and we won't ever see starlight again."

"See?" Zhiying said. "Pathetic." She gestured, and the girl crumpled like the man before her. The soldiers dragged the body away, and brought the old San-Tay man. Zhiying paused; and turned back to Anshi. "You're angry."

"Yes," Anshi said. "I did not join this so we could kill our own countrymen."

Zhiying's mouth twisted in a bitter smile. "Collaborators," she said. "How do you think a regime like the San-Tay continues to exist? It's because they take some of their servants, and set them above others. Because they make us complicit in our own oppression. That's the worst of what they do, little sister—turn us against each other."

No. The thought was crystal-clear in Anshi's mind, like a blade held against starlight. That's not the worst. The worst is that, to fight them, we have to best them at their own game.

She watched the old man as he died; and saw nothing in his eyes but the reflection of that bitter knowledge.

WHITE HORSE Hall is huge, so huge that it's a wonder Wen didn't see it from afar—more than a hundred stories, and more unveil as her floater lifts higher and higher, away from the crowd massed on the ground. Above the cloud cover, other white-clad floaters weave in and out of the traffic, as if to the steps of a dance only they can see.

She's alone: her escort left her at the floater station—the older man with a broad smile and a wave, and the second man with a scowl, looking away from her. As they ascend higher and higher, and the air thins out—to almost the temperature of Felicity—Wen tries to relax, but cannot do so. She's late; and she knows it—and they probably won't admit her into the hall at all. She's a stranger here; and Mother is right: she would be better off in Felicity with Zhengyao, enjoying her period of rest by flying kites, or going for a ride on Felicity's River of Good Fortune.

At the landing pad, a woman is waiting for her: small and plump, with hair shining silver in the unfiltered sunlight. Her face is frozen in careful blankness, and she wears the white of mourners, with none of the markers for the family of the dead.

"Welcome," she says, curtly nodding to acknowledge Wen's presence. "I am Ho Van Nhu.",

"Grandmother's friend," Wen says.

Nhu's face twists in an odd expression. "You know my name?" She speaks perfect Galactic, with a very slight trace of an accent—heard only in the odd inflections she puts on her own name.

Wen could lie; could say that Mother spoke of her often; but here, in this thin, cold air, she finds that she cannot lie—any more than one does not lie in the presence of the Honoured Leader. "They teach us about you in school," she says, blushing.

Nhu snorts. "Not in good terms, I'd imagine. Come," she says. "Let's get you prepared."

There are people everywhere, in costumes Wen recognizes from her history lessons—oddly old-fashioned and formal, collars flaring in the San-Tay fashion, though the five panels of the dresses are those of the Mheng high court, in the days before the San-Tay's arrival.

Nhu pushes her way through the crowd, confident, until they reach a deserted room. She stands for a while in the center, eyes closed, and bots crawl out of the interstices, dragging vegetables and balls of rolled-up dough—black and featureless, their bodies gleaming like knife-blades, their legs moving on a rhythm like centipedes or spiders.

Wen watches, halfway between fascination and horror, as they cut up the vegetables into small pieces—flatten the dough and fill up dumplings, and put them inside small steamer units that other bots have dragged up. Other bots are already cleaning up the counter, and there is a smell in the room—tea brewing in a corner. "I don't—" Wen starts. How can she eat any of that, knowing how it was prepared? She swallows, and forces herself to speak more civilly. "I should be with her."

Nhu shakes her head. Beads of sweat pearl on her face; but she seems to be gaining color as the bots withdraw, one by one—except that Wen can still *see* them, tucked away under the cupboards and the sink, like curled-up cockroaches. "This is the wake, and you're already late for it. It won't make any difference if you come in quarter of an hour later. And I would be a poor host if I didn't offer you any food."

There are two cups of tea on the central table; Nhu pours from a teapot, and pushes one to Wen—who hesitates for a moment, and then takes it, fighting against a wave of nausea. Bots dragged out the pot; the tea leaves. Bots touched the liquid that she's inhaling right now.

"You look like your mother when she was younger," Nhu says, sipping at the tea. "Like your grandmother, too." Her voice is matter-of-fact; but Wen can feel the grief Nhu is struggling to contain. "You must have had a hard time, at school."

Wen thinks on it for a while. "I don't think so," she says. She's had the usual bullying, the mockeries of her clumsiness, of her provincial accent. But nothing specifically directed at her ancestors. "They did not really care about who my grandmother was." It's the stuff of histories now; almost vanished—only the generation of the Honored Leader remembers what it was like, under the San-Tay.

"I see," Nhu says.

An uncomfortable silence stretches, which Nhu makes no effort to break.

Small bots float by, carrying a tray with the steamed dumplings—like the old vids, when the San-Tay would be receiving their friends at home. Except, of course, that the Mheng were doing the cutting-up and the cooking, in the depths of the kitchen.

"They make you uncomfortable," Nhu says.

Wen grimaces. "I—we don't have bots, on Felicity."

"I know. The remnants of the San-Tay—the technologies of servitude, which should better be forgotten and lost." Her voice is light, ironic; and Wen realizes that she is quoting from one of the Honored Leader's speeches. "Just like High Mheng. Tell me, Wen, what do the histories say of Xu Anshi?"

Nothing, Wen wants to say; but as before, she cannot bring herself to lie. "That she used the technologies of the San-Tay against them; but that, in the end, she fell prey to the lure of their power." It's what she's been told all her life; the only things that have filled the silence Mother maintains about Grandmother. But, now, staring at this small, diminutive woman, she feels almost ashamed. "That she and her followers were given a choice between exile, and death."

"And you believe that?"

"I don't know," Wen says. And, more carefully, "Does it matter?"

Nhu shrugs, shaking her head. "Mingxia—your mother once asked Anshi if she believed in reconciliation with Felicity. Anshi told her that reconciliation was nothing more than another word for forgetfulness. She was a hard woman. But then, she'd lost so much in the war. We all did."

"I'm not Mother," Wen says, and Nhu shakes her head, with a brief smile. "No. You're here."

Out of duty, Wen thinks. Because someone has to come, and Mother won't. Because someone should remember Grandmother, even if it's Wen—who didn't know her, didn't know the war. She wonders what the Honored Leader will say about Grandmother's death, on Felicity—if she'll mourn the passing of a liberator, or remind them all to be firm, to reject the evil of the San-Tay, more than sixty years after the foreigners' withdrawal from Felicity.

She wonders how much of the past is worth clinging to.

See how the gilded Heavens are covered
With the burning bitter tears of our departed
Cast away into darkness, they contradict no truths
Made mute and absent, they denounce no lies

Anshi gave this poem into our keeping on the night after her daughter left her. She was crying then, trying not to show it—muttering about ungrateful children, and their inability to comprehend any of what their ancestors had gone through. Her hand shook, badly; and she stared into her cup of tea, as hard as she had once stared into the black hole and its currents, dragging everything into the lightless depths. But then, as on Shattered Pine, the only thing that came to her was merciless clarity, like the glint of a blade or a claw.

It is an old, old composition, its opening lines the last Anshi wrote on Felicity Station. Just as the first poem defined her youth—the escaped prisoner, the revolution's foremost bot-handler—this defined her closing decades, in more ways than one.

The docks were deserted; not because it was early in the station's cycle, not because the war had diminished interstellar travel; but because the docks had been cordoned off by Mheng loyalists. They gazed at Anshi, steadily—their eyes blank; though the mob behind them brandished placards and howled for her blood.

"It's not fair," Nhu said. She was carrying Anshi's personal belongings—Anshi's bots, and those of all her followers, were already packed in the hold of the ship. Anshi held her daughter Mingxia by the hand: the child's eyes were wide, but she didn't speak. Anshi knew she would have questions, later—but all that mattered, here and now, was surviving this. "You're a heroine of the uprising. You shouldn't have to leave like a branded criminal."

Anshi said nothing. She scanned the crowd, wondering if Zhiying would be there, at the last—if she'd smile and wish her well, or make one last stab of the knife. "She's right, in a way," she said, wearily. The crowd's hatred was palpable, even where she stood. "The bots are a remnant of the San-Tay, just like High Mheng. It's best for everyone if we forget it all." Best for everyone but them.

"You don't believe that," Nhu said.

"No." Not any of that; but she knew what was in Zhiying's heart, the hatred of the San-Tay that she carried with her—that, to her elder sister, she would be nothing more than a collaborator herself—tainted by her use of the enemy's technology.

"She just wants you gone. Because you're her rival."

"She doesn't think like that," Anshi said, more sharply than she'd intended; and she knew, too, that she didn't believe that. Zhiying had a vision of the Mheng as strong and powerful; and she'd allow nothing and no one to stand in its way.

They were past the cordon now, and the maw of the ship gaped before them—the promise of a life somewhere else, on another planet. Ironic, in a way—the ship was from the San-Tay High Government, seeking amends for their behavior on colonized stations. If someone had ever told her she'd ride one of those as a guest…

Nhu, without hesitation, was heading up towards the dark tunnel. "You don't have to come," Anshi said.

Nhu rolled her eyes upwards, and made no comment. Like Anshi, she was old guard; a former teacher in the Mheng schools, fluent in High Mheng, and with a limited ability to control the bots. A danger, like Anshi.

There was a noise behind them—the beginning of a commotion. Anshi turned; and saw that, contrary to what she'd thought, Zhiying had come.

She wore the sash of Honored Leader well; and the stars of Felicity's new flag were spread across her dress—which was a shorter, less elaborate version of the five-panel ceremonial garb. Her hair had been pulled up in an elegant bun, thrust through with a golden phoenix pin, the first jewel to come out of the station's new workshops—she was unrecognizable from the gaunt, tall prisoner Anshi remembered, or even from the dark, intense leader of the rebellion years.

"Younger sister." She bowed to Anshi, but did not come closer; remaining next to her escort of black-clad soldiers. "We wish you happiness, and good fortune among the stars."

"We humbly thank you, Your Reverence," Anshi said—keeping the irony, and the hurt from her voice. Zhiying's eyes were dark, with the same anger Anshi remembered from the night of the Second Ring riots—the night when the girl had died. They stood, staring at each other, and at length Zhiying gestured for Anshi to move.

Anshi backed away, slowly, pulling her daughter by the hand. She wasn't sure why she felt…drained, as if a hundred bots had been pumping modifiers into her blood, and had suddenly stopped. She wasn't sure what she'd expected—an apology? Zhiying had never been one for it; or for doubts of any kind. But still—

Still, they'd been on Shattered Pine together; had escaped together; had preached and written the poetry of the revolution, and dared each other to hack into Felicity's network to spread it into every household, every corridor screen.

There should have been something more than a formal send-off; something more than the eyes boring into hers—dark and intense, and with no hint of sorrow or tears.

We do not weep for the enemy, Anshi thought; as she turned, and passed under the wide metal arc that led into the ship, her daughter's hand heavy in hers.

IN THE small antechamber, Wen dons robes of dark blue—those reserved for the mourners who are the closest family to the dead. She can hear, in the distance, the drone of prayers from the priests, and the scuttling of bots on the walls, carrying faint music until the entire structure of the hall seems to echo with it. Slowly, carefully, she rises, and stares at her pale, wan self in the mirror—with coiled bots at its angles, awaiting just an order to awaken and bring her anything she might desire. Abominations, she thinks, uneasily, but it's hard to see them as something other than alien, incomprehensible.

Nhu is waiting for her at the great doors—the crowd has parted, letting her through with an almost religious hush. In silence, Wen kneels, her head bent down—an honor to the dead, an acknowledgement that she is late and that she must make amends, for leaving Grandmother's ghost alone.

She hears a noise as the doors open—catches a flash of a crowd dressed in blue; and then she is crawling towards the coffin, staring at the ground ahead of her. By her side, there are glimpses of dresses' hems, of shoes that are an uneasy meld of San-Tay and Mheng. Ahead, a steady drone from the monks at the pulpit, taken up by the crowd; a prayer in High Mheng, incomprehensible words segueing into a melodious chant; and a smell of incense mingled with something else, a flower she cannot recognize. The floor under her is warm, soft—unlike Felicity's utilitarian metal or carpets, a wealth of painted ostentation with patterns she cannot make out.

As she crawls, Wen finds herself, incongruously, thinking of Mother.

She asked, once, why Mother had left San-Tay Prime—expecting Mother to rail once more at Grandmother's failures. But Mother merely pulled a low bench, and sat down with a sigh. "There was no choice, child. We could dwindle away on San-Tay Prime, drifting further and further away from Felicity with every passing moment. Or we could come back home."

"It's not Grandmother's home," Wen said, slowly, confusedly—with a feeling that she was grappling with something beyond her years.

"No," Mother said. "And, if we had waited too long, it wouldn't have been your home either."

"I don't understand." Wen put a hand on one of the kitchen cupboards—the door slid away, letting her retrieve a can of dried, powdered shrimp, which she dumped into the broth on the stove.

"Like two men carried away by two different currents in the river—both ending in very different places." She waved a dismissive hand. "You'll understand, when you're older."

"Is that why you're not talking with Grandmother?"

Mother grimaced, staring into the depths of her celadon cup. "Grandmother and I...did not agree on things," she said. "Sometimes I think..." She shook her head. "Stubborn old woman. She never could admit that she had lost. That the future of Felicity wasn't with bots, with High Mheng; with any of what the San-Tay had left us."

Bots. High Mheng—all of the things that don't exist anymore, on the new Felicity—all the things the Honored Leader banished, for the safety and glory of the people. "Mother…" Wen said, suddenly afraid.

Her mother smiled; and for the first time Wen saw the bitterness in her eyes. "Never mind, child. This isn't your burden to carry."

Wen did not understand. But now…now, as she crawls down the aisle, breathing in the unfamiliar smells, she thinks she understands. Reconciliation means forgetfulness, and is it such a bad thing that they forget, that they are no longer chained to the hatreds of the past?

She reaches the coffin, and rises—turns, for a brief moment, to stare at the sea of humanity before her—the blurred faces with bots at the corner of their eyes, with alien scents and alien clothes. They are not from Felicity anymore, but something else—poised halfway between the San-Tay and the culture that gave them birth; and, as the years pass, those that do not come back will drift further and further from Felicity, until they will pass each other in the street, and not feel anything but a vague sense of familiarity, like long-lost families that have become strangers to each other.

No, not from Felicity anymore—and does it matter, any of it?

Wen has no answer—none of Mother's bleak certainties about life. And so she turns away from the crowd, and looks into the coffin—into the face of a stranger, across a gap like a flowing river, dark and forever unbridgeable.

I am in halves, dreaming of a faraway home
Not a dry spot on my moonlit pillow
Through the open window lie the stars and planets
Where ten thousand family members have scattered
Along the River of Heaven, with no bridges to lead them home
The long yearning
Cuts into my heart

THIS IS the last poem we received from Xu Anshi; the last one she composed, before the sickness ate away at her command of High Mheng, and we could no longer understand her subvocalised orders. She said to us then, "it is done"; and turned away from us, awaiting death.

We are here now, as Wen looks at the pale face of her grandmother. We are not among our brethren in the crowd—not clinging to faces, not curled on the walls or at the corner of mirrors, awaiting orders to unfold.

We have another place.

We rest on the coffin with Xu Anshi's other belongings; scattered among the paper offerings—the arch leading into the Heavens, the bills stamped with the face of the King of Hell. We sit quiescent, waiting for Xu Wen to call us up—that we might flow up to her like a black tide, carrying her inheritance to her, and the memories that made up Xu Anshi's life from beginning to end.

But Wen's gaze slides right past us, seeing us as nothing more than a necessary evil at the ceremony; and the language she might summon us in is one she does not speak and has no interest in.

In silence, she walks away from the coffin to take her place among the mourners—and we, too, remain silent, taking our understanding of Xu Anshi's life into the yawning darkness.

"With apologies to Qiu Jin, Bei Dao and the classical
Tang poets for borrowing and twisting their best lines"

Immersion

IN THE MORNING, YOU'RE NO LONGER QUITE SURE WHO YOU ARE.

You stand in front of the mirror—it shifts and trembles, reflecting only what you want to see—eyes that feel too wide, skin that feels too pale, an odd, distant smell wafting from the compartment's ambient system that is neither incense nor garlic, but something else, something elusive that you once knew.

You're dressed, already—not on your skin, but outside, where it matters, your avatar sporting blue and black and gold, the stylish clothes of a well-travelled, well-connected woman. For a moment, as you turn away from the mirror, the glass shimmers out of focus; and another woman in a dull silk gown stares back at you: smaller, squatter and in every way diminished—a stranger, a distant memory that has ceased to have any meaning.

QUY WAS on the docks, watching the spaceships arrive. She could, of course, have been anywhere on Longevity Station, and requested the feed from the network to be patched to her router—and watched, superimposed on her field of vision, the slow dance of ships slipping into their pod cradles like births watched in reverse. But there was something about standing on the spaceport's concourse—a feeling of closeness that she just couldn't replicate by standing in Golden Carp Gardens or Azure Dragon Temple. Because here—here, separated by only a few measures of sheet metal from the cradle pods, she could feel herself teetering on the edge of the vacuum, submerged in cold and breathing in neither air nor oxygen. She could almost imagine herself rootless, finally returned to the source of everything.

Most ships those days were Galactic—you'd have thought Longevity's ex-masters would have been unhappy about the station's independence, but now that the war was over Longevity was a tidy source of profit. The ships came; and disgorged a steady stream of tourists—their eyes too round and straight, their jaws too square; their faces an unhealthy shade of pink, like undercooked meat left too long in the sun. They walked with the easy confidence of people with immersers: pausing to admire the suggested highlights for a second or so before moving on to the transport station, where they haggled in schoolbook Rong for a ride to their recommended hotels—a sickeningly familiar ballet Quy had been seeing most of her life, a unison of foreigners descending on the station like a plague of centipedes or leeches.

Still, Quy watched them. They reminded her of her own time on Prime, her heady schooldays filled with raucous bars and wild weekends, and late minute revisions for exams, a carefree time she'd never have again in her life. She both longed for those days back, and hated herself for her weakness. Her education on Prime, which should have been her path into the higher strata of the station's society, had brought her nothing but a sense of disconnection from her family; a growing solitude, and a dissatisfaction, an aimlessness she couldn't put in words.

She might not have moved all day—had a sign not blinked, superimposed by her router on the edge of her field of vision. A message from Second Uncle.

"Child." His face was pale and worn, his eyes underlined by dark circles, as if he hadn't slept. He probably hadn't—the last Quy had seen of him, he had been closeted with Quy's sister Tam, trying to organise a delivery for a wedding—five hundred winter melons, and six barrels of Prosper Station's best fish sauce. "Come back to the restaurant."

"I'm on my day of rest," Quy said; it came out as more peevish and childish than she'd intended.

Second Uncle's face twisted, in what might have been a smile, though he had very little sense of humour. The scar he'd got in the Independence War shone white against the grainy background—twisting back and forth, as if it still pained him. "I know, but I need you. We have an important customer."

"Galactic," Quy said. That was the only reason he'd be calling her, and not one of her brothers or cousins. Because the family somehow thought that her studies on Prime gave her insight into the Galactics' way of thought—something useful, if not the success they'd hoped for.

"Yes. An important man, head of a local trading company." Second Uncle did not move on her field of vision. Quy could *see* the ships moving through his face, slowly aligning themselves in front of their pods, the hole in front of them opening like an orchid flower. And she knew everything there was to know about Grandmother's restaurant; she was Tam's sister, after all; and she'd seen the accounts, the slow decline of their clientele as their more genteel clients moved to better areas of the station; the influx of tourists on a budget, with little time for expensive dishes prepared with the best ingredients.

"Fine," she said. "I'll come."

AT BREAKFAST, you stare at the food spread out on the table: bread and jam and some coloured liquid—you come up blank for a moment, before your immerser kicks in, reminding you that it's coffee, served strong and black, just as you always take it.

Yes. Coffee.

You raise the cup to your lips—your immerser gently prompts you, reminding you of where to grasp, how to lift, how to be in every possible way graceful and elegant, always an effortless model.

"It's a bit strong," your husband says, apologetically. He watches you from the other end of the table, an expression you can't interpret on his face—and isn't this odd, because shouldn't you know all there is to know about expressions—shouldn't the immerser have everything about Galactic culture recorded into its database, shouldn't it prompt you? But it's strangely silent, and this scares you, more than anything. Immersers never fail.

"Shall we go?" your husband says—and, for a moment, you come up blank on his name, before you remember—Galen, it's Galen, named after some physician on Old Earth. He's tall, with dark hair and pale skin—his immerser avatar isn't much different from his real self, Galactic avatars seldom are. It's people like you who have to work the hardest to adjust, because so much about you draws attention to itself—the stretched eyes that crinkle in the shape of moths, the darker skin, the smaller, squatter shape more reminiscent of jackfruits than swaying fronds. But no matter: you can be made perfect; you can put on the immerser and become someone else, someone pale-skinned and tall and beautiful.

Though, really, it's been such a long time since you took off the immerser, hasn't it? It's just a thought—a suspended moment that is soon erased by the immerser's flow of information, the little arrows drawing your attention to the bread and the kitchen, and the polished metal of the table—giving you context about everything, opening up the universe like a lotus flower.

"Yes," you say. "Let's go." Your tongue trips over the word—there's a structure you should have used, a pronoun you should have said instead of the lapidary Galactic sentence. But nothing will come, and you feel like a field of sugar canes after the harvest—burnt out, all cutting edges with no sweetness left inside.

OF COURSE, Second Uncle insisted on Quy getting her immerser for the interview—just in case, he said, soothingly and diplomatically as always. Trouble was, it wasn't where Quy had last left it. After putting out a message to the rest of the family, the best information Quy got was from Cousin Khanh, who thought he'd seen Tam sweep through the living quarters, gathering every piece of Galactic tech she could get her hands on. Third Aunt, who caught Khanh's message on the family's communication channel, tutted disapprovingly. "Tam. Always with her mind lost in the mountains, that girl. Dreams have never husked rice."

Quy said nothing. Her own dreams had shrivelled and died after she came back from Prime and failed Longevity's mandarin exams; but it was good to have Tam around—to have someone who saw beyond the restaurant, beyond the narrow circle of family interests. Besides, if she didn't stick with her sister, who would?

Tam wasn't in the communal areas on the upper floors; Quy threw a glance towards the lift to Grandmother's closeted rooms, but she was doubtful Tam would have gathered Galactic tech just so she could pay her respects to Grandmother. Instead, she went straight to the lower floor, the one she and Tam shared with the children of their generation.

It was right next to the kitchen, and the smells of garlic and fish sauce seemed to be everywhere—of course, the youngest generation always got the lower floor, the one with all the smells and the noises of a legion of waitresses bringing food over to the dining room.

Tam was there, sitting in the little compartment that served as the floor's communal area. She'd spread out the tech on the floor—two immersers (Tam and Quy were possibly the only family members who cared so little about immersers they left them lying around), a remote entertainment set that was busy broadcasting some stories of children running on terraformed planets, and something Quy couldn't quite identify, because Tam had taken it apart into small components: it lay on the table like a gutted fish, all metals and optical parts.

But, at some point, Tam had obviously got bored with the entire process, because she was currently finishing her breakfast, slurping noodles from her soup bowl. She must have got it from the kitchen's leftovers, because Quy knew the smell, could taste the spiciness of the broth on her tongue—Mother's cooking, enough to make her stomach growl although she'd had rolled rice cakes for breakfast.

"You're at it again," Quy said with a sigh. "Could you not take my immerser for your experiments, please?"

Tam didn't even look surprised. "You don't seem very keen on using it, big sis."

"That I don't use it doesn't mean it's yours," Quy said, though that wasn't a real reason. She didn't mind Tam borrowing her stuff, and actually would have been glad to never put on an immerser again—she hated the feeling they gave her, the vague sensation of the system rooting around in her brain to find the best body cues to give her. But there were times when she was expected to wear an immerser: whenever dealing with customers, whether she was waiting at tables or in preparation meetings for large occasions.

Tam, of course, didn't wait at tables—she'd made herself so good at logistics and anything to do with the station's system that she spent most of her time in front of a screen, or connected to the station's network.

"Lil' sis?" Quy said.

Tam set her chopsticks by the side of the bowl, and made an expansive gesture with her hands. "Fine. Have it back. I can always use mine."

Quy stared at the things spread on the table, and asked the inevitable question. "How's progress?"

Tam's work was network connections and network maintenance within the restaurant; her hobby was tech. Galactic tech. She took things apart to see what made them tick; and rebuilt them. Her foray into entertainment units had helped the restaurant set up ambient sounds—old-fashioned Rong music for Galactic customers, recitation of the newest poems for locals.

But immersers had her stumped: the things had nasty safeguards to them. You could open them in half, to replace the battery; but you went no further. Tam's previous attempt had almost lost her the use of her hands.

By Tam's face, she didn't feel ready to try again. "It's got to be the same logic."

"As what?" Quy couldn't help asking. She picked up her own immerser from the table, briefly checking that it did indeed bear her serial number.

Tam gestured to the splayed components on the table. "Artificial Literature Writer. Little gadget that composes light entertainment novels."

"That's not the same—" Quy checked herself, and waited for Tam to explain.

"Takes existing cultural norms, and puts them into a cohesive, satisfying narrative. Like people forging their own path and fighting aliens for possession of a planet, that sort of stuff that barely speaks to us on Longevity. I mean, we've never even seen a planet." Tam exhaled, sharply— her eyes half on the dismembered Artificial Literature Writer, half on some overlay of her vision. "Just like immersers take a given culture and parcel it out to you in a form you can relate to—language, gestures, customs, the whole package. They've got to have the same architecture."

"I'm still not sure what you want to do with it." Quy put on her immerser, adjusting the thin metal mesh around her head until it fitted. She winced as the interface synched with her brain. She moved her hands, adjusting some settings lower than the factory ones—darn thing always reset itself to factory, which she suspected was no accident. A shimmering lattice surrounded her: her avatar, slowly taking shape around her. She could still see the room—the lattice was only faintly opaque—but ancestors, how she hated the feeling of not quite being there. "How do I look?"

"Horrible. Your avatar looks like it's died or something."

"Ha ha ha," Quy said. Her avatar was paler than her, and taller: it made her look beautiful, most customers agreed. In those moments, Quy was glad she had an avatar, so they wouldn't see the anger on her face. "You haven't answered my question."

Tam's eyes glinted. "Just think of the things we couldn't do. This is the best piece of tech Galactics have ever brought us."

Which wasn't much, but Quy didn't need to say it aloud. Tam knew exactly how Quy felt about Galactics and their hollow promises.

"It's their weapon, too." Tam pushed at the entertainment unit. "Just like their books and their holos and their live games. It's fine for them—they put the immersers on tourist settings, they get just what they need to navigate a foreign environment from whatever idiot's written the Rong script for that thing. But we—we worship them. We wear the immersers on Galactic all the time. We make ourselves like them, because they push, and because we're naive enough to give in."

"And you think you can make this better?" Quy couldn't help it. It wasn't that she needed to be convinced: on Prime, she'd never seen immersers. They were tourist stuff, and even while travelling from one city to another, the citizens just assumed they'd know enough to get by. But the stations, their ex-colonies, were flooded with immersers.

Tam's eyes glinted, as savage as those of the rebels in the history holos. "If I can take them apart, I can rebuild them and disconnect the logical circuits. I can give us the language and the tools to deal with them without being swallowed by them."

Mind lost in the mountains, Third Aunt said. No one had ever accused Tam of thinking small. Or of not achieving what she set her mind on, come to think of it. And every revolution had to start somewhere—hadn't Longevity's War of Independence started over a single poem, and the unfair imprisonment of the poet who'd written it?

Quy nodded. She believed Tam, though she didn't know how far. "Fair point. Have to go now, or Second Uncle will skin me. See you later, lil' sis."

As you walk under the wide arch of the restaurant with your husband, you glance upwards, at the calligraphy that forms its sign. The immerser translates it for you into "Sister Hai's Kitchen", and starts giving you a detailed background of the place: the menu and the most recommended dishes—as you walk past the various tables, it highlights items it thinks you would like, from rolled-up rice dumplings to fried shrimps. It warns you about the more exotic dishes, like the pickled pig's ears, the fermented meat (you have to be careful about that one, because its name changes depending on which station dialect you order in), or the reeking durian fruit that the natives so love.

It feels...not quite right, you think, as you struggle to follow Galen, who is already far away, striding ahead with the same confidence he always exudes in life. People part before him; a waitress with a young, pretty avatar bows before him, though Galen himself takes no notice. You know that such obsequiousness unnerves him; he always rants about the outdated customs aboard Longevity, the inequalities and the lack of democratic government—he thinks it's only a matter of time before they change, adapt themselves to fit into Galactic society. You—you have a faint memory of arguing with him, a long time ago, but now you can't find the words, anymore, or even the reason why—it makes sense, it all makes sense. The Galactics rose against the tyranny of Old Earth and overthrew their shackles, and won the right to determine their own destiny; and every other station and planet will do the same, eventually, rise against the dictatorships that hold them away from progress. It's right; it's always been right.

Unbidden, you stop at a table, and watch two young women pick at a dish of chicken with chopsticks—the smell of fish sauce and lemongrass rises in the air, as pungent and as unbearable as rotten meat—no, no, that's not it, you have an image of a dark-skinned woman, bringing a dish of steamed rice to the table, her hands filled with that same smell, and your mouth watering in anticipation...

The young women are looking at you: they both wear standard-issue avatars, the bottom-of-the-line kind—their clothes are a garish mix of red and yellow, with the odd, uneasy cut of cheap designers; and their faces waver, letting you glimpse a hint of darker skin beneath the red flush of their cheeks. Cheap and tawdry, and altogether inappropriate; and you're glad you're not one of them.

"Can I help you, older sister?" one of them asks.

Older sister. A pronoun you were looking for, earlier; one of the things that seem to have vanished from your mind. You struggle for words; but all the immerser seems to suggest to you is a neutral and impersonal pronoun, one that you instinctively know is wrong—it's one only foreigners and outsiders would use in those circumstances. "Older sister," you repeat, finally, because you can't think of anything else.

"Agnes!"

Galen's voice, calling from far away—for a brief moment the immerser seems to fail you again, because you *know* that you have many names, that Agnes is the one they gave you in Galactic school, the one neither Galen nor his friends can mangle when they pronounce it. You remember the Rong names your mother gave you on Longevity, the childhood endearments and your adult style name.

Be-Nho, Be-Yeu. Thu—Autumn, like a memory of red maple leaves on a planet you never knew.

You pull away from the table, disguising the tremor in your hands.

Second Uncle was already waiting when Quy arrived; and so were the customers.

"You're late," Second Uncle sent on the private channel, though he made the comment half-heartedly, as if he'd expected it all along. As if he'd never really believed he could rely on her—that stung.

"Let me introduce my niece Quy to you," Second Uncle said, in Galactic, to the man beside him.

"Quy," the man said, his immerser perfectly taking up the nuances of her name in Rong. He was everything she'd expected; tall, with only a thin layer of avatar, a little something that narrowed his chin and eyes, and made his chest slightly larger. Cosmetic enhancements: he was good-looking for a Galactic, all things considered. He went on, in Galactic, "My name is Galen Santos. Pleased to meet you. This is my wife, Agnes."

Agnes. Quy turned, and looked at the woman for the first time—and flinched. There was no one here: just a thick layer of avatar, so dense and so complex that she couldn't even guess at the body hidden within.

"Pleased to meet you." On a hunch, Quy bowed, from younger to elder, with both hands brought together—Rong-style, not Galactic—and saw a shudder run through Agnes' body, barely perceptible; but Quy was observant, she'd always been. Her immerser was screaming at her, telling her to hold out both hands, palms up, in the Galactic fashion. She tuned it out: she was still at the stage where she could tell the difference between her thoughts and the immerser's thoughts.

Second Uncle was talking again—his own avatar was light, a paler version of him. "I understand you're looking for a venue for a banquet."

"We are, yes." Galen pulled a chair to him, sank into it. They all followed suit, though not with the same fluid, arrogant ease. When Agnes sat, Quy saw her flinch, as though she'd just remembered something unpleasant. "We'll be celebrating our fifth marriage anniversary, and we both felt we wanted to mark the occasion with something suitable."

Second Uncle nodded. "I see," he said, scratching his chin. "My congratulations to you."

Galen nodded. "We thought—" he paused, threw a glance at his wife that Quy couldn't quite interpret—her immerser came up blank, but there was something oddly familiar about it, something she ought to have been able to name. "Something Rong," he said at last. "A large banquet for a hundred people, with the traditional dishes."

Quy could almost feel Second Uncle's satisfaction. A banquet of that size would be awful logistics, but it would keep the restaurant afloat for a year or more, if they could get the price right. But something was wrong—something—

"What did you have in mind?" Quy asked, not to Galen, but to his wife. The wife—Agnes, which probably wasn't the name she'd been born with—who wore a thick avatar, and didn't seem to be answering or ever speaking up. An awful picture was coming together in Quy's mind.

Agnes didn't answer. Predictable.

Second Uncle took over, smoothing over the moment of awkwardness with expansive hand gestures. "The whole hog, yes?" Second Uncle said. He rubbed his hands, an odd gesture that Quy had never seen from him—a Galactic expression of satisfaction. "Bitter melon soup, Dragon-Phoenix plates, Roast Pig, Jade Under the Mountain…" He was citing all the traditional dishes for a wedding banquet—unsure of how far the foreigner wanted to take it. He left out the odder stuff, like Shark Fin or Sweet Red Bean Soup.

"Yes, that's what we would like. Wouldn't we, darling?" Galen's wife neither moved nor spoke. Galen's head turned towards her, and Quy caught his expression at last. She'd thought it would be contempt, or hatred; but no; it was anguish. He genuinely loved her, and he couldn't understand what was going on.

Galactics. Couldn't he recognise an immerser junkie when he saw one? But then Galactics, as Tam said, seldom had the problem—they didn't put on the immersers for more than a few days on low settings, if they ever went that far. Most were flat-out convinced Galactic would get them anywhere.

Second Uncle and Galen were haggling, arguing prices and features; Second Uncle sounding more and more like a Galactic tourist as the conversation went on, more and more aggressive for lower and lower gains. Quy didn't care anymore: she watched Agnes. Watched the impenetrable avatar—a red-headed woman in the latest style from Prime, with freckles on her skin and a hint of a star-tan on her face. But that wasn't what she was, inside; what the immerser had dug deep into.

Wasn't who she was at all. Tam was right; all immersers should be taken apart, and did it matter if they exploded? They'd done enough harm as it was.

Quy wanted to get up, to tear away her own immerser, but she couldn't, not in the middle of the negotiation. Instead, she rose, and walked closer to Agnes; the two men barely glanced at her, too busy agreeing on a price. "You're not alone," she said, in Rong, low enough that it didn't carry.

Again, that odd, disjointed flash. "You have to take it off." Quy said, but got no further response. As an impulse, she grabbed the other woman's arm—felt her hands go right through the immerser's avatar, connect with warm, solid flesh.

YOU HEAR them negotiating, in the background—it's tough going, because the Rong man sticks to his guns stubbornly, refusing to give ground to Galen's onslaught. It's all very distant, a subject of intellectual study; the immerser reminds you from time to time, interpreting this and this body cue, nudging you this way and that—you must sit straight and silent, and support your husband—and so you smile through a mouth that feels gummed together.

You feel, all the while, the Rong girl's gaze on you, burning like ice water, like the gaze of a dragon. She won't move away from you; and her hand rests on you, gripping your arm with a strength you didn't think she had in her body. Her avatar is but a thin layer, and you can see her beneath it: a round, moon-shaped face with skin the colour of cinnamon—no, not spices, not chocolate, but simply a colour you've seen all your life.

"You have to take it off," she says. You don't move; but you wonder what she's talking about.

Take it off. Take it off. Take what off?

The immerser.

Abruptly, you remember—a dinner with Galen's friends, when they laughed at jokes that had gone by too fast for you to understand. You came home battling tears; and found yourself reaching for the immerser on your bedside table, feeling its cool weight in your hands. You thought it would please Galen if you spoke his language; that he would be less ashamed of how uncultured you sounded to his friends. And then you found out that everything was fine, as long as you kept the settings on maximum and didn't remove it. And then…and then you walked with it and slept with it, and showed the world nothing but the avatar it had designed—saw nothing it hadn't tagged and labelled for you. Then…

Then it all slid down, didn't it? You couldn't program the network anymore, couldn't look at the guts of machines; you lost your job with the tech company, and came to Galen's compartment, wandering in the room like a hollow shell, a ghost of yourself—as if you'd already died, far away from home and all that it means to you. Then—then the immerser wouldn't come off, anymore.

"What do you think you're doing, young woman?"

Second Uncle had risen, turning towards Quy—his avatar flushed with anger, the pale skin mottled with an unsightly red. "We adults are in the middle of negotiating something very important, if you don't mind." It might have made Quy quail in other circumstances, but his voice and his body language were wholly Galactic; and he sounded like a stranger to her—an angry foreigner whose food order she'd misunderstood—whom she'd mock later, sitting in Tam's room with a cup of tea in her lap, and the familiar patter of her sister's musings.

"I apologise," Quy said, meaning none of it.

"That's all right," Galen said. "I didn't mean to—" he paused, looked at his wife. "I shouldn't have brought her here."

"You should take her to see a physician," Quy said, surprised at her own boldness.

"Do you think I haven't tried?" His voice was bitter. "I've even taken her to the best hospitals on Prime. They look at her, and say they can't take it off. That the shock of it would kill her. And even if it didn't…" He spread his hands, letting air fall between them like specks of dust. "Who knows if she'd come back?"

Quy felt herself blush. "I'm sorry." And she meant it this time.

Galen waved her away, negligently, airily, but she could see the pain he was struggling to hide. Galactics didn't think tears were manly, she remembered. "So we're agreed?" Galen asked Second Uncle. "For a million credits?"

Quy thought of the banquet; of the food on the tables, of Galen thinking it would remind Agnes of home. Of how, in the end, it was doomed to fail, because everything would be filtered through the immerser, leaving Agnes with nothing but an exotic feast of unfamiliar flavours. "I'm sorry," she said, again, but no one was listening; and she turned away from Agnes with rage in her heart—with the growing feeling that it had all been for nothing in the end.

"I'M SORRY," the girl says—she stands, removing her hand from your arm, and you feel like a tearing inside, as if something within you was struggling to claw free from your body. Don't go, you want to say. Please don't go. Please don't leave me here.

But they're all shaking hands; smiling, pleased at a deal they've struck—like sharks, you think, like tigers. Even the Rong girl has turned away from you; giving you up as hopeless. She and her uncle are walking away, taking separate paths back to the inner areas of the restaurant, back to their home.

Please don't go.

It's as if something else were taking control of your body; a strength that you didn't know you possessed. As Galen walks back into the restaurant's main room, back into the hubbub and the tantalising smells of food—of lemongrass chicken and steamed rice, just as your mother used to make—you turn away from your husband, and follow the girl. Slowly, and from a distance; and then running, so that no one will stop you. She's walking fast—you see her tear her immerser away from her face, and slam it down onto a side table with disgust. You see her enter a room; and you follow her inside.

They're watching you, both girls, the one you followed in; and another, younger one, rising from the table she was sitting at—both terribly alien and terribly familiar at once. Their mouths are open, but no sound comes out.

In that one moment—staring at each other, suspended in time—you see the guts of Galactic machines spread on the table. You see the mass of tools; the dismantled machines; and the immerser, half spread-out before them, its two halves open like a cracked egg. And you understand that they've been trying to open them and reverse-engineer them; and you know that they'll never, ever succeed. Not because of the safeguards, of the Galactic encryptions to preserve their fabled intellectual property; but rather, because of something far more fundamental.

This is a Galactic toy, conceived by a Galactic mind—every layer of it, every logical connection within it exudes a mindset that might as well be alien to these girls. It takes a Galactic to believe that you can take a whole culture and reduce it to algorithms; that language and customs can be boiled to just a simple set of rules. For these girls, things are so much more complex than this; and they will never understand how an immerser works, because they can't think like a Galactic, they'll never ever think like that. You can't think like a Galactic unless you've been born in the culture.

Or drugged yourself, senseless, into it, year after year.

You raise a hand—it feels like moving through honey. You speak—struggling to shape words through layer after layer of immerser thoughts.

"I know about this," you say, and your voice comes out hoarse, and the words fall into place one by one like a laser stroke, and they feel right, in a way that nothing else has for five years. "Let me help you, younger sisters."

To Rochita Loenen-Ruiz, for the conversations that inspired this

The Waiting Stars

THE DERELICT SHIP WARD WAS IN AN ISOLATED SECTION OF Outsider space, one of the numerous spots left blank on interstellar maps, no more or no less tantalising than its neighbouring quadrants. To most people, it would be just that: a boring part of a long journey to be avoided—skipped over by Mind-ships as they cut through deep space, passed around at low speeds by Outsider ships while their passengers slept in their hibernation cradles.

Only if anyone got closer would they see the hulking masses of ships: the glint of starlight on metal, the sharp, pristine beauty of their hulls, even though they all lay quiescent and crippled, forever unable to move—living corpses kept as a reminder of how far they had fallen; the Outsiders' brash statement of their military might, a reminder that their weapons held the means to fell any Mind-ships they chose to hound.

On the sensors of *The Cinnabar Mansions*, the ships all appeared small and diminished, like toy models or avatars—things Lan Nhen could have held in the palm of her hand and just as easily crushed. As the sensors' line of sight moved—catching ship after ship in their field of view, wreck after wreck, indistinct masses of burnt and twisted metal, of ripped-out engines, of shattered life pods and crushed shuttles—Lan Nhen felt as if an icy fist were squeezing her heart into shards. To think of the Minds within—dead or crippled, forever unable to move…

"She's not there," she said, as more and more ships appeared on the screen in front of her, a mass of corpses that all threatened to overwhelm her with sorrow and grief and anger.

"Be patient, child," *The Cinnabar Mansions* said. The Mind's voice was amused, as it always was—after all, she'd lived for five centuries, and would outlive Lan Nhen and Lan Nhen's own children by so many years that the pronoun "child" seemed small and inappropriate to express the vast gulf of generations between them. "We already knew it was going to take time."

"She was supposed to be on the outskirts of the wards," Lan Nhen said, biting her lip. She had to be, or the rescue mission was going to be infinitely more complicated. "According to Cuc..."

"Your cousin knows what she's talking about," *The Cinnabar Mansions* said.

"I guess." Lan Nhen wished Cuc was there with them, and not sleeping in her cabin as peacefully as a baby—but *The Cinnabar Mansions* had pointed out Cuc needed to be rested for what lay ahead; and Lan Nhen had given in, vastly outranked. Still, Cuc was reliable, for narrow definitions of the term—as long as anything didn't involve social skills, or deft negotiation. For technical information, though, she didn't have an equal within the family; and her network of contacts extended deep within Outsider space. That was how they'd found out about the ward in the first place...

"There." The sensors beeped, and the view on the screen pulled into enhanced mode on a ship on the edge of the yard, which seemed even smaller than the hulking masses of her companions. *The Turtle's Citadel* had been from the newer generation of ships, its body more compact and more agile than its predecessors: designed for flight and manoeuvres rather than for transport, more elegant and refined than anything to come out of the Imperial Workshops—unlike the other ships, its prow and hull were decorated, painted with numerous designs from old legends and myths, all the way to the Dai Viet of Old Earth. A single gunshot marred the outside of its hull—a burn mark that had transfixed the painted citadel through one of its towers, going all the way into the heartroom and crippling the Mind that animated the ship.

"That's her," Lan Nhen said. "I would know her anywhere."

The Cinnabar Mansions had the grace not to say anything, though of course she could have matched the design to her vast databases in an eyeblink. "It's time, then. Shall I extrude a pod?"

Lan Nhen found that her hands had gone slippery with sweat, all of a sudden; and her heart was beating a frantic rhythm within her chest, like temple gongs gone mad. "I guess it's time, yes." By any standards, what they were planning was madness. To infiltrate Outsider space, no matter how isolated—to repair a ship, no matter how lightly damaged…

Lan Nhen watched *The Turtle's Citadel* for a while—watched the curve of the hull, the graceful tilt of the engines, away from the living quarters; the burn mark through the hull like a gunshot through a human chest. On the prow was a smaller painting, all but invisible unless one had good eyes: a single sprig of apricot flowers, signifying the New Year's good luck—calligraphied on the ship more than thirty years ago by Lan Nhen's own mother, a parting gift to her great-aunt before the ship left for her last, doomed mission.

Of course, Lan Nhen already knew every detail of that shape by heart, every single bend of the corridors within, every little nook and cranny available outside—from the blueprints, and even before that, before the rescue plan had even been the seed of a thought in her mind—when she'd stood before her ancestral altar, watching the rotating holo of a ship who was also her great-aunt, and wondering how a Mind could ever be brought down, or given up for lost.

Now she was older; old enough to have seen enough things to freeze her blood; old enough to plot her own foolishness, and drag her cousin and her great-great-aunt into it.

Older, certainly. Wiser, perhaps; if they were blessed enough to survive.

THERE WERE tales, at the Institution, of what they were—and, in any case, one only had to look at them, at their squatter, darker shapes, at the way their eyes crinkled when they laughed. There were other clues, too: the memories that made Catherine wake up breathless and disoriented, staring at the white walls of the dormitory until the pulsing, writhing images of something she couldn't quite identify had gone, and the breath of dozens of her dorm-mates had lulled her back to sleep. The craving for odd food like fish sauce and fermented meat. The dim, distant feeling of not fitting in, of being compressed on all sides by a society that made little sense to her.

It should have, though. She'd been taken as a child, like all her schoolmates—saved from the squalor and danger among the savages and brought forward into the light of civilisation—of white sterile rooms and bland food, of awkward embraces that always felt too informal. Rescued, Matron always said, her entire face transfigured, the bones of her cheeks made sharply visible through the pallor of her skin. Made safe.

Catherine had asked what she was safe from. They all did, in the beginning—all the girls in the Institution, Johanna and Catherine being the most vehement amongst them.

That was until Matron showed them the vid.

They all sat at their tables, watching the screen in the centre of the amphitheatre—silent, for once, not jostling or joking among themselves. Even Johanna, who was always first with a biting remark, had said nothing—had sat, transfixed, watching it.

The first picture was a woman who looked like them—smaller and darker-skinned than the Galactics—except that her belly protruded in front of her, huge and swollen like a tumour from some disaster movie. There was a man next to her, his unfocused eyes suggesting that he was checking something on the network through his implants—until the woman grimaced, putting a hand to her belly and calling out to him. His eyes focused in a heartbeat, and fear replaced the blank expression on his face.

There was a split second before the language overlays kicked in—a moment, frozen in time, when the words, the sounds of the syllables put together, sounded achingly familiar to Catherine, like a memory of the childhood she never could quite manage to piece together—there was a brief flash, of New Year's Eve firecrackers going off in a confined space, of her fear that they would burn her, damage her body's ability to heal... And then the moment was gone like a popped bubble, because the vid changed in the most horrific manner.

The camera was wobbling, rushing along a pulsing corridor—they could all hear the heavy breath of the woman, the whimpering sounds she made like an animal in pain; the soft, encouraging patter of the physician's words to her.

"She's coming," the woman whispered, over and over, and the physician nodded—keeping one hand on her shoulder, squeezing it so hard his own knuckles had turned the colour of a muddy moon.

"You have to be strong," he said. "Hanh, please. Be strong for me. It's all for the good of the Empire, may it live ten thousand years. Be strong."

The vid cut away, then—and it was wobbling more and more crazily, its field of view showing erratic bits of a cramped room with scrolling letters on the wall, the host of other attendants with similar expressions of fear on their faces; the woman, lying on a flat surface, crying out in pain—blood splattering out of her with every thrust of her hips—the camera moving, shifting between her legs, the physician's hands reaching into the darker opening—easing out a sleek, glinting shape, even as the woman screamed again—and blood, more blood running out, rivers of blood she couldn't possibly have in her body, even as the *thing* within her pulled free, and it became all too clear that, though it had the bare shape of a baby with an oversized head, it had too many cables and sharp angles to be human...

Then a quiet fade-to-black, and the same woman being cleaned up by the physician—the thing—the baby being nowhere to be seen. She stared up at the camera; but her gaze was unfocused, and drool was pearling at the corner of her lips, even as her hands spasmed uncontrollably.

Fade to black again; and the lights came up again, on a room that seemed to have grown infinitely colder.

"This," Matron said in the growing silence, "is how the Dai Viet birth Minds for their spaceships: by incubating them within the wombs of their women. This is the fate that would have been reserved for all of you. For each of you within this room." Her gaze raked them all; stopping longer than usual on Catherine and Johanna, the known troublemakers in the class. "This is why we had to take you away, so that you wouldn't become brood mares for abominations."

"We", of course, meant the Board—the religious nuts, as Johanna liked to call them, a redemptionist church with a fortune to throw around, financing the children's rescues and their education—and who thought every life from humans to insects was sacred (they'd all wondered, of course, where they fitted into the scheme).

After the class had dispersed like a flock of sparrows, Johanna held court in the yard, her eyes bright and feverish. "They faked it. They had to. They came up with some stupid explanation on how to keep us cooped here. I mean, why would anyone still use natural births and not artificial wombs?"

Catherine, still seeing the splatters of blood on the floor, shivered. "Matron said that they wouldn't. That they thought the birth created a special bond between the Mind and its mother—but that they had to be there, to be awake during the birth."

"Rubbish." Johanna shook her head. "As if that's even remotely plausible. I'm telling you, it has to be fake."

"It looked real." Catherine remembered the woman's screams; the wet sound as the Mind wriggled free from her womb; the fear in the face of all the physicians. "Artificial vids aren't this…messy." They'd seen the artificial vids; slick, smooth things where the actors were tall and muscular, the actresses pretty and graceful, with only a thin veneer of artificially generated defects to make the entire thing believable. They'd learnt to tell them apart from the rest; because it was a survival skill in the Institution, to sort out the lies from the truth.

"I bet they can fake that, too," Johanna said. "They can fake every-thing if they feel like it." But her face belied her words; even she had been shocked. Even she didn't believe they would have gone that far.

"I don't think it's a lie," Catherine said, finally. "Not this time."

And she didn't need to look at the other girls' faces to know that they believed the same thing as her—even Johanna, for all her belligerence—and to feel in her gut that this changed everything.

CUC CAME online when the shuttle pod launched from *The Cinnabar Mansions*—in the heart-wrenching moment when the gravity of the ship fell away from Lan Nhen, and the cozy darkness of the pod's cradle was replaced with the distant forms of the derelict ships. "Hey, cousin. Missed me?" Cuc asked.

"As much as I missed a raging fire." Lan Nhen checked her equipment a last time—the pod was basic and functional, with barely enough space for her to squeeze into the cockpit, and she'd had to stash her various cables and terminals into the nooks and crannies of a structure that hadn't been meant for more than emergency evacuation. She could have asked *The Cinnabar Mansions* for a regular transport shuttle, but the pod was smaller and more controllable; and it stood more chances of evading the derelict ward's defences.

"Hahaha," Cuc said, though she didn't sound amused. "The family found out what we were doing, by the way."

"And?" It would have devastated Lan Nhen, a few years ago; now she didn't much care. She *knew* she was doing the right thing. No filial daugh-ter would let a member of the family rust away in a foreign cemetery—if she couldn't rescue her great-aunt, she'd at least bring the body back, for a proper funeral.

"They think we're following one of Great-great-aunt's crazy plans."

"Ha," Lan Nhen snorted. Her hands were dancing on the controls, plotting a trajectory that would get her to *The Turtle's Citadel* while leaving her the maximum thrust reserve in case of unexpected manoeuvres.

"I'm not the one coming up with crazy plans," *The Cinnabar Mansions* pointed out on the comms channel, distractedly. "I leave that to the young. Hang on—" she dropped out of sight. "I have incoming drones, child."

Of course. It was unlikely the Outsiders would leave their precious war trophies unprotected. "Where?"

A translucent overlay gradually fell over her field of vision through the pod's windshield; and points lit up all over its surface—a host of fast-moving, small crafts with contextual arrows showing basic kinematics information as well as projected trajectory cones. Lan Nhen repressed a curse. "That many? They really like their wrecked spaceships, don't they."

It wasn't a question, and neither Cuc nor *The Cinnabar Mansions* bothered to answer. "They're defence drones patrolling the perimeter. We'll walk you through," Cuc said. "Give me just a few moments to link up with Great-great-aunt's systems…"

Lan Nhen could imagine her cousin, lying half-prone on her bed in the lower decks of *The Cinnabar Mansions*, her face furrowed in that half-puzzled, half-focused expression that was typical of her thought processes—she'd remain that way for entire minutes, or as long as it took to find a solution. On her windshield, the squad of drones was spreading—coming straight at her from all directions, a dazzling ballet of movement meant to overwhelm her. And they would, if she didn't move fast enough.

Her fingers hovered over the pod's controls, before she made her decision and launched into a barrel manoeuvre away from the nearest incoming cluster. "Cousin, how about hurrying up?"

There was no answer from Cuc. Demons take her, this wasn't the moment to overthink the problem! Lan Nhen banked, sharply, narrowly avoiding a squad of drones, who bypassed her—and then turned around, much quicker than she'd anticipated. Ancestors, they moved fast, much too fast for ion-thrust motors. Cuc was going to have to rethink her trajectory. "Cousin, did you see this?"

"I saw." Cuc's voice was distant. "Already taken into account. Given the size of the craft, it was likely they were going to use helicoidal thrusters on those."

"This is all fascinating—" Lan Nhen wove her way through two more waves of drones, cursing wildly as shots made the pod rock around her—as long as her speed held, she'd be fine… She'd be fine… "—but you'll have noticed I don't really much care about technology, especially not now!"

A thin thread of red appeared on her screen—a trajectory that wove and banked like a frightened fish's trail—all the way to *The Turtle's Citadel* and its clusters of pod-cradles. It looked as though it was headed straight into the heart of the cloud of drones, though that wasn't the most worrying aspect of it. "Cousin," Lan Nhen said. "I can't possibly do this—" The margin of error was null—if she slipped in one of the curves, she'd never regain the kinematics necessary to take the next.

"Only way." Cuc's voice was emotionless. "I'll update as we go, if Great-great-aunt sees an opening. But for the moment…"

Lan Nhen closed her eyes, for a brief moment—turned them towards Heaven, though Heaven was all around her—and whispered a prayer to her ancestors, begging them to watch over her. Then she turned her gaze to the screen, and launched into flight—her hands flying and shifting over the controls, automatically adjusting the pod's path—dancing into the heart of the drones' swarm—into them, away from them, weaving an erratic path across the section of space that separated her from *The Turtle's Citadel*. Her eyes, all the while, remained on the overlay—her fingers speeding across the controls, matching the slightest deviation of her course to the set trajectory—inflecting curves a fraction of a second before the error on her course became perceptible.

"Almost there," Cuc said—with a hint of encouragement in her voice. "Come on, cousin, you can do it—"

Ahead of her, a few measures away, was *The Turtle's Citadel*: its pod cradles had shrivelled from long atrophy, but the hangar for docking the external shuttles and pods remained, its entrance a thin line of grey across the metallic surface of the ship's lower half.

"It's closed," Lan Nhen said, breathing hard—she was coming fast, much too fast, scattering drones out of her way like scared mice, and if the hangar wasn't opened… "Cousin!"

Cuc's voice seemed to come from very far away; distant and muted somehow on the comms system. "We've discussed this. Normally, the ship went into emergency standby when it was hit, and it should open—"

"But what if it doesn't?" Lan Nhen asked—the ship was looming over her, spreading to cover her entire windshield, close enough so she could count the pod cradles, could see their pockmarked surfaces—could imagine how much of a messy impact she'd make, if her own pod crashed on an unyielding surface.

Cuc didn't answer. She didn't need to; they both knew what would happen if that turned out to be true. Ancestors, watch over me, Lan Nhen thought, over and over, as the hangar doors rushed towards her, still closed—ancestors watch over me…

She was close enough to see the fine layers of engravings on the doors when they opened—the expanse of metal flowing away from the centre, to reveal a gaping hole just large enough to let a small craft through. Her own pod squeezed into the available space: darkness fell over her cockpit as the doors flowed shut, and the pod skidded to a halt, jerking her body like a disarticulated doll.

It was a while before she could stop shaking for long enough to unstrap herself from the pod; and to take her first, tentative steps on the ship.

The small lamp in her suit lit nothing but a vast, roiling mass of shadows: the hangar was huge enough to hold much larger ships. Thirty years ago, it had no doubt been full, but the Outsiders must have removed them all as they dragged the wreck out there.

"I'm in," she whispered; and set out through the darkness, to find the heartroom and the Mind that was her great-aunt.

"I'M SORRY," Jason said to Catherine. "Your first choice of posting was declined by the Board."

Catherine sat very straight in her chair, trying to ignore how uncomfortable she felt in her suit—it gaped too large over her chest, flared too much at her hips, and she'd had to hastily readjust the trouser-legs after she and Johanna discovered the seamstress had got the length wrong. "I see," she said, because there was nothing else she could say, really.

Jason looked at his desk, his gaze boring into the metal as if he could summon an assignment out of nothing—she knew he meant well, that he had probably volunteered to tell her this himself, instead of leaving it for some stranger who wouldn't care a jot for her—but in that moment, she didn't want to be reminded that he worked for the Board for the Protection of Dai Viet Refugees; that he'd had a hand, no matter how small, in denying her wishes for the future.

At length Jason said, slowly, carefully—reciting a speech he'd no doubt given a dozen times that day, "The government puts the greatest care into choosing postings for the refugees. It was felt that putting you onboard a space station would be—unproductive."

Unproductive. Catherine kept smiling; kept her mask plastered on, even though it hurt to turn the corners of her mouth upwards, to crinkle her eyes as if she were pleased. "I see," she said, again, knowing anything else was useless. "Thanks, Jason."

Jason coloured. "I tried arguing your case, but…"

"I know," Catherine said. He was a clerk; that was all; a young civil servant at the bottom of the Board's hierarchy, and he couldn't possibly get her what she wanted, even if he'd been willing to favour her. And it hadn't been such a surprise, anyway. After Mary and Olivia and Johanna…

"Look," Jason said. "Let's see each other tonight, right? I'll take you someplace you can forget all about this."

"You know it's not that simple," Catherine said. As if a restaurant, or a wild waterfall ride, or whatever delight Jason had in mind could make her forget this.

"No, but I can't do anything about the Board." Jason's voice was firm. "I can, however, make sure that you have a good time tonight."

Catherine forced a smile she didn't feel. "I'll keep it in mind. Thanks."

As she exited the building, passing under the wide arches, the sun sparkled on the glass windows—and for a brief moment she wasn't herself—she was staring at starlight reflected in a glass panel, watching an older woman running hands on a wall and smiling at her with gut-wrenching sadness... She blinked, and the moment was gone; though the sense of sadness, of unease remained, as if she were missing something essential.

Johanna was waiting for her on the steps, her arms crossed in front of her, and a gaze that looked as though it would bore holes into the lawn.

"What did they tell you?"

Catherine shrugged, wondering how a simple gesture could cost so much. "The same they told you, I'd imagine. Unproductive."

They'd all applied to the same postings—all asked for something related to space, whether it was one of the observatories, a space station; or, in Johanna's case, outright asking to board a slow-ship as crew. They'd all been denied, for variations of the same reason.

"What did you get?" Johanna asked. Her own rumpled slip of paper had already been recycled at the nearest terminal; she was heading north, to Steele, where she'd join an archaeological dig.

Catherine shrugged, with a casualness she didn't feel. They'd always felt at ease under the stars—had always yearned to take to space, felt the same craving to be closer to their home planets—to hang, weightless and without ties, in a place where they wouldn't be weighed, wouldn't be judged for falling short of values that ultimately didn't belong to them. "I got newswriter."

"At least you're not moving very far," Johanna said, a tad resentfully.

"No." The offices of the network company were a mere two streets away from the Institution.

"I bet Jason had a hand in your posting," Johanna said.

"He didn't say anything about that—"

"Of course he wouldn't." Johanna snorted, gently. She didn't much care for Jason; but she knew how much his company meant to Catherine—how much more it would come to mean, if the weight of an entire continent separated Catherine and her. "Jason broadcasts his failures because they bother him; you'll hardly ever hear him talk of his successes. He'd feel too much like boasting." Her face changed, softened. "He cares for you, you know—truly. You have the best luck in the world."

"I know," Catherine said—thinking of the touch of his lips on hers; of his arms, holding her close until she felt whole, fulfilled. "I know."

The best luck in the world—she and Jason and her new flat, and her old haunts, not far away from the Institution—though she wasn't sure, really, if that last was a blessing—if she wanted to remember the years Matron had spent hammering proper behaviour into them: the deprivations whenever they spoke anything less than perfect Galactic, the hours spent cleaning the dormitory's toilets for expressing mild revulsion at the food; or the night they'd spent shut outside, naked, in the growing cold, because they couldn't remember which Galactic president had colonised Longevity Station—how Matron had found them all huddled against each other, in an effort to keep warm and awake, and had sent them to Discipline for a further five hours, scolding them for behaving like wild animals.

Catherine dug her nails into the palms of her hands—letting the pain anchor her back to the present; to where she sat on the steps of the Board's central offices, away from the Institution and all it meant to them.

"We're free," she said, at last. "That's all that matters."

"We'll never be free." Johanna's tone was dark, intense. "Your records have a mark that says 'Institution'. And even if it didn't—do you honestly believe we would blend right in?"

There was no one quite like them on Prime, where Dai Viet were unwelcome; not with those eyes, not with that skin colour—not with that demeanour, which even years of Institution hadn't been enough to erase.

"Do you ever wonder..." Johanna's voice trailed off into silence, as if she were contemplating something too large to put into words.

"Wonder what?" Catherine asked.

Johanna bit her lip. "Do you ever wonder what it would have been like, with our parents? Our real parents."

The parents they couldn't remember. They'd done the maths, too—no children at the Institution could remember anything before coming there. Matron had said it was because they were really young when they were taken away—that it had been for the best. Johanna, of course, had blamed something more sinister, some fix-up done by the Institution to its wards to keep them docile.

Catherine thought, for a moment, of a life among the Dai Viet—an idyllic image of a harmonious family like in the holo-movies—a mirage that dashed itself to pieces against the inescapable reality of the birth vid. "They'd have used us like brood mares," Catherine said. "You saw—"

"I know what I saw," Johanna snapped. "But maybe..." Her face was pale. "Maybe it wouldn't have been so bad, in return for the rest."

For being loved; for being made worthy; for fitting in, being able to stare at the stars without wondering which was their home—without dreaming of when they might go back to their families.

Catherine rubbed her belly, thinking of the vid—and the *thing* crawling out of the woman's belly, all metal edges and shining crystal, coated in the blood of its mother—and, for a moment she felt as though she were the woman—floating above her body, detached from her cloak of flesh, watching herself give birth in pain. And then the sensation ended, but she was still feeling spread out, larger than she ought to have been—looking at herself from a distance and watching her own life pass her by, petty and meaningless, and utterly bounded from end to end.

Maybe Johanna was right. Maybe it wouldn't have been so bad, after all.

THE SHIP was smaller than Lan Nhen had expected—she'd been going by her experience with *The Cinnabar Mansions,* which was an older generation, but *The Turtle's Citadel* was much smaller for the same functionalities.

Lan Nhen went up from the hangar to the living quarters, her equipment slung over her shoulders. She'd expected a sophisticated defence system like the drones, but there was nothing. Just the familiar slimy feeling of a quickened ship on the walls, a sign that the Mind that it hosted was still alive—albeit barely. The walls were bare, instead of the elaborate decoration Lan Nhen was used to from *The Cinnabar Mansions*—no scrolling calligraphy, no flowing paintings of starscapes or flowers; no ambient sound of zither or anything to enliven the silence.

She didn't have much time to waste—Cuc had said they had two hours between the moment the perimeter defences kicked in, and the moment more hefty safeguards were manually activated—but she couldn't help herself: she looked into one of the living quarters. It was empty as well, its walls scored with gunfire. The only colour in the room was a few splatters of dried blood on a chair, a reminder of the tragedy of the ship's fall—the execution of its occupants, the dragging of its wreck to the derelict ward—dried blood, and a single holo of a woman on a table, a beloved mother or grandmother: a bare, abandoned picture with no offerings or incense, all that remained from a wrecked ancestral altar. Lan Nhen spat on the ground, to ward off evil ghosts, and went back to the corridors.

She truly felt as though she were within a mausoleum—like that one time her elder sister had dared her and Cuc to spend the night within the family's ancestral shrine, and they'd barely slept—not because of monsters or anything, but because of the vast silence that permeated the whole place amidst the smell of incense and funeral offerings, reminding them that they, too, were mortal.

That Minds, too, could die—that rescues were useless—no, she couldn't afford to think like that. She had Cuc with her, and together they would…

She hadn't heard Cuc for a while.

She stopped, when she realised—that it wasn't only the silence on the ship, but also the deathly quiet of her own comms system. Since—since she'd entered *The Turtle's Citadel*—that was the last time she'd heard her cousin, calmly pointing out about emergency standby and hangar doors and how everything was going to work out, in the end...

She checked her comms. There appeared to be nothing wrong; but whichever frequency she selected, she could hear nothing but static. At last, she managed to find one slot that seemed less crowded than others. "Cousin? Can you hear me?"

Noise on the line. "Very—badly." Cuc's voice was barely recognisable. "There—is—something—interference—"

"I know," Lan Nhen said. "Every channel is filled with noise."

Cuc didn't answer for a while; and when she did, her voice seemed to have become more distant—a problem had her interest again. "Not—noise. They're broadcasting—data. Need—to..." And then the comms cut. Lan Nhen tried all frequencies, trying to find one that would be less noisy; but there was nothing. She bit down a curse—she had no doubt Cuc would find a way around whatever blockage the Outsiders had put on the ship, but this was downright bizarre. Why broadcast data? Cutting down the comms of prospective attackers somehow didn't seem significant enough—at least not compared to defence drones or similar mechanisms.

She walked through the corridors, following the spiral path to the heart-room—nothing but the static in her ears, a throbbing song that erased every coherent thought from her mind—at least it was better than the silence, than that feeling of moving underwater in an abandoned city—that feeling that she was too late, that her great-aunt was already dead and past recovery, that all she could do here was kill her once and for all, end her misery...

She thought, incongruously, of a vid she'd seen, which showed her great-grandmother ensconced in the heartroom—in the first few years of *The Turtle's Citadel*'s life, those crucial moments of childhood when the ship's mother remained onboard to guide the Mind to adulthood. Great-grandmother was telling stories to the ship—and *The Turtle's Citadel* was struggling to mimic the spoken words in scrolling texts on her walls, laughing delightedly whenever she succeeded—all sweet and young, unaware of what her existence would come to, in the end.

Unlike the rest of the ship, the heartroom was crowded—packed with Outsider equipment that crawled over the Mind's resting place in the centre, covering her from end to end until Lan Nhen could barely see the glint of metal underneath. She gave the entire contraption a wide berth—the spikes and protrusions from the original ship poked at odd angles, glistening with a dark liquid she couldn't quite identify—and the Outsider equipment piled atop the Mind, a mass of cables and unfamiliar machines, looked as though it was going to take a while to sort out.

There were screens all around, showing dozens of graphs and diagrams, shifting as they tracked variables that Lan Nhen couldn't guess at—vital signs, it looked like, though she wouldn't have been able to tell what.

Lan Nhen bowed in the direction of the Mind, from younger to elder—perfunctorily, since she was unsure whether the Mind could see her at all. There was no acknowledgement, either verbal or otherwise.

Her great-aunt was in there. She had to be.

"Cousin." Cuc's voice was back in her ears—crisp and clear and uncommonly worried.

"How come I can hear you?" Lan Nhen asked. "Because I'm in the heartroom?"

Cuc snorted. "Hardly. The heartroom is where all the data is streaming from. I've merely found a way to filter the transmissions on both ends. Fascinating problem…"

"Is this really the moment?" Lan Nhen asked. "I need you to walk me through the reanimation—"

"No you don't," Cuc said. "First you need to hear what I have to say."

THE CALL came during the night: a man in the uniform of the Board asked for Catherine George—as if he couldn't tell that it was her, that she was standing dishevelled and pale in front of her screen at three in the morning. "Yes, it's me," Catherine said. She fought off the weight of nightmares—more and more, she was waking in the night with memories of blood splattered across her entire body; of stars collapsing while she watched, powerless—of a crunch, and a moment where she hung alone in darkness, knowing that she had been struck a death blow—

The man's voice was quiet, emotionless. There had been an accident in Steele; a regrettable occurrence that hadn't been meant to happen, and the Board would have liked to extend its condolences to her—they apologised for calling so late, but they thought she should know…

"I see," Catherine said. She kept herself uncomfortably straight—aware of the last time she'd faced the board—when Jason had told her her desire for space would have been unproductive. When they'd told Johanna…

Johanna.

After a while, the man's words slid past her like water on glass—hollow reassurances, empty condolences, whereas she stood as if her heart had been torn away from her, fighting a desire to weep, to retch—she wanted to turn back time, to go back to the previous week and the sprigs of apricot flowers Jason had given her with a shy smile—to breathe in the sharp, tangy flavour of the lemon cake he'd baked for her, see again the carefully blank expression on his face as he waited to see if she'd like it—she wanted to be held tight in his arms and told that it was fine, that everything was going to be fine, that Johanna was going to be fine.

"We're calling her other friends," the man was saying, "but since you were close to each other…"

"I see," Catherine said—of course he didn't understand the irony, that it was the answer she'd given the Board—Jason—the last time.

The man cut off the communication; and she was left alone, standing in her living room and fighting back the feeling that threatened to overwhelm her—a not-entirely unfamiliar sensation of dislocation in her belly, the awareness that she didn't belong here among the Galactics; that she wasn't there by choice, and couldn't leave; that her own life should have been larger, more fulfilling than this slow death by inches, writing copy for feeds without any acknowledgement of her contributions—that Johanna's life should have been larger...

Her screen was still blinking—an earlier message from the Board that she hadn't seen? But why—

Her hands, fumbling away in the darkness, made the command to retrieve the message—the screen faded briefly to black while the message was decompressed, and then she was staring at Johanna's face.

For a moment—a timeless, painful moment—Catherine thought with relief that it had been a mistake, that Johanna was alive after all; and then she realised how foolish she'd been—that it wasn't a call, but merely a message from beyond the grave.

Johanna's face was pale, so pale Catherine wanted to hug her, to tell her the old lie that things were going to be fine—but she'd never get to say those words now, not ever.

"I'm sorry, Catherine," she said. Her voice was shaking; and the circles under her eyes took up half of her face, turning her into some pale nightmare from horror movies—a ghost, a restless soul, a ghoul hungry for human flesh. "I can't do this, not anymore. The Institution was fine; but it's got worse. I wake up at night, and feel sick—as if everything good has been leeched from the world—as if the food had no taste, as if I drifted like a ghost through my days, as if my entire life held no meaning or truth. Whatever they did to our memories in the Institution—it's breaking down now. It's tearing me apart. I'm sorry, but I can't take any more of this. I—" she looked away from the camera for a brief moment, and then back at Catherine. "I have to go."

"No," Catherine whispered, but she couldn't change it. She couldn't do anything.

"You were always the strongest of us," Johanna said. "Please remember this. Please. Catherine." And then the camera cut, and silence spread through the room, heavy and unbearable, and Catherine felt like weeping, though she had no tears left.

"Catherine?" Jason called in a sleepy voice from the bedroom. "It's too early to check your work inbox..."

Work. Love. Meaningless, Johanna had said. Catherine walked to the huge window pane, and stared at the city spread out below her—the mighty Prime, centre of the Galactic Federation, its buildings shrouded in light, its streets crisscrossed by floaters; with the bulky shape of the Parliament at the centre, a proud statement that the Galactic Federation still controlled most of their home galaxy.

Too many lights to see the stars; but she could still guess; could still feel their pull—could still remember that one of them was her home.

A lie, Johanna had said. A construction to keep us here.

"Catherine?" Jason stood behind her, one hand wrapped around her shoulder—awkwardly tender as always, like that day when he'd offered to share a flat, standing balanced on one foot and not looking at her.

"Johanna is dead. She killed herself."

She felt rather than saw him freeze—and, after a while, he said in a changed voice, "I'm so sorry. I know how much she meant..." His voice trailed off, and he too, fell silent, watching the city underneath.

There was a feeling—the same feeling she'd had when waking up as a child, a diffuse sense that something was not quite right with the world; that the shadows held men watching, waiting for the best time to snatch her; that she was not wholly back in her body—that Jason's hand on her shoulder was just the touch of a ghost, that even his love wasn't enough to keep her safe. That the world was fracturing around her, time and time again—she breathed in, hoping to dispel the sensation. Surely it was nothing more than grief, than fatigue—but the sensation wouldn't go away, leaving her on the verge of nausea.

"You should have killed us," Catherine said. "It would have been kinder."

"Killed you?" Jason sounded genuinely shocked.

"When you took us from our parents."

Jason was silent for a while. Then: "We don't kill. What do you think we are, monsters from the fairytales, killing and burning everyone who looks different? Of course we're not like that." Jason no longer sounded uncertain or awkward; it was as if she'd touched some wellspring, scratched some skin to find only primal reflexes underneath.

"You erased our memories." She didn't make any effort to keep the bitterness from her voice.

"We had to." Jason shook his head. "They'd have killed you, otherwise. You know this."

"How can I trust you?" Look at Johanna, she wanted to say. Look at me. How can you say it was all worth it?

"Catherine…" Jason's voice was weary. "We've been over this before. You've seen the vids from the early days. We didn't set out to steal your childhood, or anyone's childhood. But when you were left—intact… accidents happened. Carelessness. Like Johanna."

"Like Johanna." Her voice was shaking now; but he didn't move, didn't do anything to comfort her or hold her close. She turned at last, to stare into his face; and saw him transfixed by light, by faith, his gaze turned away from her and every pore of his being permeated by the utter conviction that he was right, that they were all right and that a stolen childhood was a small price to pay to be a Galactic.

"Anything would do." Jason's voice was slow, quiet—explaining life to a child, a script they'd gone over and over in their years together, always coming back to the same enormous, inexcusable choice that had been made for them. "Scissors, knives, broken bottles. You sliced your veins, hanged yourselves, pumped yourselves full of drugs… We had to…we had to block your memories, to make you blank slates."

"Had to." She was shaking now; and still he didn't see. Still she couldn't make him see.

"I swear to you, Catherine. It was the only way."

And she knew, she'd always known he was telling the truth—not because he was right, but because he genuinely could not envision any other future for them.

"I see," she said. The nausea, the sense of dislocation, wouldn't leave her—disgust for him, for this life that trapped her, for everything she'd turned into or been turned into. "I see."

"Do you think I like it?" His voice was bitter. "Do you think it makes me sleep better at night? Every day I hate that choice, even though I wasn't the one who made it. Every day I wonder if there was something else the Board could have done, some other solution that wouldn't have robbed you of everything you were."

"Not everything," Catherine said—slowly, carefully. "We still look Dai Viet."

Jason grimaced, looking ill at ease. "That's your *body*, Catherine. Of course they weren't going to steal that."

Of course; and suddenly, seeing how uneasy he was, it occurred to Catherine that they could have changed that, too, just as easily as they'd tampered with her memories; made her skin clearer, her eyes less distinctive; could have helped her fit into Galactic society. But they hadn't. Holding the strings to the last, Johanna would have said. "You draw the line at my body, but stealing my memories is fine?"

Jason sighed; he turned towards the window, looking at the streets. "No, it's not, and I'm sorry. But how else were we supposed to keep you alive?"

"Perhaps we didn't want to be alive."

"Don't say that, please." His voice had changed, had become fearful, protective. "Catherine. Everyone deserves to live. You especially."

Perhaps I don't, she thought, but he was holding her close to him, not letting her go—her anchor to the flat—to the living room, to life. "You're not Johanna," he said. "You know that."

The strongest of us, Johanna had said. She didn't feel strong; just frail and adrift. "No," she said, at last. "Of course I'm not."

"Come on," Jason said. "Let me make you a tisane. We'll talk in the kitchen—you look as though you need it."

"No." And she looked up—sought out his lips in the darkness, drinking in his breath and his warmth to fill the emptiness within her. "That's not what I need."

"Are you sure?" Jason looked uncertain—sweet and innocent and naïve, everything that had drawn her to him. "You're not in a state to—"

"Ssh," she said, and laid a hand on his lips, where she'd kissed him. "Ssh."

Later, after they'd made love, she lay her head in the hollow of his arm, listening to the slow beat of his heart like a lifeline; and wondered how long she'd be able to keep the emptiness at bay.

"It goes to Prime," Cuc said. "All the data is beamed to Prime, and it's coming from almost every ship in the ward."

"I don't understand," Lan Nhen said. She'd plugged her own equipment into the ship, carefully shifting the terminals she couldn't make sense of—hadn't dared to go closer to the centre, where Outsider technology had crawled all over her great-aunt's resting place, obscuring the Mind and the mass of connectors that linked her to the ship.

On one of the screens, a screensaver had launched: night on a planet Lan Nhen couldn't recognise—an Outsider one, with their sleek floaters and their swarms of helper bots, their wide, impersonal streets planted with trees that were too tall and too perfect to be anything but the product of years of breeding.

"She's not here," Cuc said.

"I—" Lan Nhen was about to say she didn't understand, and then the true import of Cuc's words hit her. "Not here? She's alive, Cuc. I can see the ship; I can hear her all around me…"

"Yes, yes," Cuc said, a tad impatiently. "But that's…the equivalent of unconscious processes, like breathing in your sleep."

"She's dreaming?"

"No," Cuc said. A pause, then, very carefully: "I think she's on Prime, Cousin. The data that's being broadcast—it looks like Mind thought-processes, compressed with a high rate and all mixed together. There's probably something on the other end that decompresses the data and sends it to… Arg, I don't know! Wherever they think is appropriate."

Lan Nhen bit back another admission of ignorance, and fell back on the commonplace. "On Prime." The enormity of the thing; that you could take a Mind—a beloved ship with a family of her own—that you could put her to sleep and cause her to wake up somewhere else, on an unfamiliar planet and an alien culture—that you could just transplant her like a flower or a tree… "She's on Prime."

"In a terminal or as the power source for something," Cuc said, darkly.

"Why would they bother?" Lan Nhen asked. "It's a lot of power expenditure just to get an extra computer."

"Do I look as though I have insight into Outsiders?" Lan Nhen could imagine Cuc throwing her hands up in the air, in that oft-practised gesture. "I'm just telling you what I have, Cousin."

Outsiders—the Galactic Federation of United Planets—were barely comprehensible in any case. They were the descendants of an Exodus fleet that had hit an isolated galaxy: left to themselves and isolated for decades, they had turned on each other in huge ethnic cleansings before emerging from their home planets as relentless competitors for resources and inhabitable planets.

"Fine. Fine." Lan Nhen breathed in, slowly; tried to focus at the problem at hand. "Can you walk me through cutting the radio broadcast?"

Cuc snorted. "I'd fix the ship, first, if I were you."

Lan Nhen knelt by the equipment, and stared at a cable that had curled around one of the ship's spines. "Fine, let's start with what we came for. Can you see?"

Silence; and then a life-sized holo of Cuc hovered in front of her—even though the avatar was little more than broad strokes, great-great-aunt had still managed to render it in enough details to make it unmistakably Cuc. "Cute," Lan Nhen said.

"Hahaha," Cuc said. "No bandwidth for trivialities—gotta save for detail on your end." She raised a hand, pointed to one of the outermost screens on the edge of the room. "Disconnect this one first."

It was slow, and painful. Cuc pointed; and Lan Nhen checked before disconnecting and moving. Twice, she jammed her fingers very close to a cable, and felt electricity crackle near her—entirely too close for comfort.

They moved from the outskirts of the room to the centre—tackling the huge mount of equipment last. Cuc's first attempts resulted in a cable coming loose with an ominous sound; they waited, but nothing happened. "We might have fried something," Lan Nhen said.

"Too bad. There's no time for being cautious, as you well know. There's...maybe half an hour left before the other defences go live." Cuc moved again, pointed to another squat terminal. "This goes off."

When they were finished, Lan Nhen stepped back, to look at their handiwork.

The heartroom was back to its former glory: instead of Outsider equipment, the familiar protrusions and sharp organic needles of the Mind's resting place; and they could see the Mind herself—resting snug in her cradle, wrapped around the controls of the ship—her myriad arms each seizing one rack of connectors; her huge head glinting in the light—a vague globe shape covered with glistening cables and veins. The burn mark from the Outsider attack was clearly visible, a dark, elongated shape on the edge of her head that had bruised a couple of veins—it had hit one of the connectors as well, burnt it right down to the colour of ink.

Lan Nhen let out a breath she hadn't been aware of holding. "It scrambled the connector."

"And scarred her, but didn't kill her," Cuc said. "Just like you said."

"Yes, but—" But it was one thing to run simulations of the attack over and over, always getting the same prognosis; and quite another to see that the simulations held true, and that the damage was repairable.

"There should be another connector rack in your bag," Cuc said. "I'll walk you through slotting it in."

After she was done, Lan Nhen took a step back; and stared at her great-aunt—feeling, in some odd way, as though she were violating the Mind's privacy. A Mind's heartroom was their stronghold, a place where they could twist reality as they wished, and appear as they wished to. To see her great-aunt like this, without any kind of appearance change or pretence, was...more disturbing than she'd thought.

"And now?" she asked Cuc.

Even without details, Lan Nhen knew her cousin was smiling. "Now we pray to our ancestors that cutting the broadcast is going to be enough to get her back."

ANOTHER NIGHT on Prime, and Catherine wakes up breathless, in the grip of another nightmare—images of red lights, and scrolling texts, and a feeling of growing cold in her bones, a cold so deep she cannot believe she will ever feel warm no matter how many layers she's put on.

Johanna is not there; beside her, Jason sleeps, snoring softly; and she's suddenly seized by nausea, remembering what he said to her—how casually he spoke of blocking her memories, of giving a home to her after stealing her original one from her. She waits for it to pass; waits to settle into her old life as usual. But it doesn't.

Instead, she rises, walks towards the window, and stands watching Prime—the clean wide streets, the perfect trees, the ballet of floaters at night—the myriad dances that make up the society that constrains her from dawn to dusk and beyond—she wonders what Johanna would say, but of course Johanna won't ever say anything anymore. Johanna has gone ahead, into the dark.

The feeling of nausea in her belly will not go away: instead it spreads, until her body feels like a cage—at first, she thinks the sensation is in her belly, but it moves upwards, until her limbs, too, feel too heavy and too small—until it's an effort to move any part of her. She raises her hands, struggling against a feeling of moving appendages that don't belong to her—and traces the contours of her face, looking for familiar shapes, for anything that will anchor her to reality. The heaviness spreads, compresses her chest until she can hardly breathe—cracks her ribs and pins her legs to the ground. Her head spins, as if she were about to faint; but the mercy of blackness does not come to her.

"Catherine," she whispers. "My name is Catherine."

Another name, unbidden, rises to her lips. *Mi Chau*. A name she gave to herself in the Viet language—in the split instant before the lasers took her apart, before she sank into darkness: Mi Chau, the princess who unwittingly betrayed her father and her people, and whose blood became the pearls at the bottom of the sea. She tastes it on her tongue, and it's the only thing that seems to belong to her anymore.

She remembers that first time—waking up on Prime in a strange body, struggling to breathe, struggling to make sense of being so small, so far away from the stars that had guided her through space—remembers walking like a ghost through the corridors of the Institution, until the knowledge of what the Galactics had done broke her, and she cut her veins in a bathroom, watching blood lazily pool at her feet and thinking only of escape. She remembers the second time she woke up; the second, oblivious life as Catherine.

Johanna. Johanna didn't survive her second life; and even now is starting her third, somewhere in the bowels of the Institution—a dark-skinned child indistinguishable from other dark-skinned children, with no memories of anything beyond a confused jumble...

Outside, the lights haven't dimmed, but there are stars—brash and alien, hovering above Prime, in configurations that look *wrong*; and she remembers, suddenly, how they lay around her, how they showed her the way from planet to planet—how the cold of the deep spaces seized her just as she entered them to travel faster, just like it's holding her now, seizing her bones—remembers how much larger, how much wider she ought to be...

There are stars everywhere; and superimposed on them, the faces of two Dai Viet women, calling her over and over. Calling her back, into the body that belonged to her all along; into the arms of her family.

"Come on, come on," the women whisper, and their voices are stronger than any other noise; than Jason's breath in the bedroom; than the motors of the floaters or the vague smell of garlic from the kitchen. "Come on, great-aunt!"

She is more than this body; more than this constrained life—her thoughts spread out, encompassing hangars and living quarters; and the liquid weight of pods held in their cradles—she remembers family reunions, entire generations of children putting their hands on her corridors, remembers the touch of their skin on her metal walls; the sound of their laughter as they raced each other; the quiet chatter of their mothers in the heartroom, keeping her company as the New Year began; and the touch of a brush on her outer hull, drawing the shape of an apricot flower, for good luck...

"Catherine?" Jason calls behind her.

She turns, through sheer effort of will; finding, somehow, the strength to maintain her consciousness in a small and crammed body alongside her other, vaster one. He's standing with one hand on the doorjamb, staring at her—his face pale, leeched of colours in the starlight.

"I remember," she whispers.

His hands stretch, beseeching. "Catherine, please. Don't leave."

He means well, she knows. All the things that he hid from her, he hid out of love; to keep her alive and happy, to hold her close in spite of all that should have separated them; and even now, the thought of his love is a barb in her heart, a last lingering regret, slight and pitiful against the flood of her memories—but not wholly insignificant.

Where she goes, she'll never be alone—not in the way she was with Jason, feeling that nothing else but her mattered in the entire world. She'll have a family; a gaggle of children and aunts and uncles waiting on her, but nothing like the sweet, unspoiled privacy where Jason and she could share anything and everything. She won't have another lover like him—naïve and frank and so terribly sure of what he wants and what he's ready to do to get it. Dai Viet society has no place for people like Jason—who do not know their place, who do not know how to be humble, how to accept failure or how to bow down to expediency.

Where she goes, she'll never be alone; and yet she'll be so terribly lonely.

"Please," Jason says.

"I'm sorry," she says. "I'll come back—" a promise made to him; to Johanna, who cannot hear or recognise her anymore. Her entire being spreads out, thins like water thrown on the fire—and, in that last moment, she finds herself reaching out for him, trying to touch him one last time, to catch one last glimpse of his face, even as a heart she didn't know she had breaks.

"Catherine."

He whispers her name, weeping, over and over; and it's that name, that lie that still clings to her with its bittersweet memories, that she takes with her as her entire being unfolds—as she flies away, towards the waiting stars.

Memorials

CAM FINDS PHAM THI THANH HA IN HER HOUSE, AS SHE EXPECTED. BY now, she doesn't question the aunts' knowledge or how they came by it. She does what she's told to, an obedient daughter beholden to her elders, never raising a fuss or complaining—the shining example of filial piety extolled in the tales her girlfriend Thuy so painstakingly reconstitutes in her spare hours.

Thanh Ha is a big woman, who must tower over her extended family—though right now, her cheeks are hollowed with grief, and the black band of mourning on her sleeve seems to have sucked all joy from her. "Younger niece…Cam." She hesitates over the name, a subtle way to make it clear that Cam had better get to the purpose of her visit quickly. "Be welcome here."

They sit in Thanh Ha's private rooms, away from the rest of the family—Cam has been doing this long enough to know what to pay attention to, and she's made sure to mention private business, delicately enough that Thanh Ha has sent away inquisitive aunts and cousins, and that even the wall-screens and the implants have been turned off, all the network connections quiescent, with no spike of activity that could relate to a recording or the transmission of one.

Thanh Ha pours tea in a practised gesture, and the delicate smell of lotus flowers fills the room; Cam bows her head, acknowledging the hospitality. "My condolences on your loss, younger aunt."

Thanh Ha bows her head, and says nothing.

Well, there's nothing for it. Cam takes a deep breath, and says, "Heaven sends us wind and rain as it will, and we weather the storm as a family. Sometimes, however..." She pauses, then, as if questing for words. "Sometimes...the wind becomes trapped under our roof, and we must acknowledge the help of strangers to bear it away."

Thanh Ha's hand has stopped halfway to the cup; she raises her gaze, no doubt looking straight at Cam (Cam herself, of course, has remained properly respectful with her gaze cast down towards the table). "Your meaning," she says, as harshly, as impolitely as a Galactic—using the familiar pronouns reserved for inferiors or servants. "In plain words."

Not so traditional then—contaminated, as all of them, by the society they have found refuge in. Cam files the thought away for later, and says, simply, with the same brash impoliteness, "When your revered grandmother died, one of the doctors came to you—a Galactic one, with a face young enough to be one of your sons. He waited until you were alone, out of the presence of your elders. He said he was sorry, that perhaps it was inappropriate—"

She hears more than sees Thanh Ha's sharp indrawn breath, and knows that she has her.

"—that he knew she'd refused perpetuation, but surely she'd made a mistake, that everyone wanted to live forever, and that she hadn't been all right in the end, not in full possession of her mind..."

The noise Thanh Ha makes as she puts her cup back on its saucer is like a gunshot in the room. "I told him he was a fool. That my grandmother's soul was in the Hell of the underworld, wending its way towards reincarnation, and that perpetuation was nothing but a record, a broken image of who she'd been, no better than a vid or a still."

Cam puts her own cup back on the table, and leans with both elbows on the rough metal surface. "But still, you took the chip. You kept it, and breathed not a word to your elders. Not during the preparations, not during the procession or the burial, or the hundred days of burning incense for her soul."

Thanh Ha's hands shake, for a bare moment before she stills them. "Assuming this is true…"

Cam smiles. "Be assured that it is. I can produce the testimony of Doctor Elliott at the Marion Sims hospital, if this becomes necessary."

Doctor Elliott meant well, Cam knows—they always do. He thought Thanh Ha would find a suitable virtual universe for her grandmother— give her a second life in which her grandsons and granddaughters could visit her, in a place where the rules are more elastic than in the physical world. For most Galactics, there is no shame in being a Perpetuate; or, indeed, much difference between Perpetuates and the living. Perpetuates hold bank accounts and run businesses; and even gather into families of their own. They can't reproduce, or leave their host universes, but surely that's such a small price to pay for life after death?

The problem is that Doctor Elliott isn't a Rong—and didn't see what someone like Cam or Thanh Ha would think.

"Fine. What is it that you want?" Thanh Ha asks.

She's afraid—believing that Cam will give her away, denounce her to her elders, or hold this knowledge against her as blackmail. Cam breathes out, presents her blandest face to Thanh Ha. "You have no use for the chip."

"You want it?" Thanh Ha's laughter is as biting as lime juice on open wounds. "You think I'd give it up?"

"It's a bother, isn't it?" Cam keeps her voice pleasant, as if they were discussing the weather or their children. "You could snap it in two with a mere gesture, but that would be like tearing apart a picture of a revered ancestor—a sin that wouldn't be forgiven. You could look for a virtual universe open to Perpetuates, and give her a new life, but you would have to admit to your elders what you have done…" And they both know, here in the sanctuary of this room, that Thanh Ha won't do that. "Or you could give it to me."

Thanh Ha cocks her head, watching Cam like a cock ascertaining a rival's intentions. "I could. But I don't know you, do I? You could take it apart as surely as I would snap it—selling memories and feelings piece by piece to eager Galactics, like bits of code or war stories."

She doesn't say it, but the name of Steven Carey hovers in the room like a white-garbed, unpropitiated ghost—all the interviews with Rong refugees Carey did, all the war memories he got out from elderly Rong, promising them something grand, something that would capture the experience of their loss—all that, culminating in the bitterness that is the Memorial. "I'm not like that," Cam says, simply.

"And I'm supposed to trust you?"

She could say the truth, then; could say she doesn't know who the aunts are, or why they direct her here and there; that she's as beholden to them as Thanh Ha is to her deceased grandmother, except that the bonds are not of love or of filial piety, but something far coarser—greed and threats and the fear of losing everything. But the aunts pay her to lie, and so she does. "No," Cam says. "You're right that you can't. But I'll give you my word that I'm not after the chip to take it apart."

Words mean something; they weigh, like contracts between families in the olden times. Cam uses them cheaply, for they're the weapon by which she makes her way in life.

Thanh Ha's hands twitch; her face contracts—but Cam is used to reading the myriad ways of the human heart, and she knows how this will go, as inevitable as a flood—that Thanh Ha will argue and make excuses, and protest about being a filial granddaughter; but that, in the end, she'll yield to temptation, and give Cam the chip with her grandmother's simulacrum rather than be left with her silent, unshareable guilt. That's how it goes; how it always ends.

This is all why she hates herself.

CAM COMES home late, with the chip wrapped up in her handbag: an unwelcome reminder of what she's doing—of everything she's embroiled into, the lies she keeps telling, day after day; the fear of what the aunts are doing, taking apart Perpetuates for parts, for memories. There is a healthy market for all of these, not least of which is the sim-movies Galactics so love—Perpetuates are plundered for unusual, exotic memories that can give frissons to even the most jaded of immersed viewers. It's illegal, but until Perpetuates have joined a virtual universe and submitted to its law strictures, there's little they can do to defend themselves. It's almost natural, the aunts would say.

Cam knows the truth: that none of it is right—that Perpetuates might just be echoes of real people, but that nothing justifies selling them. But she likes the money too much to give it up.

She finds Thuy at her desk: her girlfriend is sitting on her haunches before the low table, delivering a staccato report to Daphne Reynolds, a Perpetuate colleague at her workplace—she speaks at a speed that seems blinding to Cam, but must surely be slow by Perpetuate standards. The flat's bots have already cleaned the place, and the jasmine rice in the cooker has scented the air with its rich, promising fragrance—overlaid with the mingled garlic and fish sauce from the omelette in the pan.

After a while, Thuy finishes, and looks up. "Lil' sis."

"Big sis. How did it go?"

"I think I solved the security flaw, but I could be wrong." Thuy grimaces.

It never ceases to amaze Cam that Thuy—who has a doctorate in Network Security—can have so little trust in herself. By most standards, Cam is the one who is the family failure: she barely went past the minimum amount of studies Galactics impose on their citizens, and went from small, ill-paid job to small, ill-paid job in Landsfall. News trawler, compartment cleaner, low-level network support: she's done them all, and has little to show for it but a memory of how much it hurts, to live cramped in a room with three other Rong students, and never knowing where the money is coming in.

"I'm sure it's fine," Cam says, coming closer and kissing her—drinking in deep from Thuy's lips. "Did you see the physician?"

Thuy frees herself from Cam and shrugs. She grabs one of the two coconut water glasses on the table, and gestures to Cam to pick the other one—she's older than Cam, and has always had a tendency to boss her around. "Of course I did. Everything is normal. You fuss too much."

"It's serious," Cam protests.

"It shouldn't be. Having a child is a natural process." Thuy doesn't really appear to be in a mood to discuss her pregnancy; she sips at her glass, her gaze lost towards the floor. "How did your day go?" she asks.

Cam shrugs, feigning a nonchalance she doesn't feel. "As usual. Not much to tell."

"You never tell anything anyway." Thuy is convinced that Cam works for Galactic Intelligence; a lie Cam has carefully cultivated. Her other, outer cover for Mother is feeds writer, but any lie for Thuy has to be much closer to the truth. "Come on, drink your coconut water. I'm sure your day was as thrilling as usual."

She looks at Cam with such love—with such unmitigated pride—that it makes Cam's stomach churn. How can she tell Thuy that she does none of what her girlfriend imagines—that she's a thief and a taker of lives, that she subsists entirely on deceiving others and taking advantage of their wrecked lives?

She can't tell Thuy. She can't tell the child; and she's running out of options, as Thuy's pregnancy becomes more and more visible, twisting every aspect of their lives like woven cloth. But still, she forces herself to smile, in a way she knows is unconvincing. "Thank you."

As usual, Cam meets the aunts in the Memorial.

She doesn't know why they insist on this meeting place; though she suspects that part of it is mocking her and the choices she makes—for, after all, what better place than the Memorial for accusation of betrayals?

She takes a circuitous route to go there, casting an eye over her shoulder for policemen. It's absurd, but several times she's had the feeling of being followed—of seeing the same face too many times in the crowds that brush past—and she can't be sure, but there have been a few too many police air-cars and shuttles parked near her. Or perhaps it's simply her guilt, pointing out every police presence in Landsfall that it can see.

These days, entrance to the Memorial is free, its upkeep funded by donations from rich Galactic families. Cam joins the queue of Galactics at the entrance—not many Rong there, she might as well be the only one. It's early morning on a day like any other; not the anniversary of any significant battle or the remembrance of any atrocities; and there are few people, all of them disinclined to make any conversation.

Good, for Cam doesn't know if she could stand to speak.

In the physical reality, the Memorial isn't much: a squat building crouching above the servers that keep it alive—like a toad over treasure. Inside, a long spiral wends its way to the access chambers—as the virtual reality gradually asserts itself, the Memorial reminds visitors of the war and the Rong exodus. It starts as images on wall-screens; and, by the end, has become full three-dimensional representations that presage the virtual universe. This serves two purposes: to place the Memorial in "proper" context, and to transition the visitors from physical reality to virtual universe in a soft, non-intrusive manner.

Both are failures.

The context, like everything else, has been provided by Galactics, and they so gracefully elide their own part in setting off tinder to the war between the Western and Eastern Continent, presenting themselves as heroes who failed to save the benighted locals, and deploring the exodus even as they hide their part in causing it, or the atrocities their own troops committed on Moc Hau Tinh under the pretence of keeping the peace.

The transition, if one isn't paying attention to the context, is anything but seamless, the virtual universe replacing reality in a series of jerks; and, at the last, the slimy, cold feeling of electrodes being fitted over one's head by bots; the uncomfortable sensation of every muscle crumpling at once, as if one were a tree that had just been felled.

And, at last, Cam stands in the Memorial, shivering and shaking and attempting to bring numbed muscles back to wakefulness. Around her, the other visitors are straightening: carrying flowers or paper cards in their hands, little keepsakes bought from the online vendors as they wended their way upstairs; offerings to honour the dead veterans, the innocent victims of the exodus—dead children, Cam's history teachers used to say, as if dead children were somehow more worthy of remembrance and pity than everyone else who perished in the fall of Xuan Huong, in the invasion of the Eastern Continent.

Cam's hands, as usual, are empty. She leaves the arrival area without a backward glance, heading deeper and deeper into the Memorial.

In a way, the Memorial is Xuan Huong—it's the city on the eve before the war, its streets crisscrossed by a flood of aircars and private shuttles, its buildings rearing upwards, like gilded spears held against the Heavens— and the shadow of the orbitals overhead, the houses of the rich and powerful looking down on the planetary bustle with amusement.

In so many ways, it's not Xuan Huong.

It's not the city that Cam's grandmother waxed lyrical about, not the memories that her mother carried away when she left as a child in her parents' arms. It's a city of fashionable, glitzy hotels frequented by the Galactic expatriates; of quaint and exotic temples, with Buddhist rituals described by someone who couldn't understand what it means to believe in the bodhisattva Quan Am, in the weight of one's sin and in reincarnation. Its family feasts are seen through the eyes of Galactics, who cannot comprehend the value of food or of filial piety; even its small alleyways are sordid and unclean instead of being families' beloved homes—in every way it's subtly and jarringly wrong, a travesty of what the Rong deem precious.

He meant well, is what the Rong will say about Steven Carey when they feel charitable. He genuinely thought that his project would help the Rong exiles, that it would bring their plight to the knowledge of the world (as if their plight wasn't real until the world learnt all about it, all its sordid details and secrets shrouded in grief).

Cam walks up Le Loi Street, with its overblown temple to the God of War Quan Vu; and its ghostly Galactic women shadowed by their Rong attendants—towards her meeting with the aunts.

They're always in the same place: in a small alley behind the old Galactic Ansible Station, seated on plastic chairs in the small, battered stall of a food-seller, with bowls of steaming soup in front of them—the food smells of beef and anise star, the only thing within the Memorial that doesn't feel processed through a Galactic mindset. They're squat and dark-skinned, with the reassuring solidity of visitors to the Memorial—not the ghostly, shimmering avatars that are part of the virtual universe.

Of course, they're not aunts—probably not Rong, and maybe not even women. The Memorial, like all virtual universes, comes with avatar options, and it's an easy enough thing to colour flesh differently, give a different timbre to a voice or even change one's species entirely and appear as a winged horse or a lion, though Cam has never seen the point of any of it.

"Child," the eldest aunt says. "Sit down."

Cam doesn't. It's such a small, pathetic gesture, such a doomed attempt to assert her authority on them. "I left it in a holding box at the shuttleport. Number 868."

"As usual." The eldest aunt smiles, an expression that doesn't quite reach her eyes. "Well done. You're worth every credit we pay you, child." She gestures again to the chair, the only one unoccupied—it's red, the colour of good fortune and good news, an uncomfortable reminder of New Year's Eve and family reunions. "Won't you sit down? The soup is good, here."

"Which can't be said of many things here," a younger aunt says, her face set in a frown.

"Now, now, ssh," the eldest aunt says. "This child doesn't need to hear old women complaining, she's too young."

Cam isn't young anymore—past the age to contract a marriage, past the age to straighten her life—past the age where she'd swallow lies, unthinkingly. But she says nothing of that.

"I trust everything went well?" the eldest aunt inquires, conversationally, with the same casualness Cam's own aunts use when asking about her work.

Cam thinks back to Pham Thi Thanh Ha—to the expression on her face as she handed over her grandmother's chip against Cam's payment—that face twisted halfway between guilt and fear—knowing Cam, in spite of her sweet words, couldn't be trusted. "It went as expected. There was no particular trouble."

"About payment…" Cam says.

They smile at this, as if they knew exactly how she felt inside—all twisted up and nauseous, taking that kind of pay because she has no choice. One of the middle-aged aunts opens her hand, presenting to her a sheaf of paper notes: the old ones with the image of the President stamped upon them—a sharp-faced man, wrinkled and bowed with the knowledge of the impending war. "All there," the middle-aged aunt says. "A million credits, as we agreed."

It's good money—very good money, when Rong struggle to make even a hundredth of this—when so many of them hold dingy restaurants in dingy parts of Prime, or work as private cooks for the richer exiles, saving every single credit to make their children's lives better than their own. It's hers, under two conditions: that she do her job, and keep her mouth shut about the aunts.

Both of which, of course, are getting harder and harder.

Cam reaches out for it, closes her hand over it—feeling, for a second, the coolness of the aunt's skin against her own, as dry as the scales of a snake. The notes melt like sugar onto her skin, and she doesn't need to connect to the network to know it's gone into her bank account.

"Don't thank us." The middle-aged aunt sounds amused. "Now, we have another job coming up, but it won't be for a week at least, which should please you. Time for you and your girlfriend to enjoy yourselves with your family."

Cam isn't surprised—of course they would keep a tight watch on her and her life. Of course they have other agents, to pick up the chips from the holding boxes. Of course they'll know about Thuy; that the day after tomorrow is her grandmother's death anniversary; that, like every year, Cam and Thuy are headed towards her family's home in Greenhaven, to pay their respects at the ancestral altar.

What comes next, though…

"And the baby," one of the younger aunts says. "Don't forget the baby!"

The baby. How do they know—? The baby is a secret; something not even Cam's mother knows about, a fragile promise, a prayer for a better future. Cam's hands clench, a movement she can't control. "How—how do you know?"

"It's all in your files, dearie," the middle-aged aunt says. "Don't worry, we won't tell anyone."

They'll hold this, hoard it like a tool they might use—they'll feed on anything, any scrap of Cam's life that they can turn against her. "I know you won't tell," Cam says, drily, fighting back anger.

The middle-aged aunt laughs, a rasping sound like leather tearing itself apart. She gestures towards the soup. "You should eat that, before it grows cold." Another of the aunts is noisily slurping noodles from her bowl, with an expression of satisfaction; it would make Cam hungry herself, in other circumstances.

"I don't want soup," Cam says.

"Oh yes, I forget," the middle-aged aunt says. "You're always angry after your jobs."

"I'm not angry," Cam says.

"Leave the child alone." The eldest aunt frowns. "Forgive us. You know the old can be…intrusive. Of course, we have no lives of our own anymore, so we take what distractions we can, child."

"I see."

A ghostly waiter brings three-colour dessert pudding in glass cups— the mixture sports a lurid, aggressive green, nothing like the appetising colour of pandanus leaves, and even its red beans are the dark colour of blood. The smell is…off, somehow, though Cam would be hard pressed to pinpoint why; and, as the bowls of soup are swept up, only that sense of wrongness remains.

Not for the first time, she curses Steven Carey and all his work.

The eldest aunt dips a spoon in the cup, twirls it around an invisible axis. Cam hears a sound like ice cubes crushed together, though it's impossible anyone could have such strength. "You don't see," the eldest aunt says. The colours of the pudding are melding and running together, the green fracturing into a dozen disharmonious threads, reminding Cam of nothing so much as network cables cut off at the root. "But never mind, child. I'll tell you about this next job, it'll keep your mind nice and sharp."

"I don't—" Cam starts, and then stops, aghast at what words might come out of her mouth. *I don't want my mind sharp. I don't want to hear about this next job. I want to be rid of you.*

The eldest aunt is watching her; and so are the others—cruelly amused, like birds of prey watching a mortally wounded tiger stumble and pick itself up, time and time again.

No. She can't afford to antagonise them. Slowly, carefully, she says, "Fine. Tell me about the next job."

CAM LEAVES late for Greenhaven—not a surprise, as the meeting with the aunts took more time than expected. She'd expected Thuy to still be around in the flat; but she's gone, leaving a message on the console that she hitched a ride with Cam's mother, and telling Cam not to forget the basket of fruit they special-ordered from the spaceport.

Cam is past the Lynbrook Bridge and into Westborough province before she notices the police shuttle trailing her. At first, she thinks nothing of it; traffic is dense, and the police are everywhere. As she veers upwards, onto the high-speed lane, Cam sees the shuttle do the same; and when she lowers her altitude again, to catch a bite at a rest area halfway up a skyscraper, the shuttle is still there.

It's nothing unusual—Cam has been stopped more times than she can count, simply because she looks different, because she's driving a new, expensive car that most Rong shouldn't be able to afford. Mother always hunched over when that happened—speaking in short, heavily accented sentences; consumed by the fear that Prime would send her back. Cam isn't afraid; or she wouldn't be, if she was at ease. If she didn't know in her heart of hearts that she walks enshrouded in lies, every word that she utters lengthening the shadows under her feet.

She sits at the terrace of the skyscraper, watching the dance of aircars below her—dense traffic towards Landsfall, as always, people going to their jobs, to the Festival of Arts in Lynbrook, to white-walled, disinfectant-clean supermarkets where the smell of bleach overpowers that of meat or fish.

"Excuse me, miss?"

Towering over her is the figure of a police officer—one and a half times her size, easily, with flaming hair and a spattering of freckles, with skin so pale and translucent it's tinged with the red of blood vessels. Her heart leaps in her throat—remains stuck halfway there, beating at a frantic rhythm. "Yes, Officer?"

The policewoman—who introduces herself as Lieutenant George— sits down, putting her coffee cup by Cam's right hand. Cam inhales the sickening, bitter smell of the coffee at the table, stifling an urge to retch or run away.

"What do you want, Lieutenant George?"

"To speak of Perpetuates."

"I don't know what you mean." Cam has been lying for long enough not to let anything she feels show on her face.

Lieutenant George's eyes narrow. "Let's no be coy with each other, Miss Nguyen. I am speaking of Rong Perpetuates—rare and precious by the standards of those who trade in memories." She smiles. "I'm sure you know what I'm speaking of."

It's a dance that's all too familiar to Cam—she's done it so many times she knows it all by heart. But knowing doesn't help, doesn't do anything save make the ending more inevitable—for, in the end, this is no bluff—this is all about who holds power over whom.

She forces herself to sip at her tea—sip after sip after sip, burning her lips and her tongue, the bitter taste sliding down her stomach.

Lieutenant George says, "Rong Perpetuates, as you can imagine, are eagerly sought after—they fetch high prices on the black market, and I'm sure you're well aware many of the recent releases in sim-vids were enhanced by Rong, especially the older generation. There's something about the anguish of war that makes them...irresistible."

The anguish of war—how casually she dismisses everything that Cam's family went through, in a single, weaselly Galactic word that means nothing. "I don't watch sim-vids," Cam says. She forces herself to remain still in her chair, but she sees Lieutenant George smile—showing her teeth like a shark that has sighted prey.

"You don't say." Lieutenant George pauses, nudging her coffee cup out of the way—as if imparting a secret confidence to Cam. "Anyway, there have been...rumours in the black market. Rong Perpetuates being harder and harder to find—which leads to my presence here; and to you, Miss Nguyen."

Cam says nothing. She's seen the trap; perhaps, if she holds still for long enough, she might dodge its jaws—perhaps... Foolish, Thuy would say, but Thuy isn't there no matter how desperately Cam wishes for the weight of her presence.

"I'll be blunt," Lieutenant George says—as if she weren't blunt enough already, with all the subtlety of a bomb. "You run errands for a well-organised gang, Miss Nguyen, and I have enough evidence to send you to Active Re-education for a while."

But she won't. An icy clarity descends over Cam's world, each thought as clear and as brittle as pulled sugar. "What do you want, Lieutenant?"

Lieutenant George smiles. "I have no interest in the riffraff. I want the people who pay you; and you'll help me."

This is a dance Cam has done often enough, with so many other people—enough to know every one of its steps by heart. "Why should I help you? I'll end up in Active Re-education anyway, and it'll be far less danger to me. As you said—they are a well organised gang. I doubt they are fools."

Lieutenant George shakes her head, drily amused—she's not stupid, else they wouldn't have sent her. "There are...dispensations that can be made. Ways and means of acknowledging your help to the Galactic police."

"Immunity," Cam says, putting both elbows on the table.

"I can't offer immunity. As I said—I have evidence. You can't erase that."

A bluff. "A police lieutenant is a powerful individual. I'm sure you can arrange things." Cam keeps her voice even. "Evidence—assuming there is any—can be lost. Destroyed." If it were just her, she'd give herself up, to atone for what she's done—but there is Thuy. There is the unborn child.

Lieutenant George grimaces. "Six months in Active Re-education."

"Two months," Cam says, reckless—and, when silence stretches, knows she's gone too far.

"Three months. Far less than you deserve, Miss Nguyen." Lieutenant George's voice is filled with disgust. "The offer is as it stands."

Three months. It's not so much, all things considered—three months on some deserted planet, away from all communications—from Thuy, from the baby. But it's still time that will appear on her papers; that will hamper her in her search for another job—of course, supposing the aunts don't take her down with them. She wouldn't be surprised to know they have a contingency plan for everything from sickness to betrayal.

When Cam doesn't answer, Lieutenant George shakes her head. "Think on it. Three months, and some risk to your precious person. Or five years without risk—that's the minimum you'd get for trafficking in Perpetuates, and I would be pushing for more than this, personally." She rises, cradling her coffee cup against her chest. "I've left you my contact details. Tell me within the week what your life will look like in the next few years, Nguyen Thi Cam."

CAM ARRIVES late, and finds the family gathered in the kitchen. Mother is putting the last of the rice cakes into boiling water with Father by her side, who interjects advice and reproaches as she slides each cake into the huge cooking pot. Thuy and Cousin Hanh are rolling up the twine that served them to wrap the cakes, while Cousin Vien is putting plates and bowls into the automatic washer. The uncles and aunts are nowhere to be seen—probably they're in the living room, tidying up offerings on the ancestral altar.

"Lil' sis." Thuy nods to Cam. "Sorry for not waiting."

Cam shakes her head. "No, it's me. I had an appointment I couldn't put off." She puts the basket of fruit on the table, and greets her mother and father, and then the cousins in order of age. "Sorry for arriving late."

Mother snorts. "Plenty of hands to help with the cooking, even though most of them are rather clumsy." She peers at the basket, curious. "What did you girls get?"

Dragon fruit, and mangoes—fruit that have grown ever so expensive as the years pass, making the exodus a distant memory in the minds of the elders. None of them grow well on Landsfall, and it takes a dedicated environment and a crew of biologists to make sure the other crops don't cannibalise them before they have a chance to grow. "Oh, you shouldn't have. It's too expensive, children," Mother says. Cam knows she's well pleased in spite of her protests, to see her daughters and nieces cajoling her with delicacies; all the signs of happiness that Heaven has decreed, the rewards of old age.

Father peers at the fruit, and nods, gruffly. "Go put a few in a plate, would you? Your grandmother could use nice things."

After Cam has left her offerings on the ancestral altar, everything seems to dissolve in a whirl of activities: she walks the gardens with Mother, seeing how the bots prune the trees and collect herbs from the hothouses; she and Cousin Vien help Father install his newest network connection, and get a membership into a virtual universe for Encirclement fanatics. And, all the while, she skirts around the truth, jokingly speaking of security contracts to Mother, just as she does with Thuy—lies, every word out of her mouth, every rivet in the wall of her life.

On the second day, they hold the remembrance of Xuan Huong.

They stand in silence, bowed before the altar—watching the holo of Grandmother's face, the furrows of grief traced on her skin; the bowed shoulders, as if she still labours under the weight of exile even among the ancestors. "We thank you for your blessings," Mother says, lighting a stick of incense and bowing three times. "For the gift of food, which we took with us to a new planet. For the gift of money, which gathered us all to escape the war. For the gift of love, which did not die with Xuan Huong."

They're meant to meditate on Xuan Huong: Mother and Father and Cam's aunts and uncles all have tears in their eyes, thinking of a city they knew that is now cut off from them; and of all the dead littering the streets like rice shoots cut off before they could bear food.

Cam finds her mind drifting to the Memorial; to the aunts and the sound of ice being crushed against a glass, faster and more casually than should be humanly possible… She wonders what Grandmother would have thought of her, of what she does; if she'd have forgiveness in her heart for her wayward granddaughter. But, of course, there's only the darkness of her own thoughts, and her own worries about the future.

On the last evening of the death anniversary, Cam and Thuy find themselves alone in the living room, scraping food off plates before piling them into the kitchen.

She wants to tell Thuy about Lieutenant George, about the choice between flood and fire; but she can't—she's trapped by her own lies, by the weight of her own failures.

Thuy, though, is nothing but observant. "Is anything wrong?"

"It's work-related," Cam says—and watches as the words dry up in Thuy's mouth.

"Oh. I'm sorry. I shouldn't have asked."

"No, it's all right." Cam hesitates. "Only—I might have to go away for a while."

"On a mission?" Thuy's eyes gleam with that painful, earnest enthusiasm that Cam finds hard to bear.

"Of a kind." Cam sighs. Nothing will be pleasant in the future, no matter how she turns it. "I—It might be a long while. The child—"

Thuy's hand strays to her belly, rubs it as if for luck. "You won't be back for the birth."

"I don't know." Cam feels as if she wants to cry, but all water seems to have been wrung out of her. "Ancestors, I don't know." Her hands are shaking, so hard that the plates she's carrying chink against each other.

"I see." Thuy says nothing for a while; she doesn't look happy.

As they take the last of the plates out, Cam steals a glance at the ancestral altar—Grandmother's gaze seems to follow her, wherever she goes. "Do you think—" she pauses, hesitating. Grandmother scrapped and begged and did what she had to, to get her family out of Moc Hau Tinh before war made the planet inaccessible—in so many ways, they know that they'll never be as worthy as her. "Do you think she'd approve of us?"

Thuy gathers chopsticks in her clenched hand, weighs them, thoughtfully. "Of what we've grown into? Every generation is less than the one who came before them; and more, too. Every chain of hands, reaching back to the beginning of time…" She frowns, rubs her belly again. "Lil' sis…"

"Yes?"

"About the birth—we'll talk about it later. I know it's not easy."

You don't know anything, Cam thinks, and blinks furiously, to make the world clearer. "I'm sorry." The plates are wobbling in her hands; carefully, she sets them on the ground, and stares at the ancestral altar, seeking words that have deserted her.

"Oh, Cam." Thuy covers the space that separates them in a heartbeat, and kisses her, hard. "You're a fool."

"So are you," Cam says, struggling to smile.

They finish the rest of the cleaning in silence, and tiptoe back to their room. Later, Cam lies in bed by Thuy's side, staring at the ceiling, and thinks of what lies ahead. She thinks of Lieutenant George; of the Memorial and the aunts—and it all slides with her into sleep, melds and merges into a confused jumble, with the noise of bombs and the sound of spaceships lifting from the spaceport, instants before the Western Continent soldiers march through the streets of Xuan Huong—into Grandmother's face, the old woman staring at her as if weighing her worth; before she turns away, and walks ahead into darkness...

Cam wakes up with a start, shaking her head to dismiss the last of her nightmare. Outside, it's still night, and she can smell the just-cooked rice porridge from the kitchen, and hear Mother shuffle about, no doubt looking for a bowl and a spoon. She'll get up and go into the kitchen, and say more lies about coming back home for work, that she has an important job to do at her company, that they need her to save the project...

Lies.

But not for long; not anymore.

IT'S ALL the same, the same as it ever was: Cam walks down the streets of Xuan Huong, breathing in the sweet, sharp smell of apricot trees—garlands of Tet yellow flowers drape the streets, and the year is that of the Yin Wood Tiger, the year of the fall. She brushes past young girls in five-panel costumes, giggling at Galactics in shirts and trousers: the streets are pristine, not even stained by flower petals, unreal—as ghostly as the artificial intelligences populating them.

She can't help but glance at her hands as she walks: the sniffer Lieutenant George has given her is invisible in the Memorial, though it glowed red against her skin when George injected it into her palm. *Transfer it with a thought sequence*, George had said—running through the steps of it with Cam, over and over again. *It'll embed itself in the target's hand, and start emitting—we'll be able to follow them wherever they go. We'll arrest them when they exit the Memorial.*

She didn't tell Cam to be careful, or to come back safe—of course she wouldn't. Of course she doesn't care, one way or another.

In the alleyway behind the Ansible Station, the aunts are waiting for her, though there are no bowls of steaming soup in front of them. They're dressed differently, too—wearing what looks like Galactic garb, long flowing dresses that hug their frail bodies, outlining curves they ought not to have. It feels…

Wrong, Cam wants to say, but the words don't get past her lips. Instead she wonders, for a heart-stopping moment, if she's given herself away; if George's sniffer can be detected on her, if that's the reason why the aunts have changed their behaviour. But no, that is impossible; she hasn't activated it yet. The aunts can't know…

She pulls a chair; hearing it scrape against the pavement. "No soup today?" she asks, keeping her voice light.

"It's too early for soup, child." The eldest aunt smiles, as toothy as a tiger on the prowl. "Tell me how it went with Nguyen Thi Sao."

Cam shrugs. "There isn't much to say. I left you the chip in the shuttleport. Holding box 121."

"Good." The eldest aunt frowns, and the air around her seems to tighten in menace. "That certainly was fast. I expected you to have more difficulties."

Cam shakes her head, not trusting herself to speak. It was hard, in truth—harder than it's ever been, to sit in a chair and lie and cajole, knowing that all she had to do was wait a few more days, a few more hours—and that she would finally be free of them.

"About payment," she says—and waits, her heart hammering in her chest, for the eldest aunt to extend her hand across the table, for the exchange of money to take place. She doesn't glance at her own hand.

The eldest aunt does not move. That's it, then; she's overplayed it; been too flippant, too confident—she's given the game away. She shouldn't have…

Finally, the eldest aunt shakes her head, and slowly extends her hand to her, with old-fashioned notes on her palm. Bracing herself, Cam reaches out—there's a tingle as the money changes hand, and another tingle as the sniffer leaves her and attaches itself to its target.

The eldest aunt is frowning, looking at her hand as if something were bothersome—there's nothing here, she can't possibly see it—it's impossible...

"Mmm." The eldest aunt compresses her lips—tightens her hand hard enough to crush whatever is inside it. "Is there anything else you want to tell us, child?"

Cam clamps down the first flippant response that comes to mind; and says, instead, "No. What about the next assignment?"

"We'll contact you." The eldest aunt is still staring at her hand, as if she could actually detect the sniffer; which is impossible. She and her companions rise, and walk away without a backward glance.

Cam remains behind, struggling to control the mad drum beats of her heart. They haven't seen anything, they can't possibly have seen anything...

She waits for the aunts to drop out of sight—then she takes a deep breath, and activates the sniffer.

Nothing happens—at least, nothing that she can see, but she knows that outside the Memorial, something has come online in Lieutenant George's van—that her team is now assembling, ready to track the aunts; to make the arrest George hungers for, the one that will make the world a little safer for Perpetuates. Cam has done her part. She can turn back, and leave the Memorial much as she came into it—empty-handed, braced for the worst to happen to her.

And yet...

And yet she has to know. And yet, somehow, she finds herself walking after the aunts—hearing the same litany echo in her skull until it takes the place of everything else. She's in the Memorial. In a virtual universe with no set rules for death. There's nothing they can do to her; nothing that will terminate her existence or harm her for more than a few transitory moments. Nothing. Unless...

Unless they've managed to hack into it.

No. That's impossible. No one can…

But they're the aunts—whoever they are, they know everything, have access to all the files, to all the details of Cam's life. Surely, hacking into a virtual universe, even one so tightly circumscribed as the Memorial, isn't beyond their powers?

She walks in sunlight, into little alleyways filled with compartments—with houses that advertise their wares on battered holo-screens, past bots that scuttle into bolt-holes. A sleek aircar zooms by, stopping briefly to extrude a counter and dispense some crab noodle soup to a middle-aged woman.

This far into the simulation, Galactics are not there at all—there are only Rong, from the mechanic who carries bots slung over his shoulder to the seller of barbecued pork sandwiches; from the young man lost in his virtual games, to the old woman descending from an aircar, attended by her whole family.

The smell of food is overwhelming—of steamed rice and garlic and fish sauce, of broth simmering away in the myriad restaurants she walks by. Cam should be on her knees by now, gagging with the wrongness of it—but she's not.

Cam turns a corner, still struggling to work out what is wrong, what she's not seeing—and all but bumps into the aunts.

They have stopped—are waiting for her, their arms crossed over their chests. The eldest aunt is a little apart from them, holding out her hand, in which flashes a red light—George's tracker made manifest.

It's impossible—they shouldn't…

"Did you think we wouldn't see, child?" The eldest aunt asks. Her voice is deceptively mild; she might have been talking about the weather.

Cam stops—no use waiting for help, for it won't come. She's alone now, and in spite of the innocuous environment she's never been so frightened in her life. "I had no choice. I could come down with you, or I could follow their orders."

The eldest aunt peers into her hand, thoughtfully. "I see. Galactic police coding. Shoddy work—you can tell, it's full of corrupt packages."

Abruptly she's standing by Cam's side, pressing down on her shoulder with what seems like little strength; but it feels as though something is tearing inside her. The eldest aunt is only a small, diminutive woman; how can she be so strong—how can she—?

"You *know* I can't stand on your side." Cam forces the words out between clenched teeth—the eldest aunt is still pressing on her, and gradually her body is buckling, her knees giving way, bowing her closer to the ground. "For Heaven's sake, you buy Perpetuates to take them apart!"

"And you're nothing." The eldest aunt's voice is contemptuous. "You were happy enough to take our money, and ask no questions, and all of a sudden you decide to betray us? That won't do, child."

Cam is kneeling on the ground now, brought down by the weight of the eldest aunt's hands on her shoulder; and her breath comes in gasps and shudders. She's truly, desperately alone—Lieutenant George, even if she suspects something is wrong, won't react, won't do anything to save her— she's made it clear enough what she thinks of Cam's acts.

As Cam struggles for breath, for words, she sees everything with preternatural clarity—every detail of her surroundings, the bystanders throwing curious glances at the group stuck in the middle of the wide, paved street— the eldest aunt's robes, billowing in the breeze; every little stitch of the cloth, every cut of the scissors and every little embroidery on the hem of the sleeves—they're not Galactic patterns, but rather a thin chain of lotus flowers, going all the way around the hem like prayer beads.

Rong. They're Rong patterns.

And she sees, then—not with her eyes, but with her heart and mind. She sees that the aunts are wearing the clothes her grandmother wore, every day of her life—a melding of Galactic and Rong influences. Those are the clothes her friends' grandparents wore, the ones they brought from Moc Hau Tinh when the planet burnt in civil war.

And, around her...

She doesn't look around her. She doesn't need to. She knows that everyone she saw—the noodle soup seller, the seller of sandwiches, the housewives in the aircar—they all have the solidity of real, living people.

"You're Rong," she says. "You're all Rong."

"Of course we're Rong," the eldest aunt says. "What did you think we were, child?"

Cam kneels, breathing in the smell of garlic and fish sauce and all the myriad things of home. Everyone in the street seems to have gathered around them, a circle of pressed people that is making her dizzy—she catches bits and pieces, fragments of faces that look familiar and yet are not—

No.

She sees them. She sees all of them, clustered at the back of the crowd—Thanh Ha's grandmother, and Pham Huu Hieu's brother, and Le Thi Quoc's mother, and all the others she's bargained away from their families, given flesh and blood in the Memorial, a feat that should have been impossible.

"Perpetuates," she breathes, knowing that this, too, is true. "You're all Perpetuates."

"This is our home," the eldest aunt says. "The place we have made for ourselves." She's withdrawn from Cam; stands staring at the streets around her. Cam sucks in breath through burning lungs, struggling to make sense of what she's seen.

They...they have hacked the Memorial *from within*. They have hidden themselves in its codes and processes, and built their own enclave. They have...

They're not supposed to be here at all. No wonder they hide; no wonder they tell no one what they are or what they are doing. The Memorial is not a virtual universe open to Perpetuates. It is a museum: a place to visit, not a place to live in or be hosted—not a place where you're allowed to painstakingly build your own home city within the city, year after year—

The enormity of it shocks her—that Perpetuates should have the power and desire to take the Memorial back; to expand, layer after layer, into Steven Carey's masterwork, and claim it back for themselves... That she should have helped in that, all the while thinking that she was helping the aunts taking Perpetuates apart. That she...

That she sold the aunts out, just as she sold off the chips; gave them away with scarcely a thought to ensure her own, selfish future...

It's too much to take in all at once.

"I'm sorry," she whispers—in Rong, using the pronoun reserved for young, ignorant, children. "I didn't know."

One of the middle-aunts speaks, in the growing silence, "Not so easy, is it, to find out what you have done?"

"I'm sorry," Cam says, again, knowing the words to be meaningless—cheaply bandied weapons, promises as brittle as burnt clay.

She stands, shivering, in bright sunlight in the city of Xuan Huong—not the quaint place of Steven Carey's fantasies, not the poverty-ridden, powerless victim of the war seen through Galactic eyes; but the home of Mother and Grandmother and all her ancestors; the bustling, multifaceted city that shaped her people and her family, the continuation of the history that she and Thuy carry with them, words and images carved into the grooves of their hearts.

And she knows, then, with a certainty she's never felt before in her life—she knows that she'll pay whatever price needs to be paid to preserve this; to make sure that the Memorial still contains that corner of living history; the thread, elusive and thin and yet more solid than any steel, which still binds the Rong to their homeland—the thread which is the truth of the war and the truth of their past.

Cam holds out her hand to the eldest aunt. "Let me make this right."

The eldest aunt turns; the sniffer glowing in the palm of her hand—the colour of maple leaves and New Year's lanterns. "Let me help," Cam says, again. "If I take it from you—"

"Why should we trust you?" the eldest aunt asks. "You've amply demonstrated that you'll betray us, time and time again, when your own life hangs in the balance."

Betrayals—of the Rong, of the Rong Perpetuates, not once but many, many times—selling her people to what she thought was a criminal ring, time and time again—betrayals, and selfishness, and greed...

Cam spreads her hands—speechless, for once.

"What do you advocate?" the middle-aged aunt says.

"Isn't it obvious?" The eldest aunt is standing once more by Cam's side, one hand casually raised, only a few inches from her throat. With a mere gesture, she could crush Cam's windpipe—this deep into the Memorial, Cam doesn't doubt that she'd die for real. That Thuy would wait and wait, and raise a child on her own—and be unable to tell that child anything, anything at all about Cam that would be meaningful. "Silence is gold; and the only silence we can trust is that of the grave."

"She's Rong," the middle-aged aunt says.

"She's nothing. She lies and cheats for a living."

"We all do, don't we? We all lie and deceive and cheat, elder sister—as we did to this child."

"Not for selfish motives."

"Our own survival, you mean?" The middle-aged aunt's smile is bitter. "Tell me that's not selfish. Look me in the eye and tell me it's not."

The eldest aunt says nothing.

"Please," Cam says. "Else they'll come in and find you."

The eldest aunt's gaze turns to her; and it's Grandmother's gaze, dark and unfathomable, weighing every inch of Cam's life from beginning to end. "Do you know what you're asking for, child?"

Cam thinks of Lieutenant George; of re-education—and of Thuy and their child, and of each generation being less and more than the one that came after them. She had so many ideas of what she wanted; and all of them, after all, turned out to be wrong. For, when she does this—when she walks out of the Memorial with the sniffer still in the palm of her hand, looking properly downcast and ashamed and afraid for Lieutenant George—her life will once again revolve on lies; once again be shrouded in the half-truths and evasions she's become so good at.

What matters is this: they won't be the shadow lies, the worms eating at her from within, but the other kind of lies—the ones that give weight and heft and meaning to the secret part of her life.

"Yes. Of course I know what I'm doing." And, reaching out, she takes the eldest aunt's hand in her own; and stands in sunlight on the eve of the war, in the city of her ancestors—feeling the dried, gnarled flesh against hers like a fount of strength for the future.

The Breath of War

GOING INTO THE MOUNTAINS HAD NEVER BEEN EASY. EVEN IN
Rechan's first adult years, when the war was slowly burning itself to
smouldering embers, every Spring Festival had been a slow migration in
armed vehicles, her aunts and uncles frequently stopping in every roadside
shop, taking stock of what ambushes or roadblocks might lie ahead.

The war might be over—or almost so, the planet largely at peace, the
spaceports disgorging a steady stream of Galactic and Rong visitors onto
Voc—but the pace was just as frustratingly slow.

They'd made good time at first: coming out of the city early in the morning and becoming airborne at the first of the authorised takeoff points, the
steady stream of soldiers repatriated from the front becoming smaller and
smaller as they flew higher, like insects on the intense brown of the road; zig-
zagging on the trails, laughing with relief as they unpacked the fried dough
Rechan had baked for lunch, almost forgetting that they weren't setting on
an adventure but on something with far longer-reaching consequences.

And then the flyer's motor made a funny sound, and the entire vehicle
lurched downwards with a sickening crunch that jolted Rechan against the
wall. And before they knew it, they were stranded on a dusty little road
halfway up the mountains, leaving Rechan's niece Akanlam bartering with
a local herder for a repair point.

By the sounds of it, the bartering was not going well.

Rechan sat against a large rock outcropping, rubbing the curve of her belly for comfort; feeling the familiar heaviness, the weight of the baby's body in her womb like a promise. *You'll be fine*, she thought, over and over, a saying that had become her lifeline, no matter how much of a lie it might be. *You'll be fine.*

"We should be able to solve this," Mau said. The stonewoman's face was as impassive as ever. Her eyes didn't crinkle as she spoke, her mouth didn't quirk; there was only the slow, quiet sound of her breath.

"You think so?" Rechan shook her head, trying not to think of her dreams. It was so many years since she'd carved Sang—so many years since she'd gone into the mountains with little more than rations and carving tools—but, with the particular link that bound a woman to her breath-sibling, she could feel him every night: blurred images of him hovering over the uplands, never venturing far from the place of his birth. A relief, because he was her only hope.

On Voc, it took a stoneman's breath to quicken a baby at birth—and not any stoneman's, but the mother's breath-sibling, the one she had carved on accession to adulthood and entrusted with her breath. Without Sang, her baby would be stillborn.

"We'll find a vehicle," Mau said.

Rechan watched her niece from a distance. The discussion was getting animated and Akanlam's hand gestures more and more frantic. "Help me up," she said to Mau.

The stonewoman winced. "You shouldn't—"

"I've spent a lifetime doing what I shouldn't," Rechan said; and after a while Mau held out a hand, which she used to haul herself up. The stonewoman's skin was *lamsinh*—the same almost otherworldly translucency, the same coolness as the stone; the fingers painstakingly carved with an amount of detail that hadn't been accessible to Rechan's generation. Mau was Akanlam's breath-sibling; and Akanlam had put into her carving the same intensity she always put in her art. Unlike most stonemen, nothing in her looked quite human, but there was a power and a flow in the least of Mau's features that made her seem to radiate energy, even when sitting still.

"What is going on here?" Rechan asked, as she got closer.

Akanlam looked up, her face red. "He says the nearest repair point is two days down."

Rechan took in the herder: craggy face, a reflection of the worn rocks around them; a spring in his step that told her he wasn't as old as he looked. "Good day, younger brother," she said.

"Good day, elder sister." The herder nodded to her. "I was telling the younger aunt here—you have to go down."

Rechan shook her head. "Going down isn't an option. We have to get to the uplands."

The herder winced. "It's been many years since city folks came this way."

"I know," Rechan said, and waited for the herder to discourage her. She'd gotten used to that game. But, to her surprise, he didn't.

"Exhalation?" he asked. "There are simpler ways."

"I know," Rechan said. He'd mistaken Mau as her breath-sibling and not Akanlam's—an easy mistake to make, for in her late stage of pregnancy, having a breath-sibling at hand would be crucial. "But it's not exhalation. She's not my breath-sibling; she's *hers.*"

The herder looked from her to Mau and then back to Akanlam. "How far along are you?" he asked.

Too far along; that was the truth. She'd waited too long, hoping a solution would present itself; that she wouldn't need to go back into the mountains. A mistake; hope had never gotten her anywhere. "Eight months and a half," Rechan said, and heard the herder's sharp intake of breath. "My breath-sibling is in the mountains." Which was...true, in a way.

The herder grimaced again, and looked at the bulge of her belly. "I can radio the nearest village," he said, finally. "They might have an aircar, or something you can borrow, provided you return it."

Rechan nodded, forcing her lips upwards into a smile. "Perfect. Thank you, younger brother."

THE VILLAGE didn't have an aircar, or a cart, or any contrivance Rechan could have used. They did have mules and goats, but in her advanced state of pregnancy she dared not risk a ride on an animal. So they radioed the next village, which promised to send their only aircar. Rechan thanked them, and hunkered with Akanlam down in the kitchen to help with the communal cooking. There was a wedding feast that night, and the community would need the travellers' hands as much, if not more, than their money.

Mau came by the kitchen later, having spent the afternoon gossiping with the village elders. "They say there's rebel activity on the uplands," she said, handing Rechan a thin cutting knife.

"Hmm." Rechan took a critical look at the seafood toasts on the table. Half of them looked slightly crooked; hopefully in the dim light the guests wouldn't mind too much.

"Herders don't take their beasts into the mountains, and especially not on the *lamsinh* uplands. They say people go missing there. Crossfire, probably. They say on quiet nights you can hear the sounds of battle."

Rechan thought of her dreams—of Sang's savage thoughts, the thrill of the hunt, the release of the kill, permeating everything until she woke up sweating. What kind of being had he become, left to his own devices on the uplands? "You're not trying to discourage me, are you?"

Mau shifted positions; the light caught her face, frozen into the serene enigmatic smile that had been Akanlam's as a child. "Ha. I've since long learnt how useless that is. No, I just thought you'd like to know exactly what we're going into."

"War," Akanlam said from her place at the stove, her voice dour. "The last remnants of it, anyway."

The Galactic delegation had arrived a couple of days earlier, to formalise the peace agreement between the government and the rebels; the spaceports were being renovated, the terminals and pagodas painstakingly rebuilt. "I guess," Rechan said. "It always comes back to the mountains, doesn't it?" She shifted positions, feeling the baby move within her, a weight as heavy as stone. "Legend says that's where we all came from."

"The prime colony ark?" Akanlam scoffed, chopping vegetables into small pieces. "That was debunked years ago."

A cheer went up outside. Rechan shifted, to see onto the plaza. A gathering of people in silk clothes, clustered around the lucky trio. She was young, even younger than Akanlam; wearing a red, tight-fitting tunic with golden embroidery, and beaming; and her groom even younger than her, making it hard to believe he had cleared adolescence. The breath-sibling was a distinguished, elderly gentleman in the robes of a scholar, who reminded Rechan of her own grandfather. He was standing next to the bride, smiling as widely as she was. The sunlight seemed to illuminate his translucent body from within: it had been a beautiful block of stone he'd been carved from, a white shade the colour of Old Earth porcelain; likely, so close to the uplands they could pick their blocks themselves, rather than rely on what the traders brought them.

By their side was someone who had to be the bride's sister, carrying a very young infant in her arms. The baby's face was turned towards the couple, eyes wide open in an attempt to take everything in; and a little brother in fur clothes was prevented, with difficulty, from running up to the bride. The baby was three months, four months old, perhaps? With the pudgy fingers and the chubby cheeks—her own child would be like that one day, would look at her with the same wide-eyed wonder.

"Life goes on," Akanlam said, her face softening. "Always."

"Of course." That was why Rechan had gotten herself inseminated, against the family's wishes: she might have been a failure by their standards, thirty years old and unmarried—for who would want to marry someone without a breath-sibling? But, with the war over, it was time to think of the future; and she didn't want to die childless and alone, without any descendants to worship at her grave. She wanted a family, like the bride; like the bride's sister: children to hold in her arms, to raise as she had been raised, and a house filled with noise and laughter instead of the silence of the war, when every month had added new holos to the altar of the ancestors.

"I'll go present our respects," Akanlam said.

"You never had much taste for cooking," Mau pointed out, and Akanlam snorted.

"Elder Aunt cooks quite well," she said with a smile. "Better to leave everyone do what they excel at, no?"

"You impossible child," Rechan said as she so often did, with a little of her usual amusement. Akanlam was the niece with the closest quarters to her own; and she and Mau and Rechan often got together for dinners and after-work drinks—though none of them ever let Akanlam cook. As Mau had said: not only did she not have much taste for it, but left without supervision she'd burn a noodle soup to a charred mess before anyone could intervene. She did mix superb fruit chunks, though. "What are you going to do when you get married?"

"You're assuming I want to get married," Akanlam said, without missing a beat. "And even if I did, I'd stay with you. You're going to need help with raising those children of yours. How many did you say you wanted?"

"I'd be lucky to have one," Rechan said, finally. But she'd dreamt of a larger family; of the dozens brothers and sisters and cousins of her youth, before war carved a swathe through them—a horde of giggling children always ready to get into trouble. If she could find her breath-sibling again... "And I'm old enough to do what I'm doing."

"Oh, I have no doubt. But it's still a job for two people. Or three." Akanlam smiled. "I'll see you outside."

After Akanlam had gone, Mau swung from her wooden stool and came to stand by Rechan. "Let me have a look."

Rechan almost said no, almost asked what the point was. But she knew; too many things could go wrong at this stage. It wasn't only birth without her stoneman that could kill her baby.

Mau's hands ran over the bulge of her belly, lingered on a point above her hips. "The head is here," she said, massaging it. "He's shifted positions. It's pointing downwards, into your birth canal. It's very large."

"I know," Rechan said. "My doctor said the same after the scan. Said I'd have difficulty with the birth." There were new systems; new scanners brought by the Galactics, to show a profusion of almost obscene details about the baby in her belly, down to every fine hair on its skin. But none of them had the abilities and experience of a stoneman.

"Mmm." Mau ran her hands downwards. "May I?" After a short examination, she looked up, and her face lay in shadow.

"What is it?" Rechan asked. What could she possibly have found?

"You're partly open," Mau said, finally. "You'll have to be careful, elder aunt, or you're going to enter labour early."

"I can't—" Rechan started, and then realised how ridiculous it would sound to Mau, who could do little more in the way of medical attention. "I have to get back to the uplands."

Mau shook her head. "I didn't tell Akanlam—because you know this already—but the path gets impracticable by aircar after a while. You'll have to walk."

As she had, all those years ago. "You're right," Rechan said. "I did know." She braced herself for Mau to castigate her, to tell her she couldn't possibly think of taking a mountain trail in her state. But the stonewoman's face was expressionless, her hands quite still on Rechan's belly.

"You'll have to be careful," she repeated at last.

She couldn't read Mau at all. Perhaps it came from never having lived with a breath-sibling of her own. "You never told me why you came," Rechan said. "Akanlam—"

"—came because she's your niece, and because she knew it was important to you." Mau nodded. Was it Rechan's imagination, or was the baby stirring at her touch? Mau was Akanlam's breath-sibling, not hers. She could deliver the baby, but couldn't give it the breath that would quicken it—yet still, perhaps there was something all stonewomen shared, some vital portion of the planet's energy, a simmering, life-giving warmth, like that stone she'd touched all those years ago before she started her carving. "I came because I was curious. You're a legend in the family, you know."

Rechan snorted. "The one without a breath-sibling? That's hardly worth much of anything."

Mau turned, so that the light caught on the stone of her arms, throwing every vein of the rock into sharp relief. "But you do have a breath-sibling, don't you, elder aunt?"

How much did she know, or suspect? Rechan's official story had always been she couldn't remember, and perhaps that had been the truth, once upon a time, but now that they were in the mountains again—now that the sky lay above them like a spread cloth, and the air was sharp with the tang of smoke—memories were flooding back.

"I know the story," Mau said. "They measured you when you came back down, attached electrodes to your chest and listened to the voice of your heart. You had no breath left in you; even if they gave you *lamsinh*, you wouldn't have been able to bring a carving to life. You'd already given it to someone. Or something." Her gaze was shrewd.

So that was it, the reason she'd come with them: knowledge. Akanlam was happy with her art gallery and her shows; but of all the curious apathy she could show with life, none of it had gone into her breath-sibling. "You were curious," Rechan said.

Mau smiled, that odd expression that didn't reach her eyes. "You carved something in the mountains—came back covered in stone dust. What was it, elder aunt?"

SHE REMEMBERED her last trip into the mountains as if it was yesterday: going barefoot in the morning, with a curt message left on her parents' comms unit. She'd taken the set of carving tools that had been given to her on her sixteenth birthday—the straight cutter, the piercer, the driller, and all that would be necessary for her exhalation ceremony. It was a beautiful set, given by Breath-Mother: the finest hardened glass, as translucent as the best *lamsinh* stone, and hardly weighed anything on her back. As she walked away through the sparse scattering of buildings on the edge of the city, she heard, in the distance, the rumble of bombs hitting the Eastern District—the smell of smoke, the distant wail of militia sirens—and turned her head westwards, towards the mountains.

The mountains, of course, weren't better—just further away from any hospital, Flesh-Mother and Father would say with a frown—more isolated, so that if you were captured no one would know where you were for days and days. They'd have a block of *lamsinh* brought to her for the exhalation; everyone did, paying militia and soldiers and the occasional daredevil to cart the life-sized stone into the city. She just had to wait, and she'd be safe.

Rechan could not wait.

She was young, and impatient; and tired of being cooped up for her own safety. She should have been off-planet by now, sent off to Third Aunt for a year's apprenticeship in the ship-yards; except that the previous summer all spaceport traffic had been halted when a bomb exploded in the marketplace; and the apprenticeship went to some other relative who wasn't from Voc, who didn't have to cope with bombs and battles and food shortages. By now—if it hadn't been for those stupid rebels—she could have had her hands in motor oil; could have climbed into pilots' cabins, running her hands on the instruments and imagining what it would be like, hanging suspended in the void of space with only the stars for company.

Life wasn't fair, and she certainly wasn't going to wait any longer to become an adult.

THERE PROBABLY was a divinity somewhere watching over thoughtless adolescents; for Rechan had made it into the mountains, and to the uplands, without any major trouble. She hitched a ride on a peddler's cart—so many things that could have gone wrong there, but the peddler was nice and friendly, and glad for the company—and then, when there no longer were villages or people, she walked. From time to time, she'd had to duck when a flyer banked over the path. At this height, it had to be rebels, and they'd kill her if they found her, as they had killed Second Uncle and Seventh Aunt, and Cousin Thinh and Cousin Anh; all the absences like gaping wounds in the fabric of family life. Demons take the rebels, all of them; how much simpler would life be if none of them were here.

And then she stood on the uplands—her feet hurting, her bag digging into the small of her back, her breath coming in fiery gasps—and it didn't matter, any of it, because there was the stone.

She'd only seen the blocks the traders brought down. The one for her cousin's exhalation had been roughly the size of a woman; of course, with *lamsinh* at such a dear price, people would buy only what was necessary. But here were no such constraints. The stone towered over her, cliffs as tall as the Temple of Mercy, broken bits and pieces ranging from the size of a skyscraper to the size of her fist; colours that ranged from a green so deep it was almost black, to the translucent shades Flesh-Mother so valued, the same colour used for all the family's breath-siblings—all the stone's veins exposed, streaks of lighter and darker nuances that seemed to be throbbing on the same rhythm as her own frantic heartbeat.

She walked among them, letting her hand lightly trail on the smooth surfaces, feeling the lambent heat; the faint trembling of the air where the sun had heated them through, like an echo of her own breath. People had always been vague about exhalation: they'd said you'd know, when you saw your block of stone, what kind of breath-sibling you wanted to carve, what kind of birth master you wanted to give to your children yet to come. But here she didn't just have one block of stone, but thousands; and she wandered into a labyrinth of toppled structures like the wreck of a city, wondering where she could settle herself, where she could make her first cut into the incandescent mass around her.

And then she rounded the edge of the cliff, and saw it, lying on the ground.

It was huge, easily ten times her size, with streaks the colour of algae water, and a thousand small dots, almost as if the stone had been pock-marked; a pattern of wounds that reminded her, for some absurd reason, of a tapestry that had used to hang on Seventh Aunt's wall, before the bomb tore her apart in the marketplace.

In all the stories she'd heard, all the tales about girls running off to have adventures, there was always this moment; this perfect moment when they reached the uplands, or when someone showed them a block of stone, and they just *knew*, staring at it, what it would look like when whittled down to shape; when they'd freed, measure by agonising measure, the limbs and head and body of their breath-sibling, the one who would be their constant companion as they travelled over the known planets. In the stories, they didn't carve; they revealed the stone's secret nature, gave it the life it had always longed for.

Rechan had never given that credence. She was the daughter of an engineer, and believed in planning and in forethought; and had brought sketches with her, of how her own stoneman would look, with delicate hands like her mother, and large strong arms that would be able to carry her to hospital if the delivery went badly.

Except that then, she stood in front of the stone, and saw into its heart. And *knew*, with absolute certainty, that it wasn't a stoneman that she needed or wanted to carve.

LATER, MUCH later, when she thought about it all, she wondered how she'd endured it—months up in the uplands with scant rations, sleeping rough, sheltering under the rock face when the rain came—day after day of rising and going back to her block of stone; carving, little by little, what would become her breath-sibling.

She did the outside first: the sleek, elegant hull, tapering to a point; the shadow of the twin engines at the back, every exhaust port and every weapons slit rendered in painstaking detail. Then she turned inwards, and from the only door into the ship, made corridors inch by agonising inch, her tools gnawing their way through the rock. All the while, she imagined it hanging in space—fast and deadly, a predator in a sea of stars, one who never had to cower or shelter for fear of bombs or flyers; one who was free to go where she wished, without those pointless restrictions on her life, those over-solicitous parents and breath-mothers who couldn't understand that bombs happened, that all you could do was go out and pray, moment after moment, that they wouldn't fall on you.

It was rough carving. She didn't have the tools that would be available to the generation after hers—not the fineness of Akanlam's carving, who would be able to give Mau fingernails, and a small pendant on her chest, down to the imprint of the chain that held it. She carved as she could—hour after hour, day after day, lifted into a place where time had no meaning, where only the ship existed or mattered; stopping only when the hunger or thirst brought themselves to her attention again, snatching a ration and then returning, hermit-like, to the translucent corridors she was shaping.

Until one day, she stepped back, and couldn't think of anything else to add.

There was probably something meaningful one was supposed to say, at an exhalation's close. She'd read speeches, all nonsense about "your breath to mine" and meters and meters of bad poetry. It didn't seem to matter very much what one said, truth be told.

"Well," she said to the ship, laying a hand on the hull, "this is it." Winter had come by then, settling in the mountains, a vice around her lungs; and her breath hung in ragged gasps above her. "I'm not sure—"

The stone under her hand went deathly cold. What—? She tried to withdraw her hand, but it had become fused to the *lamsinh*; and the veins shifted and moved, as lazily as snakes underwater.

There was a light, coming from the heart of the stone, even as the breath was drained out of her, leaving her struggling to stand upright—a light, and a slow, ponderous beat like a gigantic heart. *Breath-sister,* the stone whispered, and even that boomed, as if she stood in the Temple of Mercy, listening to the gong reminding the faithful to grow in wisdom. *Breath-sister.*

Her hand fell back; and the ship rose, casting its shadow over her.

He was sleek elegant beauty—everything she had dreamt of, everything she had carved, all the release she sought—and he didn't belong on Voc, anymore than she did.

Come with me, the ship whispered; and she had stood there in the growing cold, trembling, and unable to make any answer.

"A SHIP," Mau said, thoughtfully.

Rechan shivered. It had made sense at the time. "I named him Sang," she said at last. *Illumination,* in the old language of the settlers—because he had stood over her, framed by light.

"I didn't even know you could carve ships."

"Anything living," Rechan said, through clenched teeth. She was going to feel sick again. Was it the baby, or the memories, or both? "Stonemen are tradition, but we could have carved cats or dogs or other Old Earth animals if we felt like it."

"Whoever you'd want assisting at the birth of your children," Mau said with a nod. She smiled, her hand going to the impression of the pendant on her chest. "I suppose I should be grateful Akanlam followed tradition. Being an animal wouldn't have been very—exciting."

But you wouldn't know, Rechan thought, chilled. You'd be quite happy, either way. That's what you were carved for, to give your breath to Akanlam's babies, and even if you hadn't been born knowing it, everyone in our society has been telling you that for as long as you can remember. How much responsibility did they have for their carvings? How much of themselves had they put into them; and how much had they taught them?

And what did Sang owe her, in the end—and what did she owe him?

"Your ship is still up there," Mau said. Her voice was quiet, but it wasn't difficult to hear the question in her words.

"Yes," Rechan said. "The crossfire you heard about, it's not between the rebels and the government soldiers. It's Sang mopping rebels up." It hadn't been what she'd dreamt of, when she'd carved him; she'd wanted a space-ship, not a butcher of armies. But, consciously or unconsciously, she hadn't put that into her carving.

"The ship you carved?" Mau lifted an eyebrow.

"I was young once," Rechan said. "And angry. I don't think I'd carve the same, if I had to do it again." Though who could know, really. She'd always wondered what would have happened, if she'd answered the ques-tion Sang had asked; if she'd said yes. Would she still be on Voc, still going over the bitter loneliness of her life? Would she be elsewhere on some other planet, having the adventures she'd dreamt of as a teenager? If she could do it again...

"Anyway," she said, "I don't have much choice. If we don't reach the uplands in time..." She didn't dare say it, didn't dare voice the possibility; but she felt as though someone had closed a fist of ice around her heart.

THEY WERE halfway to Indigo Birds Pass, where they would have to aban-don the car, when the noise of a motor made everyone sit up.

"That's not good," Akanlam said. "We're sitting targets here." She didn't stop the aircar, but accelerated. The noise got closer, all the same: not a flyer but a swarm of drones, dull and tarnished by dust. They banked above the overhang ahead and were gone so quickly it was hard to believe they'd been there at all. Akanlam made a face. "Rebels. Our army has Galactic drones."

"Let's go on," Rechan suggested. They would get to the pass in half a day. Surely that was enough time, before the drones sent their analyses onwards to their masters. Surely...

Not half an hour later, the drones came back, and hung over the aircar for what seemed like an eternity. Rechan found herself clenching Mau's hand, so hard that the stone hurt her fingers.

When the drones left, Akanlam killed the motor. "That's it. We have to go on foot. Under the cliffs, where they'll have trouble sending flyers. Come on."

Mau shot Rechan a warning glance. Rechan spread her hands, helplessly. Yes, she had to be careful, but what else could she do?

"There's a path," Akanlam called from the shelter of the overhang. "A goat trail, probably, but it'll be sheltered. At least for a while."

Rechan slid down from the aircar and walked to the overhang. There *was* a path, twisting along the side of the mountain and vanishing between two large stones. It was steep and thin, and one look at it would have made her doctor's face pale.

But there was no choice. There had never been any choice: everything had been set from the moment she'd walked into the insemination centre; or perhaps even earlier, when she'd lain in the silence of her room and known that she couldn't bear it forever. She laid her hands on her belly, whispered "hang on" to the unborn baby, and set her feet on the path.

She'd forgotten how tiring it had been, ten years earlier. Her breath burnt in her lungs after only four steps, and her legs ached after eight; and then there was only the path ahead of her, her eyes doggedly on every rock and particle of dust, making sure of her step—perpetually off-balance, struggling to keep the curve of her belly from betraying her as rocks detached under her feet—she mustn't trip, mustn't fall, mustn't let go…

After a while, the pain came on. At first, she thought it was just the aches from the unusual exercise, but it didn't abate, washing over her in a huge, belly-clenching wave, cutting her breath until she had to halt. Touching her belly, she found it hard, pointed, and the baby a compressed weight under her hands. A contraction. She was entering labour. No, not now—it was too early. She couldn't afford—couldn't lose everything—

"Elder aunt?" Mau was by her side, suddenly, her hands running over her belly.

"It's starting," she said.

"Yes." Mau's voice was grave, expressionless. Rechan didn't want to look at Akanlam, who'd always been bad at disguising her emotions. "It's your first one, elder aunt. This can go on for hours. There is still time, but you have to walk."

"I can't—" she whispered through clenched teeth, bracing herself against the next contraction. "Too—tired—" And they were going to reach that plateau, and she was going to find there was no ship, that her dreams were lies, that it had never been there—how she wanted to be the ship now, hanging under the vastness of the heavens, without heaviness, without pain, without a care in the world…

Mau's hands massaged her, easing the knots of pain in her back. "One an hour at first, elder aunt. Or more apart. There is still time. But you have to walk."

"The drones?" she asked, and it was Akanlam who answered.

"They haven't come back."

Not yet, she thought, tasting bile and blood on her tongue. She hauled herself as upright as she could, gently removing Mau's hands. "Let's walk," she said, and even those words were pain.

There was a divinity, watching over thoughtless teenagers; there had to be one for thoughtless adults, too; or perhaps it was her ancestors, protecting her from their distant altar—her thoughts wandering as she walked, step after step on the path, not knowing how far the ending lay, not caring anymore—step after step, with the occasional pause to bend over, gasping, while the contraction passed, and then resuming her painful, painstakingly slow walk to the top.

She found her mind drifting—to the ship, to his shadow hanging over her, remembering the coldness of the stone against her hand, the breath that seemed to have left her altogether; remembering the voice that had boomed like ten thousand storms.

Come with me, breath-sister.

Come with me.

He was there on the plateau, waiting for her, and what would she tell him?

They climbed in silence. There was just Mau's hands on her, guiding her, supporting her when she stumbled; and Akanlam's tunic, blue against the grey of the rock, showing her the way forward.

She was barely aware of cresting a rise—of suddenly finding herself not flush against a cliff face, but in the middle of a space that seemed to stretch forever, a vast expanse of *lamsinh* rocks caught by the noon sun—all shades of the spectrum, from green to palest white; and a trembling in the air that mirrored that of her hands.

"There is no ship," Akanlam said, and her voice was almost accusatory.

Shaking, Rechan pulled herself upwards. "He'll be deeper into the plateau. Where I carved him. We have to—"

"Elder Aunt," Mau said, low and urgent.

What? she wanted to ask; but, turning to stare in the same direction as Mau, she saw the black dots silhouetted against the sky—growing in size, fast, too fast...

"Run."

She would have, but her legs betrayed her—a contraction, locking her in place, as frozen as the baby within her womb, as helpless as a kid to the slaughter—watching the dots become the sleek shape of flyers, hearing the whine of the motors getting louder and louder...

Run run run, she wanted to shout to Mau and Akanlam—there's no need for you to get caught in this. Instead, what came out of her was a scream: a cry for help, a jumble of incoherent syllables torn out of her lungs, towards the Heavens; a deep-seated anger about life's unfairness she'd last felt when carving the ship. It echoed around the plateau, slowly fading as it was absorbed by the *lamsinh* stone.

Her hand was cold again, her breath coming in short gasps—and, like an answer to a prayer, she saw the ship come.

He was sleek, and elegant, and deadly. Banking lazily over the plateau—illuminated by the noonday sun, as if with an inner fire—he incinerated the flyers, one by one, and then hovered over Mau and Akanlam, as if unsure what to do about them. "No you don't!" Rechan screamed, and then collapsed, having spent all her energy.

Breath-sister. The ship—Sang—loomed over her once more.

She'd forgotten how beautiful Sang was; how terribly wrong, too—someone that didn't belong on Voc, that shouldn't have been here. He should have hung, weightless, in space; instead he moved sluggishly, crushed by gravity; and his hull was already crisscrossed by a thousand fracture lines, barely visible against the heat of the stone. The *lamsinh* was weathered and pitted, not from meteorite strikes but from weapons—in fact, dusty and cracked he looked like a rougher, fuzzier version of the rebel flyers he'd incinerated.

You need me, the ship said, and came lower, hull almost touching her outstretched hands. *Let me give you your breath back.*

It was wrong, all wrong—everything she had desired, the breath she needed for her baby, the birth she'd been bracing herself for—and yet… "You shouldn't be here," she said. "You're a spaceship, not a flyer." She was barely aware of Mau standing by her side, looking up at Sang with wide eyes; of Akanlam, spreading her tunic on the ground.

I waited for you.

"You can't—" But he could, couldn't he? He could do exactly what she'd thought of, when she'd carved him—all her anger at the war, at the rebels, at the unfairness of it all—year after year of hunting down rebels because that's what she'd wanted at the time; not a breath-sibling to help her with a birth, but someone born of her anger and frustration, of her desire to escape the war at any cost.

Come with me.

She'd wondered what she would do, were Sang to ask that question of her again, but of course there was only one possible answer. The world had moved on; she had moved on; and only Sang remained, the inescapable remains of her history—a sixteen-year-old's grandiloquent, thoughtless, meaningless gesture.

"You have to go," she said, the words torn out of her before she could think. "Into space. That's what I carved you for. Not this—this butchery."

The ship came close enough for her to touch the exhaust ports: there was a tingle on her hands, and a warmth she'd forgotten existed—and, within her, for the first time, the baby quickened, kicking against the confines of her womb. She ought to have felt relief, but she was empty—bracing herself against the next contractions and trying to crane her head upwards to see Sang.

You need me, he said. *Breath to breath, blood to blood. How else will you bear your children? Come with me. Let's find the stars together.*

"I can't. You have to go," she said, again. "On your own."

You will not come with me? The disappointment, in other circumstances, would have been heartbreaking.

"Go, Sang. When this is over—go find the stars. That's all you've ever dreamt of, isn't it?"

The contractions were hitting in waves now—one barely over before the next one started. *Your child is coming,* Sang said.

"I know." Someone—Akanlam—grabbed her, laid her on the ground—no, not on the ground, on the tunic she'd spread out. It was becoming hard to think, to focus on anything but the act of giving birth.

What will you do, for your other children? You need me.

She did; and yet... "I'll find you," she said, struggling for breath. "If I need you." Of course she wouldn't; even with her link to him, all she'd have to go on would be fuzzy dream-images; she wouldn't leave Voc, wouldn't venture among ten thousand planets and millions of stars in a fruitless search. But it didn't matter. Sang would finally be free.

Sang was silent, for a while. *I will come back,* he said.

He wouldn't. Rechan knew this with absolute certainty—Sang was the desire to escape, the burning need for flight that she'd felt during her adolescence. Once he found space, he would be in the home he'd always been meant for; and who could blame him for not looking back? "Of course," she lied—smoothly, easily. "You can always come back."

There would not be other babies beyond this one, no large family she could raise; not enough to fill the emptiness of the house. But did it matter, in the end? She'd had her wish, her miracle—her birth. Could she truly ask for anything else?

I am glad.

"So am I." And it almost didn't feel like a lie. Rechan relaxed, lying flat on her back; and she settled herself down to wait for the beautiful, heart-breaking sound of her child's first breath.

The Days of the War,
as Red as Blood, as Dark as Bile

In the old days, the phoenix, the vermillion bird, was a sign of peace and prosperity to come; a sign of a virtuous ruler under whom the land would thrive.

But those are the days of the war; of a weak child-Empress, successor to a weak Emperor; the days of burning planets and last-ditch defences; of moons as red as blood and stars as dark as bile.

WHEN THIEN BAO WAS TWELVE YEARS OLD, SECOND AUNT CAME to live with them.

She was a small, spry woman with little tolerance for children; and even less for Thien Bao, whom she grudgingly watched over while Mother worked in the factories, churning out the designs for new kinds of sharp-kites and advance needle ships.

"You are over pampered," she'd say, as she busied herself at the stove preparing the midday meal. "An only child, indeed." She didn't approve of Thien Bao's name, either—it was a boy's name that meant "Treasure from Heaven", and she thought Mother shouldn't have used it for a girl, no matter how much trouble she and Father might have had having children at all.

Thien Bao asked Mother why Second Aunt was so angry; Mother looked away for a while, her eyes focused on something Thien Bao couldn't see. "Your aunt had to leave everything behind when she came here."

"Everything?" Thien Bao asked.

"Her compartment and her things; and her husband." Mother's face twisted, in that familiar way when she was holding back tears. "You remember your Second Uncle, don't you?"

Thien Bao didn't: or perhaps she did—a deep voice, a smile, a smell of machine oil from the ships, which would never quite go away. "He's dead," she said, at last. Like Third Aunt, like Cousin Anh, like Cousin Thu. Like Father; gone to serve at the edge of Empire-controlled space, fallen in the rebel attack that had overwhelmed the moons of the Eighth Planet. "Isn't he?"

Those were the days of the dead; when every other morning seemed to see Grandmother adding new holos to the ancestral altar; every visitor spoke in hushed voices, as if Thien Bao weren't old enough to understand the war, or the devastation it brought.

Mother had the look again, debating whether to tell Thien Bao grown-up things. "He was a very brave man. He could have left, but he waited until everyone had finished evacuating." Mother sighed. "He never left. The rebel ships bombed the city until everything was ashes; your aunt was on the coms with him when—" she swallowed, looked away again. "She saw him die. That's why she's angry."

Thien Bao mulled on this for a while. "They had no children," she said, at last, thinking of Second Aunt sitting before the altar, grumbling that it was wrong to see him there, that he had died childless and had no place among the ancestors. But of course, the rules had changed in the days of the dead.

"No," Mother said.

It was a sad thought, bringing a queer feeling in Thien Bao's belly. "She can remarry, can't she?"

"Perhaps," Mother said, and Thien Bao knew it was a lie. She resolved to be nicer to Second Aunt from now on; and to pray to her ancestors so that Second Aunt would find another husband, and have children to comfort her in her old age.

That night, she dreamt of Second Uncle.

He stood in some shadowy corridor, one hand feverishly sending instructions to the structure's command nodes—speaking fast and in disjointed words, in a tone that he no doubt wanted to be reassuring. Thien Bao couldn't make out his face—it was a dark blur against the shaking of the walls; but she felt the impact that collapsed everything, like a spike-punch through reality, strong enough to shatter her bones—and heard the brief burst of static, the silence falling on the coms, as he died.

The dream changed, after that. She was soaring above a green planet, watching two huge attack ships confronting one another. There was no telling who was the rebels and who was the Empire. With the clarity of dreams she knew that one ship was scanning the other for antimatter weapons; and that the other ship, who had none, was preparing pinhead bombs, in the hopes of breaching the hull at its one weak point. Below, on the planet—again, with that strange clarity—people as tiny as ants were evacuating, struggling to fit onto a few aged shuttles that would carry them no further than the minuscule moon above.

They didn't matter—or, rather, they couldn't be allowed to matter, not if the mission were to be accomplished. Somehow, in the dream, she knew this; that, even if she had been ordered to save them, she wouldn't have been capable of it, wouldn't have made the slightest difference.

She floated closer, unfurling iridescent wings as wide as the trail of a comet; and prepared to unleash her own weapons, to put an end to the fight.

The scene seemed to freeze and blur, disintegrating like a hundred water droplets on a pane of glass—each droplet was a character, one of the old fashioned ones from Old Earth that no one save elite scholars knew how to read—column upon column of incomprehensible words in a red as bright as the vermillion of imperial decrees, scrolling downwards until they filled her entire field of vision—and they, too, faded, until only a few words remained—and though they were still in the old script, she *knew* in her heart of hearts what they meant, from beginning to end.

Little sister, you are fated to be mine.

Mine.

And then the words were gone, and she woke up, shaking, in the embrace of her own cradle-bed.

THERE WERE four mindships, built in the finest workshops of the Empire, in a time when the numbered planets were scattered across dozens of solar systems—when court memorials reached the outer stations, and magistrates were posted in far-flung arms of the galaxy.

Four mindships; one for each cardinal direction, raised by the best scholars to be the pride of the Empire; their claimers of tribute from barbaric, inferior dominions; the showcase of their technological apex, beings of grace and beauty, as terrible to behold as any of the Eight Immortals.

AFTER THAT, the dreams never stopped. They came irregularly—once a week, once a month—but they always came. In every one of them she was in a different place—above a planet, orbiting a moon, approaching a space station—and every time the war was in her dreams. In every dream she watched ships attack one another; soldiers fighting hand to hand in a desperate defence of a city's street, their faces featureless, their uniforms in bloody tatters without insignia, impossible to differentiate. She scoured clean the surface of planets, rained war-kites on devastated temple complexes, disabled space domes' weapons—and woke up, shivering, staring at the imprint of words she shouldn't have been able to understand.

Mine.

Come to me, little sister. Come to me and put an end to all of this.

And yet; and yet, the war still went on.

By daylight, Mother and Second Aunt spoke in hushed tones of the fall of planets; of the collapse of orbitals; of the progress of rebel forces across the Empire—ever closer to the First Planet and the Purple Forbidden City.

"The Lily Empress will protect us," Thien Bao said. "Won't she?"

Mother shook her head, and said nothing. But later, when Thien Bao was playing *The Battle for Indigo Mountain*, her implants synched with the house's entertainment centre, she heard them—Grandmother, Mother and Second Aunt, talking quietly among themselves in the kitchen around pork buns and tea. She froze the game into a thin, transparent layer over her field of vision, and crept closer to listen in.

"You should have said something," Grandmother said.

"What do you want me to say?" Mother sounded tired; angry, but the scary kind of anger, the bone-deep one that lasted for days or months. "Everything would be a lie."

"Then learn to lie," Second Aunt said, drily. There was the sound of chewing: betel leaf and areca, the only luxury she'd allow herself. "For her sake."

"You think I haven't tried? She's a bright child. She'll figure it out the moment I open my mouth. Her wealthier schoolmates have all left, and she's got to realise what a desert the city is becoming. Everyone is leaving."

"I know," Second Aunt said. "If we had the money…"

Mother sighed, and got up to pour more tea into her fist-sized cup. There was no money, Thien Bao knew; all of Grandmother's savings had gone into paying for the watered down food in the markets; for the rice mixed with blackened grit and ashes; for the fish sauce cut with brown colouring, which never tasted right no matter how much lime or sugar Thien Bao added to it.

Mother said, finally, "Money might not matter anymore soon. There's word at the factories—that Magistrate Viec wants to evacuate."

Silence; and then Grandmother, in a hushed voice, "They can't—the rebel fleet is still not in the solar system, is it?"

"No," Second Aunt said. "But it's getting closer; and they have mind-ships. If they wanted to hit us, they could send those as advance scouts. Wouldn't be enough to take the planet, but it would cost us much."

"The magistrate said the Lily Empress will send her armies next month, after the end of the rainy season." Mother's voice was still uncertain.

"Ha," Second Aunt said. "Maybe she will , maybe she won't. But even if she did; do you truly believe that will be enough to save us, little sister? The armies are badly run, and overwhelmed as it is."

Mother said, at last, "All we need is one victory. One message to tell the rebels that their advance stops here, at the Sixth Planet; that to go further into the Empire will cost them dearly. They're overstretched, too, it wouldn't take much to make them stop..." Her voice was pleading.

"They might be overstretched," Second Aunt said, and there was pity in her voice. "And you're right. Maybe all it would take is a crushing victory; but we don't have that within our grasp, and you know it."

There was silence, then, as heavy as the air before the monsoon. Thien Bao turned back to her game; but it all seemed fake now, the units aligned on the artificial landscape, the battles where no one bled, which you could start, again and again, until you succeeded in the assigned mission—where no one ever felt fear like a fist of ice tightening in their guts; or the emptiness of loss, drawing closer with every passing hour.

In the first days of the war, the mindships were lost; their crews scattered by court decrees, recalled in haste to defend planets that had already fallen; their cradle pods neglected by the alchemists and programmers; their missions assigned irregularly, and then not at all.

One by one, they fell.

Golden Tortoise *trying to evade pursuit by a vast rebel fleet, dove into deep spaces with an aged pilot as his only crew; and never re-emerged.*

Azure Dragon *went silent after the Battle of Huong He, plummeting downwards through the atmosphere in a shower of molten metal, her fragments peppering the burnt earth of the prefecture like so many seeds of grief.*

White Unicorn *completed the emergency evacuation of the Twelfth Planet, sustaining his trembling star-drives well past the point of bursting. He landed, shaking, bleeding his guts in machine-oil and torn rivets; and never flew again.*

And as for Vermillion Phoenix—*the strongest, most capable of all four ships…she, too, stopped speaking on the Empire's coms-channels; but her missions had been too well defined. She had been given leave to wage war on the Empire's enemies; and in those days when the Empire tore itself apart and brother denounced brother, father slew son and daughter abandoned mother, who could have told who the enemies of the Empire were, anymore?*

Vermillion Phoenix *went rogue.*

IT TOOK two months, in the end, for Magistrate Viec to give the evacuation order. By then, the rebel fleet had entered the solar system; and the first and second moons of the Sixth Planet had fallen. The army of the Empress retreated, its ships slowly growing larger in the sky, trailing the sickly green light of ruptured drives. The few soldiers the magistrate could spare oversaw the evacuation, their faces bored—most of their comrades were up above, fighting the last-ditch battle in the heavens.

Thien Bao stood in the huddle at the spaceport with her family; holding Grandmother's hand while the old woman engaged in a spirited talk with Second Aunt and Mother, complaining about everything from the wait to the noise of their neighbours.

She watched the army ships through the windows—and the growing shadows of the rebel mindships, creeping closer and closer—and wondered when their own evacuation ships would be ready. Around her, people's faces were tight, and they kept looking at the screens; at the queue that hadn't moved; at the impassive faces of the militia.

Ahead was a floating palanquin: an odd sight, since such a thing could only belong to a high official; but those officials would have been able to jump to the front of the queue. Thien Bao tugged at Grandmother's sleeve. "Grandmother?"

"Yes, child?" Grandmother didn't even turn.

"Who's in the palanquin?"

"Oh." Grandmother's gaze raked the palanquin from base to top, taking in the black lacquered exterior, embossed with golden birds; and the crane with spread wings atop the arched roof. "Probably Lady Oanh—you wouldn't remember her, but she and your mother were members of the same poetry club, in the days before she withdrew from public life. Always an eccentric, that woman." She frowned. "I thought she had a mindship of her own, though—funny seeing her here."

"Lady Oanh?"

But Grandmother had already turned back to her conversation with Mother and Second Aunt.

Above, the army ships hadn't moved; but Thien Bao could see the shapes of the rebel mindships more clearly, emerging from the deep spaces just long enough to power weapons. They were going to...

She knew it a fraction of a second before it happened—saw the corona of light filling the sky like an aurora above the poles—saw it spread in deathly silence, engulf the largest of the army ships—saw the ship shudder, and crack like an egg shell—the horrible thing was that it still held together, leaking a cloud of darkened fluids that spread across the surface of the sky—that it shuddered, again and again, but did not fall apart, though surely the life support systems had to be gone, with that kind of impact; though everyone onboard had to be dead, or dying, or worse...

In the silence that followed, a man screamed, his voice deep and resonant; and the crowd went mad.

Without warning, people pressed themselves closer to the docks; elbowing each other out of the way, sending others sprawling to the floor. Thien Bao found herself crushed against Grandmother, struggling to remain upright against the press—arms pushed against her, separating her from her family, and she was lost amidst unfamiliar faces, pushed and pulled until it was all she could do to stand upright; until it was all she could do to breathe—

The darkness at the edge of her field of vision descended; and the red characters of her dreams scrolled by, resolving themselves into the same, sharp, lapidary message.

Little sister. Call me. Call me, and put an end to this.

She hung in the darkness of space, the ion exhaust of her drives trailing behind her, opening like a vast fan; every part of her sharp, honed to a killing edge—a living weapon, carrying enough firepower to end it all, to make the rebel fleet cinders, to crack them open as they'd cracked open the army ship. All she had to do was call, reach out to the vast, dark part of herself that moved between the stars...

Someone grabbed her. Cold hands tightened on her shoulders, and pulled her upwards before she could stifle a scream; and it all went away, the sense of vastness; the red characters and the presence of something other than her in her own mind.

She sat in the darkness; it took her a moment to realise she was inside the palanquin, and that the slightly clearer form in front of her was an old woman.

Lady Oanh.

"Child," the old woman said. Life-support wires trailed from every end of the palanquin, as though she sat on the centre of a spider's web. The skin of her face, in the dim light, had the pallor and thinness of wet rice paper; and her eyes were two pits of deeper darkness. "Anh's and Nhu's daughter, is it not? I was a friend of your mother; in a different lifetime."

Everything was eerily silent: no noise from outside, no hint of the riot that had started on the docks—of course the palanquin would have the best ambiance systems, but the overall effect—that of hanging in the same bubble of artificially stilled time—made Thien Bao's skin crawl. "Lady Oanh. Why—?"

Mother and Second Aunt would be freaking out; they'd always told her not to trust strangers; and here she was in the middle of a riot, stuck with someone who might or might not be a friend—but then why would Lady Oanh bother to kidnap her? She was a scholar, a public figure; or had been, once. Nevertheless... Thien Bao reached into her feed, and activated the location loop—she'd sworn to Mother she was a grown up and didn't need it any longer, and now she was glad Mother hadn't listened to her.

The old woman smiled, an expression that did not reach into her eyes. "You would prefer to be outside? Trust me, it is much safer here." A feed blinked in the lower left-hand corner of Thien Bao's vision, asking for her permission to be displayed. She granted it; and saw outside.

The palanquin floated on its repulsive field, cutting a swathe through the press of people. Thien Bao knew she wouldn't have lasted a moment out there, that she'd have been mown down as others sought to reach the shuttles before her. But still...

Lady Oanh's voice was quiet, but firm. "You looked set to be trampled by the mob."

"You didn't have to—"

"No," Lady Oanh said. "You're right. I didn't."

How old was she? Thien Bao wondered. How long did it take for skin to become this pale; for eyes to withdraw this deep into the face, as if she stood on the other side of death already? And did all of it, this aging, this putting death at bay, confer any of the wisdom of Thien Bao's ancestors?

"A riot is no place for freezing," Lady Oanh said. "Though in someone your age, it can possibly be excused."

She hadn't noticed the trance then; or that anything was wrong. Then again, why should she? She was certainly wise with her years, but wisdom was not omniscience. "I'm sorry," Thien Bao said. But she remembered the sense of vastness; the coiled power within her. If it was real; if it wasn't dreams; if she could somehow answer...

Call me, little sister. Let us put an end to all this.

Thien Bao said, "Grandmother said—you had a mindship—"

Lady Oanh laughed; genuinely amused it seemed. "*The Carp that Leapt Over the Stream?* It seemed senseless to hoard her services. She's part of the fleet that will evacuate her. That's where we're going, in fact."

Lady Oanh's eyes focused on something beyond Thien Bao, and she nodded. "I'll send a message to notify your kin that I'm helping you onboard a ship. That should alleviate their worries."

If they didn't all die first from rebel fire; if the remaining army ship held—if if if...

A gentle rocking, indicating the palanquin was moving forward again—to the waiting ships, to safety—except that there was no safety, not anywhere. Outside, the remaining army ship was trying to contain the rebel mindships; shuddering, its hull pitted and cracked. From time to time, a stray shot would hit the spaceport's shields, and the entire structure around them would shudder, but it held, it still held.

But for how long?

"I hate them," Thien Bao said.

"Who? The rebels?" Lady Oanh's gaze was sharp. "It's as much the fault of the Court as theirs, child. If the Great Virtue Emperor and the Lily Empress hadn't been weak, more concerned with poetry than with their armies; if their officials hadn't encouraged them, repeating that nonsense about adherence to virtue being the only safeguard the Empire needed…"

To hear her, so casually criticising the Empress—but then Second Aunt and Mother had done the same. "I wish…" Thien Bao sounded childish, she knew; like a toddler denied a threat. "I wish someone were strong enough to stop the rebel armies. To kill them once and for all."

Lady Oanh's face did not move, but she shook her head. "Be careful, child."

How could wanting peace be a bad thing? She understood nothing, that old, pampered woman who didn't have to fight through the crowd, who didn't live with fear in her belly, with the litany of the family dead in her mind—

"Killing is easy," Lady Oanh said. "But that has never stopped the devastation of war."

"It would be a start," Thien Bao said, defiantly.

"Perhaps," Lady Oanh said. She shook her head. "It would take a great show of strength from the Empire to stop them, and this is something we're incapable of, at the present time. The seeds of our defeat were in place long before the war, I fear; and—"

She never finished her sentence. Thien Bao saw nothing; but *something* struck the shields, wringing them dry like wet laundry; and going past them, a network of cracks and fissures spreading throughout the pillars of the spaceport and the huge glass windows.

Look out, Thien Bao wanted to say; but the wall nearest to them shuddered and fell apart, dragging down chunks of the ceiling in its wake. Something struck her in the back of the head; and everything disappeared in an excruciating, sickening crunch.

WHEN SHE went silent, Vermillion Phoenix had had an officer of the Embroidered Guard as her only crew—not a blood relative, but a sworn oath-sister, who had been with the ship for decades and would never hear of abandoning her post.

There is no record of what happened to the officer. Being human, without any kind of augmentation, she likely died of old age, while the mindship—as ships did—went on, unburdened.

Unburdened does not mean free from grief, or solitude. In the centuries that followed, several people claimed to have had visions of the ship; to have heard her voice calling to them; or dreamt of battles—past and present—to which she put a brutal end. There were no connections between them; no common ancestry or closeness in space or time; but perhaps the mindship recognised something else: a soul, torn from its fragile flesh envelope and reincarnated, time and time again, until everything was made right.

THIEN BAO woke up, and all was dust and grit—choking her, bending her to the ground to convulsively cough until her lungs felt wrung dry. When she rose at last, shaking, she saw the ruins of the palanquin, half-buried under rubble; and a few cut wires, feebly waving in the dim light—and the mob, further into the background, still struggling to reach the ships. She'd thought the wall would collapse, but it stood in spite of the massive fissures crossing it from end to end; and for some incongruous reason it reminded her of the fragile celadon cups Father had so treasured, their green surface shot with such a network of cracks it seemed a wonder they still held together.

Around her, chunks of the ceiling dotted the area—and the other thing, the one she avoided focusing on—people lying still or twitching or moaning, lying half under rubble—with limbs bent at impossible angles, and the stained white of bones laid bare at the heart of bleeding wounds; and spilled guts; and the laboured breathing of those in agony…

Those were the days of the dead, and she had to be strong.

At the edge of her field of vision—as faint as her paused game of *Battle for Indigo Mountain*, in another lifetime—the red characters of her dream hovered, and a faint sense of a vast presence, watching over her from afar.

"Lady Oanh? Mother? Second Aunt?" Her location loop was still running; but it didn't seem to have picked up anything from them—or perhaps it was the spaceport network that was the problem, flickering in and out of existence like a dying heartbeat. It was nonsense anyway; who expected the network to hold, through that kind of attack.

The sky overhead was dark with the shadow of a ship—not the army ship, it had to be one of the mindships. Its hatches were open, spewing dozens of little shuttles, a ballet slowly descending towards them: rebels, come to finish the work they had started.

She had to move.

When she pulled herself upright, pain shot through her neck and arms like a knife-stab; but she forced herself to move on, half-crawling, half-walking, until she found Lady Oanh.

The old woman lay in the rubble, staring at the torn dome of the spaceport. For a moment, an impossibly long moment, Thien Bao thought she was alive; but no one could be alive with the lower half of their body crushed; and so much fluid and blood leaking from broken tubes. "I'm sorry," she said, but it wasn't her fault; it had never been her fault. Overhead, the shuttles were still descending, as slowly as the executioner's blade. There was no time. There was no safety; not anywhere; there was no justice; no fairness; no end to the war and the fear and the sick feeling in her head and in her belly.

A deafening sound in her ears, loud enough to cover the distant sounds of panic—she realised that it was her location loop, displaying an arrow and an itinerary to join whatever was left of her family; if they, like Lady Oanh, hadn't died, if there was still hope...

She managed to pull herself upwards—staggered, following the directions—left right left going around the palanquin around the dead bodies around the wounded who grasped at her with clawed hands—days of the dead, she had to be strong had to be strong...

She found Grandmother, Mother and Second Aunt standing by the barriers that had kept the queue orderly, once—which were now covered in dust, like everything else around them. There was no greeting, or sign of relief. Mother merely nodded as if nothing were wrong., and said, "We need to move."

"It's past time for that," Second Aunt said, her gaze turned towards the sky.

Thien Bao tried to speak; to say something about Lady Oanh, but no words would come out of her mouth.

Mother's eyes rolled upwards for a brief moment as she accessed the network. *"The Carp that Leapt Over the Stream,"* she said. "Its shuttles were parked at the other end of the terminal, and there'll be fewer people there. Come on."

Move move move—Thien Bao felt as though everything had turned to tar; she merely followed as Second Aunt and Mother elbowed their way through the crowd; and onto a corridor that was almost deserted compared to the press of people. "This way," Mother said.

Thien Bao turned, briefly, before they limped into the corridor, and saw that the first of the rebel shuttles had landed some way from them, disgorging a flood of yellow-clad troops with featureless helmets.

It was as if she were back in her dreams, save that her dreams had never been this pressing—and that the red words on the edge of her field of vision kept blinking, no matter how she tried to dismiss them.

Mother was right; they needed to keep moving—past the corridor, into another, wider concourse that was mostly scattered ruin, following the thin thread of people and hoping that the shuttles would still be there, that the mindship would answer to them with Lady Oanh dead. By then, they had been joined by other people, among whom a wounded woman carried on the shoulder of a soldier—no introductions, no greetings, but a simple acknowledgement that they were all in this together. It wasn't hope that kept them going; it was sheer stubbornness, one foot in front of the other, one breath and the next and the next; the fear of falling behind the others, of slowing everyone down and ruining everything.

Ahead, the mass of a shuttle, seen behind glass windows; getting agonisingly, tantalisingly closer. "This way," Second Aunt said; and then they saw the yellow-clad troops in front of them, deployed to bar the passage across the concourse—and the other troops, too, blocking the passageways, herding people off the shuttle in the eerie silence.

Mother visibly sagged. "It will be fine," she said, and her voice was a lie. "They'll just want to check our identity and process us—"

But it was the soldier with them who panicked—who turned away, lightning-fast, still carrying his wounded charge—and in the dull silence that followed, Thien Bao heard the click of weapons being armed.

"No!" Mother said, sharply. As if in a dream Thien Bao saw her move in front of the yellow-clad soldiers, with no more apparent thought than if she'd been strolling through the marketplace—and she wanted to scream but couldn't, as the weapons found their mark and Mother crumpled, bloodless and wrung dry, her corpse so small it seemed impossible that she had once been alive.

Second Aunt moved at last, her face creased with anger—not towards Mother or the soldier, but straight at the rebel troops. "How dare you—"

There was the sound again; of weapons being armed.

No.

No. No.

Everything went red: the characters from her dreams, solidifying once more in front of her; the voice speaking into her mind.

Little sister.

And, weeping, Thien Bao reached out, into the void between stars, and called to the ship.

WHEN THE child named Thien Bao was born on the Sixth Planet, there were signs—a room filled with the smell of machine-oil, and iridescent reflections on the walls, tantalising characters from a long lost language. Had the birth-master not been desperately busy trying to staunch the mother's unexpected bleeding, and calm down the distraught father, she would have noticed them.

Had she looked, too, into the newborn's eyes as she took her first, trembling breath, the birth-master would have seen the other sign: the hint of a deep, metallic light in the huge pupils; a light that spread from end to end of the eye like a wash of molten steel, a presage of things to come.

SHE WAS vast, and old, and terrible; her wings stretched around entire planets, as iridescent as pearls fished from the depths; the trail of her engines the colour of jade, of delicate celadon—and where she passed, she killed.

She disintegrated the fleet that waited on the edge of the killing field; scoured clean the surface of the small moon, heedless of the screams of those trapped upon it; descended to the upper limit of the planet's atmosphere, and incinerated the two mindships in orbit, and the fragile ship that still struggled to defend against them; and the tribunal where the militia still fought the recently landed invasion force; and the magistrate in his chambers, staring at the tactical map of the planet and wondering how to save what he could from the rebels. In the spaceport, where the largest number of people congregated, she dropped ion bombs until no sign of life remained; until every shuttle had exploded or stopped moving.

Then there was silence; and lack of strife; and then there was peace.

And then she was merely Thien Bao again, standing in the ruins of the spaceport, in the shadow of the great ship she had called on.

There was nothing left. Merely dust, and bodies—so many bodies, a sea of them, yellow-clad, black-clad, civilians and soldiers and rebels all mingled together, their blood pooling on the cracked floor; and a circle around her, where Mother lay dead; and the soldier, and the wounded woman; and the rebels who had shot her—and by her side, Second Aunt and Grandmother, bloodless and pale and unmoving. It was unclear whether it was the mindship's weapons they had died of, or the rebels', or both; but Thien Bao stood in a circle of the dead, the only one alive as far as she could see.

The only one—it couldn't—couldn't—

Little sister. The voice of the mindship was as deep as the sea. *I have come, and ended it, as you requested.*

That wasn't what she'd wanted—that—all of it, any of it—

And then she remembered Lady Oanh's voice, her wry comment. Be careful, child. Be careful.

I bring peace, and an end to strife. Is that not what the Empire should desire?

No. No.

Come with me, little sister. Let us put an end to this war.

A great victory, Thien Bao thought, hugging herself; feeling hot and cold at the same time, her bones chilled within their sheaths of flesh, a churning in her gut like the beginning of grief. Everyone had wanted a great victory over the rebels, something that would stop them, once and for all, that would tell them that the Empire still stood, still could make them pay for every planet they took.

And she'd given them that; she and the ship. Exactly that.

Come. We only have each other, the ship said, and it was the bitter truth. There was nothing left on the planet—not a living soul—and of the rebel army that had entered the solar system, nothing and no one left either, just the husks of destroyed ships drifting in the emptiness of space.

Come, little sister.

And she did—for where else could she go; what else could she do, that would have made any sense?

IN THE old days, the phoenix, the vermillion bird, was a sign of peace and prosperity to come; a sign of a virtuous ruler under whom the land would thrive.

In the days of the war, it is still the case; if one does not enquire how peace is bought, how prosperity is paid for—how a mindship and a child scour the numbered planets, dealing death to rebels and Empire alike, halting battles by bloody massacres; and making anyone who raises arms pay dearly for the privilege of killing.

Meanwhile, on the inner planets begins the painful work of reconstruction—raising pagodas and tribunals and shops from the ashes of war, and hanging New Year's Eve garlands along avenues that are still dust and ruins, praying to the ancestors for a better future; for a long life; and good fortune; and descendants as numerous as the stars in the sky.

There is no virtuous ruler; but perhaps—perhaps just, there is a manner of peace and prosperity, bought in seas of blood spilled by a child.

And perhaps—perhaps just—it is all worth it. Perhaps it is all one can hope for, in the days of the war.

The Dust Queen

Q UYNH HA HAD EXPECTED THE DUST QUEEN TO BE...TALL AND large, filling the room with her presence. But the woman sitting before her was old and frail—breathing, it was clear, only with the help of the bots clinging to her throat; her skin as pale and translucent as the best jades; the skin of her hands bearing the peculiar tightness of too many rejuv treatments.

It was hard to believe that a gesture of hers would send bots dancing; that on her command they would bank and dip and turn over the red soil of Mars, mould the clouds of dust they raised into the ephemeral figures from Quynh Ha's childhood—the boy Cuoi and his banyan, the strategist Khong Minh and his crane-feather fan. It was hard to imagine them whirling and rearing, tracing words in the flowing writing of calligraphy masters, poems like the ones hung at compartment doorways for New Year's Eve—all the wonder and the magic that filled Fire Watch Orbital once a year; that made life bearable in a world of airsuits, processed food and long watches of a planet they could not set foot on.

When she saw Quynh Ha, the Queen, Bao Lan, looked puzzled for a split second; and then her eyes narrowed, focusing on Quynh Ha with an intensity that made her shudder. "Child. You must be wondering why you're here."

Her voice was low and pleasant, with a bare trace of an Earth accent. Quynh Ha had heard it, on broadcasts after performances, commenting on the choices Bao Lan had made, elegant, cultured and refined, a scholar in an age which barely had use for them anymore. She'd never thought, from the broadcasts, that it would be so slight; and yet it had no trouble filling the room.

The Dust Queen. She was in the presence of the Dust Queen herself. She lowed her eyes as was proper; but it was hard not to scream, not to smile, not to explain to Bao Lan all that she meant to the orbital, to Quynh Ha. "Grandmother."

"I picked you because you're the best rewirer we have on Fire Watch." Bao Lan's voice was calm, thoughtful; considering a problem she couldn't solve.

"I'm not—" Quynh Ha opened her mouth to protest, and then closed it again. She wasn't a proper master, no, not like out there on the asteroids, where everyone was rewired and all companies had their rewirers; where deaders like Peter Cauley came from, having done it to themselves so many times they looked at the world with eyes like a fish on a monger's display. Out there emotions were a hindrance, for who needed to think of a husband left behind when clinging to the outside of a craft, piloting repair bots with hairbreadth's precision? On Fire Watch it was just the dregs of the profession, those who hadn't quite made the companies' cut to go further out; or people who hoped for a quick fortune and set exorbitant fees.

"I'm just an apothecary," Quynh Ha said at last. She did rewirings, sometimes, because they were a complement to the drugs Second Aunt sold; but that was hardly the core of her business. "I don't do that many rewirings."

That was it. She shouldn't have admitted it; she'd had her one chance to help Bao Lan, to speak to her, and that stupid honesty had doomed her, yet again. She braced herself for a dismissal—which didn't come.

"More than that, I should think," Bao Lan said. "I can afford the best, child. If I picked you, there is a reason."

Quynh Ha bit her lip before she could ask why. No doubt she'd know, in due time. Or perhaps she never would. It wouldn't matter one bit. "How may I help you then, Grandmother?"

There was a sound from Bao Lan: laughter or anger or both. "I picked you because you're known for your delicateness; and because you're Viet, like me, so you will understand what it is that I want. It's a simple enough thing, child.

"I want to go home, and you're the one who'll help me do it."

GOING INTO someone's brain is almost like being in space: that curious sensation of hanging, weightless, like floating in water without the water; of hanging in darkness with the stars around her like hairpin wounds in the fabric of the heavens.

Here, of course, there are no stars; but the wounds are memories—a dizzying array of them, every one of them so close she could touch them—and yet to reach out, to catch them all, would drive her insane under the weight of information and emotions that aren't hers.

She does reach out, all the same—because it's what she's here for, because it's the reason Bao Lan picked her out of the multitude—and the images come in, fast and hard, crammed so hard together that they're almost inseparable.

A family on a cyclo, father and mother and two children, weaving their way through the traffic of an overcrowded city; a New Year's Eve dinner, plates strewn over a red table cloth, wrapped rice cakes, candied coconut and lotus seeds; a quiet day out at the graveyard, burning paper money and paper houses for the ancestors' souls...

And the other, darker ones: an old woman on a roof in the midst of a flood, raising a fist at some officials in a boat; children creeping out in the kitchen one morning, and looking down at the unfamiliar sensation of wetness, to see the widening spread of water on the floor; the smell of rain as they sit under tarpaulin in a foreign city, waiting to be assigned a new compartment...

And all the memories, the good, the bad, the heartbreaking—they're all sealed under glass, tinted the colour of old, obsolete photographs—she reaches out to them, and rebounds as if she'd hit a wall, everything preserved in that unbreakable stasis, where nothing matters, where nothing hurts…

SHE CAME to with a start; to see Bao Lan looking at her, with that same weary expression she'd seen, time and time again, on her own grandmother's face; and she knew. "You want to go home," Quynh Ha said, feeling as though she were speaking through cotton. Everything felt out of sync, as it always did when she went under—unbearably sharp and cutting, every noise a wound, every object blindingly illuminated. "To a place that would mean something to you."

They'd raised the Mekong Delta again, with seawalls and embankments and sluices, rebuilding its cities from the ground up. Sixth Aunt had gone back there, to help with that effort; and Mother and Grandmother had both started to save money for a return holiday, though none of that news, none of those unfamiliar images relayed by the comms system really seemed to lift the cloud of sadness that hung over the family.

So Bao Lan could, physically, go home; but that wouldn't be what she wanted. Nothing would have emotional heft: the streets and the scents and the canals would have no particular associations; and she would walk in the city where she'd grown up, feeling a stranger to her own childhood.

Unless one could fix her.

Bao Lan nodded. "I had myself rewired, in the early days of the resettlement. It was…easier to go that way."

Easier, perhaps; avoiding all the loaded conversations between Grandmother and Mother at Tomb Sweeping festivals; when they sat at a table and spoke of graves in a cemetery that the sea had since long swallowed; of ancestors, bewildered and lost without the care of their descendants—as if ancestors couldn't be with them, regardless of where their graves were.

"Can you do it?" Bao Lan asked; and for a moment, her old, anxious face was the same as Grandmother's.

Quynh Ha said, carefully, "Theoretically, yes. I don't know how much you know about rewiring—"

"Imagine that I know nothing," Bao Lan said.

Quynh Ha doubted that. Bao Lan, who made a point on researching obscure epics for her dust cloud performances so she could get the costume details on the characters right, would not have left anything to chance; but she went on, regardless. "It's a good scrub, I'll grant them that. Worth good money at the time, I imagine."

"My first pay as a cyclo driver in Ho Chi Minh City," Bao Lan said, with a bare smile, a tightening of lips over yellowed teeth. "That was in the days before my entire life changed. I'm glad to know it wasn't all wasted."

Quynh Ha allowed herself a smile she didn't feel. It had been a good scrub, a thorough rewiring; and she wasn't altogether sure she could undo what had been done. "Rewiring is…like deadening. You can't completely suppress the emotions involved, or the person will go mad. There'll be one, or several cracks somewhere; tiny remnants of the original emotions. All I have to do is find one and amplify it—I can't give you the original back, but it will be something much like it."

It would be like a zither melody to a full orchestra: a single voice, and with none of the body and complexity of the real memories, the ones that had hurt so much. But, because it was the mind's own emotions, the brain would take them, and compensate, creating something that would, in the end, be quite close to whatever had been there before—to the love and the loss and the pain that made up home in Bao Lan's mind. The tricky part, however, would be finding a crack: a rewiring that thorough wouldn't have left large ones.

"Then that will satisfy me, yes," Bao Lan said. "We haven't discussed the matter of payment, but rest assured I will make it worth your time. If you agree, I'll call your place of work and tell them I need you."

The image of Second Aunt picking up the comms—of her face when she realised she was speaking to the Dust Queen—flashed across Quynh Ha's mind, and was gone just as swiftly. "There won't be any problem. I'm sure they'll understand—" Quynh Ha had to swallow, to sort out the words in her mind. Bao Lan. The Dust Queen needed her. Trusted her. That was worth a talk with Second Aunt, many times over. "I'll sort it out, Grandmother."

"Good. Let me know when you can start." Her voice was that of an Empress to a supplicant; and Quynh Ha nodded.

"I'm honoured by your trust." She was honoured, but she was also scared stiff, as if she were dancing tightrope outside Fire Watch with no tether. To think that she was the one in charge of something that mattered this much to Bao Lan—to the heroine of her childhood—it was almost too much on her shoulders.

Almost.

But she'd do it, because how many times in her life would she have an opportunity like this?

THERE WAS a woman, waiting for her outside the Dust Queen's quarters. She was sitting in one of the high chairs, apparently engrossed in Fire Watch's entertainment system; but she rose when Quynh Ha walked through the door.

"Miss Quynh Ha? My name is Le Anh Tuyet. I'm Bao Lan's daughter."

She was perhaps forty, fifty years old; though like Bao Lan she bore the hallmarks of numerous rejuv treatments. Her face was eerily reminiscent of her mother's, reminding Quynh Ha of the broadcasts of her youth. Her clothes had an odd, almost old-fashioned cut seen nowhere on Fire Watch; and the sheen of Earth silk, grown on mulberry trees and sunlight. "You're an Earthsider?" The words were torn out of Quynh Ha before she could think. "I'm sorry."

"That's quite all right." Tuyet smiled. "I lived here a while, but yes, I emigrated back to Earth twenty years ago."

"I see," Quynh Ha said; and wondered how much lay hidden behind that simple sentence. "You haven't told me what I can do for you."

Tuyet shook her head. "It's what you can do for Mother, younger aunt." She'd slipped, effortless, into the Vietnam vernacular, with its myriad set of pronouns.

"She's already asked—"

"I know," Tuyet said. "I came to accompany her home, to Thoi Binh." Her gaze, for a moment, was distant.

Quynh Ha's curiosity got the better of her. "Did you take part in the land reclamation?"

"In Thoi Binh, yes." Tuyet shrugged. "Mostly boring stuff, and we couldn't salvage everything. Districts Ten and Fifteen are still underwater, I'm afraid."

"It must be very different from here," Quynh Ha said before she could stop herself.

"It's home," Tuyet said, and shook her head. "Apologies. We all have homes, of course; but Thoi Binh is where I was born. You must have relatives—"

"Of course," Quynh Ha said, and bit her lip, thinking of her own grandmother. If she'd rewired herself, would she be more like Bao Lan? It wasn't fair, of course; Grandmother's wandering thoughts might as well be old age, and she'd been sharp enough when Quynh Ha was young: had established the family restaurant on Fire Watch, had paid for the schooling of her numerous grandchildren out of the money she'd saved. But lately... "Never mind that. I'll go plan the rewiring."

"You have much experience."

Quynh Ha was not about to be caught a second time; and she could hear the scepticism in Tuyet's voice. "You don't have rewiring, on Earth?"

Tuyet shrugged. "No, we do. It's just—"

Oh. Like the older generation; the ones who'd been too old at the inception of rewiring; and therefore distrusting it. "Rewiring is only dangerous if you keep doing the same rewiring all the time," Quynh Ha said. "Like the deaders? You must have seen them on the shows. That's because they keep doing it to themselves—dozens of times a day, it's more an addiction than anything, really. Otherwise, it's like anything; a tool that has its uses."

I've done it for customers; and I've done it on myself." She rewired herself periodically when making complex preparations: it was useful to be able to ignore fear and the previous memories of failure so she could focus on getting the drug proportions right.

"I see," Tuyet said. Quynh Ha could tell some of her confidence had got through. "I guess it's what Mother wants, and I won't argue with her. Not this time." Her voice was bleak.

Quynh Ha said nothing; it was obviously not her place to pry. At length Tuyet sighed. "Ah well. It's what you do, on Fire Watch, and if it makes her happy…"

Quynh Ha bowed her head. "Thank you. I'll set to work immediately."

"Great. Do you have everything you need to work?"

Quynh Ha shrugged. "I can do a lot of things from the dispensary." She had remote access to a simulacrum of Bao Lan's memories; enough to find the best places for her rewiring and test her results; though of course anything in a rewiring was unpredictable enough that only live testing would help.

"Good," Tuyet said, and handed her a piece of paper with a private handle. "Do let me know if I can do anything for you. Mother and I—" she grimaced "—have had our differences in the past, but they're over now. We both want her home, no matter the cost."

ALL REWIRINGS have cracks; points of weaknesses, where the protective fabric has been deliberately torn; where the emotions keep seeping in. If she can find one memory that feels different from the other ones—where the glass has fissured, where the colours have bled—then she'll have all she needs to unlock the Mekong Delta again.

What she finds, rifling through Bao Lan's brain, is not that, but something else entirely.

She finds the other memories: the ones associated with Fire Watch, with her role as the Dust Queen, the official entertainer for New Year's Eve: years and years of dust cloud dances all packed together like grains of sand. The Committee that rules over Fire Watch wants something to allay the frustration of Fire Watchers, forced to watch over the terraformation of a planet they're not allowed to set foot on for fear of a cross-planet contamination that would disturb the entire, delicate process mapped out a generation ago. They have decided to hold a celebration on the planet; something that will remind people that one day, when the cyanobacteria and the bots have done their jobs, humans will breathe the air of Mars.

The earlier memories are of technology in its infancy: of frustrated scientists in labs; of bots that die on the surface of Mars, choked up on dust; of implants that short circuit, almost taking out a portion of Bao Lan's brain with them. The lead scientist, Zhu Chiling, comes to hospital to apologise, and almost gives up; but Bao Lan shakes her head, and tells her she's willing to try again—and they do, and she feels the pride and the wonder when it finally works—when Bao Lan sits in the chair of the broadcasting room and makes bots crawl on the surface of Mars for the very first time.

She's with Bao Lan when they inaugurate the seventh cyanobacteria greenhouse; when everyone on Fire Watch gathers to see Bao Lan's bots weave images of villages and houses, with tiny figures running in the street, cutting the strings of kites for good fortune. And she sees every performance after that, establishing a ritual that becomes an anchor for the inhabitants of Fire Watch, a promise renewed year after year.

There's one in particular that Quynh Ha remembers; a New Year's Eve that has no special meaning—another worship of the ancestors, another meal with the family. But, nevertheless, she remembers crowding with the cousins around the huge screen in Mother's compartment; sitting, rapt, as bots dance below, retelling the story of Cuoi and his banyan tree. In the clouds of dust Cuoi meets the tiger; plants the seed of the magical banyan; and is finally whisked to the moon, clinging to the tree's roots as it rises.

And she understood, then; that they're all like Cuoi; that they rose into the Heavens and made their home there; that the banyan's roots, drawn in the dust by the bots, now cover the surface of Mars. That all of this is Bao

Lan's message, Bao Lan's hope: one day their children's children will leave their footprints in the dust and bring their own legends to life on the red soil.

But Bao Lan's home, like Mother's, like Grandmother's, isn't Fire Watch, isn't Mars: it's the land they left in the resettlement, the land that was once submerged under the sea. With difficulty, Quynh Ha tears herself from the feasts, from the beautiful dances of the bots; and goes back to the other memories, the sepia-tinted ones that she finds no purchase on.

She rifles through car rides; through afternoons by the sea at Vung Tau; expeditions to the metropolis in Can Tho. Everything is quaint and old and outmoded—no implants, no bots, just clunky machines and a network that still requires dozens of antennas to function properly. But it's Bao Lan's childhood—this small corner of Viet Nam, those gardens with pomegranate and papaya trees; those boats weaving their way on the muddy expanses of the Mekong; the smell of monsoon rain and fried dough, a promise of a meal of rolled rice cakes and dipping sauce that will be an explosion of flavour in the mouth, salty and acid and sweet all at the same time, a perfect taste that will never again be reproduced, no matter how many cakes she orders.

Quynh Ha realises, then, that she finally has the memory she was looking for. It's small and insignificant, a brief moment of a child running on a bridge clogged with cyclos, and then stopping by a food vendor's cart, but it's alive and vibrant in a way none of the others are. This is her crack; this is the emotion she was looking for. And it's also oddly familiar, in a way she can't place. It can't be shared experience, for she's never been to Can Tho, never been to Earth even, and those wide streets interspersed with trees mean nothing to her. She sets her extrapolations algorithms on it, watching as the fragile network of emotions gains body and heft with each pass—grows like crystals in caves, becoming a complex, fragile assembly of ten thousand details.

She sets up the graft, though she expects only minor issues; and logs out to await the result in the morning.

WHEN SHE gets to the compartment early in the morning, there is an error message waiting for her in the console.

For a moment, Quynh Ha freezes. There is no reason this should fail, especially not at the simulacrum stage. The hardest part had been finding a crack, but normally everything from there on should have been smooth—like a sleek craft set on ice, gathering momentum and sliding straight to its destination. Why?

She throws a glance at the shop's entrance. At this early hour, the customers aren't there yet, though old Miss Hanh should be there any moment to pick up her medication. Quynh Ha wraps the drugs in a piece of paper, and leaves them in evidence with a message for Miss Hanh: since the drugs are tailored to a client's biology, it is unlikely anyone will steal them. Then she turns on her implants, and dives back into the simulacrum.

THE MEMORIES are still there, sepia tinted and under glass, and as inaccessible as ever. There are shards of her algorithms clinging to their edges—broken bits of crystal, jagged edges that made her shudder when she brushes too close, singeing herself on their heightened intensity. But nothing seems to have grown; her graft has been summarily rejected, something alien and unacceptable.

Was the memory wrong? If it didn't belong to Bao Lan, but to the original rewirer? Sometimes things get confused when rewiring; but no, the emotions associated with it were too strong. She's seen them ten thousand times: in Grandmother's gaze when she sits with her friends playing; in the catch of Mother's voice when she speaks of her childhood; in Second Aunt's careful, fragile movements; in the weight of the air at every Tomb Sweeping festival, where the presence of the ancestors is as thick as incense smoke.

There is no reason for that failure then; it makes no sense...

She zooms in on one of the shards, staring at the details—fear and longing and happiness; and a hint of rainy skies, of heavy air. The emotions are real, or as real as Bao Lan allows them to be—the graft is what she's done a dozen times for a dozen customers, surely it shouldn't be such a difficulty?

Still…still, she stares at the shard; and remembers that feeling of familiarity when the extrapolation was being built; remembers dismissing it as of no matter. Her mistake. Every little detail matters.

The shard feels solid and transparent at the same time—the original feelings she got from the crack; the raw pain of losing home mingled with what home means—the joys and the sorrows and the dreams that made up Bao Lan's life in the Delta—the sound of cyclos on the bridge, the patter of the street vendor peddling her fried dough; the sense of vastness opening up all around her, childhood stretching like a vast, endless plain with so many adventures left—and yet already, at the fringes, is the smell and shadow of the rising sea; the inescapable knowledge that all of this is a suspended moment of grace; a fragile dream in a place doomed to vanish.

And she sees it, then. She sees why it hasn't worked; why it can never work.

"I FOUND a crack," Quynh Ha told Bao Lan.

The Dust Queen was sitting in her broadcast chair again, staring at one of the screens in front of her. Tuyet was in one of the smaller chairs, reading a printed book; an oddity on Fire Watch, where nothing was printed much anymore. She reminded Quynh Ha of Second Aunt and her brocade dresses; youthful face, but mannerisms from another generation.

On the screen was a scene from a familiar tale, rendered as in shadow theatre: a man kneeling before the Buddha, watching a hundred stems of bamboo come together to make the hundred-knot bamboo that will win him his sweetheart's hand in marriage. As Quynh Ha watched, Bao Lan made a gesture with one hand; and the scene gradually faded; and then rearranged itself, emphasising the kneeling posture of the man and the larger-than-life size of the Buddha. Then it broke apart; became the dance of bots on a simulated Mars—clouds that slowly built up the apparition of the Buddha; the surprise of the man, who attempted to throw himself backwards; the gathering of the hundred bamboo stems in the forest, so well rendered one could see the sweat on the dust-man's brow; could hear the sound of bamboo falling on the ground of the forest.

Quynh Ha found herself holding her breath, so hard it hurt.

Bao Lan made a dismissive gesture. "It's not yet ready." She pinched her lips; and made another gesture. The scene dissolved; played itself out again; the Buddha slightly larger; the man slightly smaller—and, when he went into the forest, it wasn't sweat that was falling from his brow, but tears—his fear, his anguish at the thought he might never return in time, never marry his bride…

"Better." Bao Lan shook her head. "But not quite there, I think. Sorry for making you wait, child."

"I don't mind," Quynh Ha said. Her heart still hung suspended in her chest. "Is this how you do your performances?"

"Sometimes, yes." The Dust Queen had an oddly nostalgic look in her face. "There wasn't this, in the old days: it was all gut instinct, but this helps."

"I know," Quynh Ha said, and bit her tongue.

"You've seen the memories." Bao Lan nodded.

"I didn't know you'd based it on shadow theatre."

Bao Lan shrugged. "It seemed as good an inspiration as any. I had…good memories of shadow theatre, when I was a child. There was this itinerant Hoa performer, back in Thoi Binh…" She smiled. "But never mind, we're not here for this old woman to babble on. You said you'd found a crack."

Quynh Ha would have listened to her all day; but she knew that wasn't what Bao Lan was expecting. "Yes," she said.

"And you're here to finish your work, I take it."

Quynh Ha took a deep breath. "I can't." From the corner of her eye, she saw Tuyet set aside her book, and turn her head to her, with a gaze sharp enough to pierce metal.

"I don't understand," Tuyet said. "Surely, once you've found your crack, everything else should be easy?"

It was what she'd told Bao Lan; and there was, indeed, no reason to suppose it would go otherwise. Except…

"I've extrapolated it, as I said. And I could rewire you right now, but it wouldn't take. It's not just a crack. It's everywhere."

"Everywhere?" Bao Lan shook her head. "I don't think so. When I think of my childhood, all that comes up is empty memories. Images that mean nothing. Sounds and tastes that are a stranger's."

"It's not—" Quynh Ha paused, struggling for words that seemed to have escaped her. It had seemed so clear, staring at the pattern yesterday; but that had been yesterday; and today she was in the presence of Bao Lan again, and as tongue-tied as a child. "Your crack is your art. The thing that makes your dust clouds sing, that gives them meaning, emotion, depth: it's that tiny little remnant of what it meant to lose your home."

Bao Lan opened her mouth to speak—Quynh Ha barely noticed, as she went on through her memorised speech. "You're the Dust Queen. That's who you've been, for decades. I've seen the memories. Your entire life revolves around your art." There had been memories of Tuyet in the simulacrum, but Quynh Ha had steered clear of them. They were none of her business, and she'd felt ashamed enough spying on Bao Lan's performances. Nevertheless, she'd seen enough: a lonely childhood, with a mother that had little time for her child; but who had still resented Tuyet for leaving Fire Watch—abandoning Bao Lan for the lifelong work of raising the Delta from the sea.

There was silence, in the wake of her words. Surely she'd gone too far, had been too frank, too honest? "I see," Bao Lan said at last. "And it won't take—"

"Because you won't let it," Quynh Ha said.

"What makes you so sure?"

Quynh Ha spread her hands. "The simulacrum—"

"Is a simulation." Bao Lan's voice was quiet, but forceful. Behind her, the little shadow play was still going on; the man abasing himself before the Buddha; the hundred-knot bamboo rebuilding itself, time and time again. "You can't know what will happen in real life."

"No," Quynh Ha said.

"You've known cases of divergence," Bao Lan said, softly. "Cases where the simulacrum didn't follow the patient."

"Not this way!"

Bao Lan said, softly, quietly, "I'm told there are ways and means, to make a graft take. Forcefully, if need be."

Demons take her. Of course she'd do her research; and of course she'd find out all about the more shady practises of rewiring. "We don't do this," Quynh Ha said. "Not on Fire Watch." Out there in the asteroids, perhaps—who knew what the companies got up to, when their profits were on the line? But here on the orbital, where the only thing at stake was watching Mars grow? No. "And even if we did, it would be an even more difficult procedure." To make a graft take when it didn't cling, you had to add anchors everywhere; to tie hundreds of knots in the nerve fabric, to implant emotion after emotion in such a way that they never came loose, and yet didn't damage the brain... "Hours of work, and the slightest deviation could make everything fail."

"Ah. But I did say I'd picked you out for your delicate touch, didn't I?"

She—she—"You knew," Quynh Ha said, sucking in a burning breath. "You knew all along."

"No," Bao Lan said. "But I suspected that it might come to this, yes; and I gave a long thought to what I would do, if that were the case. I knew I would ask you to go ahead."

"But I can't—" she struggled for breath and words. "Having a stable simulation is the basis of rewiring. I can't just let anything loose in your brain!"

"That would seem to be the definition of rewiring," Bao Lan said, with a tight smile. "At least as far as I'm concerned. I'm not a fool, child. All things come with their cost. I admit I didn't expect the price to be so high, but—"

"Not like that," Quynh Ha said. "Even if I make it take, you might wake up a vegetable. You might not wake up at all. You might be completely different."

"I'll be different in any case, no?"

"Yes, but—"

Bao Lan lifted a hand; and that same sense of presence filled the room; that same reminder that she was the Dust Queen, with decades of commanding the attention of Fire Watch. "I'm old, child, old enough to be your grandmother, as you and I well know. I've done my duty to Fire Watch. Now it's time for me to think of my ancestors; and to honour their graves. Tuyet is right; it's time for me to return home." She smiled a little; and in that moment the mask cracked, and the expression of vague longing on her face was the same as Grandmother's.

"The dust clouds—" Quynh Ha started, but Bao Lan shook her head.

"The dust clouds are only a thing." A brief expression of pain crossed her face, then; and was as swiftly gone. "Pieces of art I loved, yes; but if you cling too much to what you love, they destroy you in the end. I won't lie and say I won't miss them; but I can live without them."

She couldn't. She was the Dust Queen. She was—

No more dust clouds. No more performances; and worse than that, Bao Lan turning her back on them, on what they meant to Fire Watch—going home to die in obscurity, forgetting all that passion that had gone into making them; dismissing them as not important, as something that could be erased from her—no different, after all, from Mother, from Grandmother…

For a moment Quynh Ha stood frozen where she stood; and then the truth was torn out of her. "I—I can't help you. I just can't. I'm sorry." The Dust Queen stared at her, expressionless for a second; and then a look of mild disappointment gradually took over, as if Quynh Ha were six again, standing in the kitchen unit of the family compartment in a puddle of water and sugar she'd spilled on the floor—and a sense of growing, unbearable shame, unbearable fear that seemed to squeeze her heart into burning shards—and before she knew it, she was up and running out of the room, and a long way into the corridors of the orbital before she could catch her breath again.

IT WAS Tuyet who found her, later; sitting moodily at the counter of the dispensary, staring into her console as if it could yield some unfathomable truth. Second Aunt had left her some noodle soup; and the aroma of star anise and beef marrow filled the shop, strong enough to overpower even the smells of drug compounds.

"I thought I'd find you here."

"I can't do it," Quynh Ha said. "I'm sorry I ran out, but there's just no way I can do it."

"Can't, or won't?" Tuyet asked, with disturbing perspicacity. "It's her wish. Why would you deny her that?"

As though a customer with excess asked her to remove cucumber seeds from a drug preparation: would she do it, if they assured her they'd weighed the effect of the harm on their own bodies? "She'll change," Quynh Ha said. "She might even regret it."

"Perhaps. But she's given enough thought to the consequences, hasn't she? In the end, it's what she wants, now."

"What would you do?"

Tuyet shrugged. "She's my mother. Of course I would do as she asks. 'Do no harm' only applies to doctors."

And she was only an apothecary. Quynh Ha smiled, bleakly. Shouldn't the customer's well-being take precedence over everything else? "She'll never be the same."

"Of course she won't. It's a rewiring that she wants to live with. You know how I feel about rewiring. It's hardly innocuous."

"She won't do any dust art, ever again," Quynh Ha said, finally; and knew that this was the truth, the rock bottom of her existence; her own crack around which everything was built. There were other artists, other people working in dust clouds; but none of them were Bao Lan.

Tuyet's face was carefully blank. "We all have our homes. We all have our childhood treasures. I've had my share of disagreement with Mother; but this is her choice, and I won't take it away from her."

And Quynh Ha would. "I—I can't do it. I told her the truth: it's a delicate procedure." She took in a deep breath—it hurt, to admit even that. "I can give you the name of someone else—"

"She trusted you."

"I know," Quynh Ha said; reliving, again and again, her conversation with Bao Lan; that awful moment when she'd frozen, and some incoherent mush had taken over her brain. "She'll learn to live without that trust. It will be easy." Depressingly so; after all, what need had the Dust Queen for broken tools? She'd go back to working in the dispensary for Second Aunt; burying that shame, that moment of failure deep into herself. Part of wisdom, Second Aunt always said, was knowing when you were outmatched, and this was the case—she knew what ought to be done, but couldn't even bring herself to contemplate the possibility of it.

Tuyet didn't speak for a moment. "I can take that name," she said at last. "I can bring them to Mother and have them perform the procedure—"

"Then do it!"

"Just answer me one question first, younger aunt: what will it do to you, if I do this?"

"I don't understand—"

Tuyet's smile was bitter. "I know all about regrets, younger aunt. Can you look me in the eye and tell me yours won't eat you up? That you had your chance to help the Dust Queen, and passed up on it?"

"I—" She was right; Quynh Ha knew it. "You asked if I couldn't, or if I wouldn't? The answer is that I... I can't knowingly remove Bao Lan's art from her—it would hurt me too much. She's right: it requires delicacy, and absolute control. That's...not something I can provide." Not now; not ever—it was her childhood, her dreams, and how could she ever wreck them?

"As you wish." Tuyet's voice was stiff, carefully controlled. Disapproval, again. Well, she was no longer six years old, and Tuyet wasn't Mother or Second Aunt, not someone whose mere glance would induce burning shame. She would simply turn aside, and finish her soup; and go back to

Second Aunt; and feel no regrets, none at all, over failing the Dust Queen in her moment of need.

No regrets...

Quynh Ha looked at the other's emotionless face, and heard her own voice again, stating the obvious. Absolute control. Delicacy. She was completely right: she couldn't provide it. Not in her current state.

But there was always a way to change one's current state.

Carefully, she laid her chopsticks on the side of the bowl, over the sodden remnants of cold noodles and wilted coriander. "Give me a minute," she said, "and I'll be with you."

GOING INTO someone's brain is almost like being in space: that curious sensation of hanging, weightless, like floating in water without the water; of hanging in darkness with the stars around her like hairpin wounds in the fabric of the heavens.

Here, of course, there are no stars; but the wounds are memories—a dizzying array of them, every one of them so close she could touch them—and yet to reach out, to catch them all, would drive her insane under the weight of information and emotions that aren't hers.

She does reach out, all the same—because it's what she's here for, because it's the only thing she can decently do—and takes the images one by one, delicately threading her assemblage into their very fabric—adding longing and hurt and joy to memories of a cyclo weaving its way through the traffic of an overcrowded city; to images of plates strewn on red table cloth, of wrapped rice cakes, candied coconut and lotus seeds; to tombs in a graveyard, with paper money and paper houses burning in a copper dish; to an old woman on a roof in the midst of a flood, raising a fist at some officials in a boat...

And, as she does so, she sees the other memories—the ones of Cuoi and his banyan, of Khong Minh and his fan; of bots dancing in the dust, weaving images of villages and houses, with tiny figures running in the street, cutting the strings of kites for good fortune—she sees them shrivel a little, become a little smaller, a little more distant, like feelings of affection for acquaintances one sees once a year. She sees them wither and die, and knows that this is the end; that there will be no more Dust Queen, no more of her heartrending performances to tell them who they are.

It would have made her cry, once; would have stopped her in her tracks as she weaves through memory after memory, spreading the crack to every single image of the Mekong Delta. There's one performance in particular that she would have been unable to see without wrecking everything: a New Year's Eve with no special meaning; another worship of the ancestors, another meal with the family—save that this was the New Year's Eve when she understood at last—the New Year's Eve where she took Bao Lan's message into herself, when she knew with absolute certainty that the banyan's roots now were in the planet itself; that her children's children would leave their own footprints in the red dust, and bring to life their own legends on the red soil.

But all those memories of performances, the good, the bad, the heartbreaking—they're all sealed under glass, tinted the colour of old, obsolete photographs—preserved under glass in that temporary stasis, where nothing matters, where nothing hurts.

It doesn't have to be temporary, of course—she could make it last forever, but she's not Bao Lan, and she won't live with her childhood memories cut off. Bao Lan did what she had to, to survive—and, in the end, so will she. She will keep the performances, and remember the way they showed: forward, into a future where Mars belongs to her descendants; and further on, perhaps—when humanity is spread among the stars, like so many grains of rice in fallow fields.

SHE SAW them off at the spaceport, afterwards.

"We've got you something else," Bao Lan said—handing her a velvet box, which contained a piece of translucent jade the colour of the pandan leaves in Bao Lan's memories. "In addition to your payment. I know it's not much, but this is with my gratitude." She held herself hunched now, with the same familiar hurt in her eyes all the time; the same look Quynh Ha knew all too well from Mother, from Grandmother. The Dust Queen— that tall, imperious figure that had brought attention to a room by simply lifting her hand—was no more.

Quynh Ha took the jade: it was engraved, with a simple design of a man in a banyan tree. She felt queasy, as though she would weep; though it might simply have been part of the after effects of undoing her rewiring. What was it Tuyet had said? Hardly innocuous. Perhaps that was the truth of all rewirings. "Thank you. Have a safe journey home, both of you."

"We probably won't see each other again," Tuyet said. "But I hope you live a long life, with the ancestors' blessings on your health and children."

Quynh Ha nodded, accepting the traditional parting. "Thank you for believing in me," she said.

Tuyet smiled. "You were Mother's choice; and she's seldom wrong."

And then they were gone; leaving her alone once more. She came to stand before the screens, watching their shuttle depart from Fire Watch— the ion drives lighting up in the darkness, before they were altogether gone on their months-long journey back to Earth—and the huge image of Mars appeared once more on the screen, with a few dots denoting the cyanobacteria greenhouses.

No more dust clouds.

She raised the jade to the light, until the image of Cuoi in the banyan was superimposed on the red planet; and thought of Bao Lan, hunched and subdued and entirely unlike who she had been.

"Safe journeys," she whispered; and wondered if she'd ever be able to forgive herself, for sending the Dust Queen home.

Three Cups of Grief, by Starlight

Green tea: green tea is made from steamed or lightly dried tea leaves. The brew is light, with a pleasant, grassy taste. Do not over-steep it, lest it become bitter.

AFTER THE FUNERAL, QUANG TU WALKED BACK TO HIS COMPART-ment, and sat down alone, staring sightlessly at the slow ballet of bots cleaning the small room—the metal walls pristine already, with every trace of Mother's presence or of her numerous mourners scrubbed away. He'd shut down the communal network—couldn't bear to see the potted summaries of Mother's life, the endlessly looping vids of the funeral procession, the hundred thousand bystanders gathered at the grave site to say goodbye, vultures feasting on the flesh of the grieving—they hadn't known her, they hadn't cared—and all their offerings of flowers were worth as much as the insurances of the Embroidered Guard.

"Big brother, I know you're here," a voice said, on the other side of the door he'd locked. "Let me in, please?"

Of course. Quang Tu didn't move. "I said I wanted to be alone," he said.

A snort that might have been amusement. "Fine. If you insist on doing it that way…"

His sister, *The Tiger in the Banyan*, materialised in the kitchen, hovering over the polished counter, near the remains of his morning tea. Of course, it wasn't really her: she was a Mind encased in the heartroom of a spaceship, far too heavy to leave orbit; and what she projected down onto the planet was an avatar, a perfectly rendered, smaller version of herself—elegant and sharp, with a small, blackened spot on her hull which served as a mourning band. "Typical," she said, hovering around the compartment. "You can't just shut yourself away."

"I can if I want to," Quang Tu said—feeling like he was eight years old again, trying to argue with her—as if it had ever made sense. She seldom got angry—mindships didn't, mostly; he wasn't sure if that was the overall design of the Imperial Workshops, or the simple fact that her lifespan was counted in centuries, and his (and Mother's) in mere decades. He'd have thought she didn't grieve, either; but she was changed—something in the slow, careful deliberation of her movements, as if anything and everything might break her...

The Tiger in the Banyan hovered near the kitchen table, watching the bots. She could hack them, easily; no security worth anything in the compartment. Who would steal bots, anyway?

What he valued most had already been taken away.

"Leave me alone," he said. But he didn't want to be alone; not really. He didn't want to hear the silence in the compartment; the clicking sounds of the bots' legs on metal, bereft of any warmth or humanity.

"Do you want to talk about it?" *The Tiger in the Banyan* asked.

She didn't need to say what; and he didn't do her the insult of pretending she did. "What would be the point?"

"To talk." Her voice was uncannily shrewd. "It helps. At least, I'm told it does."

Quang Tu heard, again, the voice of the Embroidered Guard; the slow, measured tones commiserating on his loss; and then the frown, and the knife-thrust in his gut.

You must understand that your mother's work was very valuable...

The circumstances are not ordinary...

The slow, pompous tones of the scholar; the convoluted official language he knew by heart—the only excuses the state would make to him, couched in the over-formality of memorials and edicts.

"She—" he took a deep, trembling breath—was it grief, or anger? "I should have had her mem-implants." Forty-nine days after the funeral; when there was time for the labs to have decanted and stabilised Mother's personality and memories, and added her to the ranks of the ancestors on file. It wasn't her, it would never be her, of course—just a simulation meant to share knowledge and advice. But it would have been something. It would have filled the awful emptiness in his life.

"It was your right, as the eldest," *The Tiger in the Banyan* said. Something in the tone of her voice…

"You disapprove? You wanted them?" Families had fallen out before, on more trivial things.

"Of course not." A burst of careless, amused laughter. "Don't be a fool. What use would I have, for them. It's just—" She hesitated, banking left and right in uncertainty. "You need something more. Beyond Mother."

"There isn't something more!"

"You—"

"You weren't there," Quang Tu said. She'd been away on her journeys, ferrying people back and forth between the planets that made up the Dai Viet Empire; leaping from world to world, with hardly a care for planet-bound humans. She—she hadn't seen Mother's unsteady hands, dropping the glass; heard the sound of its shattering like a gunshot; hadn't carried her back to bed every evening, tracking the progress of the disease by the growing lightness in his arms—by the growing sharpness of ribs, protruding under taut skin.

Mother had remained herself until almost the end—sharp and lucid and utterly aware of what was happening, scribbling in the margins of her team's reports and sending her instructions to the new space station's building site, as if nothing untoward had ever happened to her. Had it been a blessing; or a curse? He didn't have answers; and he wasn't sure he wanted that awful certainty to shatter him.

"I was here," *The Tiger in the Banyan* said, gently, slowly. "At the end."

Quang Tu closed his eyes, again, smelling antiseptic and the sharp odour of painkillers; and the sour smell of a body finally breaking down, finally failing. "I'm sorry. You were. I didn't mean to—"

"I know you didn't." *The Tiger in the Banyan* moved closer to him; brushed against his shoulder—ghostly, almost intangible, the breath that had been beside him all his childhood. "But nevertheless. Your life got eaten up, taking care of Mother. And you can say you were only doing what a filial son ought to do; you can say it didn't matter. But…it's done now, big brother. It's over."

It's not, he wanted to say, but the words rang hollow in his own ears. He moved, stared at the altar; at the holo of Mother—over the offering of tea and rice, the food to sustain her on her journey through Hell. It cycled through vids—Mother, heavily pregnant with his sister, moving with the characteristic arrested slowness of Mind-bearers; Mother standing behind Quang Tu and *The Tiger in the Banyan* in front of the ancestral altar for Grandfather's death anniversary; Mother, accepting her Hoang Minh Medal from the then Minister of Investigation; and one before the diagnosis, when she'd already started to become frailer and thinner—insisting on going back to the lab; to her abandoned teams and research…

He thought, again, of the Embroidered Guard; of the words tightening around his neck like an executioner's garrotte. How dare he. How dare they all. "She came home," he said, not sure how to voice the turmoil within him. "To us. To her family. In the end. It meant something, didn't it?"

The Tiger in the Banyan's voice was wry, amused. "It wasn't the Empress that comforted her when she woke at night, coughing her lungs out, was it?" It was…treason to much as think this, let alone utter it; though the Embroidered Guard would make allowances for grief, and anger; and for Mother's continued usefulness to the service of the Empress. The truth was, neither of them much cared, anyway. "It's not the Empress that was by her side when she died."

She'd clung to his hand, then, her eyes open wide, a network of blood within the whites, and the fear in her eyes. "I—please, child…" He'd stood, frozen; until, behind him, *The Tiger in the Banyan* whispered, "The lights in Sai Gon are green and red, the lamps in My Tho are bright and dim…"—an Old Earth lullaby, the words stretched into the familiar, slow, comforting rhythm that he'd unthinkingly taken up.

"Go home to study

I shall wait nine months, I shall wait ten autumns..."

She'd relaxed, then, against him; and they had gone on singing songs until—he didn't know when she'd died; when the eyes lost their lustre, the face its usual sharpness. But he'd risen from her death-bed with the song still in his mind; and an awful yawning gap in his world that nothing had closed.

And then—after the scattering of votive papers, after the final handful of earth thrown over the grave—the Embroidered Guard.

The Embroidered Guard was young; baby-faced and callow, but he was already moving with the easy arrogance of the privileged. He'd approached Quang Tu at the grave site, ostensibly to offer his condolences—it had taken him all of two sentences to get to his true purpose; and to shatter Quang Tu's world, all over again.

Your mother's mem-implants will go to Professor Tuyet Hoa, who will be best able to continue her research...

Of course, the Empire required food; and crops of rice grown in space; and better, more reliable harvests to feed the masses. Of course he didn't want anyone to starve. But...

Mem-implants always went from parent to child. They were a family's riches and fortune; the continued advice of the ancestors, dispensed from beyond the grave. He'd—he'd had the comfort, as Mother lay dying, to know that he wouldn't lose her. Not for real; not for long.

"They took her away from us," Quang Tu said. "Again and again and again. And now, at the very end, when she ought to be ours—when she should return to her family..."

The Tiger in the Banyan didn't move; but a vid of the funeral appeared on one of the walls, projected through the communal network. There hadn't been enough space in the small compartment for people to pay their respects; the numerous callers had jammed into the corridors and alcoves, jostling each other in utter silence. "She's theirs in death, too."

"And you don't care?"

A side-roll of the avatar, her equivalent of a shrug. "Not as much as you do. I remember her. None of them do."

Except Tuyet Hoa.

He remembered Tuyet Hoa, too; coming to visit them on the third day after the New Year—a student paying respect to her teacher, year after year; turning from an unattainable grown-up to a woman not much older than either he or *The Tiger in the Banyan*; though she'd never lost her rigid awkwardness in dealing with them. No doubt, in Tuyet Hoa's ideal world, Mother wouldn't have had children; wouldn't have let anything distract her from her work.

"You have to move on," *The Tiger in the Banyan* said, slowly, gently; coming by his side to stare at the memorial altar. Bots gathered in the kitchen space, started putting together fresh tea to replace the three cups laid there. "Accept that this is the way things are. They'll compensate, you know—offer you higher-level promotions and make allowances. You'll find your path through civil service is...smoother."

Bribes or sops; payments for the loss of something that had no price. "Fair dealings," he said, slowly, bitterly. They knew exactly the value of what Tuyet Hoa was getting.

"Of course," *The Tiger in the Banyan* said. "But you'll only ruin your health and your career; and you know Mother wouldn't have wanted it."

As if... No, he was being unfair. Mother could be distant, and engrossed in her work; but she had always made time for them. She had raised them and played with them, telling them stories of princesses and fishermen and citadels vanished in one night; and, later on, going on long walks with Quang Tu in the gardens of Azure Dragons, delightedly pointing at a pine tree or at a crane flying overhead; and animatedly discussing Quang Tu's fledging career in the Ministry of Works.

"You can't afford to let this go sour," *The Tiger in the Banyan* said. Below her, the bots brought a small, perfect cup of tea: green, fragrant liquid in a cup, the cracks in the pale celadon like those in eggshells.

Quang Tu lifted the cup; breathed in the grassy, pleasant smell—Mother would love it, even beyond the grave. "I know," he said, laying the cup on the altar. The lie slipped out of him as softly, as easily as Mother's last exhaled breath.

O Long tea: those teas are carefully prepared by the tea masters to cre-
ate a range of tastes and appearances. The brew is sweet with a hint of
strength, each subsequent steeping revealing new nuances.

TUYET HOA woke up—with a diffuse, growing sense of panic and fear, before she remembered the procedure.

She was alive. She was sane. At least...

She took in a deep, trembling breath; and realised she lay at home, in her bed. What had woken her up—above the stubborn, panicked rhythm of her heart—was a gentle nudge from the communal network, flashes of light relayed by the bots in the lightest phase of her sleep cycle. It wasn't her alarm; but rather, a notification that a message classified as "urgent" had arrived for her.

Not again.

A nudge, at the back of her mind; a thread of thought that wasn't her own; reminding her she should look at it; that it was her responsibility as the new head of department to pay proper attention to messages from her subordinates.

Professor Duy Uyen. Of course.

She was as forceful in life as she had been in death; and, because she had been merely Hoa's head of department, and not a direct ancestor, she felt...wrong. Distant, as though she were speaking through a pane of glass.

Hoa was lucky, she knew—receiving mem-implants that weren't your own family's could irretrievably scramble your brain, as fifteen different strangers with no consideration or compassion fought for control of your thoughts. She could hear Professor Duy Uyen; and sometimes others of Duy Uyen's ancestors, as remote ghosts; but that was it. It could have been so much worse.

And it could have been so much better.

She got up, ignoring the insistent talk at the back of her mind, the constant urge to be dutiful; and padded into the kitchen.

The bots had already set aside Hoa's first tea of the day. She'd used to take it at work, before the procedure; in the days of Professor Duy Uyen's sickness, when Duy Uyen came in to work thinner and paler every day—and then became a succession of memorials and vid-calls, injecting her last, desperate instructions into the project before it slipped beyond her grasp. Hoa had enjoyed the quiet: it had kept the desperate knowledge of Professor Duy Uyen's coming death at bay—the moment when they would all be adrift in the void of space, with no mindship to carry them onwards.

Now Hoa enjoyed a different quiet. Now she drank her tea first thing in the morning—hoping that, at this early hour, the mem-implants had no motive to kick in.

Not that it had worked, this particular morning.

She sat down to breathe in the flavour—the faint, nutty aroma poised perfectly between floral and sweet—her hand trembling above the surface of the cup—mentally blocking out Professor Duy Uyen for a few precious minutes; a few more stolen moments of tranquillity before reality came crashing in.

Then she gave in, and opened the message.

It was from Luong Ya Lan, the researcher who worked on the water's acidity balance. On the vid relayed from the laboratory, she was pale, but perfectly composed. "Madam Hoa. I'm sorry to have to inform you that the samples in Paddy Four have developed a fungal disease..."

Professor Duy Uyen stirred in the depths of Hoa's brain, parsing the words as they came in—accessing the station's private network and downloading the pertinent data—the only mercy was that she wasn't faster than Hoa, and that it would take her fifteen to twenty minutes to parse all of it. The Professor had her suspicions, of course—something about the particular rice strain; perhaps the changes drafted onto the plant to allow it to thrive under starlight, changes taken from the nocturnal honeydreamer on the Sixteenth Planet; perhaps the conditions in the paddy itself...

Hoa poured herself another cup of tea; and stared at the bots for a while. There was silence, the voice of Duy Uyen slowly fading away to nothingness in her thoughts. Alone. At last, alone.

Paddy Four had last been checked on by Ya Lan's student, An Khang—Khang was a smart and dedicated man, but not a particularly careful one; and she would have to ask him if he'd checked himself, or through bots; and if he'd followed protocols when he'd done so.

She got up, and walked to the laboratory—still silence in her mind. It was a short trip: the station was still being built, and the only thing in existence were the laboratory and the living quarters for all ten researchers—a generous allocation of space, far grander than the compartments they would have been entitled to on any of their home stations.

Outside, beyond the metal walls, the bots were hard at work—reinforcing the structure, gradually layering a floor and walls onto the skeletal structure mapped out by the Grand Master of Design Harmony. She had no need to call up a vid of the outside on her implants to know they were out there, doing their part; just as she was. They weren't the only ones, of course: in the Imperial Workshops, alchemists were carefully poring over the design of the Mind that would one day watch over the entire station, making sure no flaws remained before they transferred him to the womb of his mother.

In the laboratory, Ya Lan was busying herself with the faulty paddy: she threw an apologetic glance at Hoa when Hoa walked in. "You got my message."

Hoa grimaced. "Yes. Have you had time to analyse?"

Ya Lan flushed. "No."

Hoa knew. A proper analysis would require more than twenty minutes. But still... "If you had to make a rough guess?"

"Probably the humidity."

"Did Khang—"

Ya Lan shook her head. "I checked that too. No contaminants introduced in the paddy; and the last time he opened it was two weeks ago." The paddies were encased in glass, to make sure they could control the environment; and monitored by bots and the occasional scientist.

"Fungi can lie dormant for more than two weeks," Hoa said, darkly.

Ya Lan sighed. "Of course. But I still think it's the environment: it's a bit tricky to get right."

Humid and dark; the perfect conditions for a host of other things to grow in the paddies—not just the crops the Empire so desperately needed. The named planets were few; and fewer still that could bear the cultivation of food. Professor Duy Uyen had had a vision—of a network of space stations like this one; of fish ponds and rice paddies grown directly under starlight, rather than on simulated Old Earth light; of staples that would not cost a fortune in resources to grow and maintain.

And they had all believed in that vision, like a dying man offered a glimpse of a river. The Empress herself had believed it; so much that she had suspended the law for Professor Duy Uyen's sake, and granted her mem-implants to Hoa instead of to Duy Uyen's son: the quiet boy Hoa remembered from her New Year's visits, now grown to become a scholar in his own right—he'd been angry at the funeral, and why wouldn't he be? The mem-implants should have been his.

"I know," Hoa said. She knelt, calling up the data from the paddy onto her implants: her field of vision filled with a graph of the temperature throughout last month. The slight dips in the curve all corresponded to a check: a researcher opening the paddy.

"Professor?" Ya Lan asked; hesitant.

Hoa did not move. "Yes?"

"It's the third paddy of that strain that fails in as many months…"

She heard the question Ya Lan was not asking. The other strain—the one in paddies One to Three—had also failed some tests, but not at the same frequency.

Within her, Professor Duy Uyen stirred. It was the temperature, she pointed out, gently but firmly. The honeydreamer supported a very narrow range of temperatures; and the modified rice probably did, too.

Hoa bit back a savage answer. The changes might be flawed, but they were the best candidate they had.

Professor Duy Uyen shook her head. The strain in paddies One to Three was better: a graft from a lifeform of an unnumbered and unsettled planet, P Huong Van—luminescents, an insect flying in air too different to be breathable by human beings. They had been Professor Duy Uyen's favoured option.

Hoa didn't like the luminescents. The air of P Huong Van had a different balance of *khi*-elements: it was rich in fire, and anything would set it ablaze—flame-storms were horrifically common, charring trees to cinders, and birds in flight to blackened skeletons. Aboard a space station, fire was too much of a danger. Professor Duy Uyen had argued that the Mind that would ultimately control the space station could be designed to accept an unbalance of *khi*-elements; could add water to the atmosphere to reduce the chances of a firestorm onboard.

Hoa had no faith in this. Modifying a Mind had a high cost, far above that of regulating temperature in a rice paddy. She pulled up the data from the paddies; though of course she knew Professor Duy Uyen would have reviewed it before her.

Professor Duy Uyen was polite enough not to chide Hoa; though Hoa could feel her disapproval like the weight of a blade—it was odd, in so many ways, how the refinement process had changed Professor Duy Uyen; how, with all the stabilisation adjustments, all the paring down of the unnecessary emotions, the simulation in her mind was utterly, heartbreakingly different from the woman she had known: all the keenness of her mind, and the blade of her finely-honed knowledge, with none of the compassion that would have made her more bearable. Though perhaps it was as well that she had none of the weakness Duy Uyen had shown, in the end—the skin that barely hid the sharpness of bones; the eyes like bruises in the pale oval of her face; the voice, faltering on words or instructions...

Paddies One to Three were thriving; the yield perhaps less than that of Old Earth; but nothing to be ashamed of. There had been a spot of infection in Paddy Three; but the bots had taken care of it.

Hoa watched, for a moment, the bots scuttling over the glass encasing the paddy; watched the shine of metal; the light trembling on the joints of their legs—waiting for the smallest of triggers to blossom into flame. The temperature data for all three paddies was fluctuating too much; and the rate of fire-*khi* was far above what she was comfortable with.

"Professor?" Ya Lan was still waiting by Paddy Four.

There was only one paddy of that honeydreamer strain: it was new, and as yet unproved. Professor Duy Uyen stirred, within her mind; pointed out the painfully obvious. The strain wasn't resistant enough—the Empire couldn't afford to rely on something so fragile. She should do the reasonable thing, and consign it to the scrap bin. They should switch efforts to the other strain, the favoured one; and what did it matter if the station's Mind needed to enforce a slightly different balance of *khi*-elements?

It was what Professor Duy Uyen would have done.

But she wasn't Professor Duy Uyen.

Minds were made in balance; to deliberately unhinge one…would have larger consequences on the station than mere atmospheric control. The risk was too high. She knew this; as much as she knew and numbered all her ancestors—the ones that hadn't been rich or privileged enough to bequeath her their own mem-implants—leaving her with only this pale, flawed approximation of an inheritance.

You're a fool.

Hoa closed her eyes; closed her thoughts so that the voice in her mind sank to a whisper. She brought herself, with a slight effort, back to the tranquillity of her mornings—breathing in the nutty aroma from her teacup, as she steeled herself for the day ahead.

She wasn't Professor Duy Uyen.

She'd feared being left adrift when Professor Duy Uyen's illness had taken a turn for the worse; she'd lain late at night wondering what would happen to Duy Uyen's vision; of what she would do, bereft of guidance.

But now she knew.

"Get three other tanks," Hoa said. "Let's see what that strain looks like with a tighter temperature regulation. And if you can get hold of Khang, ask him to look into the graft—there might be a better solution there."

The Empress had thought Duy Uyen a critical asset; had made sure that her mem-implants went to Hoa—so that Hoa would have the advice and knowledge she needed to finish the station that the Empire so desperately needed. The Empress had been wrong; and who cared if that was treason?

Because the answer to Professor Duy Uyen's death, like everything else, was deceptively, heartbreakingly simple: that no one was irreplaceable; that they would do what everyone always did—they would, somehow, forge on.

Dark tea: dark tea leaves are left to mature for years through a careful process of fermentation. The process can take anywhere from a few months to a century. The resulting brew has rich, thick texture with only a bare hint of sourness.

THE TIGER in the Banyan doesn't grieve as humans do.

Partly, it's because she's been grieving for such a long time; because mindships don't live the same way that humans do—because they're built and anchored and stabilised.

Quang Tu spoke of seeing Mother become frail and ill, and how it broke his heart; *The Tiger in the Banyan*'s heart broke, years and years ago; when she stood in the midst of the New Year's Eve celebration—as the sound of crackers and bells and gongs filled in the corridors of the orbital, and everyone hugged and cried, she suddenly realised that she would still be there in a hundred years; but that no one else around the table—not Mother, not Quang Tu, none of the aunts and uncles or cousins—would still be alive.

She leaves Quang Tu in his compartment, staring at the memorial altar—and, shifting her consciousness from her projected avatar to her real body, climbs back among the stars.

She is a ship; and in the days and months that Quang Tu mourns, she carries people between planets and orbitals—private passengers and officials on their business: rough white silk, elaborate five panel dresses; parties of scholars arguing on the merit of poems; soldiers on leave from the most distant numbered planets, who go into the weirdness of deep spaces with nothing more than a raised eyebrow.

Mother is dead, but the world goes on—Professor Pham Thi Duy Uyen becomes yesterday's news; fades into official biographies and re-creation vids—and her daughter goes on, too, doing her duty to the Empire.

The Tiger in the Banyan doesn't grieve as humans do. Partly, it's because she doesn't remember as humans do.

She doesn't remember the womb; or the shock of the birth; but in her earliest memories Mother is here—the first and only time she was carried in Mother's arms—and Mother herself helped by the birth-master, walking forward on tottering legs—past the pain of the birth, past the bone-deep weariness that speaks only of rest and sleep. It's Mother's hands that lie her down into the cradle in the heartroom; Mother's hands that close the clasps around her—so that she is held; wrapped as securely as she was in the womb—and Mother's voice that sings to her a lullaby, the tune she will forever carry as she travels between the stars.

"The lights in Sai Gon are green and red, the lamps in My Tho are bright and dim…"

As she docks at an orbital near the Fifth Planet, *The Tiger in the Banyan* is hailed by another, older ship, *The Dream of Millet*: a friend she often meets on longer journeys. "I've been looking for you."

"Oh?" *The Tiger in the Banyan* asks. It's not hard, to keep track of where ships go from their manifests; but *The Dream of Millet* is old, and rarely bothers to do so—she's used to other ships coming to her, rather than the other way around.

"I wanted to ask how you were. When I heard you were back into service—" *The Dream of Millet* pauses, then; and hesitates; sending a faint signal of cautious disapproval on the comms. "It's early. Shouldn't you be mourning? Officially—"

Officially, the hundred days of tears are not yet over. But ships are few; and she's not an official like Quang Tu, beholden to present exemplary behaviour. "I'm fine," *The Tiger in the Banyan* says. She's mourning; but it doesn't interfere with her activities: after all, she's been steeling herself for this since Father died. She didn't expect it to come so painfully, so soon, but she was prepared for it—braced for it in a way that Quang Tu will never be.

The Dream of Millet is silent for a while—*The Tiger in the Banyan* can feel her, through the void that separates them—can feel the radio waves nudging her hull; the quick jab of probes dipping into her internal network and collating together information about her last travels. "You're not 'fine'," *The Dream of Millet* says. "You're slower, and you go into deep spaces further than you should. And—" she pauses, but it's more for effect than anything else. "You've been avoiding it, haven't you?"

They both know what she's talking about: the space station Mother was putting together; the project to provide a steady, abundant food supply to the Empire.

"I've had no orders that take me there," *The Tiger in the Banyan* says. Not quite a lie; but dangerously close to one. She's been…better off knowing the station doesn't exist—unsure that she could face it at all. She doesn't care about Tuyet Hoa, or the mem-implants; but the station was such a large part of Mother's life that she's not sure she could stand to be reminded of it.

She is a mindship: her memories never grow dim or faint; or corrupt. She remembers songs and fairytales whispered through her corridors; remembers walking with Mother on the First Planet, smiling as Mother pointed out the odder places of the Imperial City, from the menagerie to the temple where monks worship an Outsider clockmaker—remembers Mother frail and bowed in the last days, coming to rest in the heartroom, her laboured breath filling *The Tiger in the Banyan*'s corridors until she, too, could hardly breathe.

She remembers everything about Mother; but the space station—the place where Mother worked away from her children; the project Mother could barely talk about without breaching confidentiality—is forever denied to her memories; forever impersonal, forever distant.

"I see," *The Dream of Millet* says. Again, faint disapproval; and another feeling *The Tiger in the Banyan* can't quite place—reluctance? Fear of impropriety? "You cannot live like that, child."

Let me be, *The Tiger in the Banyan* says; but of course she can't say that; not to a ship as old as *The Dream of Millet*. "It will pass," she says. "In the meantime, I do what I was trained to do. No one has reproached me." Her answer borders on impertinence, deliberately.

"No. And I won't," *The Dream of Millet* says. "It would be inappropriate of me to tell you how to manage your grief." She laughs, briefly. "You know there are people worshipping her? I saw a temple, on the Fifty-Second Planet."

An easier, happier subject. "I've seen one too," *The Tiger in the Banyan* says. "On the Thirtieth Planet." It has a statue of Mother, smiling as serenely as a bodhisattva—people light incense to her to be helped in their difficulties. "She would have loved this." Not for the fame or the worship, but merely because she would have found it heartbreakingly funny.

"Hmmm. No doubt." *The Dream of Millet* starts moving away; her comms growing slightly fainter. "I'll see you again, then. Remember what I said."

The Tiger in the Banyan will; but not with pleasure. And she doesn't like the tone with which the other ship takes her leave; it suggests she is going to do something—something typical of the old, getting *The Tiger in the Banyan* into a position where she'll have no choice but to acquiesce to whatever *The Dream of Millet* thinks of as necessary.

Still…there is nothing that she can do. As *The Tiger in the Banyan* leaves the orbital onto her next journey, she sets a trace on *The Dream of Millet*; and monitors it from time to time. Nothing the other ship does seems untoward or suspicious; and after a while *The Tiger in the Banyan* lets the trace fade.

As she weaves her way between the stars, she remembers.

Mother, coming onboard a week before she died—walking by the walls with their endlessly scrolling texts, all the poems she taught *The Tiger in the Banyan* as a child. In the low gravity, Mother seemed almost at ease; striding once more onboard the ship until she reached the heartroom. She'd sat with a teacup cradled in her lap—dark tea, because she said she needed a strong taste to wash down the drugs they plied her with—the heartroom filled with a smell like churned earth, until *The Tiger in the Banyan* could almost taste the tea she couldn't drink.

"Child?" Mother asked.

"Yes?"

"Can we go away—for a while?"

She wasn't supposed to, of course; she was a mindship, her travels strictly bounded and codified. But she did. She warned the space station; and plunged into deep spaces.

Mother said nothing. She'd stared ahead, listening to the odd sounds; to the echo of her own breath, watching the oily shapes spread on the walls—while *The Tiger in the Banyan* kept them on course; feeling stretched and scrunched, pulled in different directions as if she were swimming in rapids. Mother was mumbling under her breath; after a while, *The Tiger in the Banyan* realised it was the words of a song; and, to accompany it, she broadcast music on her loudspeakers.

Go home to study

I shall wait nine months, I shall wait ten autumns...

She remembers Mother's smile; the utter serenity on her face—the way she rose after they came back to normal spaces, fluid and utterly graceful; as if all pain and weakness had been set aside for this bare moment; subsumed in the music or the travel or both. She remembers Mother's quiet words as she left the heartroom.

"Thank you, child. You did well."

"It was nothing," she'd said, and Mother had smiled, and disembarked—but *The Tiger in the Banyan* had heard the words Mother wasn't speaking. Of course it wasn't nothing. Of course it had meant something;

to be away from it all, even for a bare moment; to hang, weightless and without responsibilities, in the vastness of space. Of course.

A hundred and three days after Mother's death, a message comes, from the Imperial Palace. It directs her to pick up an Embroidered Guard from the First Planet; and the destination is...

Had she a heart, this is the moment when it would stop.

The Embroidered Guard is going to Mother's space station. It doesn't matter why; or how long for—just that she's meant to go with him. And she can't. She can't possibly...

Below the order is a note, and she knows, too, what it will say. That the ship originally meant for this mission was *The Dream of Millet*; and that she, unable to complete it, recommended that *The Tiger in the Banyan* take it up instead.

Ancestors...

How dare she?

The Tiger in the Banyan can't refuse the order; or pass it on to someone else. Neither can she rail at a much older ship—but if she could—ancestors, if she could...

It doesn't matter. It's just a place—one with a little personal significance to her—but nothing she can't weather. She has been to so many places, all over the Empire; and this is just one more.

Just one more.

The Embroidered Guard is young, and callow; and not unkind. He boards her at the First Planet, as specified—she's so busy steeling herself that she forgets to greet him, but he doesn't appear to notice this.

She's met him before, at the funeral: the one who apologetically approached Quang Tu; who let him know Mother's mem-implants wouldn't pass to him.

Of course.

She finds refuge in protocol: it's not her role to offer conversation to her passengers, especially not those of high rank or in imperial service, who would think it presumption. So she doesn't speak; and he keeps busy in his cabin, reading reports and watching vids, the way other passengers do.

Just before they emerge from deep spaces, she pauses; as if it would make a difference—as if there were a demon waiting for her; or perhaps something far older and far more terrible; something that will shatter her composure past any hope of recovery.

What are you afraid of? A voice asks within her—she isn't sure if it's Mother or *The Dream of Millet*, and she isn't sure of what answer she'd give, either.

The station isn't what she expected. It's a skeleton; a work in progress; a mass of cables and metal beams with bots crawling all over it; and the living quarters at the centre, dwarfed by the incomplete structure. Almost deceptively ordinary; and yet it meant so much to Mother. Her vision for the future of the Empire; and neither Quang Tu nor *The Tiger in the Banyan* having a place within.

And yet.. and yet, the station has heft. It has meaning—that of a painting half-done; of a poem stopped mid-verse—of a spear-thrust stopped a handspan before it penetrates the heart. It begs—demands—to be finished.

The Embroidered Guard speaks, then. "I have business onboard. Wait for me, will you?"

It is a courtesy to ask; since she would wait, in any case. But he surprises her by looking back, as he disembarks. "Ship?"

"Yes?"

"I'm sorry for your loss." His voice is toneless.

"Don't be," *The Tiger in the Banyan* says.

He smiles then; a bare upturning of the lips. "I could give you the platitudes about your mother living on in her work, if I thought that would change something for her."

The Tiger in the Banyan doesn't say anything, for a while. She watches the station below her; listens to the faint drift of radio communications—scientists calling other scientists; reporting successes and failures and the ten thousand little things that make a project of this magnitude. Mother's vision; Mother's work—people call it her life work, but of course she and Quang Tu are also Mother's life work, in a different way. And she understands, then, why *The Dream of Millet* sent her there.

"It meant something to her," she says, finally. "I don't think she'd have begrudged its completion."

He hesitates. Then, coming back inside the ship—and looking upwards, straight where the heartroom would be—his gaze level, driven by an emotion she can't read: "They'll finish it. The new variety of rice they've found—the environment will have to be strictly controlled to prevent it from dying of cold, but…" He takes a deep, trembling breath. "There'll be stations like this all over the Empire—and it's all thanks to your mother."

"Of course," *The Tiger in the Banyan* says. And the only words that come to her are the ones Mother spoke, once. "Thank you, child. You did well."

She watches him leave; and thinks of Mother's smile. Of Mother's work; and of the things that happened between the work; the songs and the smiles and the stolen moments, all arrayed within her with the clarity and resilience of diamond. She thinks of the memories she carries within her—that she will carry within her for the centuries to come.

The Embroidered Guard was trying to apologise, for the mem-implants; for the inheritance neither she nor Quang Tu will ever have. Telling her it had all been worth it, in the end; that their sacrifice hadn't been in vain.

But the truth is, it doesn't matter. It mattered to Quang Tu; but she's not her brother. She's not bound by anger or rancour; and she doesn't grieve as he does.

What matters is this: she holds all of her memories of Mother; and Mother is here now, with her—forever unchanged, forever graceful and tireless; forever flying among the stars.

A Salvaging of Ghosts

T HUY'S HANDS HAVE JUST CLOSED ON THE GEM—SHE CAN'T FEEL ITS warmth with her gloves, but her daughter's ghost is just by her side, at the hole in the side of the ship's hull, blurred and indistinct—when the currents of unreality catch her. Her tether to *The Azure Serpent*, her only lifeline to the ship, stretches; snaps.

And then she's gone, carried forward into the depths.

ON THE night before the dive, Thuy goes below decks with Xuan and Le Hoa. It's traditional; just as it is traditional that, when she comes back from a dive, she'll claim her salvage and they'll have another rousing party in which they'll drink far too many gems dissolved in rice wine and shout poetry until *The Azure Serpent*'s Mind kindly dampens their incoherent ravings to give others their sleep—but not too much, as it's good to remember life; to know that others onship celebrate surviving one more dive, like notches on a belt or vermillion beads slid on an abacus.

One more. Always one more.

Until, like Thuy's daughter Kim Anh, that one last dive kills you and strands your body out there, in the dark. It's a diver's fate, utterly expected;

but she was Thuy's child—an adult when she died, yet forever Thuy's little girl—and Thuy's world contracts and blurs whenever she thinks of Kim Anh's corpse, drifting for months in the cold alien loneliness of deep spaces.

Not for much longer; because this dive has brought them back where Kim Anh died. One last evening, one last fateful set of drinks with her friends, before Thuy sees her daughter again.

Her friends… Xuan is in a bad mood. No gem-drinking on a pre-dive party, so she nurses her rice wine as if she wishes it contains other things, and contributes only monosyllables to the conversation. Le Hoa, as usual, is elated; talking too much and without focus—dealing with her fears through drink, and food, and being uncharacteristically expansive.

"Nervous, lil' sis?" she asks Thuy.

Thuy stares into the depth of her cup. "I don't know." It's all she's hoped for; the only chance she'll ever get that will take her close enough to her daughter's remains to retrieve them. But it's also a dangerous dive into deep spaces, well into layers of unreality that could kill them all. "We'll see. What about you?"

Le Hoa sips at her cup, her round face flushed with drink. She calls up, with a gesture, the wreck of the mindship they're going to dive into; highlights, one after the other, the strings of gems that the scanners have thrown up. "Lots of easy pickings, if you don't get too close to the wreck. And that's just the biggest ones. Smallest ones won't show up on sensors."

Which is why they send divers. Or perhaps merely because it's cheaper and less of an investment to send human beings, instead of small and lithe mindships that would effortlessly survive deep spaces, but each cost several lifetimes to build and properly train.

Thuy traces, gently, the contours of the wreck on the hologram—there's a big hole in the side of the hull, something that blew up in transit, killing everyone onboard. Passengers' corpses have spilled out like innards—all unrecognisable of course, flesh and muscles disintegrated, bones slowly torn and broken and compressed until only a string of gems remains to mark their presence.

Kim Anh, too, is gone: nothing left of Thuy's precocious, foolhardy daughter who struggled every morning with braiding her hair—just a scattering of gems they will collect and sell offworld, or claim as salvage and drink away for a rush of short-lived euphoria.

There isn't much to a gem—just that familiar spike of bliss, no connection to the dead it was salvaged from. Deep spaces strip corpses, and compress them into...these. Into an impersonal, addictive drug.

Still...still, divers cannibalise the dead; and they all know that the dead might be them, one day. It's the way it's always been done, on *The Azure Serpent* and all the other diver-ships: the unsaid, unbreakable traditions that bind them all.

It didn't use to bother Thuy so much, before Kim Anh died.

"Do you know where she is?" Xuan asks.

"I'm not sure. Here, perhaps." Thuy points, carefully, to somewhere very near the wreck of the ship. "It's where she was when—"

When her suit failed her. When the comms finally fell silent.

Xuan sucks in a sharp breath. "Tricky." She doesn't try to dissuade Thuy, though. They all know that's the way it goes, too.

Le Hoa attempts, forcefully, to change the subject. "Two more dives and Tran and I might have enough to get married. A real couple's compartment, can you imagine?"

Thuy forces a smile. She hasn't drunk enough; but she just doesn't feel like rice wine: it'll go to her head, and if there's any point in her life when she needs to be there; to be clear-headed and prescient... "We'll all get together and give you a proper send-off."

All their brocade clothes retrieved from storage, and the rice wine they've been saving in long-term compartments onboard the ship taken out, sipped at until everything seems to glow; and the small, round gem-dreams dumplings—there's no actual gems in them, but they're deliberately shaped and positioned like a string of gems, to call for good fortune and riches to fall into the newlyweds' hands, for enough that they can leave the ship, leave this life of dives and slow death...

Kim Anh never had a chance for any of this. When she died, she'd barely begun a relationship with one of the older divers—a fling, the kind that's not meant to last onboard *The Azure Serpent*. Except, of course, that it was cut short, became frozen in grief and regrets and recriminations.

Thuy and Kim Anh's ex seldom speak; though they do get drunk together, sometimes. And Cong Hoan, her eldest son, has been posted to another diver-ship. They talk on comms, and see each other for festivals and death anniversaries: he's more distant than she'd like, but still alive—all that matters.

"You're morbid again," Xuan says. "I can see it in your face."

Thuy makes a grimace. "I don't feel like drinking."

"Quite obviously," Le Hoa says. "Shall we go straight to the poetry?"

"She's not drunk enough," Xuan says before Thuy can open her mouth.

Thuy flushes. "I'm not good at poetry, in any case."

Le Hoa snorts. "I know. The point isn't that you're good. We're all terrible at it, else we would be officials on a numbered planet with scores of servants at our beck and call. The point is forgetting." She stops, then, looks at Thuy. "I'm sorry."

Thuy forces a shrug she doesn't feel. "Doesn't matter."

Le Hoa opens her mouth, and then closes it again. "Look…" she says. She reaches inside her robes and withdraws something—Thuy knows, even before she opens her hand, what it will be.

The gem is small, and misshapen: the supervisors won't let them keep the big, pretty ones as salvage; those go to offworld customers, the kind rich enough to pay good money for them. It glistens like spilled oil in the light of the teahouse; and in that light, the dumplings on the table and the tea seem to fade into the background; to recede into tasteless, odourless insignificance. "Try this."

"I—" Thuy shakes her head. "It's yours. And before a dive…"

Le Hoa shrugs. "Screw tradition, Thuy. You know it's not going to change anything. Besides, I have some stash. Don't need this one."

Thuy stares at it—thinking of dropping it in the cup and watching it dissolve; of the warmth that will slide down into her stomach when she drinks; of the rising euphoria seizing all her limbs until everything seems to shake with the bliss of desire—of how to step away, for a time; away from tomorrow and the dive, and Kim Anh's remains.

"Come on, lil' sis."

Thuy shakes her head. She reaches for the cup of rice wine, drains it in one gulp; leaving the gem still on the table.

"Time for poetry," she says, aloud. *The Azure Serpent* doesn't say anything—he so seldom speaks, not to the divers, those doomed to die—but he dims the lights and the sound as Thuy stands up, waiting for words to well up from the empty pit in her chest.

Xuan was right: you need to be much drunker than this, for decent verses.

THUY KNOWS where her parents died. The wreck they were scavenging from is on her ancestral altar, at the end of the cycling of holos that shows First and Second Mother go from newlyweds flushed with drink and happiness, to older, greyer women holding their grandchild in their arms, their smile cautious; tentative; as if they already know they will have to relinquish her.

Aboard *The Azure Serpent*, they're legends, spoken of in hushed tones. They went deeper, farther into unreality than anyone else ever has. Divers call them The Long Breathers, and they have their own temple, spreading over three compartments and always smelling of incense. On the temple walls, they are depicted in their diving suits, with the bodhisattva Quan Am showing them the way into an empty cabin; where divers leave offerings praying for good fortune and prosperity.

They left nothing behind. Their suits crumbled with them, and their bodies are deep within the wreck of that mindship: two scatterings of gems in a cabin or a corridor somewhere, forever irretrievable; too deep for anyone to survive retrieval, even if they could be located anymore, in the twenty-one years since they died.

On the altar is Bao Thach: her husband, not smiling but stern and unyielding, as utterly serious in death as he was mischievous and whimsical in life.

She has nothing left of him, either.

Kim Anh... Kim Anh is by her father's side; because she died childless and unmarried; because there is no one else who will mourn her or say the prayers to ease her passage. Thuy isn't the first, or the last, to do this onboard the ship.

There's a box, with enough space for a single gem. For what Thuy has earned the right to salvage from her daughter's body: something tangible, palpable that she can hold onto, not the holos or her own hazy-coloured and shrivelled memories—holding a small, wrinkled baby nursing at her breast and feeling contentment well up in her, stronger than any gem-induced euphoria—Kim Anh at age ten, trying to walk in a suit two sizes too big for her—and a few days before her death, the last meal she and Thuy had in the teahouse: translucent dumplings served with tea the colour of jade, with a smell like cut grass on a planet neither of them will ever live to see.

Kim Anh isn't like Thuy's mothers: she died outside a different mindship, far enough from the wreck that it's possible to retrieve her. Tricky, as Xuan said; but what price wouldn't Thuy pay, to have something of her daughter back?

IN THE darkness at the hole in the ship's hull, Thuy isn't blind. Her suit lights up with warnings—temperature, pressure, distortions. That last is what will kill her: the layers of unreality utterly unsuited to human existence, getting stronger and stronger as the current carries her closer to the wreck of the mindship, crushing her lungs and vital organs like crumpled paper when her suit finally fails.

It's what killed Kim Anh on her last dive; what eventually kills most divers. Almost everyone on *The Azure Serpent*—minus the supervisors, of course—lives with that knowledge, that suspended death sentence.

Thuy would pray to her ancestors—to her mothers the Long Breathers—if only she knew what to ask for.

Thuy closes her hand over the gem. She deactivates the suits' propulsion units and watches her daughter's remains, floating beside her.

Gems and more gems—ranging from the small one she has in her hand to the larger, spherical ones that have replaced the organs in the torso. It's a recent death compared to that of the mindship: the gems still form something vaguely like a human shape, if humans could be drawn in small, round items like droplets of water; or like tears.

And, as the unreality readings spike, the ghost by her side becomes sharper and sharper, until she sees, once more, Kim Anh as she was in life. Her hair is braided—always with the messy ends, the ribbon tied haphazardly; they used to joke that she didn't need a tether, because the ribbon would get caught in the ship's airlock in strands thick and solid enough to bring her back. Her eyes are glinting—with tears, or perhaps with the same oily light as that of a gem.

Hello, Mother.

"Child," Thuy whispers, and the currents take her voice and scatter it—and the ghost nods, but it might as well be at something Thuy can't see.

Long time no see.

They're drifting apart now: hurtling down some dark, silent corridor into the wreck that dilates open like an eye—no no no, not after all of this, not after the certainty she'll lose her own life to the dive—and Thuy shifts, making the propulsion units in the suit strain against the currents, trying to reach Kim Anh; to hold her, to hold *something* of her, down there in the dark...

And then something rushes at her from behind, and she feels a sharp, pressing pain through the nape of the suit—before everything fades away.

WHEN THUY wakes up—nauseous, disoriented—the comms are speaking to her.

"Thuy? Where are you?" It's Xuan's voice, breathless and panicking. "I can help you get back, if you didn't drift too far."

"I'm here," she tries to say; and has to speak three times before her voice stops shaking; becomes audible enough. There is no answer. Wherever she is—and, judging by the readings, it's deep—comms don't emit anymore.

She can't see Kim Anh's body—she remembers scrabbling, struggling to remain close to it as the currents separated them, but now there is nothing. The ghost, though, is still there, in the same room, wavering in the layers of unreality; defined in traceries of light that seem to encompass her daughter's very essence in a few sharp lines.

Thuy still has the gem in her hand, tucked under the guard of her wrist. The rest of her daughter's gems—they've fallen in and are now floating somewhere in the wreck, somewhere far away and inaccessible, and...

Her gaze, roaming, focuses on where she is; and she has to stop herself from gasping.

It's a huge, vaulted room like a mausoleum—five ribs spreading from a central point, and racks of electronics and organics, most of them scuffed and knocked over; pulsing cables converging on each other in tight knots, merging and parting like an alchemist's twisted idea of a nervous system. In the centre is something like a chair, or a throne, all ridges and protrusions, looking grown rather than manufactured. Swarms of repair bots lie quiescent; they must have given up, unable to raise the dead.

The heartroom. The centre of the ship, where the Mind once rested—the small, wilted thing in the throne is all that's left of its corpse. Of course. Minds aren't quite human; and they were made to better withstand deep spaces.

"Thuy? Please come in. Please..." Xuan is pleading now, her voice, growing fainter and fainter. Thuy knows about this too: the loss of hope.

"Thuy? Is that your name?"

The voice is not Xuan's. It's deeper and more resonant; and its sound make the walls shake—equipment shivers and sweats dust; and the cables writhe and twist like maddened snakes.

"I have waited so long."

"You—" Thuy licks dry lips. Her suit is telling her—reassuringly, or not, she's not certain—that unreality has stabilised; and that she has about ten minutes left before her suit fails. Before she dies, holding onto her daughter's gem, with her daughter's ghost by her side. "Who are you?"

It's been years, and unreality has washed over the ship, in eroding tide after eroding tide. No one can have survived. No one, not even the Long Breathers.

Ancestors, watch over me.

"*The Boat Sent by the Bell,*" the voice says. The walls of the room light up, bright and red and unbearable—characters start scrolling across walls on all sides of Thuy, poems and novels and fragments of words bleeding from the oily metal, all going too fast for her to catch anything but bits and pieces, with that touch of bare, disquieting familiarity. "I—am—was—the ship."

"You're alive." He…he should be dead. Ships don't survive. They die, just like their passengers. They—

"Of course. We are built to withstand the farthest, more distorted areas of deep spaces."

"Of course." The words taste like ashes on her mouth. "What have you been waiting for?"

The ship's answer is low, and brutally simple. "To die."

Still alive. Still waiting. Oh, ancestors. When did the ship explode? Thirty, forty years ago? How long has the Mind been down here, in the depths—crippled and unable to move, unable to call out for help; like a human locked in their own body after a stroke?

Seven minutes, Thuy's suit says. Her hands are already tingling, as if too much blood were flooding to them. By her side, Kim Anh's ghost is silent, unmoving, its shape almost too sharp; too real; too alien. "Waiting to die? Then that makes two of us."

"I would be glad for some company." *The Boat Sent by the Bell's* voice is grave, thoughtful. Thuy would go mad, if she were down here for so long—but perhaps mindships are more resistant to this kind of thing. "But your comrades are calling for you."

The comms have sunk to crackles; one of her gloves is flickering away, caught halfway between its normal shape and a clawed, distorted paw with fingers at an impossible angle. It doesn't hurt; not yet. "Yes." Thuy swallows. She puts the gem into her left hand—the good one, the one that's not disappearing, and wraps her fingers around it, as if she were holding Kim Anh. She'd hold the ghost, too, if she could grasp it. "It's too deep. I can't go back. Not before the suit fails."

Silence. Now there's pain—faint and almost imperceptible, but steadily rising, in every one of her knuckles. She tries to flex her fingers; but the pain shifts to a sharp, unbearable stab that makes her cry out.

Five minutes.

At length the ship says, "A bargain, if you will, diver."

Bargains made on the edge of death, with neither of them in a position to deliver. She'd have found this funny, in other circumstances. "I don't have much time."

"Come here. At the centre. I can show you the way out."

"It's—" Thuy grits her teeth against the rising pain—"useless. I told you. We're too deep. Too far away."

"Not if I help you." The ship's voice is serene. "Come."

And, in spite of herself—because, even now, even here, she clings to what she has—Thuy propels herself closer to the centre; lays her hand, her contracting, aching right hand, on the surface of the Mind.

She's heard, a long time ago, that Minds didn't want to be touched this way. That the heartroom was their sanctuary; their skin their own private province, not meant to be stroked or kissed, lest it hurt them.

What she feels, instead, is…serenity—a stretching of time until it feels almost meaningless, her five minutes forgotten; what she sees, for a bare moment, is how beautiful it is, when currents aren't trying to kill you or distort you beyond the bounds of the bearable, and how utterly, intolerably lonely it is, to be forever shut off from the communion of ships and space; to no longer be able to move; to be whole in a body that won't shift, that is too damaged for repairs and yet not damaged enough to die.

I didn't know, she wants to say, but the words won't come out of her mouth. The ship, of course, doesn't answer.

Behind her, the swarms of bots rise—cover her like a cloud of butterflies, blocking off her field of view; a scattering of them on her hand, and a feeling of something sucking away at her flesh, parting muscle from bone.

When *The Boat Sent by the Bell* releases her, Thuy stands, shaking—trying to breathe again, as the bots slough away from her like shed skin and settle on a protuberance near the Mind. Her suit has been patched and augmented; the display, flickering in and out of existence, tells her she has twenty minutes. Pain throbs, a slow burn in the flesh of her repaired hand; a reminder of what awaits her if she fails.

On the walls, the characters have been replaced by a map, twisting and turning from the heartroom to the breach in the hull. "Thirteen minutes and fifty-seven seconds," the ship says, serenely. "If you can propel fast enough."

"I—" She tries to say something, anything. "Why?" is the only thought she can utter.

"Not a gift, child. A bargain." The ship's voice has that same toneless, emotionless serenity to it—and she realises that *The Boat Sent by the Bell* has gone mad after all; cracks in the structure small and minute, like a fractured porcelain cup, it still holds water, but it's no longer *whole*. "Where the bots are…tear that out, when you leave."

"The bots could have done that for you," Thuy says.

If the ship were human, he would have shaken his head. "No. They can repair small things, but not.. this."

Not kill. Not even fix the breach in the hull, or make the ship mobile. She doesn't know why she's fighting back tears—it's not even as if she knew the ship, insofar as anyone can claim to know a being that has lived for centuries.

She moves towards the part the bots have nestled on, a twisted protuberance linked to five cables, small enough to fit into her hand, beating and writhing, bleeding iridescent oil over her fingers. The bots rise, like a swarm of bees, trying to fight her. But they're spent from their repairs, and their movements are slow and sluggish. She bats them away, as easily as one would bat a fly—sends them flying into walls dark with the contours of the ship's map, watches them bleed oil and machine guts all over the heart-room, until not one remains functional.

When she tears out the part, *The Boat Sent by the Bell* sighs, once—and then it's just Thuy and the ghost, ascending through layers of fractured, cooling corpse.

LATER—MUCH, MUCH later, after Thuy has crawled, breathless, out of the wreck, with two minutes to spare—after she's managed to radio Xuan—after they find her another tether, whirl her back to the ship and the impassive doctor—after they debrief her—she walks back to her compartment. Kim Anh's ghost comes with her, blurred and indistinct; though no one but Thuy seems to be able to see it.

She stands for a while in the small space, facing the ancestral altar. Her two mothers are watching her, impassive and distant—the Long Breathers, and who's to say she didn't have their blessing, in the end?

Kim Anh is there too, in the holos—smiling and turning her head to look back at something long gone—the box on the altar awaiting its promised gem; its keepsake she's sacrificed so much for. Someone—Xuan, or Le Hoa, probably—has laid out a tray with a cup of rice wine, and the misshapen gem she refused back in the teahouse.

"I didn't know," she says, aloud. *The Azure Serpent* is silent, but she can feel him listening. "I didn't know ships could survive."

What else are we built for? whispers *The Boat Sent by the Bell*, in her thoughts; and Thuy has no answer.

She fishes inside her robes, and puts Kim Anh's gem in the palm of her right hand. They allowed her to keep it as salvage, as a testament to how much she's endured.

The hand looks normal, but feels…odd, distant, as if it were no longer part of her, the touch of the gem on it an alien thing, happening to her in another universe.

Her tale, she knows, is already going up and down the ship—she might yet find out they have raised her an altar and a temple, and are praying to her as they pray to her mothers. On the other side of the table, by the blind wall that closes off her compartment, her daughter's ghost, translucent and almost featureless, is waiting for her.

Hello, Mother.

She thinks of *The Boat Sent by the Bell*, alone in the depths—of suits and promises and ghosts, and remnants of things that never really die, and need to be set free.

"Hello, child," she whispers. And, before she can change her mind, drops the gem into the waiting cup.

The ghost dissolves like a shrinking candle-flame; and darkness closes in—silent and profound and peaceful.

Pearl

I<small>N</small> D<small>A</small> T<small>RANG</small>'<small>S</small> <small>NIGHTMARES</small>, P<small>EARL</small> <small>IS</small> <small>ALWAYS</small> <small>LEAVING</small>—<small>DARTING</small> away from him, toward the inexorable maw of the sun's gravity, going into a tighter and tighter orbit until no trace of it remains—he's always reaching out, sending a ship, a swarm of bots—calling upon the remoras to move, sleek and deadly and yet too agonizingly slow; to do anything, to save what they can.

Too late. Too late.

It wasn't always like this, of course.

In the beginning…in the beginning…his thoughts fray and scatter away, like cloth held too close to a flame. How long since he's last slept? The Empress's courtier was right—but no, no, that's not it. The Empress doesn't understand. None of them understand.

In the beginning, when he was still a raw, naive teenager, there was a noise, in the hangar. He thought it was just one of the countless remoras, dipping in and out of the room—his constant companions as he studied for the imperial examination, hovering over his shoulder to stare at the words; nudging him when one of them needed repairs they couldn't provide themselves. And once—just after Inner Grandmother's death, when Mother had been reeling from the loss of her own mother and, when he'd come running to the hangar with a vise around his chest—he'd seen them weaving and dancing in a pattern beautiful beyond words as he stood transfixed, with tears running down his cheeks.

"Can you wait?" Da Trang asked, not looking away from the text in his field of vision. "I'm trying to work out the meaning of a line." He was no scholar, no favored to be graced with a tutor or with mem-implants of his ancestors: everything he did was like moving through tar, every word a tangle of meanings and connotations he needed to unpack, every clever allusion something he needed to look up.

A nudge, then; and, across his field of vision, lines—remoras didn't have human names, but it was the one he thought of as Teacher, because it was one of the oldest ones; and because it was always accompanied by a swarm of other remoras with which it appeared to be in deep conversation.

>Architect. Need to see.<

Urgent, then, if Teacher was attempting to communicate—remoras could use a little human speech, but it was hard work, tying up their processes—they grew uncannily still as they spoke, and once he'd seen a speaking remora unable to dodge another, more eager one.

He raised his gaze, and saw...

Teacher and another remora, Slicer; both with that same look of intent sleekness, as if they couldn't hold still for long without falling apart—and, between them, a third one, looking...somehow wrong. Patched up, like all remoras—leftovers from bots and ships that had gone all but feral, low-level intelligences used for menial tasks. And yet...

The hull of the third remora was painted—engraved with what looked like text at first, but turned out to be other characters, long, weaving lines in a strange, distorted alphabet Da Trang couldn't make out.

>Is Pearl,< Teacher said, on the screen. >For you.<

"I don't understand," Da Trang said slowly. He dismissed the text; watched the third remora—something almost graceful in the way it floated, like a calligraphy from a master, suggesting in a few strokes the shape of a bird or of a snake. "Pearl?"

Pearl moved; came to stand close to him—nudging him, like a pet or favorite bot—he'd never felt that or done that, and he felt obscurely embarrassed, as if he'd given away some intimacy that should have been better saved for a parent, a sibling, or a spouse.

>Architect.< Pearl's lines were the same characters as on its hull for a brief moment; and then they came into sharp focus as the remora lodged itself on his shoulder, against his neck—he could feel the heat of the ship, the endless vibrations of the motor through the hull, like a secret heartbeat. >Pleased. Will help.<

Da Trang was about to say he didn't need help; and then Pearl burrowed close to him—a sharp, painful stab straight into his flesh; and before he had time to cry out, he saw—

The hangar, turned into flowing lines like a sketch of a Grand Master of Design Harmony; the remoras, Slicer and Teacher, already on the move, with little labels listing their speed, their banking angles; their age and the repairs they'd undergone—the view expanding, taking in the stars beyond the space station, all neatly labeled, every wavelength of their spectrum cataloged—he tried to move, to think beyond the confines of the vision the ship had him trapped in; to remember the poem he'd been reading— and abruptly the poem was there, too, the lines about mist over the water and clouds and rain; and the references to sexual foreplay, the playfulness of the writer trying to seduce her husband—the homage to the famed poetess Dong Huong through the reuse of her metaphor about frost on jade flowers, the reference to the bird from Viet on Old Earth, always looking southward…

And then Pearl released him; and he was on his knees on the floor, struggling for breath. "What—what—" Even words seemed to have deserted him.

>Will help,< Pearl said.

Teacher, firmer and more steady, a rock amidst the turmoil in his mind. >Built Pearl for you, Architect. For…examinations?< A word the remora wasn't sure of; a concept Da Trang wasn't even sure Teacher understood.

>For understanding,< Slicer said. >Everything.< If it had been human, the remora would have sounded smug.

"I can't—" Da Trang pulled himself upward; looked at Pearl again. "You made it?"

>Can build others,< Teacher said.

"Of course. I wasn't doubting that. I just—" He looked at Pearl again and finally worked out what was different about it. The others looked cobbled together of disparate parts—grabbing what they could from space debris and scraps and roughly welding it into place—but Pearl was...not perfect, but what you would get if you saved the best of everything you found drifting in space, and put it together, not out of necessity, not out of a desire for immediate survival or return to full functionality—but with a carefully thought-out plan; a desire for...stability? "It's beautiful," he said at last.

>We built,< Teacher said. >As thanks. And because...< A pause, and then another word, blinking on the screen. >We can build *better*.<

Not beauty, then; but hope, and longing; and the best for the future. Da Trang found his lips twisting in a bitter smile; shaping words of comfort, or something equally foolish to give a remora—some human emotions to a being that had none.

Before he could speak up, though, there came the patter of feet. "Lil' brother, lil' brother!" It was his sister Cam, out of breath. Da Trang got up— Pearl hovering again at his shoulder, the warmth of metal against his neck.

"What—" Cam stopped, looked at him. "What in heaven is this?"

Pearl nudged closer; he felt it nip the surface of his skin—and some of that same trance rose in him again, the same sense that he was seeing the bones of the orbital, the breath of the dragon that was the earth and the void between the stars and the universe—except oddly muted, so that his thoughts merely seemed far away to him, running beneath a pane of glass. He could read Cam—see the blood beating in her veins, the tension in her hands and in her arms. Something was worrying her; beyond her usual disapproval of a brother who dreamt big and spent his days away from the family home. Pearl?

"This is Pearl," Da Trang said awkwardly.

Cam looked at him—in Pearl's trance, he saw her face contract; saw electrical impulses travel back and forth in her arms. "Fine," she said, with a dismissive wave of her hand. "You were weird enough without a remora pet. Whatever."

So it wasn't that which worried her. "What's on your mind?" Da Trang asked.

Cam jerked. There was no other word for it—her movement would have been barely visible, but Pearl's trance magnified everything; so that for a moment she seemed a puppet on strings, and the puppet master had just stopped her from falling. "How do you know?"

"It's obvious," Da Trang said, trying to keep his voice steady. If he could read her—if he could read people—if he could remember poems and allusions and speak like a learned scholar...

"The Empress is coming," Cam said.

"And?" Da Trang was having a hard time seeing how that related to him. "We're not scholars or magistrates, or rich merchants. We're not going to see her unless we queue up for the procession."

"You don't understand." Cam's voice was plaintive. "The whole Belt is scraping resources together to make an official banquet, and they asked Mother to contribute a dish."

Da Trang was going to say something funny, or flippant, but that stopped him. "I had no idea." Pearl was showing him things—signs of Cam's stress, the panic she barely kept at bay, the desire to flee the orbital before things got any more overwhelming—but he didn't need Pearl for that. Imperial favor could go a long way—could lift someone from the poorer, most outward orbitals of the Scattered Pearls Belt all the way to the First Planet and the Imperial Court—but it could also lead someone into permanent disgrace; into exile and death. It was more than a dish; it would be a statement made by Mother's orbital, by the Belt itself; something they would expect to be both exquisite, and redolent with clever allusions—to the Empress's reign name; to her campaigns, to her closest advisers or her wives...

"Why did they ask Mother?"

"I don't know," Cam said. Blood flowed to her face, and her hands were moments away from clenching. "Because there was no one else. Because they wanted us to fail. Take your pick. What matters is that we can't say no, lest we become disgraced."

"Can you help?" he asked, aloud; and saw Cam startled; and then her face readjusting itself into a complex mixture of—contempt, pity—as she realized he was talking to the remora.

"You really spend too much time here," she said, shaking her head. "Come on."

"Can you help?" Da Trang asked again, and felt Pearl huddle more closely against him; the trance rising to dizzying heights as the remora bit deeper.

>Of course, Architect.<

Days blur and slide against one another; Da Trang's world shrinks to the screen hovering in front of him, the lines of code slowly turning into something else—from mere instructions and algorithms to semiautonomous tasks—and then transfigured, in that strange alchemy where a programmed drone becomes a remora, when coded behaviors and responses learnt by rote turn into something else: something wild and unpredictable, as pure and as incandescent as a newborn wind.

Movement, behind him—a blur of robes and faces, and a familiar voice calling his name, like red-hot irons against the nape of his neck: "Councillor Da Trang."

Da Trang turns—fighting the urge to look at the screen again, at its scrolling lines that whisper he'll fix it if he can write just a few more words, just a few more instructions. "Your Highness." Forces his body into a bow that takes him, sliding, to the floor, on muscles that feel like they've turned to jelly—words surface, from the morass of memory, every one of them tasting like some strange foreign delicacy on his tongue; like something the meaning of which has long since turned to meaningless ashes. "May you reign ten thousand years."

A hand, helping him up: for a moment, horrified, he thinks it's the Empress, but it's just one of the younger courtiers, her face shocked under its coat of ceruse. "He hasn't slept at all, has he? For days. Councillor—"

There's a crowd of them, come into the hangar where he works, on the outskirts of the capital: the Empress and six courtiers, and bodyguards, and attendants. One of the courtiers is staring all around him—seeing walls flecked with rust, maintenance bots that move only slowly: the dingy part of the city, the unused places—the spaces where he can work in peace. There is no furniture: just the screen, and the pile of remoras—the failed ones—stacked against one of the walls. There's room for more, plenty more.

The Empress raises a hand, and the courtier falls silent. "I'm concerned for you, councillor."

"I—" He ought to be awed, or afraid, or concerned, too—wondering what she will do, what she can do to him—but he doesn't even have words left. "I have to do this, Your Highness."

The Empress says nothing for a while. She's a small, unremarkable woman—looking at her, he sees the lines of deep worry etched under her eyes, and the shape of her skull beneath the taut skin of the face. Pearl, were it still here, were it still perching on his shoulder, would have told him—about heartbeats, about body temperature and the moods of the human mind, all he would have needed to read her, to convince her with a few well-placed words, a few devastating smiles. "Pearl is gone, councillor," she says, her voice firm, stating a fact or a decree. "Your remora was destroyed in the heart of the sun."

No, not destroyed. Merely hiding—like a frightened child, not knowing where to find refuge. All he has to do is find the right words, the right algorithms…"Your Highness," he says.

"I could stop it," the Empress said. "Have you bodily dragged from this room and melt every piece of metal here into scrap." Her hand makes a wide gesture, encompassing the quivering remoras stacked against the walls; the one he's working on, with bits and pieces of wires trailing from it, jerking from time to time, like a heart remembering it has to beat on.

No. "You can't," he starts, but he's not too far gone as to forget who she is. Empress of the Dai Viet Empire, mistress of all her gaze and her mindships survey, protector of the named planets, raised and shaped to rule since her birth. "You—" and then he falls silent.

The Empress watches him for a while but says nothing. Is that pity in her face? Surely not. One does not rise high in the Imperial Court on pity or compassion. "I won't," she says at last, and there is the same weariness in her voice, the same hint of mortality within. "You would just find another way to waste away, wouldn't you?"

He's not wasting away. He's...working. Designing. On the verge of finding Pearl. He wants to tell her this, but she's no longer listening—if she ever was.

"Build your remoras, councillor." The Empress remains standing for a while, watching him. "Chase your dreams. After all—" And her face settles, for a while, into bleak amusement. "Not many of us can genuinely say we are ready to die for those."

And then she's gone; and he turns back to the screen, and lets it swallow him again, into endless days and endless nights lit only by the glare of the nearby star—the sun where Pearl vanished with only its cryptic good-bye.

He isn't building a single remora, but a host of them, enough that they can go into the sun; enough to comb through layer after layer of molten matter, like crabs comb through sand—until they finally find Pearl.

None of them comes back, or sends anything back; but then it doesn't matter. He can build more. He must build more—one after another and another, until there is no place in the sun they haven't touched.

The first Da Trang knew of the banquet was footsteps, at the door of the hangar—Mother, Pearl's trance said, analyzing the heavy tread, the vibrations of the breathing through the hangar's metal walls. Worried, too; and he didn't know why.

"Child," Mother said. She was followed by Cam, and their sister Hien; and a host of aunts and uncles and cousins. "Come with me." Even without Pearl, he could see her fear and worry, like a vise around his heart.

"Mother?" Da Trang rose, dismissing the poetry he'd been reading—with Pearl by his side, it was easier to see where it all hung together; to learn, slowly and painstakingly, to enjoy it as an official would; teasing apart layers of meaning one by one, as though eating a three-color dessert.

Mother's face was white, bloodless; and the blood had left her hands and toes, too. "The Empress wants to see the person who cooked the Three Blessings."

Three Blessings: eggs arranged around a hen for happiness and children; deer haunches with pine nuts for longevity; and carp with fishmint leaves cut in the shape of turtle leaves, for prosperity and success as an official. "You did," Da Trang said mildly. But inwardly, his heart was racing. This was…opportunity: the final leap over the falls that would send them flying as a dragon; or tumbling down to earth as piecemeal, broken bodies.

"And you want me to come."

Mother made a small, stabbing gesture—one that couldn't disguise her worry. It was…unsettling to see her that way; hunched and vulnerable and mortally afraid. But Da Trang pushed the thought to the back of his mind. Now wasn't the time. "You were the one who told me what to cook." Her eyes rested on Pearl; moved away. She disapproved; but then she didn't understand what Pearl could do. "And…" She mouthed silent words, but Pearl heard them, all the same.

I need you.

Da Trang shook his head. He couldn't—but he had to. He couldn't afford to let this pass him by. Gently, slowly, he reached for Pearl—felt the remora shudder against his touch, the vibrations of the motors intensifying—if it were human, it would be arching against his touch, trying to move away—he didn't know why Pearl should do this now, when it was perfectly happy snuggling against him, but who could tell what went through a remora's thought processes?

"It's all right," he whispered; and pressed the struggling remora closer to him—just a little farther, enough for his mind to float, free of fear—free of everything, except that strange exhilaration like a prelude of larger things to come.

The banquet room was huge—the largest room in the central orbital—filled with officials in five-panel dresses, merchants in brocade dresses; and, here and there, a few saffron-dressed monks and nuns, oases of calm in the din. Pearl was labeling everyone and everything—the merchants' heart rate and body temperature; the quality of the silk they were wearing; the names of the vast array of dishes on the table and how long each would have taken to prepare. And, beyond the walls of the orbital—beyond the ghostly people and the mass of information that threatened to overwhelm him, there was the vast expanse of space; and remoras weaving back and forth between the asteroids and the Belt, between the sun and the Belt—dancing, as if on a rhythm only they could hear.

At the end of the banquet room was the Empress—Da Trang barely caught a glimpse of her, large and terrible, before he prostrated himself to the ground along with Mother.

"Rise," the Empress said. Her voice was low, and not unkind. "I'm told you're the one who cooked the Three Blessings."

"I did," Mother said. She grimaced, then added, "It was Da Trang who knew what to do."

The Empress's gaze turned to him; he fought the urge to abase himself again, for fear he would say something untoward. "Really," she said. "You're no scholar." If he hadn't been drunk on Pearl's trance, he would have been angry at her dismissal of him.

"No, but I hope to be." Mother's hands tightening; her shame at having such a forward son; such unsuitable ambitions displayed like a naked blade.

The Empress watched him for a while. Her face, whitened with ceruse, was impassive. Beyond her, beyond the courtiers and the fawning administrators, the remoras were slowing down; forming up in a ring that faced toward the same direction—neither the sun nor the Belt, but something he couldn't identify. Waiting, he thought, or Pearl thought, and he couldn't tell what for.

"Master Khong Tu, whose words all guide us, had nothing to say on ambition, if it was in the service of the state or of one's ancestors," the Empress said at last. She was...not angry. Amused, Pearl told him, tracking the minute quirking of the lips, the lines forming at the corner of her eyes. "You are very forward, but manners can be taught, in time." Her gaze stopped at his shoulder, watching Pearl. "What is that?"

"Pearl," Da Trang said slowly.

One of the courtiers moved closer to the Empress—sending her something via private network, no doubt. The Empress nodded. "The Belt has such delightful customs. A remora?"

To her, as to everyone in the room, remoras were low-level artificial intelligences; smaller fishes to the bulk and heft of the mindships who traveled between the stars—like trained animals, not worth more than a moment's consideration. "Yes, Your Highness," Da Trang said. On his shoulder, Pearl hesitated; for a moment he thought it was going to detach itself and flee; but then it huddled closer to him—the trance heightened again, and now he could barely see the Empress or the orbital; just the remoras, spreading in a circle. "Pearl helps me."

"Does it?" The Empress's voice was amused again. "What wisdom does it hold, child? Lines of code? Instructions on how to mine asteroids? That's not what you need to rise in the Imperial Court."

They were out there—waiting—not still, because remoras couldn't hold still, but moving so slowly they might as well be—silent, not talking or communicating with one another, gathered in that perfect circle, and Pearl was feeling their sense of anticipation too; like a coiled spring or a tiger waiting to leap; and it was within him, too, like a flower blossoming in a too-tight chest, pushing his ribs and heart outward, its maddened, confused beating resonating like gunshots in the room.

"Watch," he whispered. "Outside the Belt. It's coming."

The Empress threw him an odd glance—amusement mingled with pity.

"Watch," he repeated, and something in his stance, in his voice, must have caught her, for she whispered something to her courtier; and stood.

Outside, in the void of space; in the freezing cold between orbitals, the remoras waited—and, in the center of their circle, a star caught fire.

It happened suddenly—one moment a pinpoint of light, the next a blaze—and then the next a blaring of alarms aboard the station—the entire room seeming to lurch and change, all the bright lights turned off, the ambient sound drowned by the alarms and the screaming; the food tumbling from the tables, and people clinging to one another as the station lurched again—a merchant lost her footing in a spill of rice wine and fell, her brocade dress spread around her.

On Da Trang's shoulder, Pearl surged—as if it was going outside, as if it was going to join the other remoras watching the star ignite—but then it fell back against Da Trang; and he felt something slide into him: needles with another liquid, which burnt like fire along his spine. At the next lurch of the station, his feet remained steady; his body straight, as if standing at attention; and his muscles steadfastly refusing to answer him—even his vocal cords feeling frozen and stiff. >Don't move.<

Da Trang couldn't have moved, even if he'd wished to; even if he wasn't standing apart, observing it all at a remote, high on Pearl's trance and struggling to make sense of it all—no fear, no panic, merely a distant curiosity. A star wildfire; light waves that were destabilizing the station, frying electronics that had never been meant for such intensity—Pearl's readouts assured him the shielding held, and that radiation levels within the room remained nonlethal for humans, poor but welcome reassurance in the wake of the disaster.

In front of him, the Empress hadn't moved either; with each lurch of the station, she merely sidestepped, keeping her balance as if it were nothing. Of course she would have augments that would go far beyond her subjects', the best her Grand Masters and alchemists could design.

Abruptly, the station stopped lurching, and the lights slowly came back on—though they were white and blinding, nothing like the quiet and refined atmosphere of the banquet; and instead of the ambient sound there was only the low crackle of static. The Empress gazed at him levelly; and then went on, as if their conversation had been merely stopped by someone else's rude interruptions, "In all of the Dai Viet Empire, there is no one who can predict a star wildfire. We can determine when the conditions for the ignition are met, of course; but the scale of such predictions is millennia, if not millions of years. And yet you knew."

Da Trang shook his head. Pearl had withdrawn; he could still see the remoras outside, now utterly still, though Pearl's readouts assured him they were not broken—merely oddly, unnaturally still. Merely...content. Who knew that remoras basked in wildfire? "Pearl knew," he said. "You asked how it helped me. That's how."

The Empress watched him for a while; watched Pearl nestled on his shoulder, the remora's prow wedged in the hollow where his collarbone met his neck. "I see. I think," she said, slowly, softly, "it would be best for you to take your things and come back with us, child."

And like that—just like that, with two simple sentences, and a polite piece of advice that might as well be a command—Da Trang started his rise at the Imperial Court.

Da Trang is watching his latest remora, a sleek, small thing with a bent thruster—even as he does, he sees it move, and the thruster *flows* back into place; and the remora dips its prow, a movement that might as well be a nod; and is gone through the open doorway, following the path of the previous ones—pulling itself upward into the sky, straight toward the sun. Toward silence.

>Architect. We are here.< Da Trang's head jerks up. The words are blinking, in a corner of his field of vision, insistent; and the remora saying this is close by too. It's not one of the ones he made; but it's one he's seen before, a vision from his past when he was still repairing remoras and studying for the imperial examinations—before Pearl, before the Empress. Pitted metal and those broken thrusters at the back; and the wide gash on the right side, that he's never managed to patch; the nub on the prow and the broken-off wing, clumsily repaired with only a basic welder bot...

"Teacher," he whispers, addressing the remora by the name he gave it, all those years ago. "I'm sorry."

Remoras don't have feelings, don't have human emotions. They lie somewhere halfway between ships and bots, outside the careful order of numbered planets; cobbled together from scraps, looking as though they're going to burst apart at any moment.

Behind Teacher is Slicer, and Tumbler, and all the rest of the remoras: the ones who were with him at the very beginning, the ones who made and gave him Pearl.

Teacher's image wavers in and out of focus, and Da Trang fights the urge to turn away, to go back to his code; because he owes Teacher that much. Because Pearl was given to him for safekeeping, and he has lost it.

"I'm sorry," Da Trang says again, though he doesn't even know if Teacher can understand him.

>New things are more easily broken,< Teacher says. Something very like a shrug, and the remora weaving closer to him. >Don't concern yourself, Architect.<

"Are you—are you building another?" Da Trang knows the answer even before he asks.

>Like Pearl? No.< Teacher is silent for a while. >It was flawed, Architect. Too…much vested into a single vessel. We will ponder how to build otherwise.<

Da Trang cannot wait. Cannot stand to be there, with the emptiness on his shoulder, where Pearl used to rest; to gaze at the remoras and the hangar and have nothing about them, no information about their makeup or their speed; all the things Pearl so easily, effortlessly provided him. If he closes his eyes, he can feel again the cold shock of needles sliding into his neck; and the sharpening of the world before the trance kicked in, and everything seemed glazed in light.

Slicer weaves its way to the first pile of remoras in the corner of the hangar: the flawed ones, the ones that wouldn't lift off, that wouldn't come to life, or that started only to crash and burn. It circles them, once, twice, as if fascinated—it never judges, never says anything, but Da Trang can imagine, all too well, what it sees: hubris and failure, time and time again. He's no Grand Master of Design Harmony, no Master of Wind and Water: he can repair a few remoras, but his makings are few, and pitiful, and graceless; nothing like Pearl.

"I have to try," Da Trang whispers. "I have to get it back."

>It was flawed,< Teacher says. >Will not come back.<

They know too, more than the Empress does, that it will take more than a sun's warmth to destroy a remora. That Pearl is still there. That he can still reach it, talk to it—make it come back.

Teacher moves, joins Slicer around the pile of stillborn remoras. >Architect. Use of this?<

No scraps of metal left unused, of course—they scavenge their own dead, make use of anything and everything to build. Once, Da Trang would have found it disquieting; but now all he feels is weariness, and impatience that they're keeping him from his algorithms. "I don't need them anymore. They're...flawed. Take them."

>Architect. Thank you.< He'd have thought they didn't know gratitude, but perhaps they do. Perhaps they've learnt, being so close to humans. Or perhaps they're merely doing so to appease him—and would it really make a difference if that was the case? So many things human are fake and inconstant—like favors. >We will return. Much to ponder.<

"Wait," Da Trang calls, as the remoras move away from his discarded scraps; from the blurred, indistinct remnants of his failures. "Tell me—"

>Architect?<

"I need to know. Was it my fault?" Did he ignore Pearl—was there some harbinger of the things to come—were the odd times the remora fell silent, with its prow pointed toward the sun, a sign of what it secretly yearned for?

Could he...could have stopped it, had he known?

Silence. Then Teacher's answer, slow and hesitant. >We built. We made, from metal and electronics to the spark of life. We didn't *determine*, Architect. It went where it willed. We do not know.<

No answer then, but why had he thought it would be so easy?

On the morning of the day he was to be raised to councillor, Da Trang got up early, with an unexpected queasiness in his stomach—fear of what would happen; of Mother and her dire warnings about Empresses' fickle favorites being right?—no, that wasn't it.

Pearl was gone. He reached out, scratching the callus on his neck, in the place where it usually rested—scanning the room and finding nothing, not even a trace of its presence. "Pearl? Pearl?"

Nothing under the sheets, nothing in the nooks and crannies of the vast room—he turned off everything, every layer of the Purple Forbidden City's communal network, and still he couldn't see Pearl.

Impossible. It wasn't human; it didn't have any desires of its own except to serve Da Trang; to serve the whims of the Empress and her endless curiosity about anything from stellar phenomena to the messages passed between remoras and bots; to the state of the technologies that underpinned the communal network—to be shown off to scientists and alchemists and engineers, its perceptions and insights dissected and analyzed for anything of use to the Empire. It couldn't just go wandering off. It—

Da Trang threw open the doors of his room, startling one of the servants who'd been carrying a tray with a cup of tea—almost absentmindedly, he reached out and straightened the tray before moving on. "Pearl? Pearl?"

Courtiers, startled out of their impassivity, turned their heads to follow him as he ran into courtyard after courtyard, finding nothing but the usual bustle of the court, the tight knots of people discussing politics or poetry or both—an endless sea of officials with jade-colored sashes barely paying attention to him—and still no Pearl, no trace of it or word on his coms.

It was only two bi-hours until the ceremony; and what would he say to the Empress, if Pearl wasn't there—if he couldn't perform any of the feats of use to her, and that distinguished him from the mass of upstart courtiers?

"Pearl?"

He found the remora, finally, in the quarters of the Master of Rites and Ceremonies. The Master was deep in discussion with her students; pointing to something on an interface Da Trang couldn't see. Pearl was in the small room at the end, where they had gathered the necessary supplies for the ceremony.

"Pearl?"

It stood, watching the clothes on the mannequin in the center of the room: the five-panel robe made from the finest brocade with the insignia of the sparrow on the chest—not an official rank attained through merit and examinations, but one reserved for special cases; for emperors' and empresses' fickle favors. On the shoulder was a rest for Pearl, with a small model of the remora.

"What are you doing here?"

Pearl didn't move, or acknowledge him in any way. It was…that same particular intent stillness it had had, back at the time of the first star wild-fire. Waiting—what for? "Is something going to happen? Pearl?"

>Architect.< The words were hesitant—letter after letter slowly materializing in his field of vision. And still Pearl didn't move; didn't head to Da Trang's shoulder, to fill the empty space he couldn't get used to. >Need. Time.<

"What for? The ceremony is in two bi-hours—"

Pearl shifted; and he realized, then, that it had been standing in a shaft of sunlight, its prow turned toward the heavens. >Not meant for this.<

"You were built for this," Da Trang said. Why the strange mood—fear or nervousness? But remoras couldn't feel any of that, surely?

But, then, Pearl wasn't just any remora. *We can build better,* Teacher had said. Better, or merely more unstable? "Come," Da Trang said.

Pearl hovered to the shoulder of the mannequin—nudging the small model they'd made of it, which looked nothing like a remora: bedecked with silk and scraps of translucent cotton. >Not meant for this.< Its prow rose again, toward the sun. >Space. The song of stars. The heartbeat of the universe.<

"We'll be going into space," Da Trang said. "Often enough. I promise." It scared him, now—the Imperial Court wasn't a place to hear the song of the stars or the rhythm of the universe or whatever else it was going on about. "Come."

>Not the same.< Pearl made a small whirring noise.

"They built you to help me," Da Trang said. And, without Pearl, he was nothing—just another dull-witted poor boy, the Empress's favor soon forgotten. "Pearl. Come on." He fought an urge to bodily drag it from the room, like a disobedient child; but it would have been unkind. "Remember Teacher and Slicer and the other remoras? They said they'd built you for me. For the examinations. For understanding."

Come on, come on, come on—if Pearl left him, he didn't know what he'd do, what he'd become; what he could make of the shambles that would be his life—

>Understanding.< Pearl's prow dipped again, toward the mannequin. >Building better.< Again, the same slowness to the words, as if it were considering; and then, to Da Trang's relief, it flew back to him, and the familiar weight settled on his shoulder—the familiar ice-cold feeling of needles biting into his shoulder, the sense of reality becoming unbearably sharp, unbearably clear, everything labeled and parceled and analyzed, from the Master of Rites and Ceremonies' minute frown to the student fighting off sleep in the first row—from the cut and origin of the silk to the fluctuating intensity of the sunlight in the room.

>Can help.< But as Da Trang turned away, he felt Pearl's weight on his shoulder—felt the remora, looking upward at the sun—the pull of the motors, barely suppressed; and he knew that he hadn't managed to quell Pearl's yearnings.

He doesn't sleep—only so many hours in a day, and there are ways to enjoy them all. Not for long, of course, not with the drugs he's pumped himself full of; but what does he care for more time? He *needs* Pearl back, so badly it's like a vise, squeezing his ribs into bloodied shards. Without Pearl, he's nothing: an ex-favorite of the Empress, fallen from her regard—an overambitious boy from the outer edges of the Empire, overreaching and tumbling over the waterfalls instead of soaring, dragonlike, in the wake of imperial favor. But it's Pearl that the Empress was truly interested in—its tidbits on stellar phenomenon, on technologies, on ships and what made them work—what Pearl called the understanding of the universe, with an earnestness that didn't seem to belong in a remora: everything that they put into always moving, never stopping, it put into intent stillness; in that posture on its shoulder where its eyes, if it'd had any, would have bored holes into steel or diamond.

It's still there, in the heart of the sun. Waiting. For him, or for something else; but if Pearl is there, that means he can find it. That means... He doesn't know what he will do when he finds Pearl, how he'll beg or plead or drag it from the sun—but he'll find a way.

It was a routine journey, a shuttle ride between the First Planet and the White Clouds orbital; and the Empress, of course, insisted her new Councillor come with her, to show her the wonders of space.

Da Trang came, because he had no choice—in spite of deep unease—because Pearl had been restless and distant, because he'd tossed and turned at night, trying to think of what he could do and thinking of nothing.

Halfway through the trip, the Empress called for him.

She was in her cabin, surrounded by her courtiers—they were all sitting on silk cushions and sipping tea from a cup as cracked as eggshells. In front of her was a hologram of space as seen from the prow of the ship. As Da Trang entered, the view blurred and shifted, and became the outside of the orbital—except that the stars were dimmer than they ought to have been.

"Councillor," the Empress said. "I thought you would enjoy seeing these."

Pearl snuggled closer to Da Trang—needles extended, the blissful cold spreading outward from the pinpricks, the trance rising—extending to the outside, narrowing until he could see the bots maneuvering nano-thin filaments, unfolding a large, dark shape like a spread cloth behind the orbital.

Void-nets. Da Trang had sat in nightlong sessions with the Ministry of War's engineers, describing to them what Pearl saw—what Pearl thought—how the remora could even analyze the dust of stars, the infinitesimal amounts of matter carried by the wind in the void of space—and how, in turn, those could be trapped.

He hadn't thought—

"Your Highness," Da Trang said, struggling to remember how to bow. "I had no idea this was such a momentous occasion."

"The Ministry of War has been testing prototypes for a while—but it is the first time a void-net is deployed in the vicinity of a Numbered Planet, to be sure." The Empress was almost...thoughtful. "All to your credit, and Pearl's."

Another nudge; but he had no need to see heartbeats or temperature to catch the anger of the other courtiers. As if they'd ever be capable of matching him...

"Tell us," the Empress said. "What will we find, in your nets?"

A brief moment of panic, as nothing happened—as Pearl didn't move, the thought that it was going to be today, of all days, when the remora failed him—and then a stab so deep under his collarbone it was almost painful—and the view shifting, becoming dotted with hundreds of pinpoints of colored lights, each labeled with a name and concentration. "Suffocating metal 5.3 percent," he whispered. "Frozen water 3 percent. Gray adamantine crystals 9.18 percent..." On and on, a litany of elements, labeled and weighed: everything the Empire would decant to fuel its machines and stations and planets, names and images and every use they could be put to, a flood of information that carried him along—such a terrible, breathless sense of being the center, of knowing everything that would come to pass...

He came to with a start, finding Pearl all but inert against him; softly vibrating on his shoulder. The Empress was looking at him and smiling—her face and body relaxed, her heartbeat slow and steady. "A good take. The Ministry of War should be satisfied, I should think." She watched the screens with mild curiosity. "Tell me what you see."

"Colors," Da Trang said. Even with Pearl quiescent, he could make them out—slowly accreting, the net bulging slightly outward as it filled—the bots straining under the pressure. "A dance of lights—"

He never got to finish the sentence.

On his shoulder, Pearl surged—gone before Da Trang's flailing arms could stop it, tearing through the cabin—and then, with scarcely a pause, through the walls of the ship as if they were nothing more than paper;

alarms blaring, the Empress and him thrown to the ground as the cabin sealed itself—but Pearl was already gone. Fumbling, Da Trang managed to call up a view from ships around the orbital—a slow zoom on Pearl, weaving and racing toward the stars, erratic and drunken; stopping for a bare moment, and then plunging toward the heart of the sun.

>Architect. Farewell. Must be *better*. Must show them.<

And then there was nothing—just emptiness on his shoulder like a hole in his own heart, and the memory of those words—and he could not tell if they were angry or sad or simply a statement of fact.

Nothing.

Days blur and slide against one another; his world shrinks to the screen hovering in front of him, the lines of code slowly turning into something else. He can barely read them now, he's merely inputting things from rote—his hands freeze, at odd intervals; and his vision goes entirely black, with whole chunks of time disappearing—everything oddly disjointed.

Except for his remoras.

They're sleek and beautiful and heartbreaking now, moving with the grace of officials and fighter-monks—one by one, pulling themselves from the floor, like dancers getting up and stretching limb after limb—still for a heartbeat, their prows turned toward him, and then gone toward the sun, a blur of speed he cannot follow anymore—as darkness grows and encroaches on his field of vision.

He must build more.

Remoras come and go: Teacher, Slicer, and all the others, taking from the pile of scraps, making small noises as they see a piece of metal or a connector; slowly, determinedly taking apart his earlier efforts—the tearing sound of sheets of metal stretched past the breaking point; the snapping of cables wrenched out of their sockets; the crackling sound of ion thrusters taken apart—his failures, transfigured into life—patched onto other remoras, other makings; going on and on and on, past Da Trang's pitiful, bounded existence—going on, among the stars.

"Tell me," he says, aloud.

>Architect. What should I tell you?< One of them—Slicer, Teacher, he's not sure he can tell them apart anymore: save for his own remoras, everything seems small and blurred, diminished into insignificance. Everything seems dimmer and smaller, and even his own ambitions feel shriveled, far away, belonging to someone else, a stranger with whom he shares only memories.

"Pearl wanted to be better than you. It said so, before it left. Tell me what it means."

Silence, for a while. Then letters, steadily marching through his darkening field of vision. >Everything strives. It couldn't be better than us, Architect. It is—<

"Flawed. I know."

>Then you understand.<

"No, I don't. That's not what I want. I want to—I need to—" He stops, then; thinks of remoras; of scarce resources that have to be endlessly recycled; of that hunger to rebuild themselves, to build others, that yearning that led to Pearl's making.

And he sees it, then. "It doesn't matter. Thank you, Slicer." He stifles a bitter laugh. Everything strives.

>I am Teacher.<

Its words are almost gentle, but Da Trang no longer cares. He stares ahead, at the screen; at the blurred words upon it, the life's blood he fed into his remoras; making them slowly, painstakingly, and sending them one by one into the heart of the sun. He thinks of the remoras' hopes for the future; and of things that parents pass on to their children, and makers to their creations. He knows now that Pearl, in the end, is like Teacher, like Slicer, no better or no different; moved by the same urges and hungers. He thinks of the fires of the sun, the greatest forge in the system; and of Pearl, struggling to understand how things worked, from the smallest components of matter to mindships and humans—he'd thought it was curiosity, but now he sees what drove it. What still drives it.

If you know how things work, you can make them.

Darkness, ahead and behind him; slowly descending upon the screen—the remoras dancing before him, scavenging their own to survive, to make others.

Yearnings. Hunger. The urge to build its own makings, just as it was once built.

Must be better.

Must build better.

And as he slides into shadows—as his nerveless fingers leave the keyboard, his body folding itself, hunched over as if felled by sleep—he thinks of the other remoras, taking their own apart—thinks of the ones he made, the ones he sent into the heart of the sun; and he sees, with agonizing clarity, what he gave Pearl.

Not tools to drag it back or to contact it; but offerings—metal and silicon chips and code; things to be taken apart and grafted; to be scavenged for anything salvageable—the base from which a remora can be forged.

As his eyes close—just for a moment, just for a heartbeat, he sees Pearl—not the remora he remembers, the sleek making of Teacher and Slicer, but something else—something *changed*, reshaped by the heat of the sun, thickened by accreted metal scooped from the heart of a star; something slick and raw and incandescent, looming over him like a heavenly messenger, the weight of its presence distorting the air.

Darkness, ahead and behind him—rising to fill the entire world; and everything he was, his lines of code, his remoras, scattering and fragmenting—into the fires of the sun, to become Pearl's own makings, reforged and reborn; and with no care for human toil or dreams or their petty ambitions.

There is no bringing Pearl back. There is no need to.

And as his eyes close for the last time, he smiles, bitterly—because it is not what he longed for, but it is only fair.

>Farewell, Architect.<

And Pearl's voice, booming, becomes his entire world, his beginning and his ending—and the last thing he hears before he is borne away, into the void between the stars.

Author's Note

I DON'T remember where I first heard the tale of Dã Tràng and the Pearl, but it's been rattling around my head for a while. I was always struck by its final few lines: after the loss of the pearl, Dã Tràng exhausts himself looking for it, dies, and is reincarnated as a small sand-digger crab (which bears his name in Vietnamese). I've always had a weakness for metamorphosis tales, and this was a particularly dramatic one! I wanted to retell it as a spare opera, because it's what I usually do: a lot of my science fiction has roots both in fairy tales and in science. It seemed pretty natural to me that the equivalent of animals in a fairy tale would be low-level AIs: the remoras, who have formed a parallel society on the edge of the human one; and that Pearl would be, not a thing, but a living being—a special remora made by a class of beings who kept remaking and modifying themselves as necessity dictated (there's more than a hint of the golem in Terry Pratchett's *Feet of Clay* in Pearl). Once I had that nailed into place, the story pretty much wrote itself. (Okay, no. There was blood, sweat, and tears, but that's business as usual!)

Children of Thorns,
Children of Water

With thanks to Stephanie Burgis, Fran Wilde and Kate Elliott

IT WAS A LARGE, MAGNIFICENT ROOM WITH INTRICATE PATTERNS OF ivy branches on the tiles, and a large mirror above a marble fireplace, the mantelpiece crammed with curios from delicate silver bowls to Chinese blue-and-white porcelain figures: a clear statement of casual power, to leave so many riches where everyone could grab them.

Or rather, it would have been, if the porcelain hadn't been cut-rate— the same bad quality the Chinese had foisted on the Indochinese court in Annam—the mirror tarnished, with mould growing in one corner, spread down far enough that it blurred features, and the tiling cracked and chipped in numerous places—repaired, but not well enough that Thuan couldn't feel the imperfections under his feet, each one of them a little spike in the *khi* currents of magic around the room.

Not that Thuan was likely to be much impressed by the mansions of Fallen angels, no matter how much of Paris they might claim to rule. He snorted disdainfully, an expression cut short when Kim Cuc elbowed him in the ribs. "Behave," she said.

"You're not my mother." She was his ex-lover, as a matter of fact; and older than him, and never let him forget that.

"Next best thing," Kim Cuc said, cheerfully. "I can always elbow further down, if you insist."

Thuan bit down the angry retort. The third person in the room—a dusky-skinned, young girl of Maghrebi descent, who'd introduced herself as Leila—was looking at them with fear in her eyes. "We're serious," he said, composing his face again. "We're not going to ruin your chances to enter House Hawthorn, promise."

They were a team: that was what they'd been told, as the House dependents separated the crowd before the House in small groups; that their performance would be viewed as a whole, and their chance to enter the House weighed accordingly. Though no rules had been given, and nothing more said, either, as dependents led them to this room and locked them in. At least he was still with Kim Cuc, or he'd have been hopelessly lost.

For people like Leila—for the Houseless, the desperate—it was their one chance to escape the streets, to receive food and shelter and the other tangible benefits of a House's protection.

For Thuan and Kim Cuc, though…the problem was rather different. Their fate, too, would be rather different, if anyone found out who they really were. No House in Paris liked spies, and Hawthorn was not known for its leniency.

"You're relatives?" Leila asked.

"In a manner of speaking." Kim Cuc was cheerful again, which meant she was about to reproach him once more. "He's the disagreeable one. We work in the factories." They'd agreed on this as the most plausible cover story: they had altered their human shapes, slightly, to make their hands thinner and more scarred. They didn't need to fake the gaunt faces and brittle hair: in the days after the war that had devastated the city, magical pollution affected everyone.

"The factories. The ones behind the stations?"

Kim Cuc nodded. She looked at her lap, thoughtfully. "Yes. Only decent jobs there are, for Annamites in this city."

"That's—" Leila started. The House factories by the ruined train stations employed a host of seamstresses and embroiderers, turning them blind and crooked-handed in a short span. "People don't last long in there."

Kim Cuc looked at her lap again as if embarrassed. "It sucks the life out of you, but it pays well. Well, decent considering it's not for House dependents." She fingered her bracelet. It and its matching twin on the other side looked like cheap, gilded stuff, the kind of wedding gifts the Annamite community gave each other, but they were infused with a wealth of Fallen magic. If found out and pressed, she'd say they were savings for an upcoming operation—not an uncommon thing in devastated Paris, where the air corroded lungs and caused strange fungi to bloom within bones and muscle. "What about you?"

Leila's face froze as she exhaled. "Gang," she said, shortly. "The Deep Underground Dreamers, before they got beaten by the Red Mambas."

"Ah," Kim Cuc said. "And the Red Mambas didn't want you?"

Leila's gaze was answer enough: haunted and taut, and more adult than it should have been. Beneath her hemp shirt and patched-up skirt, her body was thin, and no doubt bruised. Thuan felt obscurely ashamed. He and Kim Cuc were only playing at being Houseless. The dragon kingdom under the waters of the Seine might be weakened, its harvests twisted out of shape by Fallen magic, but they still had enough to eat and drink, and beds to sleep in they didn't need to fight or trade favours for. "Sorry," he said.

"Don't be," Leila said. And, when the silence got too awkward, "So what are we supposed to do?"

"Damned if I know." Thuan got up, and picked up one of the figurines from the mantelpiece. It was a shepherdess with a rather improbable waistline, carrying a small and perfectly fashioned lamb in her arms. One of her eyes was slightly larger than the other, an odd effect that most mortals wouldn't have picked up on.

There is one day of the year when House Hawthorn takes in the Houseless, and trains them as servants or potential dependents. One of you needs to get in.

Hawthorn was the kingdom's closest and most uncomfortable neighbour, and they were getting more and more pressing. Till recently, they had shown no interest in the Seine or its underwater cities. But now they were encroaching on dragon territory, and no one at the imperial court had any idea of why or what the stakes were.

We need an agent in the House.

Kim Cuc was fascinated by Fallen magic and by the Houses. Thuan—a dragon, but a minor son of a minor branch of the imperial family—just happened to be the definition of convenient and expendable.

He'd have cursed, if he hadn't been absolutely sure that Kim Cuc would elbow him again. Or worse, continue the small talk with Leila, picking up on all of Thuan's imperfections as if he weren't there. Trust her to share secrets with someone who wasn't even a dragon, or a relative.

The door opened. Thuan, startled, put the shepherdess back on the mantelpiece, and straightened up, feeling for all the world as though he'd been caught stealing dumplings from the kitchens by one of his aunts.

The newcomer was a Fallen, with a round, plump face, and the same slight radiance to her skin as all former angels, a reminder of the magic swirling through them. She turned to look at all of them in turn, her brown eyes lingering longer on Thuan, as if she knew exactly what he'd been doing when he entered the room. "My name is Sare," she said. "I'm the alchemist of the House, and in charge of these tests."

The one in charge of making all their magical artefacts, and turning Fallen corpses into magic for dependents. She *definitely* reminded Thuan of Third or Fourth Aunt, except that his aunts wouldn't kill him for stealing or snooping where he wasn't meant to—no, they'd come up with something far worse.

Sare waited for them to introduce themselves, which they did, awkwardly and in a growing silence. Leila's eyes were wide. Kim Cuc, by the looks of her, was unimpressed and trying not to show it.

"So you want to enter Hawthorn," Sare said. She didn't wait, this time. "Let me tell you a little about how it works. I'll pick a few people from everyone who showed up today: the ones who show the most resourcefulness. The House will take you in, feed you, clothe you and teach you. If not..." She shrugged. "The streets are full of the Houseless. Any questions?"

"Dividing us into teams..." Thuan said, slowly.

"Because a House stands together," Sare said. The look she gave him could have frozen lava. "Intrigues are allowed, but nothing that threatens our unity. Am I clear?"

She wasn't, but Thuan nodded all the same.

"What are we supposed to do?" Kim Cuc asked.

"To start with?" Sare gestured, gracefully, towards the large table in the centre of the room. "You'll find supplies in the cupboard on the right, and other materials in the room on the left. You have an hour to come up with something that impresses me."

"Something—?" Thuan asked.

Sare shook her head. "Resourcefulness. I look forward to seeing what you make."

He shouldn't have, but he raised his gaze to meet hers. Brown eyes, with light roiling throughout the irises, flecks of luminescence that looked like scattered stars. "I'm sure you won't be disappointed," he said.

Something creaked in the corridor outside the room, and Sare looked away for a moment, startled. When she came back to Thuan, something had changed in her gaze, a barely perceptible thing, but Thuan was observant.

"Cocky," Sare said. "I'm not too sure I like that, Thuan. But we'll see, won't we?"

And then she was gone, and it was just the three of them, staring at each other.

Kim Cuc was the first to move, towards the cupboard Sare had shown them. She opened it, and stared at its contents. Thuan heard her suck in a deep breath. "Well, that should be interesting."

Thuan wasn't sure what he'd expected—some kind of dark and twisted secrets, weapons or knives or something, but of course that was nothing more than fancies born of nightmares. Inside the cupboard were metal bowls and plates, and a series of little packets of powder.

"Is that—" Leila asked.

"Yes," Kim Cuc said. "Flour, sugar and salt." Her face was carefully composed again, mostly so she didn't laugh. She looked, again, at the table in the centre of the room, a fragile contraption with the curved legs characteristic of the Louis XV style, except that they'd been broken once already, and that the white marble surface was soot-encrusted. "I'm assuming we should make our best effort not to break that."

Servants. Kitchen hands. Of course.

Leila pushed open the door of the other room, came back. "There's a sink and a small stove in there." Her face was closed again, pinched and colourless. "I can't cook. We never saw all of this, outside—" On the streets of Paris, flour was grit-filled and grey, butter thin and watered-down, and sugar never seen. As tests went, it was actually quite a good one: how would you handle cooking with so much more wealth than you'd ever seen in your life?

Clever, Thuan thought, and then he remembered that he wasn't supposed to admire the House that was his enemy.

Kim Cuc was gazing at him, levelly. "You're in luck," she said to Leila. "Because I can't cook either. But Thuan was paying way too much attention to old recipes, back when he was trying to seduce the family cook."

"It did work," Thuan said, stung. Not for long, true. It had soured when Thuan was called to the innermost chambers of the court, and last he'd heard, the cook had found himself another lover. He'd have been bitter if he could have afforded to, but that wasn't the way to survive in the intrigues of the imperial court.

"It always works," Kim Cuc said. "Until it doesn't." She stopped, then, as if aware she was on the cusp of going too far.

"You said you weren't keeping score," Thuan said.

Kim Cuc shrugged. "Do you want me to?"

"No." They'd parted on good terms and she wasn't jealous or regretful, but she did have way too much fun teasing him.

"Fine," Kim Cuc said. "What can we do in one hour?"

Thuan knelt, to stare at the contents of the cupboard. "An hour is short. Most recipes will want more than that. And…" the supplies were haphazard, bits and scraps scavenged from the kitchens, he assumed. He had to come up with something that wasn't missing an ingredient, and that could be significantly sped up by three people working on it at the same time. And that was a little more impressive than buttered toast.

"Chocolate éclairs," he said, finally. "Leila and I on the dough, Kim Cuc on the cream. We'll sort out the chocolate icing while the dough cools down." Time was going to be tight and the recipe wasn't exactly the easiest one he had, but the cake—pâte à choux filled with melted pastry cream and iced with chocolate—was an impressive sight, and probably a better thing than the other teams would come up with. Assuming, of course, that everyone had been assigned a cooking challenge, which might not be the case.

The downside was that, unless they were very fast, they'd leave the place a mess. One hour definitely didn't include time for clean up. Better, however, to be ambitious and fail, rather than come back with a pristine room and nothing achieved.

But, all the while, as he directed Leila to beat eggs and sugar together— as he attempted to prevent Kim Cuc from commenting on his strings of previous lovers and their performances as she boiled butter and water together—he remembered Sare's eyes, the way she'd moved when the floor in the corridor creaked.

It had been fear and worry in her gaze, something far beyond the annoyance of having to deal with the Houseless in the course of a routine exam she must have been used to supervising every year. And, for a moment, as she'd turned, the magic within her had surged, layer after layer of protective spells coming to life in Thuan's second sight, spells far too complex and sturdy to be wasted on the likes of them.

"Something is wrong," he said, to Kim Cuc, in Viet. They couldn't keep that conversation up for long, or Leila would get suspicious.

Kim Cuc's eyes narrowed. "I know. The *khi* currents in the wing are weird. I noticed it when we stepped in."

"Weird how?"

"They should be almost spent," Kim Cuc said. "Devastated like the rest of Paris. But they're like a nest of hornets. Something's got them stirred up."

"Something?"

"Someone. Someone is casting a spell, and it's a large one." Her voice was thoughtful. "Keep an eye out, will you?" Fortunately, questions in Viet sounded like any other sentence to foreigners, marked only by a keyword that was no different from the usual singsong rhythm.

"Of course." Whatever it was, they were locked in a room somewhere near the epicentre of it.

Great. What ancestor had he offended lately, to get such a string of bad luck?

THUAN WAS down to making an improvised piping bag with baking parchment when Kim Cuc said, sharply, "Younger uncle."

"Is anything wrong—" he started, and then stopped, because the *khi* currents had shifted. Water had given way to an odd mixture of water and wood, something with sharp undertones Thuan had never felt before.

The key turned in the lock again: it was Sare, her smooth, perfect face expressionless, but with the light of magic roiling beneath her skin, so strongly it deepened the shadows around the room. "Out," she said. Her voice was terse and unfriendly.

Leila, startled, looked up with her hands full of congealed chocolate. Kim Cuc merely flowed into a defensive stance, gathering the rare strands of *khi* water in the room to herself. Thuan just waited, not sure of what was happening. Except that the ground beneath his feet felt...prickly, as if a thousand spikes had erupted from it and he was walking on a carpet of broken glass. "What's wrong?" he asked.

"Enough," Sare said. She looked at Thuan and Kim Cuc for a moment, her gaze suspicious—surely she couldn't have found out what they were, surely dragon magic was as alien to Fallen as the sky was to fish? But then she shook her head, as if a bothersome thought had intruded. "We're evacuating the wing, and you're coming with us."

"Caring about the Houseless?" Kim Cuc's voice was mildly sarcastic, the remark Thuan had clamped down on as being too provocative.

"Corpses are a mess to clean." Sare's gaze was still hard. "I see both of you are equally cocky. Don't give me a hard time, please."

Kim Cuc grabbed him, as they came out. "It's over the entire wing," she said, in Viet.

"Not the House?"

She shook her head. "Don't think so." Her hands moved, smoothly, teasing out a pattern of *khi* water out of the troubled atmosphere. "This smooths out the *khi* currents. Got it?"

Thuan's talent for magic was indifferent, but his memory for details was excellent. "Yes."

"Good. Now hold on tight. This could get messy."

In the corridor, a crowd of other Houseless mingled, waiting in a hubbub of whispers, until Sare clapped her hands together and silence spread like a thrown cloth. "We're going into the gardens. Follow the dependents— the grey-and-silver uniforms. And don't dawdle."

And still no mention of whatever was causing the evacuation—no one who'd dared ask, either. Thuan fell in line behind two gaunt men in white bourgerons and blue aprons, Leila and Kim Cuc following a little behind. His neighbour was one of the House's dependents, a middle-aged woman with a lean, harsh face who didn't seem inclined to make conversation. She held a magical artefact in her clenched hand, but by the faint translucency of her skin she'd already inhaled its contents. Bad enough for everyone to be prepared for magic, then.

He still felt, under him, the spikes. They were moving, slowly weaving a pattern like snakes as he stepped over them, pushing upwards to trap his ankles. Their hold easily snapped as he stepped away, but it kept getting stronger and stronger. How far away were the gardens, how much time did they have? And what would happen, if he faltered and stopped? Something was trying to invade this part of the House, was trying to find a weakness, but he couldn't see anything or anyone.

He glanced behind him. A small, skeleton-thin girl in a torn hempen dress had stumbled, and one of the dependents, cursing under her breath, was trying to help him up. Magic surged through her chest and arms, a light that threw the girl's cheekbones into sharp relief. "Get up," the dependent said, and the girl stumbled on.

So he wasn't the only one, then. And it wasn't only people with magic, Fallen or dragon who were feeling this.

Something moved, at the back. For a moment Thuan thought it was a child who'd gotten left behind, but it was too small and agile, and its joints didn't seem to flex in the right way. Its eyes glittered in the growing shadows. And then, as swiftly as it had appeared, it vanished.

A child. The shape of a child. And—Thuan's memory was unfortunately excellent on details like this—not something made of flesh and muscles and bones, but a construct of parquet wood, prickling with the thorns of brambles.

Of hawthorns, he thought, suddenly chilled.

When he turned to look again, the shadows had lengthened, and there were more of them, trailing the group, here one moment and gone the next, flickering in and out of existence like lights wavering in the wind. He scanned the crowd. Most Houseless appeared oblivious; but, here and there, people stared with growing fear. The House dependents didn't appear to see the children of thorns at all.

That wasn't good.

But, as they moved forward—always driven, always following the elusive light of Sare's magic, following a corridor that twisted and turned and seemed to have no end—Thuan couldn't help looking back again. Every time he looked, the children of thorns were more solid, more sharply defined. And not flickering in and out of existence, but more and more *there*.

The shadows at their back lengthened, until the light of the dependents' magic seemed the only safety in the entire world. And the spikes—the branches, weren't they?—grabbed his ankles and slowed him down, and more and more people stumbled, and they weren't making good enough time, they were going to slow down and fall…

Someone grabbed Thuan's hand. And it was definitely not human, or Fallen, or dragon—a dry, prickling touch like kindling wood. Thuan fought the urge to grab his hand away. "What are you?" he asked, and—where its breath should have been coming from—there was only the loud creak of floorboards.

It whispered something that might have been a name, that might have been a curse, but didn't let go. "Stay," it whispered. "Or the House will fail you as it failed its children."

Thuan's feet felt as though he was stuck to the parquet floor. With his free hand he called up *khi* water—it came slowly, agonisingly slowly—and wove it into the pattern Kim Cuc had shown him, throwing it over the spikes like a blanket. The currents smoothed themselves out. He lifted his feet, trying to stamp some circulation back into them, but he couldn't get rid of the hand in his.

"Enough," Sare said. She turned, ahead of them, to face the group. Light streamed from her face, from her arms beneath the grey and silver dress she wore—a radiance that grew steadily blinding, a faint suggestion of wings at her back, a halo around her fair hair.

By Thuan's side, there was a sharp, wounded sound like wood snapping, and the hand withdrew from his as if scalded. He didn't wait to see if it would come back, and neither did his companions. They ran, slowly at first and then picking up speed—not looking back, one should never look back—leaving the darkness behind and heading for the end of the corridor, door after door passing them, dust-encrusted rooms, rotten panelling, broken sofas and torn carpets and burnt wallpaper—and finally emerged, gasping and struggling to breathe, in the grey light of the gardens.

They stared at each other. Leila was dishevelled and pale, breathing heavily. Thuan was still trying to shake the weird feeling from his hand. When he raised it to the light he saw a dozen pinpricks, already closing. He'd never been so happy for dragons' healing powers.

Sare stood on the steps of the wing, eyes shaded to look at the rest of the House. "Just this wing," she said, half to herself. She gestured to one of the dependents. "Get a message to Lord Asmodeus."

"He said—" the dependent started, with fear in her voice.

"I know what he said," Sare said. She sounded annoyed. "He's grieving and doesn't want to be disturbed. But this is an emergency." She breathed in, a little more calmly. "No, you're right. Iaris. Get Iaris. She'll sort this mess out."

Thuan showed no sign he'd understood what was going on. From his briefings he knew that Iaris was the House's chief doctor, and Asmodeus's right hand, seconding him in his work of ruling the House.

Sare turned back to Thuan and the others, huddled on the steps, struggling to catch their breath. "We'll find you some food until this gets sorted out."

Of course. They weren't going to be allowed to leave, were they? Just in case one of them turned out to be responsible for whatever had happened.

Leila withdrew something from her pocket: it was soggy and broken in half, and left trails of chocolate in her hand. "They'd have tasted great," she said, forlornly.

"We can always do them later," Thuan said. And then he stopped, as his brain finally caught up with him. "Where's Kim Cuc?"

She. She wasn't there. He hadn't seen her since the hand had grabbed him in the corridor. A fist of ice was squeezing his innards into mush. Where. Where was she?

He moved, half-running across the steps, gently shoving people out of his way—a gaunt girl with the round belly of starvation, an older man from the factories, his clothes slick and stained from machine oil—no Kim Cuc, no other Annamite, not anywhere. "Older aunt!"

She wasn't there. She wasn't anywhere. She...he stopped at last, staring at the Houseless on the steps, at the grey, overcast sky, so unlike the rippling blue one of the dragon kingdom under the Seine. Gone. Stuck inside. With the children of thorns and the floorboards and whatever else was going on inside.

Stay.

No.

"What do you think you're doing?" Sare, towering over him, with the remnants of the magic she'd used to extricate them from the wing, a dark, suffocating presence far too close for comfort. Within him, the *khi* water rose, itching for a fight, for anything to take his mind off the reality. But he couldn't. Even if he'd been the most powerful among the dragon kingdom, he couldn't take on a Fallen within her House.

"My friend," Thuan said.

Sare was quick on the uptake. Her gaze moved, scanned the crowd. "Not here. All right. Is anyone else missing?" she called out.

It should have been chaos, but fear of what Sare would do kept them all in check. At length, after some hurried, whispered talks among themselves, the other Houseless established that, if anyone had gone missing, it was someone who'd come alone, and whom they hadn't noticed.

Great.

Thuan looked at the wing they'd just come out of. The doors were a classic: a lower half of faded wooden panels, once a shade of purple but now just flaking off to reveal pale, mouldy wood underneath, and broken window panes on the top half.

But, around the handles...faint and translucent, and barely visible in the autumn light, was the imprint of thorn branches. Thuan sucked in a deep, burning breath. "What's going on?" he asked Sare.

Her face was hard. He thought she'd brush him off, put him in his place with the other Houseless, but he must have caught her at an unguarded moment. "I don't know. This wing has been odd since Lord Asmodeus came home from House Silverspires. Since..." she stopped herself, then.

Grieving. Thuan thought back to his mission briefing. Asmodeus's long-time lover, Samariel, had died in House Silverspires. He wouldn't have thought the head of House Hawthorn was the type to mourn, but clearly he'd been wrong. He opened his mouth, closed it, and then chose his words a little more carefully. "They say he lost his lover, in House Silverspires."

"Yes." Sare was still in that oddly contemplative mood.

"Does this have anything to do with it?"

Sare's face closed. "Perhaps. Perhaps not." She looked at him; seeing him, not as a Houseless, not as a candidate to join the House, but as a person—a scrutiny he might not be able to afford, no matter how good his disguise was. "Cocky and curious. Who are you, Thuan?"

The only thing that came out of him was the truth. "I'm the one whose friend is stuck inside the wing. Assuming she's even there anymore." Assuming she was even alive anymore. Assuming...

"Don't do anything you'll regret later." Sare gestured to the other Houseless, who'd fanned out on the steps. Someone had found a deck of cards, and a raucous game of tarot had started, cheered on by half the crowd, though the atmosphere was still subdued. "Now go wait, will you? Iaris has got a lot of experience at cleaning messes." She looked as though she'd roll her eyes upwards, but stopped just short of actual disrespect. "You'll be just fine."

It was gently phrased, but it was an order. Thuan walked back to the group, and found Leila a little way from the doors, leaning on the railing. The éclair had vanished. He guessed she'd eaten it. Good on her, this wasn't a time to waste food.

"Thuan. Did she—"

Thuan shook his head. "They don't know what's happening." And neither did he. He eased, cautiously, into his second sight, trying to see what was happening with the *khi* currents. Wood and water, curling around the door; but weakened, just an after-effect of what was happening within the wing. And those same little spikes everywhere, like a field of thistles underfoot, but nothing that made sense.

"I'm sorry," Leila said.

"It's all right," Thuan said. It wasn't. He should have paid more attention to Kim Cuc, but of course he'd assumed she'd take care of herself, because it was what Kim Cuc always did. He squeezed her hand, briefly. "Why don't you watch the tarot game?"

Leila made a face. "Not interested." She slid down the railing, her eyes on Sare. "I'd rather know what they will do."

"The House?" Thuan shrugged. He didn't expect much from the House. They weren't its dependents, and Sare had hardly seemed heartbroken to lose someone.

A tall, auburn-haired magician with an elegant dress in the House's colours had arrived. She was huddled in conversation with Sare, a frown on her wrinkled face, fingering a filigreed pendant around her neck as if debating whether she should inhale the magic contained within. Leila watched them, fascinated.

Thuan turned his gaze, instead, on the wing they'd just come out of.

Kim Cuc would have joked about his inability to see further. She'd have teased him, infuriating as always, and told him to keep his head down, to not make waves. Better to remain hidden and safe, as the kingdom was hidden from Fallen.

Except, of course, that the kingdom wasn't safe anymore, and that Houses Silverspires and Hawthorn had both encroached on its territory. Except that, like the Houses, they were ruined and decaying, and so desperate they had no choice but to send Thuan and Kim Cuc on a dangerous mission to infiltrate a House.

Stay safe. Stay hidden. As if that'd ever worked.

He crept closer to the handles. Sare was still in conversation with the magician, who was tracing a circle in the dust-choked earth of the gardens, while Sare was interjecting suggestions that the magician didn't appear to approve of. Leila had crept closer to them, her gaze still full of that enraptured fascination.

Thuan's hand closed, gently, on the left handle. The spikes of *khi* wood shifted, lay parallel to his fingers. His palm prickled, where the hand had held him, but nothing bled again, more like the memory of a wound than a real one.

He looked, again, at the steps. The Houseless were engrossed in the tarot game or in their own private thoughts, and Sare was still arguing with the magician. He could imagine what Kim Cuc would have said if she'd seen him. She'd have known exactly what he was thinking, and would have told him, in so many words, exactly how foolish it all was.

But, then again, if their situations were reversed, she'd still charge in.

Thuan turned the handle, slowly. Greased, it barely creaked as he pushed the door open and slipped, invisible and forgotten, into the wing they'd just evacuated.

INSIDE, IT was dark. Not merely the gloom of dust-encrusted rooms, but shadows, lengthening as he walked, and his own footsteps, echoing in the silence. Doors opened, on either side, on splendid and desolate rooms, with fungus spreading on chairs upholstered with red velvet, and a pervading smell of humidity, as if everything hadn't been aired properly after a rainy day.

And, as he walked, he became aware he wasn't alone.

It was only one presence at first, but soon there were dozens of them, easily keeping pace with him: the same lanky, dislocated shapes of children made of thorns, their eyes glittering like gems in the darkness. They didn't speak. They didn't need to. It was creepy enough. Thuan could feel the spikes beneath his feet, dormant. Of course, he wasn't trying to escape the wing. He was headed back into it.

He didn't even want to think of all the sarcastic words Kim Cuc was going to come up with, after this one.

"Where is she?" he asked, aloud.

They seemed…made of *khi* wood and *khi* water, of old things and memories, cobbled together by someone with only a rudimentary idea of what was human. The *khi* currents didn't pool around their feet, but went straight through them, as if they were extensions of the floor, and the only noise they made as they walked was the creaking of wood. "You're not human," he said, slowly, carefully, and again, there was no answer. It was a stupid thing to say, in any case. Sare wasn't human, and neither was Thuan, and they were vastly different beings.

What there was, instead, was a bright, blinding light, coming from behind him. And loud footsteps, from someone brash enough to think discretion didn't matter. The children scattered—no, not quite, they merely stepped back into the shadows, flowing back into them like smaller pools of ink rejoining a bigger one. Thuan mentally added that to his growing list of worries. Though so far, they didn't seem aggressive. It was going to be rather different when they tried to leave.

"I told you not to do anything you'd regret," a familiar voice said, behind Thuan.

Sare was alone, but, with so much magic flowing through her, she didn't need to be accompanied. A pendant swung over the collar of her dress, shining in Thuan's vision: an alchemical container she'd emptied for its preserved power. As she moved, the faint outline of wings followed her—an inverted afterimage, all that would remain after staring too long at blinding radiance.

He was in the middle of a wing invaded by magic, unsure of whether he'd ever be able to escape it, looking for Kim Cuc and with no leads whatsoever. He no longer had any room for fear of Sare. He didn't even have room to worry about whether she'd choose him for Hawthorn. "Regret. You mean rescuing my friend? I think I won't regret that on my deathbed."

"That's assuming you get a deathbed and not a violent death." Sare shook her head, as if amused by the antics of a child. The sort of thing that might be borne by mortals, who were younger than she was and in awe of her. But Thuan was immortal and over three hundred years old, and running out of patience, fast.

"I thought you were waiting for Iaris," Thuan said.

"I was," Sare shrugged. "She might be a while, though. She's currently entertaining the envoys of another House, and she needs to extricate herself gracefully."

"Why are you here?"

"Curiosity. Also…" she shook her head. "We take turns administering the tests, every year. And because this year I'm the one in charge, I am responsible for whatever you get up to."

"You don't care about the Houseless." Thuan *was* annoyed. Normally he wouldn't have let the words get past his lips.

"No, but I do take my responsibilities seriously. And Iaris wouldn't see it kindly if I were to lose two of you, not to mention an entire wing of the House."

"The magician—"

"Albane? She's preparing a spell, don't worry. Now, you seemed to know where you were going."

"No," Thuan said. *"They* knew."

"Who?" Sare turned, to look at the corridor. There was nothing but motes of dust in the dim light.

So she still couldn't see them. And Thuan could. Which wasn't good. A heartbeat, perhaps less, passed, and then Sare said, with a frown, "You're not a magician."

"No," Thuan said, with perfect honesty. He had no need of angel breath or other adjuncts to perform magic, and he drew on *khi* water, a power Sare couldn't see and wouldn't be able to make sense of. But it wasn't the *khi* currents that made him able to see the children, because the Houseless had also seen them.

But the House dependents hadn't. Because of their magic?

Sare's gaze held him, for a while. She couldn't see through him. She couldn't even begin to guess what he was. He was in human shape, with not a hint of scales showing on his dark skin, not a hint of antlers on his head or pearl beneath his chin.

At last, after what felt like an eternity, Sare asked, "What did you see?"

"Thorns," Thuan said. "Beings of thorns."

"Thorns don't—" Sare started, then stopped. "You mean trees that moved."

"No," Thuan said. "Children. They were children. They said…they said the House would fail me as it had failed its children."

Sare said nothing. Thuan considered asking her whether it meant anything to her, decided against it. He would gain nothing, and only make her suspicious. "Let's have a look," she said, carefully.

Room after room, deserted reception rooms with conversation chairs draped in mouldy coverings, closed pianos that looked as though they wouldn't even play a note, and harps with strings as fragile as spun silk, rooms with moth-eaten four-poster beds, bathrooms with cracked tiles and yellowed tubs…

As they turned into the servants' part of the wing—narrower rooms with shabbier sloped ceilings, all with that air of decayed grandeur—Thuan spoke up. "What's this wing?" he asked.

Sare's eyes narrowed. "You mean why here?"

"Yes."

Her gaze held him, for a while. Beneath him, he could feel the spikes, quiescent. Waiting. Like the children, in the shadows, the ones he couldn't see.

"I don't know," Sare said. "It's the water wing—the one with the spring and the pump room—but it's not the only one."

The spring. He could feel it, distantly—*khi* water, far, far underground, all reserved for the House's use, a trove of power that would never be his. But Sare was right: there were other springs, too, that he could feel on the edges of his thoughts, other currents of *khi* water being funnelled into the House.

"Then that can't be it."

Sare's gaze was hard. "You want everything to make sense, don't you."

Thuan fingered dust on a marble table, followed it down the curve of verdigried legs. "I want to understand."

"Then this is what I want to understand," Sare said, closing the door behind her. "How come only your friend vanished, Thuan? What made her so special?"

She was clever. But then, he'd expected nothing less of her. She hadn't gotten where she was—head of the alchemy laboratory, in charge of Hawthorn's vast troves of stored magic—by being a fool.

"I don't know," he said, thoughtfully. It couldn't be that she was a dragon, or Thuan would have vanished, too. He wasn't stronger than she was. "They tried to hold us all."

"Yes," Sare said. "But they gave up when we proved no easy prey. Except they did snatch your friend, who presumably fought back, same as everyone. Why?"

"I don't know."

"You're the only Annamites."

"Yes," Thuan said, startled. This wasn't where he'd wanted the conversation to go. The immediate threat of the thorn children had receded, but Sare's grilling almost made him regret the creepy escort. "But not the only colonials. And *I* didn't vanish."

"No," Sare said. "But perhaps you're stronger than her."

Thuan snorted. "No. If anything, I'm weaker than she is." He hesitated, then said, "She's been the one always looking out for me."

"Like a mother?" Sare's gaze was sharp.

Children of thorns. No. Thuan shook his head. "She wasn't the only motherly figure in that crowd, was she? That's a rather facile explanation."

"That children want mothers? It seems to me rather natural," Sare said, with the ease of someone who'd never actually have any children. All Fallen were sterile.

Mothers, perhaps not. He thought, again, of the bracelets on Kim Cuc's arms, of the wealth of Fallen magic stored there, something most Houseless would never see. In Paris, the Houses had hoarded nearly all the magic, and the rare artefacts went on the black market for a fortune. But no, that couldn't be it. Otherwise Sare and the other dependents would have been the first to vanish. "Why children? They can't possibly be the only dependents the House has failed."

He thought Sare was going to berate him, but instead she walked a little further down the corridor, and stared at the darkness in front of her. "You're here, aren't you?" she called, magic streaming out of her like light. "I can feel you."

Again, that odd feeling in his feet, as if the floor itself were twisting and disgorging something; and two children, stepping out of the darkness to gaze levelly back at her. Their arms were branches woven together, their hands three-fingered, and their bodies merely frames on which hung flowers the colour of rot. And, in the gauntness of their faces, they had no eyes, just pinpoints of light.

"Stay," the one on the left said.

"Where is she?" Sare asked. The light that came out of her was subdued, but Thuan could still feel the power; could still feel it pushing against the children, compelling them to answer.

She might as well have been pushing on thin air.

"Where we all go," the rightmost one said. "Into darkness, into earth."

Thuan opened his mouth to ask why they'd taken her, and then closed it, because it wasn't what mattered.

"Show me," Sare said.

A slow ponderous nod from both of them, perfectly synchronised, and two hands extending towards her.

"Sare, wait—"

But she was already moving—before Thuan could grab her away, or even finish his warning—extending both arms to clasp them.

There was a sound like cloth ripping, and then only shadows, extending to cover the corridor where Sare had been.

Thuan gave up, and used all the colourful curses Second Aunt forbade him to utter in her presence. It seemed more than appropriate.

HE DIDN'T know how long he remained there, staring at the darkness, which stubbornly refused to coalesce again into anything meaningful. But, gradually, some order swam out of the morass of his thoughts, a sense that he had to do something rather than succumb to despair. He was—no matter how utterly laughably inappropriate this might seem—their best chance at a rescue.

Where we all go.

Into darkness, into earth.

Sare was right: there were other wings with a spring, and a water room. But this was also the wing where the House received the Houseless. Which meant the expendable one. And—if he was to hazard a guess—the one least protected by the wards.

And Asmodeus, the head of the House and its major protector, was shut in his rooms, grieving and not paying attention to what was going on within the House. An opening, for something that had lain in wait for years? An attempt to seize a weak and unprotected part of the House, or to weaken Hawthorn?

Demons take them all. He didn't want to help the House, didn't want to involve himself in its politics. But, if he didn't, Kim Cuc wouldn't come back.

Thuan closed his eyes, and sought out the spring again. It was muzzled, bound by layer after layer of Fallen magic—wards that would singe him, if he so much as thought of touching them. It flowed, steadily, into the House, giving it everything it had, the diseased, polluted waters of the Parisian underground, sewage no one would have thought of drinking before the war and its devastation.

The House will fail you as it failed its children.

The only thing Thuan wanted the House to do for him was to forget he existed, and not look too closely. He hardly expected any protection, or wanted to pledge it any allegiance. Not that Second Aunt would let him, mind you. She'd carve out chunks of his hide before she allowed this to happen.

A comforting thought: there were things scarier than unknown children of thorns with shadowy agendas.

Thuan walked downwards, towards the spring.

THERE WERE two children waiting for him outside the corrugated doors of the water room. They didn't appear, or fade: they were just there, like guards standing at attention. By their size, the human children they were mimicking couldn't have been more than five or six.

"What are you?" he asked, again.

He hadn't expected an answer, but they both bowed to him, perfectly synchronised. "The Court," they said.

"The Court." Thuan's voice was flat.

"The Court of Birth."

Thuan was abysmal at a number of things, but his memory for details was excellent, and he'd been briefed on the history of the House before being sent there. Before he became head of the House, Asmodeus had been leader of the Court of Birth.

Children. The Court of Birth was in charge of the education of children and young Fallen. In charge of their protection. "There is a Court of Birth," he said, slowly. "In the House." Not here, in this deserted wing filled with thorns and shadows.

There was no answer. Thuan grabbed the doors, and pushed.

He didn't know what he'd expected. It was a low room with several rusted pumps, their steady hum a background to his own breath. The air was saturated with humidity, the tiles on the walls broken in numerous places—repaired so many times they looked like jigsaws, with yellowed grouting running at odd angles through the painted windmills and horse-drawn carts.

In a corner of the room, Sare was fighting children of thorns—small, agile shapes who dodged, effortlessly, the spells she threw at them. The pipes lit up with magic, showing, at intervals, the flow of water going upwards through the pumps.

And, in the centre of the room…

Thuan walked faster, his heart in his throat.

It was an empty octagonal basin of water, the *khi* currents within it all but extinguished, except where Kim Cuc was. She wasn't looking at him, but kneeling, her hands flat on old, cracked mosaics. The *khi* water within her, the currents running in her veins and major organs, was slowly spreading to cover the entire surface of the mosaics. Her green bracelets were fused to the floor, the light from them spreading across the mosaics. She—

She was taking root in the basin.

This wasn't good.

"Big sis—" Thuan started. He didn't get to finish his sentence, because someone else spoke up first.

"So you're her friend."

Thuan turned around, sharply, hands full of *khi* water—or rather, they would have been, if all the water within the room hadn't been either extinguished or claimed. There was nothing in his palms but a faint, pathetic tug, as if he held a dog on a distant leash.

The being of thorn who stood in front of him was tall; taller than Thuan, and rake-thin. When it bowed, the gesture wasn't like that of the others, smooth and synchronised and in no way human. This was elegant and slow, with a hint of mockery, as if the being couldn't quite disguise amusement. It reminded Thuan of…

In fact, it reminded Thuan of nothing so much as Sare's demeanour. "You don't have wings," he said—a stab in the dark, but given where he was it could hardly get worse.

"No." The being straightened from its bow, stared at Thuan. The face wasn't just branches arranged to have eyes and nose. This was someone's face, carefully sculpted in wood and thorns: plump cheeks, and a round shape, someone who must have been pleasantly baby-faced and young, except that now not a single muscle moved as it spoke, and the eyes were nothing but pits of darkness, like the orbits of a skull. "We don't keep them, when we Fall. As you well know."

"I don't know," Thuan said. He pulled on *khi* water, and found barely anything that would answer him. Not good at all. "You were alive once, weren't you?"

The being cocked its head, watching him like a curiosity. "You ask the wrong questions," it said, at last.

"Fine," Thuan said, exhaling. "Then why are we here? Because the House failed you?"

He thought the other was going to make him some mocking answer about following his friend in harm's way, but it merely shook its head. "The House didn't fail me."

"You make no sense," Thuan said.

The being was still watching him. It made no move to seize or stop him. "She was willing."

Thuan took in a deep, burning breath. Willing to do what, and what questions had it asked, before binding Kim Cuc to the basin's floor? Words had power here, which was good, because they seemed to be all he had to bargain with.

He hesitated—every instinct he had telling him not to do such a stupid thing—but then turned his back on the being, to look at the basin. Kim Cuc's eyes were closed, her breathing slow, even. "Big sis. Big sis."

He wanted to shake her, but he wasn't a complete idiot. She'd put her hands in the basin, on the mosaics, and it had seized her. She didn't need Thuan caught in the spell, either.

She shouldn't have needed Thuan at all, demons take her. She should have been in charge; fighting, like Sare, trying to figure out the riddle that had Thuan stumped.

"We asked her to help," the being said, behind him. It'd still made no move to take Thuan. And though Sare was fighting, she wasn't harmed, either.

Magic. Fallen magic. That was why they seemed summarily uninterested in Thuan, or in any of the other Houseless: Thuan's magic was invisible to them. But they hadn't taken Sare, or the other House dependents. He'd thought it was something dark, something the House couldn't keep at bay, but…

But when Sare had pushed against the children of thorns, Thuan had seen nothing, in the *khi* currents.

And none of the House dependents had seen them, or been threatened by them.

He breathed in, slowly. It was as if they were part of the House, weren't they. Ghosts or spirits or constructs that hadn't been made by any magicians. And they hadn't taken Sare or the other House dependents, because theirs was a power already bound to the House. As Kim Cuc wasn't.

"You're the House," he said.

"A small part of it." Its smile would have been dazzling, if it hadn't been made of branches and twigs.

"Willing. You asked her if she wanted to be part of the House," Thuan said, slowly. "That's why she's here."

The voice that answered him was mocking. "Was there any need to ask? She was there, taking the tests."

In order to enter the House, not to become subsumed within its foundations. But he doubted the being would know, or care about the difference. "She's not House," he said, carefully. A glance upwards: Sare had dispatched one of the two children, but it was already reforming.

What did he have, to bargain with? Not the kingdom: even if he'd been willing to expose and sell it, it'd have no value to a House of Fallen and magicians. Not his magic, for the same reasons. Sare, possibly, but how did you bargain with something the other already owned? "You don't need her," he said, slowly.

"In ordinary circumstances, no."

"Because Asmodeus is grieving for Samariel? All grief passes, in time."

"The grief of Fallen?" The being's voice was mocking again. "That could last an eternity." Thuan found a word—a name—on the tip of his tongue, forced himself not to utter it. The being wasn't Samariel any more than any of the children of thorns had been flesh and bones, or real children. They were all just masks the House wore as a convenience. "And meanwhile, our protections weaken."

"He's head of the House," Thuan said. "He won't leave you undefended."

It was going nowhere. He couldn't negotiate from a position of weakness, and he couldn't share his only strengths for fear of being caught out. "If you start taking people, they'll tear the wing apart stone by stone."

"Would they? They're Houseless," the being said. "Not likely to be much missed, in the scheme of things."

Spoken as only a House-bound could.

"What you take, they could give freely."

A low, rumbling noise mingling with that from the pumps. Thuan realised it was laughter. "No one ever gives freely. There's always an expectation of being paid, in one currency or another."

"You're..." Thuan fought a rising sense of frustration. "You're the House. All you do is take!" He pointed to Sare, flowing in and out of combat with unearthly grace, her pale skin lit up with the radiance of magic, the white shape of bones delineated under her taut skin. "Do you think she'd be as useful, if you shut her in the foundations of the wing?"

A silence, then, "One day, when she's spent almost all the magic she was given when she Fell, that might be her only use." A low, amused chuckle. "But this isn't how dependents are rewarded."

He'd had lessons of diplomacy in the dragon kingdom. He should have paid more attention to them, instead of trying to come up with plans to impress his cousins. He...he'd always thought Kim Cuc would be there, and of course she was the one in need of rescue, and he couldn't come up with a single idea that would make sense. He couldn't fight off a House, or even a part of a House, all by himself—and especially not with both hands tied down, and no access to his magic lest he reveal himself.

No.

He was looking at it from the wrong way around. Because fighting or threatening wasn't what he needed to do, if he wanted to use his magic. He needed…a distraction.

Which meant Sare.

He didn't trust Sare. He couldn't even be sure she was going to follow his lead: for all he knew, she'd be happy to leave Kim Cuc there forever, if it was for the good of the House.

But.

But she'd come back for both of them, and it was the only chance he'd get. "You don't want Kim Cuc," Thuan said, slowly. There wasn't much *khi* water in the room, but he could gather it to him, slowly and methodically. He could fashion it into razor-thin blades, held within his palms. "You want Asmodeus."

A silence. "You're Houseless. You can't possibly promise me anything that involves him."

No, and neither would Thuan ever consider getting involved with the head of House Hawthorn. The last thing he needed was attention from that quarter. But it didn't matter, because all he needed to do was lie smoothly enough.

"I'm not House. But she is." He pointed to Sare but finished his gesture with a wide flourish, which enabled him to throw the blades of *khi* water in his hands towards Kim Cuc's wrists. They connected with an audible crunch.

Water was stillness and decay and death. Thuan breathed in, slowly, moving his fingers as though he were playing the zither, weaving the pattern Kim Cuc had shown him earlier. The blades slowly moved in response, digging into the green stone, their edges turning it to dust, a thin, spreading line across its surface—so agonisingly slowly it was all he could do to breathe. "Ask her," he said.

A silence, broken only by the slurping sound of the pumps. Then the being moving as gracefully as water flowing down, and the two children facing Sare vanished. She turned to Thuan, snarling, her face no longer in the semblance of anything human; and then saw the being of thorns, and sucked in a deep, audible breath.

Her mouth opened, closed. "It's a bit of the House," Thuan said, quickly. "Not…"

Sare's face was unreadable again. "Is it?" She bowed, very low. "Tell me," she said to Thuan.

Thuan gathered thoughts from where they'd fled, and put as many of them as he dared into words. "It wants Lord Asmodeus."

Sare's gaze moved to the basin, and then back to Thuan. "And, failing that, it will take the Houseless?" She showed no emotion. But then why would she have cared about Kim Cuc? Thuan waited for her to speak, to tell the being it was welcome to Kim Cuc and whatever else it saw fit to take. But Sare didn't say anything.

"We need to be strong," the being said. Thuan watched Kim Cuc's bracelets; watched the thin line that was spreading across the stone, a widening crack. He would only get one chance to seize her and run, and he couldn't even be sure that Sare would follow them. "Not distracted."

"Distracted." Sare's face was hard again. "Grief is *allowed.*"

The being said nothing. Of course it wouldn't understand.

Thuan shifted, moving closer to Kim Cuc, both arms outstretched to grab her.

"Lord Asmodeus isn't available," Sare said. "And we work on the principle that people are safe inside the House, regardless of whether they're dependents or not."

A hiss, from the being.

"Sare," Thuan said.

She looked at him, startled, as if she'd forgotten he was there, or that he would speak.

"Be ready."

The bracelets split with an audible crunch. Thuan reached out, lightning fast; grabbed Kim Cuc and pulled—she came light and unbearably fragile, a doll he could have snapped with a careless gesture—threw her over his shoulder, and ran.

He didn't look back.

The spikes under his feet tensed, but didn't surge—behind him, a blinding light, that filled the pump room until he could hardly see. He ran for the open doors, and the maze of corridors leading back to safety.

He'd expected to have to fight the children at the entrance, but they'd vanished in the wash of light. He could still see their silhouettes in the midst of the radiance, shock-still. Stunned, but recovering. He didn't have much time.

Which way had he come? The corridors all looked alike, all with that same faded flower wallpaper, and the stains of blackened mould spreading from the carvings on the ceiling. The light behind him was dying down, the spikes at his feet quiescent. Waiting.

"You're fast," Sare commented, as she caught up to him.

"You—" Thuan was breathing hard. He'd slowed down to see where he was going. He expected, at any time, to see the spikes reforming, children of thorns waiting for them in the darkness.

"I hit him hard." Sare sounded cheerful. "It was easier, knowing what I was dealing with."

"You—" Thuan found a breath, finally. "You didn't *have* to do this." It was the House. It was the wards that kept all their dependents safe. She only had to look the other way.

Sare raised an eyebrow. "As I said, I'm responsible for the safety of the Houseless during those tests. And there are some choices that I won't make. We're not monsters, Thuan."

Thuan clamped his mouth on the obvious response. "The Court of Birth," he said, instead.

"This way," Sare said, pointing to a corridor that seemed like the others, cracked parquet and faded wallpaper with an alignment of the same doors, all painted with stylised flowers. And, in the growing silence, "Children died, because Lord Uphir wouldn't protect them. Before Lord Asmodeus took the House from him. It remembers."

And Asmodeus protected children? Thuan didn't voice this question, either, but Sare answered it regardless.

"The House keeps faith with its own. Lord Asmodeus understands this," Sare said.

"Fine," Thuan said. He wasn't about to argue with her. "Any plans?"

"Yes." For someone who'd been through Hell and back, Sare was still inordinately cheerful. "My turn. Be ready to run. It's straight ahead, and left at the first intersection, the one with the two chairs and the pedestal table with the Chinese vase."

"I don't understand—" Thuan started, but she was looking past him, at what was coming up.

He turned, slightly—Kim Cuc a growing dead weight on his shoulder—and saw the maw of darkness, rising from the bottom of the wing—flowing like ink, like polluted oil, glittering with the shadows of thorns.

They couldn't possibly outrun this.

By his side, Sare was leaning against a wall—the light coming out of her pale and weakened, the artefact around her neck open, with no hint of magic left within. The shadows flowed around her, not touching her—House, she was still House, and it didn't care for her, didn't want to hurt her, just in case she turned out to be useful one day. Under Thuan, the floor seemed to have become broken glass. And, as the shadows came forward and extinguished the light, they pooled—becoming the shape of children, the shape of a Fallen.

They didn't speak, anymore: just a thin thread of sound that might have been the creaks of floorboards, the trickle of water. *Stay. Stay.*

Thuan backed away, until he stood in the centre of the corridor, with threads of magic stretching, trying to bind him to the floor, to make him part of the House as they'd tried to do with Kim Cuc. He could barely hold on to his human shape. Any moment now, he was going to lose it, and Sare was going to see antlers sprouting from his temples, scales scattered across his cheeks.

Stay. Stay.

Never.

"I told you." Sare's voice was conversational, her face utterly emotionless, as if she was merely shepherding Houseless through tests. "We guaranteed their safety. It's not an idle promise."

The being that looked like Samariel was stretching past her already, making for Thuan. Sare was leaning against the wall, winded and exhausted; but her gaze found Thuan's, held it.

Be ready to run.

There was no blinding light, no rising magic. Instead, the floor under Thuan changed—as if someone had smoothed out the broken glass, stroked raised spines until they lay flat again. The threads under his feet snapped.

He ran.

The darkness would follow him, but he couldn't do anything about that. His lungs were burning, his legs trembling. Kim Cuc wasn't heavy, but he couldn't keep carrying her forever. She kept sliding off his shoulder, head lolling against his chest.

Turn left at the next intersection. Two chairs, a pedestal table with one of those horrible Chinese porcelain vases on it. He almost tripped over one of the chairs, had to force himself to change course, calves burning.

On either side of him, the wallpapers were turning black again, the painted flowers and birds merging with the growing shadows, and he could see the shape of children, pooling from the panelling like ink, thorns and branches and a House he couldn't fight, a power that was slowly choking the dragon kingdom.

Demons take them. Demons take them. He couldn't possibly—

At the end of the corridor was the door to the garden, so close, so impossibly far. Whatever Sare had done was nothing more than a sop, a few moments' safety gained. He was never going to make it. He was going to freeze there, within sight of the exit...

He'd started to shoulder off Kim Cuc's weight, ready to stand over her and defend her—when the magic hit.

It came, not from behind him, but from the door. And it wasn't harsh, blinding light, but something smoother and softer; the voices of children, laughing and teasing each other; an echo of a lullaby, sung over and over; a smell of fried onions and warm bread, and a hint of unfamiliar spices.

In front of Thuan, the being of thorns formed, stared at the light, empty eye-sockets shining in the darkness. *Khi* water pooled around its feet, circled its shape on the parquet. It didn't move. It stood, entranced, as if listening, its head cocked.

Thuan would have run, but he had no energy left. Instead, he straightened out Kim Cuc on his shoulder, and hobbled towards the light.

An eternity of walking, with Kim Cuc growing heavier; and the spell—whatever it was—spreading around him, a warm embrace, a promise of small, ordinary things; of fire in the hearth, water and wine in crystal glasses, the smoothness of cotton sheets at the end of the day—never mind that the bed was mouldy and broken, the wine sour, the hearth cracked, it was still home.

But not his home. Never.

When Thuan stepped outside, the light blinded him for a moment. Then he saw the magician—Albane?—kneeling in the middle of a circle traced in the mud. Light streamed, highlighted the words she'd written, as fluid and as deliberate as a master's calligraphy. Leila was kneeling by the side of the circle, both hands plunged deep into the earth, the light coming up to her wrists, making her swarthy skin seem pale and colourless.

Thuan kept walking—he wasn't sure he could stop. His feet carried him down the stairs, by the side of the circle: Albane looked up at him and nodded once, grimly. Leila withdrew her hands from it and grabbed him. "Thuan!"

Thuan stopped, at a loss for words. He laid Kim Cuc on the grass, blinking once, twice, as he knelt by her side, looking for a pulse—feeling it, slow and strong. "Come on, come on," he muttered.

"She's alive," Sare said.

She must have come out of the wing straight in his wake, but he hadn't heard her. Everything felt…unbearably real, unbearably distant, and he couldn't seem to process thoughts. Magic flowed from Sare into Kim Cuc.

She convulsed, the bruises on her wrists becoming darker. "You—" Thuan said, struggling to speak.

Kim Cuc's eyes opened. "Thuan? What—what happened?"

"It's all right. You're safe." He could have wept.

"I would advise you not to bring Fallen magic into the House," Sare said. Her face was smooth once again, emotionless. "Not unless you're strong enough to use it."

Thuan looked up. The wing was quiescent once again, the thorns a fading smear of darkness against the door handles. "Sare—"

She wasn't listening to him: she'd moved, coming to meet an older woman with the same kind of smooth face, wearing a doctor's white gown over the colours of the House. "Iaris."

Iaris nodded. "Apologies for the delay. I needed to figure out how to keep this contained."

"And—?"

"A slip-up," Iaris said. "My mistake. We hadn't checked the wards on this wing for a while. It won't happen again. I've set magicians to reinforcing them. We can't have the House seeking out magic to maintain itself."

As if they'd care.

"I saw." Sare closed her eyes. "I saw him. Samariel."

Iaris's face tightened. "Samariel is dead. You'd do well to remember this. And whatever you saw is dormant now. Contained, and it will remain so for centuries, God willing."

"Let's hope so," Sare said.

"You all right?" Leila asked Thuan.

Thuan still held Kim Cuc's hand. She'd fallen back into unconsciousness, looking older than she should, weak and vulnerable and *fragile*. Any time now, she was going to open her eyes, and make some flippant, sarcastic remark. Any time.

But she didn't.

"I'm not sure," he said, finally, to Leila. "I didn't know you could use magic."

"You learn things, in the gangs." Leila squeezed his hand, briefly. "Besides…we're a team."

Thuan stifled a bitter laugh. "For the tests? I don't think these turned out very well."

"Oh, I don't know. The éclairs tasted nice, even though they were a bit wet in the middle. I gave mine to Sare, before she entered the wing."

"You—" Sare hadn't mentioned this, but why would she? "What did she say?" He didn't even know what it'd have tasted like, half-made and with the pastry filling falling out of it.

"Nothing," Leila said. She shrugged. "I know it looked horrible, but we might as well not waste our work." Her face grew serious again. "This isn't about tests."

He stared at her, for a while; thinking of the streets and how lonely they could be. "We *are* a team," he said. "Thank you." He couldn't give her everything that he wanted, but friendship? The dragon kingdom would surely let him spare that.

Except, of course, that he wouldn't be able to tell her the truth about who he was, or Kim Cuc would box his ears out. Some friend.

One problem at a time.

Beside them, Iaris and Sare were still talking. "The Court of Birth." Iaris snorted. "As if that'd have impressed Lord Asmodeus."

Sare didn't answer. She was opening and closing the clasp of her pendant. "It might have. Dredging up the past."

"We're looking to the future," Iaris said. "He has plans, believe me." Her gaze rested, for a moment, on Thuan, moved away. "The mourning period is over."

"I see." Sare closed the pendant with an audible click. "Plans. That will be good."

Plans. Thuan's ears prickled. But neither Iaris nor Sare appeared ready to discuss further. Of course. Not in front of outsiders.

"Do you want to debrief them, or shall I?" Sare said.

"You can do it," Iaris said. "Report to me afterwards, will you?"

"Yes," Sare said. "I will." Thuan held Kim Cuc's hand, and said nothing. Sare hadn't seen anything. He'd barely used any magic, and he'd smooth it over. He'd have been worried in other circumstances: but if she wanted him dead, he'd already be.

"And once the wing is shored up, we'll have to reschedule the tests." Iaris sounded annoyed.

"Oh, I don't think so." Sare turned, briefly, to look at them. "I know exactly who passed."

Iaris raised an eyebrow. "That's…unusual."

"You have objections?"

"None. It's your own business, Sare."

"My responsibility. Yes, I know."

"So these three?"

Sare shook her head. "Two."

Two. Leila and him. Thuan looked at Kim Cuc. "Sare—" he said.

"I told you," Sare said. "Resourcefulness. And strength. I appreciate your loyalty to your friend, but—"

But, from Sare's point of view, she'd been nothing but trouble.

He *needed* Kim Cuc. He couldn't possibly take on the House by himself, couldn't make it far without her support. He needed her jokes at his expense, her reminders of his failures in bed and elsewhere—and, more importantly, he needed to not be alone in Hawthorn. Leila, for all that he liked her, wasn't from the kingdom, and could never fill that role.

He…

He'd gone through this all, without her help—and now he'd have to do much, much more. The breath in his lungs burnt, as bitter as ashes and smoke. "I see," he said. "Thank you."

"Good," Sare said, briskly. "Welcome to the House, Thuan." She smiled mirthlessly. "I'm assigning you to the kitchens to start with. Your pastries were too soggy, but not that bad, considering. Never fear, you'll have plenty of classes to learn better cooking skills."

Thuan forced a smile he didn't feel. He remembered darkness flowing to fill his entire world, that feeling he would never escape the corridors.

"I'm glad I passed," he said, smoothly, slowly. He stared, in silence, at the looming shape of the House before him, at the fading imprint of thorns on the handles, and wondered how many secrets it still held—how many things waiting to bite and grasp, and never let go.

Of Birthdays, and Fungus, and Kindness

I T WAS THE BIRTHDAY PARTY THAT WAS THE PROBLEM.

It didn't start as such. Emmanuelle had envisioned a romantic dinner, something with candles and an impressive array of Selene's favourite dishes, all sprung as a surprise as Selene finished up the day's paperwork—at least, as romantic as things could be, in private quarters still overrun by banyan roots. She'd even started to have chats with Laure on what they could do, on House Silverspires' limited stocks of food: things that wouldn't too much impact the daily running of the House, or be needless extravagance that would deprive other dependents of their own pleasures.

None of this survived Lucifer Morningstar's first run of interference.

He found Emmanuelle in the library, in the early morning before the other archivists arrived. She was at the back, wedged between two banyan roots, engrossed in the cataloguing of a few new arrivals: water-logged books from the Great Market of Paris, lost marvels from the golden age before the magical war that had devastated France and Europe, with gilded spines and lavish illustrations, their bindings still miraculously intact, though the stitches were a little worse for wear. One was in Russian. They owned exactly nineteen of these in the library, and Emmanuelle was looking forward to a chance to sit down with it, parsing unfamiliar words with a tattered dictionary.

"You're going about it the wrong way," Morningstar said.

Emmanuelle didn't drop the book, but it was close. Morningstar had been power incarnate, a presence that seemed to distort and bend everything it touched, footsteps that echoed from afar and grew into deafening thunder, a trembling heat in the air as if before a storm. But he'd died and been resurrected, and the Fallen who now stood beside her had none of that. His blue eyes shone with the magic all former angels wielded, but it was like the light beneath Emmanuelle's dark skin and curled hair, a diminished and washed-out radiance. He was…weak. Ordinary. And, whatever else she'd thought of Morningstar, "ordinary" hadn't ever applied.

"What are you doing here?" she asked. He never came into the library. He'd disapproved of his promising student Selene sleeping with Emmanuelle, and had done his best to tear them apart. It wasn't because Emmanuelle, though Fallen, manifested as an African colonial—he didn't much care, either way—but because she'd defied him by walking away from him and refusing to worship at his feet.

"Laure told me about your party plans," Morningstar said.

"Party?" Emmanuelle rose, surrounded by a cloud of dust and the familiar, comforting smell of old books. "I have no idea what you mean."

Morningstar made a small, stabbing gesture with his broad hand. His blue gaze—that had once been filled with light, that had once all but forced Emmanuelle to abase herself—held nothing but faint annoyance. "She's the head of the House. Her birthday needs to be a statement."

"I hadn't thought—" Emmanuelle started, but he cut her off. Well, at least that was pure old Morningstar.

"She needs to spend some time with her closest advisers," Morningstar said. "To reward them for their trust in her. To remind them that we're still great."

"Really?" Emmanuelle said. Around them, the library shelves were half-choked by banyan roots. The supernatural tree had been summoned by Hawthorn, a rival House intent on destroying them: it was still wrapped around the ruins of Notre-Dame, and no amount of hacking and burning would remove the branches that had filled the gaps between the broken benches and the ruined altar. It was a miracle that it hadn't choked off the House completely. "I don't think we need bluster right now. And—her closest advisers?" Obviously Morningstar would include himself in them.

Morningstar shook his head—fair hair so pale it was almost white, falling to his shoulders in a great cascade. People had used to worship him, fighting for a chance, for any chance to be acknowledged and raised up. Even now, returned and diminished, they looked up to him for inspiration. Emmanuelle had never seen the point. "A select committee, obviously. Her largest supports within the House. Something real, for them."

"Look," Emmanuelle said, abandoning all attempts at subtly shepherding the conversation, never her strong suit anyway. "It wasn't a party, or a select committee, or whatever else you've got in your head. Just a quiet evening between the both of us." And God knew Selene could use one of these right now, in between tearing her hair out trying to rebuild their place in the order of things.

The various Houses of Paris, its large magical factions and oases of shelter for dependents in the ruined city, were always at each other's throats: Silverspires, who held Ile de la Cité and the Notre-Dame cathedral, had once been a major House—the first, the oldest—but after the summoning of the banyan tree and the damage it had done, they might as well have been demoted to minor status. Every other minor House had turned indifferent or hostile, even their former clients.

"I know." Morningstar's smile was dazzling. But it hadn't worked on Emmanuelle at the height of his former powers, and it wasn't going to work now. "And it was. But—as I said—I think this is a missed opportunity. You'll have quiet time to spend with her, whenever you want. You said 'bluster', and you're right. But if we're weak, the other Houses will just take us apart for scraps. It's happening now. Selene is finding it harder and harder to hold. You've seen it. She can't do it alone."

He'd changed, then. She'd expected him to be the old, boastful Morningstar, to dismiss her as of no importance; to punish her, again and again, for walking away from him, for changing her name, the old "Indigo" he'd given to her for the darkness of her skin. "So you want us to make her birthday into a prestige dinner. There are other occasions."

"None so good." Morningstar laid one hand on a banyan root climbing up a set of shelves, watching the light from his skin play on the thick bark. "Her birthday is the perfect occasion to reassure people. And, if they're reassured, they can reassure the other dependents. It would do wonders for morale."

And morale, as Emmanuelle knew all too well, was low. The House had barely survived House Hawthorn's attack. They were still finding banyan roots in all the wings and all the rooms; they might have cleared all the corpses, but she couldn't even be sure of that. He was right. They needed something to keep going. But…

She didn't want to sacrifice her planned dinner. She didn't want him to be right, again. But he was, and she was too honest to lie to herself. "Fine. Something just a little larger, then. But you're going to help me run it."

"Of course." Morningstar's smile was wide again, with a sense of coiled power, a hint of his former self, something that sent a shiver through her bones, pleasure that she'd made him happy, that his attention would turn away from her. The old him. The dead him. "I'll be quite glad to help you."

In hindsight, that was where things started to go downhill.

"YOU'RE UP to something," Selene said to Emmanuelle.

They lay together in bed after making love—Selene's short auburn hair in the hollow of Emmanuelle's dark-skinned shoulder, her grey eyes mildly curious, and far more sunken than they should have been for a Fallen. She didn't quite look mortal: her skin still translucent but never bruising, her movements graceful, effortless, with no hint of awkwardness, but all the same… All the same, Emmanuelle had seldom seen her so tired.

She should have said no to Morningstar. The House would eat Selene alive, if it could. Not literally, but so many dependents relying on her to solve their problems would drain her. Father Javier and the others in Silverspires were doing what they could, but in the end it still came back to her, to Morningstar's successor, and never mind the awkwardness of her predecessor being alive and well, and summarily uninterested in taking his old place again.

Ghost at the feast, she thought, sourly.

"I'm allowed to have a private life," she said.

"Mmm." Selene sounded amused. "It's that time of year again, and you're too often closeted with Laure."

Emmanuelle shrugged. "I'd be a poor lover if I didn't plan something." At this stage of the process, the "something" seemed to have morphed into a full buffet with what felt like half the dependents of the House, and Morningstar kept coming up with reasons for adding guests to the ranks of people who needed to see Selene. At least he was running most things for her. Nevertheless, Emmanuelle's evening prayers for a few days had included heartfelt pleas that nothing would go wrong, even if she suspected that God might well find her concerns trivial and unworthy of His time.

"Ha," Selene said. She moved, her lips seeking Emmanuelle's for a kiss, long and deep and with that faint tinge of radiant strength, Morningstar's power without any of the harshness. Emmanuelle drank it all in, a shuddering, intoxicating breath that seemed to travel from mouth to heart and fill her entire body. "Well, you know what you're doing. I look forward to being surprised."

THE FIRST hint that all wasn't well came when they were taking out the dinner service a week before the party. It was early, but Laure had grimly insisted.

"In the current climate I wouldn't be surprised if half of them had cracked."

"It's in stasis," Morningstar had said, mildly disbelieving. And, in the face of her silence, "isn't it?"

"It will be," Laure said. "When all the magic we have isn't going into reinforcing the wards and cleaning up the House. Now come."

Said service—the only one large enough for the House-wide party that Morningstar had turned her romantic dinner into—was in the pantry by the ballroom, split over two buffets and a cupboard with a frosted door, which held the crystal wine glasses.

Except that it was now hard to tell what the cupboard held, anymore. The frosted door was now covered with a greyish strain of fungus: long strands braided into the wood going all the way into the hinges, a crop of small, golden toadstools on the corners of the frame, and further on, darker roots wrapping around the stem of the wine glasses like a hundred fingers from some demented nightmare.

"I'm not sure—" Emmanuelle started, turning towards Laure and the two kitchen hands who had come with her. "Perhaps another service for the glasses?"

Morningstar pushed her aside, gently but firmly. "Here," he said. He put his hand on the fungus. Light streamed out of him, lazily, a rippling radiance like the sun on a field of ripe corn, a gold so rich it hurt to see; and the strands caught fire.

It was a thing without warmth, without body. It burnt bright, but didn't touch the wood or the glass, flowing like molten metal into the hinges, lighting up the glass from within. The air smelled, not of charring, but of burning incense and churned earth.

"There," Morningstar said, turning to Emmanuelle. And for a moment only, highlighted in the light of his power, he was his old, old self, carelessly arrogant, smiling with the confidence of one who'd always seen the world reshape itself to his needs. "You can open it now."

Maïr, one of the kitchen hands, cautiously approached, and, visibly steeling herself, threw open the glass door in one single quick gesture.

Nothing happened.

Inside were only the glasses with barely any trace of the fungus, speckled with dust, broken and cracked, but nothing unusual. "All right," Laure said. She pointed to a nearby table. "We're going to count them. If one looks like it can't hold any liquid, it probably can't. Don't try to pretend otherwise. Emmanuelle, can you look at the plates?"

The sideboard's locks had rusted shut, and there were still thin branches of banyan clinging to the handles. She knelt and tried to pry them open, hoping, all the while, that Morningstar wouldn't turn his attention her way. From the table came the clink of glasses, and Laure's occasional interjection to be careful.

"You look like you could use some help," Morningstar said, kneeling by her side.

Emmanuelle shook her head. "I can do it." Her magic was weak, and the banyan seemed to be absorbing all of it, the lock stubbornly refusing to click open. She couldn't feel any resistance, but she felt she was casting a spell into a vacuum. "You should help Laure."

She should be trying to work with him, not rehashing decades-old grudges. He was only trying to be helpful, even if his ideas of help were grandiloquent and over-dramatic. But he was going to use his power—going to bend over the locks, his magic overwhelming hers with the same old ease, her objections once again pitiful, only worthy to be disregarded...

"Look—" she started, and never got the chance to finish.

Something imploded.

A bang—the clatter of broken glass, skittering across the broken parquet—and a high-pitched scream.

Not good. Emmanuelle was on her feet, running towards the table, when Morningstar's hand on her stopped her. "You'll cut yourself."

She tried to shrug him off, but he was stronger than her. "Let go," she said, but he didn't. Ahead, near the table, Maïr was standing, blood dripping from the cuts in her hand, the shards of the broken glass at her feet. "It just broke apart—" she tried to speak, her ruddy complexion growing paler and paler, each breath coming fast, choking the one before it. Her legs were shivering, on the edge of buckling. "It—"

Laure's face was frozen in a mask of horror. "Hospital wing. Now."

The cuts? Surely not that serious. And then Emmanuelle saw the specks on Maïr's hands: greyish, glistening dots like flecks of mould on bread, a thin coat of dust that stubbornly refused to come off.

"IT'S RATHER resilient," Aragon said. House Silverspires' chief physician looked positively incensed, hopefully at the fungus rather than any of them. His swarthy skin was almost flushed darker than Emmanuelle's, and his face was a study in annoyance. "Magical, obviously. It must be a remnant from the war. I don't know what triggered it awake. Where did you say you found it?"

"Crystal glasses," Laure said, curtly. "One came apart in Maïr's hands."

"It would have," Aragon said. "The mycelium's strands bring enormous pressure..." His voice trailed away.

"It was on a cupboard," Laure said. "Morningstar burnt it away."

"Some of it," Emmanuelle said, and bit her lip. Being spiteful wasn't going to help. "Is Maïr going to be all right?" She'd gotten worse and worse as she'd walked—by the end she'd been leaning on Laure's shoulder for strength, and barely able to speak a word through the obstruction in her throat.

"I don't know," Aragon said. "There were spores in her lungs. You heard her. She couldn't breathe. The only reason she got to hospital on her own strength is because she's Fallen and therefore less vulnerable. I've cleared her lungs and given her fungicides, but it's going to take time for them to kick in." He frowned at Laure. "How far away would you say you were when the glass broke?"

"A meter or so?" Laure looked dubious. "I didn't get any glass on me."

"No," Aragon said. "But not all the spores might be that visible. Or you might have inhaled them." He gestured towards the back of the room, where rows of empty bed frames stood stripped of mattresses, remnants of a time when the hospital wing had been much busier than now. "I want to be sure that you're not going to be affected."

"You really think—" Emmanuelle started.

"It's a nasty thing to have, and you're mortal, Laure. You don't have any of Maïr's advantages. You said Morningstar burnt it away?"

"Yes," Emmanuelle said.

Aragon shook his head, and looked at Morningstar with barely a trace of amusement in his eyes. "I'd go check, if I were you."

"What worries you?" Morningstar asked. *He* didn't seem particularly worried.

"Heat is how a lot of fungus disperse spores," Aragon said. "Unless you have a large radius of action, burning isn't necessarily what I'd advocate. I'd also check the floor and the walls. The body of a fungus isn't the toadstools, it's the mycelium, and that could be threaded throughout the parquet of the pantry."

Morningstar stared at him for a long while. Aragon held his gaze without flinching. He might have respected Morningstar, but even the old head of House Silverspires would never have made Aragon question his own expertise.

Emmanuelle was braced for anger, for a roiling wave of magic that would have sent Aragon on one knee, because that was what he had always done. But Morningstar simply shook his head. "I see."

Aragon nodded, brusquely. "Good." He turned to Laure, "You're staying in observation for tonight. If you're still not showing any symptoms, you can get out on fungicides. Maïr is staying for a while longer, until the wounds are clear and I'm sure the risk of contagion is gone."

"The kitchens—"

"Will survive for a day," Aragon snapped. "I'm pretty sure the House will appreciate not having spores or strands of fungus in their meals."

"I'll go sort out that fungus," Morningstar said. "Emmanuelle?"

Emmanuelle looked at Laure, who was pale and breathing fast; and trying very hard not to show it. Afraid, and no wonder. Aragon hadn't exactly been reassuring. "Do you need me? I'd rather stay here for a while. See if Laure can find us another appropriate service." As good an excuse as any so Laure could save face.

His smile was dazzling, overpowering. "I can handle this on my own. If you'd rather stay here, I'll leave the menus on your desk tonight. You can tell me what you think tomorrow."

So much to look forward to. Emmanuelle bit off a curse, and settled down with Laure.

MORNINGSTAR ENTERED the library as Emmanuelle was straightening up the pile of menus. "I see you've had a go at them."

"Mmm," Emmanuelle said. She wanted to ask him about the fungus, but they might as well tackle the menus first. She had a feeling she wasn't going to like his answer about that: at least the menus were a relatively consensual matter. They were written in Morningstar's expansive, utterly confident handwriting, except in very, very small letters, in crooked lines that kept overlapping each other like a secret pattern for a spell. "Laure doesn't have the ingredients or money for half of these," she said. Or even a quarter of these, but she was trying very hard to be generous.

Morningstar pulled a chair, sat next to her. The warmth of his magic washed over her: Emmanuelle's fingers clenched, reflexively. He had changed. Had to; death always did that.

But, for all his mellowing, he kept trying to take over her life.

"It's a formal reception," Morningstar said. "You have to impress. Here." His finger rested, lightly, on the middle of the page.

Chicken vols-au-vent, fish bouchées, fois gras... It read like a fantasy—a fragile memory spun from the golden age before the war, the House ablaze with light, every courtyard thick with dependents, the limestone walls shining ochre under the noonday sun, a profusion of men in swallowtail jackets and women in elegant dresses and scarves, chatting about the latest fashions—all gone and ground into dust now. Emmanuelle opened her mouth to speak, and then read the words more carefully.

"It's all sleight-of-hand." Morningstar looked as smug as a cat who'd feasted on cream. "Pastry can be so impressive, even with little meat."

"If everyone in the kitchen is ready to work for hours," Emmanuelle said, more sharply than she intended to.

"Emmanuelle." Morningstar shook his head. "They want this. They want a feast."

"Something they won't take part on?"

"Of course not." He looked genuinely shocked, for once. "They're joining it, too. As soon as they've finished setting things up. It's also an occasion for them to celebrate among themselves. To remind themselves of the House at its height."

"I guess," Emmanuelle said. She was still not convinced, and still slightly resentful he'd turned her calm dinner into something unrecognisably grand; but perhaps it'd do Selene some good, to remember the House's grand past instead of their diminished present. "Selene doesn't much like red meat." She read the list, slowly, carefully. "Tapenade is good. Can Laure do anything with shrimp?"

"Dried shrimp, yes. Annamite fashion."

Better than nothing. "I can help Laure, but I'm sure she knows how to do this."

"Of course." Morningstar smiled. "I wouldn't presume to tell her to do her job. And of course she wants to impress the guests, for the good of the House."

"The dependents, you mean," Emmanuelle said, distractedly, trying to decipher the end of the line. Some kind of skewer involving mushrooms and onions, with liberally spiced sauce to hide the lack of sophistication? "That doesn't look like—" And then her brain caught up. He hadn't answered her, or contradicted her in any fashion.

She raised her gaze. He gazed back, utterly unfazed. "The guests. Who did you invite, Morningstar?"

He slid the sheet she was reading off the table, pushed off a second one towards her. "I also brought you guest lists."

One glance at it was enough. "No," Emmanuelle said. "Not the other Houses." This was supposed to be a private romantic dinner. Not... She took a deep breath.

"You said Selene needed a distraction," Morningstar said. He looked crestfallen, which was an odd and unwelcome expression. She'd expected him to argue over her, ignoring her objections wholesale. "She enjoys sparring with people."

Emmanuelle took a deep, shaking breath, trying to control herself. "You already sent the invitations."

"I had to," Morningstar said. "Considering the delays..."

Emmanuelle stared at the list again. People on it had been meticulously checked off. He'd been keeping track of who had answered, who was coming and who wasn't. So far it was only minor Houses—the only ones that caught Emmanuelle's attention were Shellac, a House in the Southeast of Paris that held the Gobelins manufacture, and who were slowly but steadily rising through the ranks, and Stormgate and Minimes, two former client Houses of theirs that Selene was doing her best to court back to their side. "No major Houses?"

No House Hawthorn, but then that wasn't surprising. They'd summoned the banyan tree, though Selene couldn't prove anything, or ask for reparations they wouldn't deign to grant. But Hawthorn wasn't the only major House in Paris.

"No major Houses so far," Morningstar said. "Most of them think we're too weak to bother indulging." Morningstar had that look again. Like a beaten puppy, except that "puppy" made him seem harmless, and he was anything but. "If we pull this off, they'll know that we're not that vulnerable, not that easy a prey. It will give us space to rebuild. Time. It'll free up Selene so she can rest and breathe. It would be the best birthday present you could give her."

"If." Emmanuelle kept her voice flat, in spite of the fact that she wanted to strangle him. "Have you seen the House?! We still have entire rooms we can't access because they're solid with banyan roots!"

Morningstar looked at her for a while. "You know that. I know that. The other Houses don't." He made a peculiar gesture, a kind of shrug with his large shoulders, flexing them as if he still had wings. "As I said, sleight of hand."

If only he hadn't been so unbearably smug. If only he hadn't been so unbearably right. Emmanuelle forced herself to exhale. It was done. They could shout at each other for a long time, but it wasn't going to change anything.

And then a horrible thought surfaced. "The fungus," she said, slowly, carefully. "You did deal with it, didn't you?"

Morningstar's face didn't move. "I'm going to need a little more time."

"We." Emmanuelle gave up. "Don't. Have. More. Time." She enunciated every word with the precision of someone throwing darts at a wall—the thunk they'd make as they sank into wood would be so satisfying. "And we don't have more space. The ballroom is the only place in the House that can put up so many people." Aragon was confident the course of fungicides he'd given Maïr was going to wipe off the traces on her hands, but so far they'd seen few results. As he'd pointed out, it would take weeks or months to clear in any case. Which was, she guessed, fine if it was House dependents; a diplomatic disaster if it involved envoys, because by the mere act of inviting them into Silverspires, they'd guaranteed their safety.

"No one has a reason to go into the pantry," Morningstar said. "Especially now."

Emmanuelle, having learnt her lesson the hard way, wasn't about to let this pass. "Especially?"

"I was thorough this time. Better to completely incinerate the wallpaper. And the furniture."

"You—" Emmanuelle stared at him. "You *burnt* the cupboard?"

"Aragon said 'large radius'. It sounded like the best way to make sure." His face was hard. Was it the same expression he'd had, when sending dependents to their deaths? She was surprised to no longer remember.

Focus on the important things. "So we have a charred pantry, and a fungus still clinging to a smouldering ruin." Or possibly worse: they had spores everywhere.

Morningstar shrugged, and smiled. He probably hoped it was winsome. Emmanuelle was too far gone to care. "As Aragon pointed out," he said, "it's surprisingly resilient. Don't worry: I checked. There are no spores in the ballroom."

Emmanuelle didn't want to know how he'd checked. She had a sneaking suspicion that he'd simply have asked a dependent to walk through the ballroom and checked whether they asphyxiated. "But there are in the pantry."

"The pantry is probably better if it's off-limits, especially to mortals, yes. But the door is small. Piling chairs and tables in front of it should hide it. And if not, I can always cast a spell of illusion."

It was far from ideal, but then again there was no good solution. There was nothing she could think of that would rescue this unmitigated disaster. "I'll have a look when we set up the room. But don't think that lets you off the hook."

Morningstar had the grace to look chastened, though clearly he still didn't understand what he'd done wrong. *Any* of what he'd done wrong. "I can tell Selene if you want."

"No." Emmanuelle bit off the angrier retort. "I'll do that. It's my job. You tell Father Javier we need the wards on the ballroom and the neighbouring corridors re-checked. And everything cleared of roots. You're going to have to convince dependents to work very, very hard in the coming six days. You have got work ahead. I'm sure you'll enjoy it." The worst thing was that he probably would. It'd have been torture to Emmanuelle, but Morningstar was like Selene, a social butterfly who relished a challenge.

Good news was, it was all uphill—for both of them.

EMMANUELLE FOUND Selene in her office, her slight frame hidden by a mountain of paperwork. She wore her usual men's clothes: swallowtail jacket over trousers, and a starched red shirt. The insignia of the House—Morningstar's large two-handed sword over the towers of Notre-Dame—was barely visible, embroidered on the collar of her jacket.

Selene raised her head when she came in, and frowned, mildly amused. "You look preoccupied."

Emmanuelle kissed her on the mouth, drinking in the smell of her, the familiar giddiness. "It's been a trying day so far."

"Morningstar?" Selene still sounded amused. Carefully, she set aside the report she was reading on a pile of other papers.

Well, nothing for it. "Hum." Emmanuelle said. "About your birthday. There have been issues."

Selene raised an eyebrow.

"Things might have got out of control. A tiny bit." Emmanuelle shook her head. "Partly my fault, partly Morningstar's."

"Ah." Selene bit her lip not to laugh. She still looked amused. "Did you bite off more than you could chew?"

"It was going to be a romantic dinner," Emmanuelle said. "And then it…grew."

Selene was still amused. "I can guess."

"You knew?"

"A party of that size in the House? I'm sorry, but you can't hope to keep that a surprise." She drew Emmanuelle to her. Emmanuelle climbed on her lap, knees on either side of Selene's hips, dark skin against light, looking into eyes that always saw too clearly. "I don't know the details, though. Dishes and such. Wine." She let the words dangle in the air.

Emmanuelle fought the temptation to kiss her again, and said, instead, running one hand up Selene's chest, "It *was* the plan. Morningstar invited the other Houses to your party."

Silence. Selene's eyes were cool, expressionless, but her lips had gone tight.

"He said we needed to show strength to others, and that your birthday would be the perfect occasion. I'm sorry. You've got other things to do than navigate the swamp."

Silence. She almost couldn't bear to look at Selene. At last her lover said, "He's not wrong, per se."

"Don't tell me—"

"That I'm happy? God, no. I'm going to have to keep smiling at envoys of Houses until my face aches. I imagine you've already reinforced security."

"We're going to rope Father Javier in," Emmanuelle said. "We've got some fungus in the pantry as well. A rather persistent strain."

"The thing that sent Maïr to hospital?" Selene shook her head. "Morningstar told me. It sounded like it was under control."

"I think so," Emmanuelle said, cautiously. It was hardly the more urgent preoccupation now. She and Morningstar could keep the fungus contained, or at least out of Selene's way, while Selene did the heavy lifting of not setting off a Houses war.

"Good," Selene said. Her face was distant, but not in that harsh, unhappy way that Emmanuelle recognised. Merely thoughtful. "Part and parcel of being head of the House. Pity I can't delegate my own presence. I don't suppose I can skip my own party?"

"You can try," Emmanuelle said.

"Until Morningstar drags me back. I suppose you've tried wringing his neck."

"He's taller than me," Emmanuelle said. "Difficult to get the better of."

"Don't I know it." Selene grimaced. "In many ways, it was simpler when he was in charge. Or not."

She hadn't wanted to be head of the House, but of course there'd been no one else—and if there was one thing about Selene, it was that she'd always do what needed to be done, no matter the cost.

Emmanuelle, of course, would never have been capable of this. She was content where she was, and the library, banyan roots and all, was her refuge and her entire world.

"You're on edge," Selene said, fondly. "Come here." And drew Emmanuelle to her, skin against skin, for a kiss that set her entire body afire—and then Emmanuelle forgot everything else, and lost herself in the urgent, comforting maelstrom of desire.

EMMANUELLE SPENT the day before the birthday party in the ballroom.

They'd cleaned it carefully. It was possibly the only place in the House, along with Selene's office, which was completely free of banyan roots. They'd glued the parquet floor back into place, although it was starting to look like an elaborate and disorderly jigsaw, polished the cracked mirrors until the reflections in them were almost free of mould, and the chandeliers were blazing with light, though a good quarter of the candles were missing, their absence disguised by a profusion of cheap glass. And the perfume and light couldn't quite disguise the persistent smell of mould, or the broken-off, tarnished carvings on the walls.

Hélène, the majordomo, was setting up tables: the large ones they kept under wraps for big occasions, with the extensions being slotted into place. Emmanuelle helped roll these into place. She had no idea what time it was when she finally looked up, hands and arms aching, to see Father Javier at her elbow.

"Did you even get anything to eat?"

"This morning," Emmanuelle said. They still had the glasses and drinks to set out, and they were running late on schedule. "What's wrong?"

Javier looked forlorn, his olive skin pale above his clerical collar. But then he'd looked the same that morning, at mass, when he'd given a sermon with none of his usual fire. Being in charge of security at a time like this was enough worries for several lifetimes. "Do you have a minute?"

Emmanuelle rose, wiping her hands against her dress—realising, too late, that they left traces of grey dust against the pristine white. She'd change later. "Of course."

Javier, unsurprisingly, led her towards the recessed door of the pantry. "I'd ask Morningstar, but—"

But Morningstar, of course, wouldn't be bothered by something so mundane as setting up tables. No, that was unfair. He was with Selene, to help her welcome the other Houses, because he'd once been the head of House Silverspires, and Selene needed the envoys to see him—at her side and clearly as a subservient adviser, rather than some true power behind the throne.

Sometimes, Selene could be ruthless.

"How does this strike you?" Javier asked.

The pantry door was behind one of the smaller tarnished mirrors, its handle hidden in the midst of garlands of grape. Only the faintest of charred marks around the mirror indicated that beyond the door lay nothing but burnt devastation. But the dark roots that had encircled the wine glasses—the rhizomorphs—were now entwined around the gilded fruit, forming garlands of their own, and a few toadstools had sprung up in the ashes—none of them larger than a finger. It was all encased in a thin, fragile layer of magical ice, and just to be sure Javier had put a table in front of it.

"It's growing much faster than ordinary fungus," Javier said. "Because of the magic, I assume. I checked with Aragon: he thought he recognised it—something that grows on wood and earth, and hates the cold. The ice should keep it contained for a while, but it's not exactly innocuous or unremarkable." Magic was rare and seldom used, and a pane of that size would draw inevitable attention. Not good.

"Aragon didn't have fungicides for it?"

"For people, yes. For the actual fungus on furniture?" Javier shook his head. "I believe his solution involved ripping off the affected parts, any neighbouring bits, and disposing of it all somewhere far, far from the House."

So, no easy solutions. Not that she'd expected them, but still. "You checked for spores."

"I'm still standing." Javier's smile was wry. "As long as it remains frozen I think we should be fine."

For various values of "fine". "How confident are you that your spell will contain it?"

"I don't know. It shouldn't be growing too fast, but that magical sheet is fragile. It won't stand up to much pressure. It's the best I can do, but—"

Emmanuelle reached out across the table. She saw Javier's hand tense, ready to snatch her away, but she stopped well short of the rhizomorphs.

"I added the table to help hide it, and to make sure no one accidentally got close to it. It's the largest one we have. As you can see, you'd have to bend completely over it to touch the wall. Hard to do in the middle of a crowd. I thought we'd pile food on it, like a huge *pièce montée* or something similar, to hide the rest." Javier said. "It's hard to keep piling furniture up near it. It just looks suspicious."

Emmanuelle shook her head. "You can't put food there. There's not much that would reach high enough to hide your spell." She looked at the rest of the room: long series of tables artfully set, and groups of chairs and sofas set in circles so people could sit in private conversations. There was nothing that looked tall or innocuous enough to hide that mass of fungus. "Let's take another approach. Can you get a large grey sheet? And more chairs?"

"What do you want?" Javier asked.

"If we can't hide it, let's minimise it. Everyone knows Silverspires is a shambles. It won't be shocking if there's a burnt space on a wall, half-covered by a sheet and blocked off by a pile of chairs."

"Why grey?"

"Rhizomorphs won't show on grey."

"You think—"

"I'd rather be ready for contingencies," Emmanuelle said. Though at that stage they might have spores in the ballroom, and hiding the fungus might well be the least of their worries. "Hopefully." Emmanuelle looked at the wall again. "You're going to need a bigger charred mark." She thought, again, of what Aragon had said about the spores. "Just try not to burn the door handle or anywhere with actual fungus. Perhaps just the space around the mirror."

Javier looked, thoughtfully, at the door, his face creased in a familiar expression—trying to solve a given problem with the few resources he had.

"All right. I'll disengage the wards for a bit." The wards over the ballroom were reinforced to prevent extensive damage: a necessary precaution, considering it was used for welcoming visiting envoys.

"Good. Let me know if you run into difficulties. I'll go see Laure."

AS IT turned out, she never made it to the kitchens: she found Laure escorting an envoy from House Harrier, her face set in a grimace that turned into sheer relief when she saw Emmanuelle. "Emmanuelle. This is Darrias. She's here for the party."

Emmanuelle's heart sank. "You're early." Harrier was a major House in the South. They'd answered, with typical arrogance, at the last minute, and there'd never been any question of refusing to accommodate them. They were much diminished by the war—the limestone of their buildings darkened by soot, their gardens on small plazas all but wiped out—but they weren't to be trifled with.

Darrias was Fallen: a woman with a shaven head, covered in intricate tattoos. She turned to Emmanuelle. A cool, brown-eyed gaze swept her up and down, and finally decided she might be worth the time. "Lord Guy wanted to make sure I was among the first to present my respects."

Which was unlikely. Guy wouldn't bother with such niceties, especially not for a House that stood at the bottom of the order of things. What was Harrier up to? "The party doesn't start for an hour, but I'll find you a room to wait in. If you'll excuse me a minute, I'll need a word with Laure first."

Laure was ill at ease, and no wonder. Harrier despised mortals. It reserved all its high-level positions for Fallen, and Laure to her would be little more than a drudge, unworthy of any respect. "You couldn't spare any Fallen to accompany her?" Emmanuelle asked, but she knew the answer already. The Fallen would have all been requisitioned by Javier, except for Maïr, who was still in hospital.

Laure pulled herself to her full height. "I'm head of the kitchens. She'd have been vexed if anyone else accompanied her." But, presumably, it hadn't been a pleasant walk.

There were various minor emergencies in the kitchen, and things that were going to require Emmanuelle's input, but all of this could wait until she'd taken Darrias to Selene and Morningstar.

She had no pity for Morningstar. He'd earned every excruciating minute of small talk with an envoy of a House who wanted to destroy them, but damn it, Selene's birthday should have been different. Emmanuelle was going to strangle Morningstar, when all was said and done. The best birthday present for her, he'd said. Some idea.

Emmanuelle walked back to Darrias, trying to compose herself as best as she could. "The ballroom isn't ready, but I'll take you to see Lady Selene."

Darrias smiled. It was a surprising expression, which transformed her entire face, pure, unadulterated delight that made her seem younger. "Why not. That's an unexpected surprise."

As they walked through the courtyards, their feet echoing on the cracked cobblestones, Darrias said, "You've been with Lady Selene a long time." Her eyes were bright and quick, taking in everything around her, her whole demeanour focused, deliberate, as if she were a weapon just out of its sheath, sharpened and hungry for blood.

Emmanuelle shrugged. "Since before the war. Have you been in House Harrier long?"

Darrias's face shifted. Emmanuelle could have sworn she'd hit a sore point, but surely the question she'd asked had been innocuous? "A century or so. I've been Lord Guy's envoy for a while. I deal with other Houses for him."

"I assume he has other envoys?" Emmanuelle said. She didn't much like Harrier. Their superciliousness grated: there was nothing inherently inferior to mortals, merely a lack of power in a city where power had become the only currency. And Guy was a dreadful bore with not much in the way of conversation. A good thing she wasn't Selene, who had to deal with him regularly.

"Some," Darrias said. She still looked oddly thoughtful, oddly unhappy, with the smug self-satisfaction all but gone. The courtyard they were in still had traces of the banyan: a few roots growing on the limestone buildings, gripping the iron-wrought balconies. The cobblestones were warm under Emmanuelle's feet, a reminder of the wards that kept them all safe, still standing in spite of other Houses' efforts to bring them down. "I'm the oldest envoy. It's dangerous work."

"Paris isn't always safe," Emmanuelle said. Part of her missed the city of her youth—wanted to buy the narrative of the gilded age before the war, but she'd been on the streets for a while, and she knew that one could starve or die of infection as easily back then as now. The only thing that had happened was that the powerful had cut themselves off from the Houseless, and that she'd joined them, as complicit as any of them.

"Oh, it was always unsafe," Darrias said, with a shrug. "The war didn't much change things, did it? Those who have nothing still starve and die."

It so startlingly echoed Emmanuelle's own thoughts that she stopped, and stared at Darrias. "Most House-bound don't pay attention to what happens outside the Houses. Or among the Houseless."

"I have to," Darrias said. "It's the difference between survival and death."

But presumably she didn't care about the Houseless. No one did.

Darrias stood, both hands loosely at her sides. "I like it out there," she said, with an expansive shrug. "Beholden to no one and nothing, and only your wits to survive. It makes people different."

It was skirting close to heresy, in House Harrier's thinking. Slowly, cautiously, Emmanuelle said, "No, it doesn't. They're not inferior or more stupid. Just good at what they do." Which was surviving on so little.

She thought Darrias was going to shake her head and change the subject of conversation, but she didn't. "Like diamonds, refined to a cutting edge. Except much less valued." She stopped, then, watched Emmanuelle warily. Gone too far, this time?

Emmanuelle said, fascinated in spite of herself—"Burning bright and exhausting themselves because someone else has stolen all the fire. The world isn't fair, is it."

Darrias looked at her, for a while. "It never is. And they're just people. Not more or less evil than any of us."

Arguable. Power came with responsibilities, didn't it? "The Houses have riches. They're the ones with the onus to share." And now they were definitely into territory she'd never would have expected of a House Harrier envoy. Or a House-bound, full stop.

Darrias laughed. It was gentle, genuinely amused, with a hint of fondness. "A real firebrand. I should have known."

Was this just her way of mocking her? But Darrias seemed sincere. "I do what I can."

"Sneaking outside with food and clothes?" Darrias said. "And giving classes to the seamstresses in the factories?"

Emmanuelle laughed, bitterly. "I think of it as doing the right thing, but Morningstar would tell you I'm trying to salve a guilty conscience."

"I'm not Morningstar." Darrias shrugged. "I'm not here to judge you, either." Her brown eyes held Emmanuelle's, a weight that twisted in her stomach. In other circumstances—if she hadn't been Harrier, if they hadn't been on opposite sides...

Emmanuelle said, curtly, "I forgot. You're here for a birthday."

"On Lord Guy's behalf." A quick, glib answer. Too quick.

Emmanuelle might not be the diplomat Selene was, but she'd picked up on a few things. "And you have business of your own."

Darrias laughed. "Of course not. Don't be ridiculous."

Emmanuelle thought back to the conversation as they started walking again, but nothing struck her. Darrias didn't appear happy about her errand. Was she angry that Guy assigned her to something as routine as this? She'd seemed to thrive on danger, on being her own mistress, none of which applied here.

She couldn't tell, but she didn't like it.

Selene and Morningstar were not in Selene's office, but in a nearby reception room, seated around a small corner table inlaid with mother-of-pearl squares.

It was a large room with faded wallpaper—a sickly beige that made it hard to differentiate between the spots of mould and the faded flower pattern. They'd almost removed all the banyan roots from this one: the parquet floor still buckled in places, but it was all but invisible. The mirror above the fireplace was cracked, fungus spreading from the bottom corner until it obscured their silhouette. It reminded Emmanuelle, all too vividly, of the fungus in the ballroom.

"Darrias has arrived early," Emmanuelle said, showing Darrias in, who was still looking at everything with that bright, hungry look, those eyes that made Emmanuelle ill at ease.

"Oh." Selene rose, made a small, perfunctory bow to Darrias's deep one. "Do have a drink," she said. She rose, to get a glass from a sideboard, pouring wine in an easy, graceful gesture, as Morningstar effortlessly engaged Darrias in small talk, drawing her attention away from the room.

Emmanuelle let out a breath she hadn't even been aware of holding. She nodded, briefly, at Selene, and slipped out to go back to the ballroom. Selene could have handled Darrias in her sleep.

Still, something was wrong with Darrias, and she couldn't tell what. So many risks, so many things that could go wrong—but it was something specific bothering her, and she couldn't put her finger on what—like a familiar pattern that refused to coalesce. And she knew that, when it did, it was going to be the kind of thing that had long, sharp, unpleasant teeth.

THE KITCHENS were almost an oasis of calm compared to the ballroom. Laure was directing an army of pastry cooks in preparing an elaborate *pièce montée*, a peacock of nougat and spun sugar, carrying the arms of House Silverspires in its mouth. The kitchen hands were running between stations, and the smell of fish and meat was rising from the kitchen, almost like the full formal banquets Emmanuelle remembered from before the war. Of course, the fish these days was dried, the meat dry and tasteless and sprinkled on top of dishes rather than being a centrepiece, and the soups more water than vegetables—but compared to the grit-filled flour of the streets it was still luxury.

Stacks of bread lay on a table, being cut into toasts for canapés: tapenade and butter and all they could scavenge. Helias was haranguing a brigade of kitchen hands, showing them how to create something that looked good and effectively disguised the fact the pantry was all but empty, the butter stretched out, the tapenade diluted with far too much oil.

All on track. Emmanuelle breathed a sigh of relief, and went to chat with Astyanax, who'd just checked in the cellars for the wines Selene pre-ferred, and then with a few of the sous-chefs, checking on the progress of individual dishes while Laure was busy.

The period of quiet lasted perhaps half an hour.

Someone knocked at the doors. No one in House Silverspires ever knocked at the doors of the kitchens, which were always kept open. The cavernous rooms under arched ceilings were busy day and night, and too many people kept going in and out of them. Emmanuelle, busy tasting a hollandaise sauce, barely noticed, until the sound of Laure's voice changed, no longer directing or correcting mistakes, but pleading. If she'd been on the verge of panic with House Harrier's envoy, now it was ten times worse.

"Excuse me," Emmanuelle said. And elbowed her way out of the kitchen station—which suddenly felt crowded with frozen sous-chefs—to find Laure talking to Asmodeus.

The Fallen head of House Hawthorn wore his usual dark grey swal-lowtail, perfectly cut. His hair, black with a touch of white at the temples, framed a lean, sharp face. His eyes, grey-green behind horn-rimmed glasses, sparkled with his usual amusement: he was a sadist and would revel in Laure's discomfort, probably regretting he couldn't actually hurt her in more direct ways.

"What are you doing here?" Emmanuelle asked. And bit her lip. So much for diplomacy. Hawthorn hadn't formally answered Morningstar's invitation, but of course she couldn't just turn Asmodeus away. They didn't need a war with Hawthorn. They couldn't afford it, no matter that Hawthorn was probably the one who'd put them in this position.

"Why, Emmanuelle," Asmodeus said. He smiled. It was sharp and unpleasant, the expression of a predator. Laure used this relief to discreetly leave. Emmanuelle couldn't blame her. "One would think you weren't happy to see me." His usual perfume, bergamot and orange blossom, saturated the room.

Careful. "Not overly, no," Emmanuelle said. He enjoyed defiance—up to a point. "I assume you're here for the party."

Asmodeus gestured. One of the two bodyguards with him brought a bottle, which he presented, bowing just a fraction, to Emmanuelle. "Romanée-Conti Grand Cru, 1910. It's been held in stasis in the cellars of the House. A bit too spicy for my personal taste, but Selene has always liked them a little harsher." He must have seen her face. "It's not poisoned."

Emmanuelle took the bottle, feeling very much as though she was holding a live snake. "And I'm supposed to just take your word for it?"

"I'm assuming you'll check. But there's really little pleasure in poisoning anyone." His gloved fingers flexed, slightly, as sharp as talons. "I suppose people like Guy might enjoy doing things at a remove. House Harrier has always been squeamish." He sounded disapproving. It was surreal. Or typical Asmodeus.

"Fine," Emmanuelle said. She left the bottle on a nearby table. She really didn't want to handle it longer than she had to. "We'll give it to Selene, and she can taste it and tell you how enjoyable it was."

"I doubt she can say anything else." He sounded amused. "Playing the game."

Emmanuelle threw a glance behind her. The kitchen staff was still watching them, with an expression she knew by heart: wanting him gone without giving them any particular notice. Asmodeus held long grudges. He wouldn't dare touch a member of another House without good motivation, but who knew, in their current situation, what he'd feel emboldened to do. He'd already taken dependents from them.

"Laure?"

Laure looked up from the table she'd settled at, her eyes filled with grim determination.

"Do you know what's going on in the ballroom?"

She'd weighed, for a split second, the wisdom of showing him into the reception room with Darrias. But while Selene could have handled Darrias in her sleep, she hated Asmodeus, and Emmanuelle just didn't have the heart to have him spoil Selene's afternoon.

Laure's gaze went from Asmodeus to Emmanuelle. When she spoke, it was clear she was picking her words with care. "Javier is there, but last I checked he was finished with what he had to do. I think—" her voice was slow, cautious—"that we're ready to accommodate guests."

Translation: Javier had probably succeeded in containing and hiding the fungus. They were going to have to pray this was enough.

Emmanuelle turned her eyes upwards for a brief moment, to the invisible Heavens. *Father, please see us safely through this.* It was going to take a miracle. Or several of them.

They didn't speak again until they were out of the kitchens, going through one of the smaller courtyards that separated two crooked buildings—each floor a little larger than the previous ones, until they joined at the top to form an arm. "You'll probably get bored here," Emmanuelle said. "It's hardly an exciting event." And she'd dearly have loved to know why he bothered to attend, but she knew he'd never answer her if she simply asked. Darrias was one thing, an envoy whose sending cost Guy very little. Asmodeus was head of his House and must have had far better things to than bothering with Silverspires.

"Oh, I can find my own entertainment, never fear." Asmodeus's smile was charming, of the butter wouldn't melt in his mouth variety. Or it would have been, if Emmanuelle didn't remember him standing in the middle of a drawing room with the animal smell of blood all around him, his white gloves gone dark, carefully wiping his glasses clean with a handkerchief that was fast turning dark red.

"I'm not worried," Emmanuelle said, tartly. "I hear you've been amply busy since you left us."

"There was a void to fill." His face was suddenly grave.

Too late, Emmanuelle remembered that his lover Samariel had died in Silverspires, caught in a spell that had shredded him like flimsy paper. "I'm sorry," she said. "That was thoughtless."

Asmodeus's sarcastic smile didn't waver. "Platitudes. Though you do mean them."

"Don't you dare reproach me for compassion."

"I don't." His gaze locked on her for a moment. She was the one who broke away, not sure if she should pity him, or be annoyed, or both. "As a matter of fact, I wanted to have a word with you."

Emmanuelle raised an eyebrow. "Really."

"I could have it with Selene, but given the current state of our relationship…"

Emmanuelle bit back the "she hates your guts" that was her first answer. "I see," she said, cautiously. "A word. What about."

"Hawthorn," Asmodeus said. He straightened his jacket, as much at ease as if he'd been walking through his own gardens. "Selene is worried."

She had a lot on her plate. "About us? It's her job," Emmanuelle said. "As head of House Silverspires."

"Mmm," Asmodeus said. "Protecting her dependents. That's a welcome change from the previous leadership of this House."

"Morningstar—"

Asmodeus laughed, curtly. "Don't pretend you're entranced by Morningstar. He sacrificed anything and anyone as long as it would keep the House safe, even his own dependents. That kind of behaviour doesn't deserve to be *worshipped.*"

He's changed, Emmanuelle wanted to say, but the words had shrivelled to ash on her tongue. "So you disapprove of us. Don't pretend that's why you tried to make us fall."

"Moral high ground?" His eyes sparkled behind his horn-rimmed glasses. "Of course not. I made you fall because you were too powerful, and anything powerful is a threat to Hawthorn. Destroying Morningstar's pride and joy in the process was merely an added attraction. Now..." he shrugged. "You're no longer powerful."

To say the least. "And your dependents are safe." She didn't bother to keep the sarcasm out of her voice.

"For the time being." Asmodeus's face was grave. "But never mind my dependents. I promised Selene I wouldn't interfere with her running of the House. I'd like to make sure she doesn't interfere with mine, either."

"With Hawthorn?" Emmanuelle would have laughed, if it hadn't been so deathly serious. She groped for a carefully worded answer, and found nothing but the truth. "Asmodeus. Does it look as though we're in any position to interfere with whatever you're doing?"

"Great things," Asmodeus said, casually. Too casually. Well, she didn't care. He had a scheme, or something similar, to climb to the top of the hierarchy of Houses, and it was going to involve a lot of pain for someone, somewhere in another House. Which suited her fine. "So long as we're agreed..." he shrugged. "Tell her to be careful with the minor Houses."

The minor Houses. The ones Selene was courting, their former satellites, and the clients of other Houses, ill disguising their glee at seeing Silverspires reduced. Shellac. Minimes. Stormgate. "I'm not biting. You're going to have to be clearer than that."

Asmodeus looked at her for a while, his head cocked like a bird of prey's. "If you wish. In the wake of what happened to Silverspires, the balance of powers has shifted. Client Houses have peeled away from major ones and formed new alliances. I've heard rumblings some of them wanted to make a mark with something spectacular."

Which meant blood or death or both. "And you think they'd involve us?"

"You're weak. Irresistible prey. And beset from within and without. Morningstar isn't necessarily an asset to you. He's got such useful experience of destroying his own, but being eager to burn people and things indiscriminately only gets you so far." He smiled, showing white, sharp teeth. Was he referring to the fungus? No, it was too indirect. He couldn't possibly know.

Emmanuelle didn't rise to the jibe. It was exactly what he'd expect. "You have a particular House in mind."

He didn't answer. All they were going to get, clearly, a barbed, useless warning. Not that much different from his usual self, then. She bit her lip, and changed tacks again. "You know Darrias."

"Guy's envoy?" Asmodeus shrugged. "Of course. She's been around for a while. I assume she's here, or you wouldn't be asking me. I look forward to catching up with her. We haven't spoken in a long time."

Casual. Too casual. Where did he and Darrias and Harrier stand? Were they allied to put Silverspires into more misery? Was he warning her about minor Houses just as misdirection, to keep her sifting through dozens of envoys until it was too late? "So you come here out of the goodness of your heart, to catch up with old friends." She didn't bother to hide the sarcasm in her voice.

"Something like that, yes." He straightened his gloves, stretching the fingers of his right hand and holding them to the light, as if admiring some handiwork.

"You said we were irresistible prey. You expect me to believe you don't want to join the vultures?" Emmanuelle's voice was sharper than it should be. Darrias, watching everything, committing to memory the layout between the kitchens and the reception room. What was going on?

"Oh, I like weakness as much as the next head of House," Asmodeus said. "But I have other business. More profitable. As I said to Selene, there's not much point in trying to wring blood out of a stone."

"Except pleasure."

"Not even that. Much trouble for few results. For one thing, if it's just my personal entertainment, I've got more than enough prisoners in the cells to indulge. Outside of the House, I prefer challenges." Asmodeus smiled. She wanted to shake him, except that he'd probably find it all amusing.

Challenges. Emmanuelle thought, for a heartbeat." Well, I've got something for you. You can keep Morningstar entertained at the party."

His expression didn't change, but she knew she'd scored a hit, given his feelings towards Morningstar.

In Emmanuelle's current mood, they were quite welcome to one another.

BY THE time she arrived with Asmodeus, the party had started.

A pile of gifts was on a table to the left of the entrance, given pride of place on a marble table with tarnished golden legs. They'd clearly been unwrapped and wrapped back together with as much care as possible. Javier was no fool, which meant they looked as though they'd been through a light wringer instead of completely shredded and flattened.

A sea of dependents in swallowtail jackets and ornate dresses mingled by the buffet, sampling the food, parting around the envoys of the other Houses like a shoal of fish around unexpected obstacles. The exception was Morningstar, who held a fluted glass of champagne, and stood in a circle with three envoys of minor Houses as though holding court.

Typical.

Selene was nowhere to be seen, but it wasn't unexpected. Of course she'd want to make a grand entrance later, for maximum effect.

Asmodeus greeted Morningstar, and they had perhaps a two-minute chat, during which Morningstar did most of the talking. Asmodeus pointedly gave short, noncommittal answers, and then made excuses and wandered to the buffet to help himself to some tapenade toasts.

Emmanuelle leant in the doorjamb for a while, watching. They were all engrossed in their private conversations. Asmodeus had drifted towards the Minimes envoy, a woman who looked impossibly young to be trusted with the business of other Houses, but held herself with impressive poise. The Shellac envoy was an older mortal woman with the smooth face of someone who did far too much angel magic. She was sipping at her fluted glass, making small talk with Darrias and the Stormgate envoy, a Fallen of indeterminate gender with sharp features and long, braided hair falling on a broad-shouldered back.

In all the time she'd been there, Asmodeus hadn't made a single move towards Darrias. But of course he knew that she'd asked. Of course he'd beware, wouldn't he?

She threw a glance towards the entrance to the pantry. It was exactly as she'd asked, hastily covered with a sheet and barricaded with a table and a pile of chairs. Javier had been thorough: the sheet hung askew over charred marks, giving the impression that they'd desperately tried to mask a large burnt area, and he'd picked a thick, mottled grey sheet that completely hid the sheet of magical ice.

She couldn't see Javier anywhere. That was odd. Surely he should have been watching over the party, making sure that nothing could go wrong? She threw another glance over the assembly. She could always get Morningstar if she couldn't find him—

Something caught her eye under the cloth of the table in front of the pantry door: a flash of red and silver, the colours of the House. Surely... No, she was definitely right. It was someone in a House uniform, and they were lying under the table.

This wasn't good.

Emmanuelle elbowed her way into the room towards Morningstar— mouthing platitudes, as Asmodeus would put it, taking news and assuring them all that the party would be something to remember. Morningstar was right, damn him. They all were searching for signs of weakness, and the House couldn't afford any.

An unconscious dependent under a table at a party probably didn't count as a strength.

She grabbed the first child dependent she could find—Charlotte, a young girl of perhaps eight, awkwardly wearing a patched red dress with mutton sleeves—and gave her the piece of paper on which she'd written her message to Morningstar.

I need a distraction. Anything you want. It doesn't need to be long.

She watched Charlotte make her way to Morningstar, watched him bend down and smile, his face not changing as he read the message. His gaze held Emmanuelle's, briefly, but he gave no other sign.

Damn him, he was good.

He bowed down to the three envoys. The Solférino envoy smiled, showing teeth filed to sharp points; the Samothrace one raised her champagne glass, thoughtfully; the Astragale one merely nodded. Then he followed Charlotte.

Emmanuelle moved towards the pantry door. She kept a wary eye on everyone else. Asmodeus was still in conversation with the Minimes envoy, and most of the other envoys were clustered near the buffet. The Astragale envoy looked in her direction for a brief moment, but dismissed her.

She'd thought Morningstar was going to use magic, something loud and grandiloquent that would catch the attention of the room—and in that she was almost right.

Almost.

There was a crackling noise, like chestnuts popping in a fire. Morningstar knelt in the centre of a ring of children of the House, all dressed in swallowtail jackets and dresses, and preternaturally silent, their faces filled with awe—and moved his hands, cradling a flame that became a leaping deer, and then a rabbit. The crowd shifted, craning to see the magic at work.

That was her cue.

Emmanuelle knelt, quickly, and pulled at the underside of the table. As she'd thought, it was an unconscious body. She was Fallen, and dragging it out from under the table was never going to be a problem.

It was Javier.

He looked a mess, his clerical collar and white shirt soaked with wet blood—too much, too fast. She couldn't see a wound, and now wasn't the time for a detailed check. She reached under the table, and lifted the sheet as discreetly as she could. The magical ice sheet was intact. The fungus—it did seem a little larger than the last time, didn't it? She couldn't be sure. But it didn't matter. Javier's spell held, and the rhizomorphs and mycelium were still encased in ice, still contained and posing no danger to the party.

And it most certainly wasn't the fungus that had wounded Javier.

His eyes opened, stared straight at her. "Emmanuelle—" his hand moved, tried to pluck at her. "Save your strength." She laid a hand on his chest, sent magic questing towards his heart, a jolt of strength that crossed his entire body, making his limbs contort and flex like twigs in a windstorm. She rose, propping him up on her shoulder, heedless of the blood spreading on her dress. "You're going to need to walk."

He hissed. Light streamed through his eyes, making the cornea as translucent as fine porcelain, his contracted pupils two pinpoints of darkness. "Emmanuelle—"

She looked at the room. Most people were still entranced with Morningstar's display. A handful of envoys had grown bored and had turned again towards the buffet; and Asmodeus was looking straight at her, face twisted in terrible amusement.

He knew. Was it because he'd put Javier there? But that was impossible. He'd been in her sights the entire time, and he most definitely hadn't been in the room when this happened.

She tottered towards the door, her shoulder supporting Javier; smiled, brightly, at people started turning towards her. "I'm awfully sorry. He fell down and hit something. I'm getting him to hospital."

Morningstar's little stunt should have obscured that she'd dragged Javier out from under the table. She couldn't do much—an unconscious and wounded man was never going to make a discreet exit from the party—but she could at least draw attention away from the pantry and its dangerous contents.

Javier didn't speak again until they were halfway to the hospital wing. Around them, the peeled-off wallpaper of the corridor rustled in an invisible wind. She could hear his breath, coming faster and faster. "Emmanuelle—"

"Yes," she said, shifting to support his full weight on her shoulder. He kept sliding off. His eyes were dark again, the magic she'd given him fading. He was in a bad state, and it was all going to sustain him, even though it couldn't actually heal him. "You're going to be all right." She said it because she had to, not because she knew it was true.

"They—they're going to—they—" How long had he been under the table, bleeding out? Too long.

"Who?" Emmanuelle asked. "Who's doing this?"

Javier's breath came in hard and fast—his lungs couldn't keep up. He was starting to choke. Emmanuelle gave up, and shifted him to her two arms. "Going to run." Had to, before he started convulsing.

"The gifts," Javier said. "Going to—ruin—party."

And then he fell silent, and didn't speak again—not even after Aragon came out of his office, face flushed with worry and anger—and laid him down on a bed, screaming at the nurses to move faster before they lost him altogether.

"HE'S LUCKY," Aragon said.

"Lucky?" Emmanuelle sat on one of the iron chairs of the hospital, watching Javier in his bed.

"Yes. Most victims stabbed in an area with so many major organs don't recover."

"Was that—"

"—where the blood was coming from? One wound on the forehead, and two stabs in the chest. Fortunately no vital organs were touched." His voice was gruff. "You did good getting him here."

"Mmm," Emmanuelle said. "Will he—"

"Live?" Aragon shrugged. "He's mortal, Emmanuelle. Insofar as chances go, they're all on his side. But something could still go wrong."

"Stab-wounds." Emmanuelle thought again of Asmodeus looking straight at her. "Someone didn't want him around."

"Obviously." Aragon took off his gloves and threw them away into a container. He glared at it for a while. "I'd have appreciated going to the party instead of getting extra work."

"Liar," Emmanuelle said, amused. "You were in your office. You've always hated parties."

"I hear we've been having a busy day?" Selene asked, from the doorway.

Emmanuelle turned. "You—" she looked at Selene. "You look stunning."

She wore a long, flowing blue dress of embroidered silk from the Indochinese colonies, with a white-flowered branch near the hem. Over her shoulders was a shawl that started with the same blue, and then shifted colours, to the shimmering, dark colour of a summer sky in the instant just before the sun set. A single large pendant hung around her neck, shining with the light of stored magic. All of Emmanuelle's worries and frustrations suddenly seemed to shrivel into insignificance, and not even Morningstar's smug face behind Selene could dampen her mood.

"You," Selene said, "look like you need to put on party clothes." She walked into the room—past row after row of empty hospital beds, rusted iron frames with threadbare mattresses—until she got to the one where Javier was.

"Yes," Emmanuelle said. "As soon as I sort things out."

Selene nodded, briefly, towards Javier. "Is he going to be all right?"

Aragon shrugged. It was apparently all Selene needed.

"Do you know who hurt him?"

"One of the envoys, or someone on their behalf," Morningstar said, before Emmanuelle could speak.

"But not who?" Selene's voice was cold. "Or why?"

Emmanuelle thought of Asmodeus, but in their current state, they couldn't afford to antagonise Hawthorn unless there was clear evidence. "He didn't say much. When he wakes up—"

"That's not going to happen for a while," Aragon said.

"I know," Emmanuelle said. "He said something about the gifts being used to ruin the party."

Selene's face had that expression again, the one that suggested that someone was going to pay for this, and no quarter given. "I don't see how. They've all been checked for spells, and the House is weak, but not that weak. Our magical protections still hold. But whoever harmed Javier will be up to further mischief in the ballroom." She nodded at Aragon. "Keep an eye on him, will you? And tell me or Morningstar if he wakes up and says anything."

And, to Emmanuelle, "You really should go and get changed." She moved closer to Emmanuelle. Her hand trailed on Emmanuelle's cheek, rested on her lips for a second. "It's your party. You should at least attempt to enjoy it."

"Yes," Emmanuelle said. "I—I worry."

"I know you do." Selene kissed her, briefly. "But we're not defenceless. Morningstar and I can hold the fort while you dip out. Just go change."

Entirely too much going wrong—too many Houses, and God only knew what Darrias and Asmodeus and the other envoys were really up to. Emmanuelle bit her lips. "Go to the ballroom. I'll see you there."

Morningstar followed her, as regal as if he'd been her privileged advisor—and perhaps he was, Emmanuelle didn't know enough about how Selene currently ran the House.

"Morningstar?" Emmanuelle called, as he was about to leave the room.

He turned, smile bright and dazzling, towering over her. "Yes?"

Emmanuelle waited a fraction of a second, to be sure that Selene had cleared the door and was out of earshot.

"You saw what Javier had done in the ballroom. The fungus—"

"Isn't dead," Aragon's voice could have frozen metal. "I told Javier already."

"It's contained," Emmanuelle said.

"I should hope so," Aragon said. "In high concentrations—as you saw with Maïr—the spores are a menace."

As if they needed that, on top of all their other problems.

"We don't have time for this," Morningstar said, impatiently. "It doesn't grow fast, does it."

"No," Aragon said. "Most funguses—"

"Then it's not relevant and not a problem," Morningstar snapped. For a fraction of a second Emmanuelle thought that Aragon was going to lose his calm—nothing he hated more than being cut mid-lecture—but then he rallied, and his face became expressionless once again. "Everything is going according to plan."

Except for Javier being stabbed. And far too many other Houses in Silverspires at a time when the House was vulnerable. But of course Morningstar would never admit to anything like that being a problem.

"What did you learn from the envoys?"

Morningstar shrugged. "You mean do I have a suspect?" he shook his head.

"You looked at the gifts," Emmanuelle said. It was merely an educated guess.

"I did give Valérie and Myra a hand." Of course. Trying to be the centre of attention once more; or perhaps she was uncharitable, and he couldn't help being the centre of attention, always burning brighter than everyone else.

"Anything stuck out? From the minor Houses?" She wasn't sure why Asmodeus would bother warning her, but she'd be a fool to ignore the obvious.

He thought, for a while. "That's most of them—"

"I know," Emmanuelle snapped. Among the major Houses, only Hawthorn and Harrier were there, and they were enough of a headache as it was.

"A bit of everything, to be honest. Shellac brought a rather large still life painting in rather poor taste, with some kind of patina spell on it to age it—make it seem older than it is." He sounded amused. "Minimes brought some carved wooden trinkets with a trigger spell—touch them and they'll sing like some rather indifferent choir. Stormgate's was an umbrella. I couldn't identify the spell on it, but I assume it's meant to help with repelling magical weather. Do you want me to go on? As I said, it's a long list."

There was no risk. The House was strong. As Morningstar said—just trinkets, toys for Selene's amusement.

But still, something wasn't right.

"What about Harrier?" The gift Darrias had brought.

"A silver limousine with inset emeralds. Half of them have rather bad inclusions, and it was rather badly tarnished. Not that, brand new, it'd look anything but tawdry. A borderline insult."

"You left it in the pile?"

Morningstar's smile was pitying, that same unbearable expression he'd had when she failed a spell or didn't understand something fast enough. Her hands had clenched into fists. She only unclenched them with an effort. "There's nothing in that gift that can hurt Silverspires or Selene," Morningstar said.

"They don't need to hurt her," Emmanuelle said, darkly. "They just need to make us look bad."

"Nevertheless… As I said, we're not that weak." Morningstar straightened up. He towered over her, large shoulders flexing as if he still wore the metal wings that had been his weapon and his prerogative. "The House has wards, and they still stand strong. I didn't design them to fail."

Emmanuelle swallowed, her heart in her throat—remembering how he'd been, how he'd really been, not this bonhomie he affected now, but effortless arrogance, effortless dominance—for who would gainsay the first and foremost among Fallen, the one who still remembered what it meant to fly in the City of Heaven?

"Morningstar—" she had to clamp her lips down not to say "master", lock her knees together to not abase herself.

And then he smiled, and it was all gone, and there was just the easygoing, smiling and bloody annoying Fallen she'd been working with for the past two weeks. "Those are very specific worries. What aren't you telling me?"

"I'm not sure," Emmanuelle said. "And the wine?"

"Hawthorn's bottle? I didn't have time for more than a cursory look before you found Javier, but it's good wine. Very good wine. The kind of thing you can't find in Paris anymore, whatever the price. I have to grant it to Asmodeus: he does have good taste in that." His tone clearly implied Asmodeus failed on so many other levels.

"I thought it could…" Emmanuelle paused, frustrated. "Poison her, or something."

"Because of the legends about Hawthorn's poison?" Morningstar shook his head. "I can assure you that's not the case. And I don't see what Asmodeus would gain."

"Me neither," Emmanuelle said. "But he's here, Morningstar. Out of all the Houses, he's the only head attending. There has to be a reason."

"Again—" Morningstar said. "You may be focusing on the wrong things, Emmanuelle. Asmodeus wasn't there when Javier was stabbed."

"I know," she said, darkly. "But he was stabbed. Which means someone is up to something." He'd seen something he shouldn't have, but what?

Morningstar's voice was pitying. Emmanuelle found, once again, her hands balled into fists. "It's a party with most of the Houses of Paris. *Everyone* is up to something."

"But someone was willing to cross a line for it. Can you keep an eye out? Please."

He nodded. Of course he would, but she knew he wasn't convinced. He believed—absolutely, obstinately—that the House he had founded was strong, that it could weather anything; and even their getting all but choked out by a magical banyan was a temporary setback, and not the beginning of a long slow slide to oblivion.

Where Emmanuelle had seen too many people who'd thought themselves invincible and indispensable, and had been, in the end, neither one or the other when everything went to Hell.

EMMANUELLE FOLLOWED Selene's advice, and changed into party clothes: a cream dress with an elaborate, V-shaped lace collar, and a belt with sharp angles that highlighted her large hips. Over this she wrapped a shawl in nuances of shimmering blue, with floral patterns entwined along its length. She couldn't find matching shoes, and had to settle for something black and shiny, a classic that would go with anything.

She walked back from their quarters to the ballroom in an increasingly deserted House. Everyone had to be gathering for the party, and she was going to be hopelessly late.

In the ballroom, Selene stood by the side of a huge cake. She was slight and of average size, but the confection dwarfed her, a tower of sugar and flour in bright colour, floor after floor of every shade of red separated with thin layers of silver frosting, and elaborate patterns of stars, lines and circles drawn on the sides. Morningstar wasn't anywhere near her: much to Emmanuelle's surprise, he'd moved to the back of the room. He was laughing and chatting with three Silverspires dependents, but his gaze was alert, and clearly focused on everything else around him.

She *had* told him to keep an eye out, but she hadn't expected him to actually take the suggestion.

Emmanuelle elbowed her way through the crowd until she found Laure, who was watching as Helias lit up the candles with magic, cradling a naked flame in her hands—all for show, of course, a reminder that the House's Fallen could afford to waste magic on something so trivial. "It's breath-taking," she said. Especially given that Laure had had next to nothing to make it.

Laure smiled. "Had to make it count."

The first candle caught fire. Helias moved slowly, deliberately, her hands passing over each one until the wick caught the warmth of the flame. Everyone seemed entranced, except for Selene, whose face had that expressionless cast Emmanuelle recognised: wariness and worry that she was heartbreakingly trying to mask.

Damn Morningstar. Perfect birthday present or not, it really shouldn't have been that way.

Emmanuelle's gaze roamed—the envoys, equally entranced, the dependents with something close to naked wonder in their eyes as the light lent a warm, comforting glow to the carvings of the ceiling, an expression that Emmanuelle hadn't seen in the House for a long, long time.

As Helias moved to the third floor of the cake, there was a muffled sound from the back of the room. Emmanuelle turned, half-distracted; and felt as though she'd just been blasted by cold water.

A dependent had just collapsed by the pantry door, and the pile of chairs was now colonised by a mixture of thick whitish mycelial strands, and dark rhizomorphs to which still clung the remnants of Javier's ice sheet. As Emmanuelle watched, the rhizomorphs actually stretched, blindly groping along the chairs' back. They were still slow, moving stubbornly rather than fast and quick, and unlikely to grab people from mid-air, but clearly the spore concentration was enough to choke lungs.

Not to mention they weren't supposed to be moving at all!

No.

No.

This was a disaster.

Emmanuelle turned, taking stock. Selene hadn't seen it. Morningstar had, and he was moving towards the pantry door: he'd shed the dependents (much easier to do, since they weren't House envoys) and was trying to make it look natural. Emmanuelle hadn't yet moved closer to Selene: a good idea, it turned out, because not as many eyes were on her. If she could gracefully get out, she should be able to help Morningstar deal with this.

And then her brain caught up with her eyes, and she realised that in the mass of entranced envoys—in the press of House colours, and extravagantly wasteful dresses and swallowtail suits—neither Asmodeus nor Darrias were present.

FOR A moment—an agonisingly long moment, like a last breath before oblivion—Emmanuelle stood petrified. Helias was lighting the candles on the fourth floor of the cake now: five floors to go until the crowd's attention wandered. And, behind her, Morningstar would be moving into position, trying to contain the damage, to stop the fungus, to do whatever it took to save the House's reputation.

All she could hear, over and over, was Asmodeus's amused warning. *Tell her to steer clear of Guy.*

You're weak. Irresistible prey.

Irresistible even to him; all his professions of good faith, his cryptic warnings, his accusations levered at minor Houses—all of it a distraction, calculated to focus their attention in the wrong direction. And now this: an attack in the ballroom, while he and Darrias slipped out in a deserted House, and—

She needed to find them. She needed to stop whatever they were doing, before it was too late.

She looked up, to meet Selene's hard gaze. Seeing that she had Emmanuelle's attention, Selene's mouth moved, barely. Within Emmanuelle, the link to House Silverspires stirred into life. *What's wrong?*

Emmanuelle couldn't answer the same way, because she wasn't head of the House. She mouthed, instead, as clearly as she could, *Emergency. Hold the fort.*

Selene glanced back at the cake, and then back at Emmanuelle. She nodded, grimly. She knew, better than Emmanuelle, what a disaster it would be if she never got to blow the candles and open the gifts. This was theatre now, sleight of hand as Morningstar would say, and the stakes were all of the House and its reputation, and ultimately their own uncertain survival.

Emmanuelle gave a brief nod to Laure, and started moving towards the back of the room.

It was slow. Agonisingly slow, because she couldn't run, couldn't savagely elbow people out of the way with no regard for protocol or etiquette— could barely keep her own panic contained. Yes, most of the people were dependents, but if they panicked, it wouldn't matter. The envoys would see. She needed to keep up appearances with them as well. She—

She needed to breathe, but she had nothing left.

She moved between groups, smiling until everything ached, making small talk about how she had to get her own gift for Selene, how glad she was they were enjoying it, how she hoped it would be the beginning of something new. They didn't buy it. They couldn't possibly buy it.

Ahead, by the pile of chairs, a second dependent had gone down, but Morningstar was nudging people out of the way with a dazzling smile.

Emmanuelle couldn't hear what he was saying, but the dependents looked more surprised than sceptical.

Thank God.

She caught Morningstar's eye, a second before she slipped out of the room. He frowned, gesturing at her to come and help, his face turned dark with anger.

No time, Emmanuelle mouthed. And, as clearly as she could, knowing there was no way she could explain any of it, *Asmodeus. In the House.*

That didn't make him happier. If she'd been closer he would have given her a verbal flaying, but she was out of reach and beyond caring.

She needed to find Asmodeus, and fast.

SHE HAD no idea where they'd gone.

The House was large, and deserted, and silent. The mouldy wallpaper—that horrible East Wing thing with the faded stylised flowers—alternated with thin strips of bare wall where they'd torn out banyan tree filaments. Around her was only the acrid smell of the angry river Seine, and a more distant one, the churned-earth one of a jungle, that same oppressive atmosphere that had now overwhelmed the Notre-Dame cathedral. Under her feet the broken parquet floor crunched like shards of glass, each step she took reminding her of how far from whole they really were.

Emmanuelle didn't have Selene's connection to the wards and couldn't tell where they'd gone weak—if they had gone weak at all, or if Asmodeus's game was just something different, some other thing that was going to explode in all their faces. What could he possibly want of House Silverspires, after gutting them two months ago? He'd seemed quite happy to stand aside and let others finish his handiwork. He—

Damn it, she was kicking herself for believing him. He'd seemed so… "sincere" was perhaps the wrong word when dealing with him, but so transparently helpful.

She should have known.

Where could he have gone? The cellars, where the wards were made manifest? The ruined Notre-Dame cathedral, where only the banyan's roots held sway?

She—

She paused, then, thought for a while.

Darrias and Asmodeus wouldn't have left the ballroom together, even if they were working together. Two envoys slipping out was too noticeable, too risky. Which meant they'd given each other a meeting point.

Which meant—

Darrias had been bright and chatty, and clearly memorising the path Emmanuelle had taken from the kitchens to Selene's office. And, no doubt, the path from Selene's office to the ballroom.

There was nothing of note on either path. So either the kitchens, or Selene's office.

She had only one chance, and she couldn't afford to get it wrong. There was no time.

Selene's office, on the face of it, was the more plausible target; the place where she kept all her papers (though not her magical artefacts, but they had no way of knowing that), and where any crucial information would be kept.

But Selene's office was also their private quarters, and Emmanuelle had come to the ballroom straight from there after changing dresses. If Darrias or Asmodeus had slipped out at any point before Emmanuelle's arrival, she should have met them in the corridors. There were magical ways to hide, but the House's wards wouldn't allow them to cast those spells.

She was almost sure—almost—that neither Asmodeus nor Darrias had been there when she'd arrived in the ballroom.

And the kitchens were deserted, weren't they? Emptied of every dependent, with Laure and the others upstairs at the party, celebrating Selene's birthday, and only the occasional dependent coming back for food. The perfect meeting place.

She hitched up her dress, making sure the embroidered hem wouldn't get in the way, tied a knot in the shawl to prevent it from slipping from her shoulders, and started running.

SHE'D FEARED she'd be too late or simply plain wrong, but when she arrived, out of breath, at the kitchen doors, the first thing she heard was Asmodeus's voice.

"It's costly for me, as you well know, but certainly doable. Unless there's something you haven't told me?"

Darrias's voice, low, tight with an emotion Emmanuelle couldn't name: "I've given you all I have."

Emmanuelle didn't wait. She ran straight through the doors, her footsteps echoing under the arches of the kitchen. Subtle and delicate, insofar as entrances went.

Spectacular, she thought, sourly.

They both looked up, startled, when they saw her. They'd grabbed two chairs at the end of one of the cooking stations, near some pans still glazed with browned sauces and meat juices. Two kitchen hands had been there too, but they now lay on the ground. They didn't look dead, but Emmanuelle couldn't be sure. Everything about this stank to high heaven. "What do you think you're doing?" Emmanuelle asked.

Darrias's voice was cool. "None of your business."

Asmodeus, of course, was more controlled. He unfolded his lean frame from the chair he was sitting in, in a cloud of orange blossom and bergamot perfume. He gave Emmanuelle a sharp, amused smile. "I could return the question," he said. His gaze swept her, up and down, seeing the flush on her cheeks, the rumpled dress, the hair shaken loose as Emmanuelle ran. "You look like you lost a fight with a clothes wringer."

Which was really all his fault. No, not quite. His and Morningstar's. And it'd be useless to point either of these out. She breathed out. "And you don't look like you're attending a party at all. You didn't come for this, did you?" She stared at him, and at Darrias. Something clicked. Looking forward to catching up. "You wanted to see Darrias."

"As I said, we're old friends."

The notion of "friends" and Asmodeus in the same sentence was bewildering, but it had been a long day. "Fine," Emmanuelle said. "And this business of yours, whatever it is, has nothing to do with Silverspires. Or Selene." She didn't bother to keep the sarcasm out of her voice.

Darrias looked at her for a while. Then she said, simply, "I want to leave Harrier."

"Darrias—" Asmodeus's tone was sharp.

"You think she's in any position to interfere?"

Asmodeus's gaze was cool, composed. He watched Emmanuelle for a while, all traces of his earlier sarcasm gone. "No. She's not ruthless enough."

Leaving Harrier. Jumping ship. Emmanuelle struggled to process. She said the first thing that came to mind, instead. "The kitchen hands—"

"Enchanted sleep." Asmodeus smiled. "I'd have a hard time explaining two dead ones."

Great. "So your warning about the minor Houses—"

"Still holds, but none of my concern. Or Darrias's."

"So—" Emmanuelle took a deep breath, considered the end of the sentence, and forged ahead anyway. Things couldn't exactly get worse, or at any rate, if they did it would have nothing to do with those two. "So you don't have anything to do with the fungus. Or Javier being stabbed."

Asmodeus raised an eyebrow. He didn't look surprised, but she suspected the day he showed anything beyond easy sarcasm Hell would freeze over. "I'm hardly the only one who'd know the interesting things you keep in your pantries. Any House worth its salt has informants in other Houses."

"You—"

Emmanuelle took a deep, shaking breath, kept her face expressionless, knowing it was useless and that he'd read her panic like an open book.

"As I told you, I have no interest in Silverspires at the moment. You're just a convenient neutral territory."

Convenient. Emmanuelle took a deep, shaking breath. "You're going to tell me what's going on."

A large, ironic smile. "Assuming I do know what's going on."

"You know who is doing it."

Asmodeus picked up his wine glass from the table, swirled it between his long, elegant fingers. "I make it my business to be well informed. Such a shame you don't—but I'll enjoy watching the fallout."

"You said you wouldn't interfere."

"Which is exactly what I'm doing, isn't it?" Again that smile she ached to remove from his face. "I can't help it if all you seem to do is thrash and flounder."

Hopeless. Any help coming their way wasn't through him. Why had she ever thought it would?

Emmanuelle looked at Darrias's face, at that carefully cultivated expression. It wasn't amusement at all, but a mask of guardedness barely masking fear. *I could tell Guy what you're doing*, she wanted to say. Perhaps she'd have done it, if it had been just Asmodeus. But Guy would probably punish or kill Darrias in an unpleasant way if Emmanuelle did speak up on this. She could see Father Javier's face if she confessed to doing this—carefully non-judgmental, because he had to, but what he really thought would be all too clear in his eyes.

Selene, she was sure, would have been suitably ruthless.

"You two are coming with me," she said, sharply. "Back to the ballroom." If nothing else, she'd keep an eye on them while they sorted things out.

Asmodeus's expression was a study in amusement as he put the wine glass back on the table. "I wouldn't dream of being anywhere else."

He strode ahead, as they walked through the House—in long, easy strides, the tail of his jacket moving like flags in a breeze. The bastard probably knew the House inside out, by now.

"Darrias." Darrias turned, her tattooed face gleaming in candlelight. "Harrier and Hawthorn…" Emmanuelle paused, trying to sort out her own thoughts. "All the same."

"Really? You'd move to Hawthorn tomorrow, then?"

Emmanuelle snorted. "No. I don't care for Asmodeus."

"He takes care of his own," Darrias said, curtly. "That's all I need to know." She was silent, for a while. "Being out of the House makes you see other things. Guy thinks I've drifted too far away from being a proper Harrier dependent."

Seeing the Houseless as people? Emmanuelle bit back on the sarcasm. It wasn't going to help, but it was hard to remain focused when all she had on her mind was worry about Selene and Silverspires. "You don't agree with him on mortals. On the Houseless."

Darrias shrugged. "As I said, things are different out there." She laughed, shortly. "You really should tell Guy, you know. Repair your relationship with Harrier, claw back a little influence with a major House…"

Emmanuelle exhaled. "I should. But that wouldn't be doing the right thing, would it?" She wished she didn't feel so much sympathy for Darrias.

Her gaze held Emmanuelle, for a while—again, that same odd twisting weight in Emmanuelle's stomach. "Firebrand," she said, almost fondly. "Doing the right thing never brought anyone anywhere."

"Perhaps we're all too focused on getting somewhere at all costs," Emmanuelle said.

"Perhaps." Darrias stared at Asmodeus, who strode on ahead, but had to hear most of what they were saying. Emmanuelle no longer cared. "A fresh start. We all deserve that, in the grand scheme of things, don't we? All I have to do is keep my head down for a little longer, and pretend I'm a proper Harrier dependent until Asmodeus sorts things out with Lord Guy."

"I see," Emmanuelle said, again. And, more carefully, "I can't wish you luck."

"Because it's not the House's official position?" Darrias smiled. "Of course. Understood."

Ahead, around the corner of the corridor—past the table with the Chinese blue-and-white vase and the wilted flowers, past this stretch of patched-up parquet, shot through with the thin filaments of some mould or fungus—was the ballroom. She couldn't hear anything: surely that was a good sign? Perhaps it was merely the low-level roar of party conversation, with nothing to sort out. Perhaps Morningstar—

No. Morningstar wasn't his old ruthless, powerful self. He was just an arrogant bastard with a tendency to get into trouble.

He—

She looked at Asmodeus: he was still walking ahead of them as if nothing were wrong. The air smelled of churned earth, and bergamot, and citruses, an unwelcome reminder of how they'd got there in the first place.

She'd been thinking she had no negotiation position, but that wasn't quite true, was it? Asmodeus was only interested in poaching Darrias from Harrier, but he didn't like Morningstar. And he was far too fond of showing off. They both were, weren't they? Real drama queens. It was just a matter of finding the right levers.

"Asmodeus?"

He didn't even bother to turn around. "What would you want from us in exchange for help?"

"From a diminished House at the bottom of the hierarchy?" He laughed, and it wasn't malicious, merely good natured, his indifference like nails on a chalkboard. It was all coming apart. Selene couldn't possibly hope to hold things together, not without any idea of what was going on, and all he could do was mock. "I don't think there's much you can offer me."

"I guess not," Emmanuelle didn't have to try very hard to sound unsure of herself. "Morningstar will deal with it. He always knows what to do."

A pause from him, barely perceptible, but she knew what to watch out for this time. She plunged on. "He'd tell me not to trust you."

"He'd be entirely right." Amusement again, but this one had an edge. They were almost at the ballroom now, and the noises she could hear weren't the hubbub of small conversations at a successful birthday party, but a diffuse, growing roar made up of a hundred panicked voices.

Please please please, let Selene be all right. Let her be in charge. Let her…

"Still think Morningstar has everything under control?" Asmodeus's voice was mocking.

Emmanuelle stared at him. And, slowly, carefully, "He was the head of the House. Selene's teacher. If anyone knows what to do…"

Asmodeus snorted. "He's gone through life thinking being the most powerful was the only tool he'd ever need to solve problems." He moved, and the shadow of large, black wings moved with him—his gaze resting on Darrias, who'd stopped a few paces behind him, out of breath and with such naked hope on her face that it squeezed Emmanuelle's heart into bloody tatters. Pinning all her hopes on him, at the mercy of his unpredictable whims—but he did keep his word. She had to grant him that. He kept his word and protected his own, and God knew what he considered Darrias to be, now.

"It won't help you," Asmodeus said, at last, shaking his head. "Too little, too late. The House is Shellac. They used to be a satellite of ours, but they drifted away from us after my predecessor's death."

Shellac. The older woman envoy, the one who'd sipped a champagne cup with Darrias. They were doing this? How?

"Too little, too late," she said. The words tasted like ashes on her tongue.

"By the sounds of it, the party is already in some disarray. I fear you'll find it difficult to rescue Silverspires's reputation from this." His smile was feral. She'd never wanted to punch him as much as now.

"You—" she breathed in, slowly. "If you showed public support—" Either him or Darrias—the only two major Houses present at the party. It would count. It had to. Assuming they could stop the fungus, somehow.

"Support to Selene? Why should I?"

"Darrias—"

Darrias's face was expressionless.

"Darrias," Asmodeus said. His voice was sharp, all amusement gone. "Be careful. Helping Emmanuelle isn't in your best interests."

Because Guy had no love for Silverspires, and certainly didn't want his envoy to play politics in his stead. "Drawing attention to herself? I think we're past that, aren't we? You both went missing at a crucial juncture. Do you truly think Guy isn't going to work things out?"

"There's a chance he might not. I don't see why we'd make things harder for ourselves, do I?"

Too little, too late. Darrias looked distinctly unhappy, but Emmanuelle couldn't possibly ask her to jeopardise things for the sake of a foreign House, no matter how much they might like each other.

Squeamish. Always squeamish.

"Forget it," she said, savagely, and ran towards the ballroom.

SHE'D EXPECTED sheer chaos in the ballroom, but it wasn't quite that.

The mass of dependents milled away from the pantry door, pushing and prodding at each other to try and get as far away from it as possible. A new sheath of ice encased the fungus's rhizomorphs. Within, Emmanuelle could still see them moving and scrabbling, knocking, the filaments leaving small, almost invisible bursts on the inside of the sheet's surface.

What had Javier said? It was fragile, and wouldn't stand much pressure. Of all the bad solutions in a bad day…

Three of the House's magicians, Valérie, Myra and Naocles, were trying to shepherd the dependents towards the end of the room. Of course they couldn't just evacuate everyone. Abandoning the party would have sent a clear message they were frightened of the fungus; that they couldn't control it and couldn't hope to get rid of it. It would have taken this from bad to unmitigated disaster.

Emmanuelle would have sought out Morningstar, but she had no need to. Because the warmth of his presence washed over the room—not warm or comforting or weak, but a pure incandescent rage that sought to drive her to her knees. He stood by Selene's side, arguing with the envoys. Words and fragments of sentences drifted to her, each one a blow that made her legs tremble. "Outrage… Payment exacted… Reparations…"

Kneel. Kneel. The same presence that she'd felt, again and again, telling her she was no good for Selene, that Morningstar's best and brightest student had no time for love, for tenderness—that she should be honed and cut and reforged until nothing was left but a weapon for the good of the House.

Her knees dipped, almost unconsciously. The fungus was scrabbling at the edges of the ice sheet, knocking against it again and again, the network of thin cracks getting wider and wider. The ice sheet was going to break. It was going to break, and then the fungus was going to spread again and more people would collapse, while Selene and Morningstar, oblivious, tried to argue with the envoys, while the magicians struggled to keep the crowd under control.

No.

She'd stood up to Morningstar once. She could do it again.

She drew in a deep, shuddering breath, remembering what it had felt like, to walk away from him; to give herself her own name and be her own self. The pressure of the words receded, and the tightness in her chest came undone.

The Shellac envoy. She sought her out: an older woman—Theliphae, Laure had said?—milling among the other envoys, a distracted frown on her face, as if she were thinking of the consequences of this for her House.

Shellac's gift. Morningstar had said…the large painting, wasn't it? Emmanuelle elbowed her way through the press until she got to the gift table.

It was, indeed, hard to miss. It would have taken half a wall in their bedroom, if pictures of rabbits with glassy eyes, and uncannily positioned grapes and apples, held any appeal. And, when she touched it, a jolt of magic like a faint memory of heat. A patina spell. Something to age the paint. Something to—

She stared at the fungus, at the hairline cracks spreading on the surface of the ice. At the rhizomorphs stretching and scrabbling, devouring wood. An aging spell. The fungus, growing and spreading, faster than it should have, on accelerated time.

And Javier, who'd examined it, who'd lifted the wards to burn it on a large surface. Had he put them back properly, before he'd been stabbed?

Would anyone have noticed, if he hadn't?

She knew the answer to that already. In the stress and panic, and one emergency after another...

House Shellac probably had planned something much smaller when they'd learnt about the fungus—some minor incident they could spin into a headache for Selene. But of course, with the wards down, their spell had succeeded in sowing discord beyond their wildest dreams.

Theliphae, the Shellac envoy, was still pretending to look at Selene. Emmanuelle sent a burst of magic into the spell. Yes. As she'd thought. It was tied to the paints used. An alchemist had infused these with angel breath or some other magic from a Fallen, and only then had the paints been applied to the canvas. If she wanted to undo it, she was going to have to take the painting apart and reshape it, slow and painstaking work that they most certainly didn't have the time for.

The sheet of ice was cracked through and through now. There was no time. She needed the fungus to stop growing, and she needed that *now*.

Or yesterday.

Her gaze, trying to avoid Theliphae, met Darrias's—the Harrier envoy was leaning against the buffet, seemingly chewing on some nougat, Asmodeus a few paces away from her with a wine glass in his hands. Darrias was cool and composed. Of course it didn't touch her. But then the world shifted, and Emmanuelle suddenly saw it very differently. It did touch her. If word got back to Guy of what she and Asmodeus was planning, Darrias wouldn't get a chance. It was her life at stake, her entire future.

What had she said, to Emmanuelle, in the corridors?

Beholden to no one and nothing, and only your wits to survive.

Breathe. Don't panic.

She needed to stop Theliphae, except she couldn't, not on her own.

She—damn it, she was going to have to trust Morningstar. There was no time to warn him of what she was planning, and no way of discreetly catching his attention, even if she'd wanted to—he was too busy supporting Selene as she tried to project strength and calm.

He would know. He had to know. She didn't like him, but surely he'd understand what she wanted—never mind that he'd never understood that, not across either of his lifetimes—that, even in the previous two weeks, he'd never *listened* to any of what she'd wanted, planning the party in spite of her and her desires...

Still think Morningstar has everything under control?

Of course he didn't. But it was the best of bad choices, and there was always a start for everything.

Emmanuelle reached out, and—in an exact copy of the spell Morningstar had used, back in the pantry—set fire to the painting. And, as she did so, screamed, "Morningstar!"

Things seemed to slow down, then; to hang, agonisingly suspended, in a moment when she felt everything was falling apart, before tumbling back on each other in a panicked jumble.

Theliphae, stumbling, her face frozen in shock—Morningstar, looking at Emmanuelle, at the burning painting, his face set in a frown—he didn't get it, she'd been wrong, of course he would never understand where she was coming from—and then he shifted, moving with an alien grace—he was standing by Theliphae as she stumbled, and doing something with his hands that went too fast to see—and Theliphae tried to catch onto something to break her fall, and ended up against him, spilling her glass of champagne on his jacket—and then slid further down, eyes rolling up in her face.

The feeling of magic on Emmanuelle's fingers died. The painting burnt, reducing itself to ashes—and as it did, the fungus's rhizomorphs slowed down and all but fell still, with the ice sheet still intact.

Emmanuelle let out a breath she wasn't even aware of holding.

She got perhaps a heartbeat of calm before the hubbub started again: she saw Morningstar whisper into Selene's ear, one hand pointing towards Theliphae. Selene nodded, and turned to the envoys. Darrias was talking, urgently, to Asmodeus, whose face was oddly still. Emmanuelle just wanted to curl up and sleep, but that wasn't going to be possible. She'd just set fire to the gifts table.

She walked, instead, slowly, carefully, towards Selene; nodded, briefly. Selene's face was cold. The Minimes envoy looked distinctly unhappy. "I had to," Emmanuelle said. "She was using the painting to…" she took in a deep, shaking breath.

Selene's face didn't move. Like Morningstar, she was fast on her feet. Had to be, to weather this kind of thing. "As you can see," she said, softly, "this incident isn't to be laid at the door of the House. House Shellac thought they could give me a surprise present."

There was laughter, but most of the envoys were still watching them with malice in their eyes. Emmanuelle and Morningstar might have stopped the fungus, but the House had just done the metaphorical equivalent of rolling over with its throat and belly bared to predators, and showing it had neither claws nor fangs left to defend itself.

"You know," the Stormgate envoy said, "I wouldn't have thought you'd be ready for something that large so soon."

Selene's face didn't move. "We're the first House," she said, grey eyes sparkling in the light from the chandelier. "The oldest. You'll find us most resilient."

"Are you?" the Minimes envoy's voice was low, amused. Her hand swept through the ballroom, the fungus under its sheet of ice, dependents cautiously moving back towards the buffet, magicians still busy transferring those who'd fainted to nurses. "I'd say you were dancing on the edge of the abyss, and you've rather badly stumbled."

Emmanuelle bit her lips not to shake Morningstar.

"Does it matter how much we've stumbled, if we recover?" Morningstar's voice was warm, with some of that same strength Emmanuelle had felt, earlier, the thoughtless energy that had kept them all safe in better days, the utter certainty that bent everything to his will. In spite of everything, she held her breath, waiting for the Minimes envoy to nod.

No longer.

The envoy's smooth face was tinged with the faintest hint of contempt. "There is such a thing as falling too low." Her pale lips pinched, bloodless, as if crushing a piece of food between them. "The first House." She sounded amused, and almost pitying. "The higher the rise…"

Selene said, coldly, "Don't be in such a hurry to carve from our corpse."

A clink of glass; a smell of bergamot and orange blossom. Asmodeus and Darrias now stood by Selene's side: Asmodeus holding out a filled glass of wine in one hand, and the bottle he'd gifted to Selene in the other; and behind him Darrias, with Harrier's silver model car.

"Time for the unwrapping of gifts, is it not?" Asmodeus's face was smooth, unreadable. Darrias's was much more expressive, taut with the fear of someone who'd just stepped into fire to rescue a stranger. There was no going back from this.

Hawthorn. Harrier. The two major Houses present at the party. The Stormgate and Minimes envoys stared at them, and then back at each other. At length they nodded to Asmodeus, who held the glass to Selene, smiling as if nothing were wrong.

Selene took it, bowing slightly, nothing in her expression betraying any of her thoughts. "Let's see how good Hawthorn's wine cellars are," she said, raising it to the light until it shone ruby red.

And this time the laughter was the one of guests appreciating a good joke—polite and relaxed, and devoid of any bite.

THEY CAME to see her, before they left—after Morningstar and the magicians renewed the ice barrier on the fungus, and Theliphae was carried back to Shellac with an official complaint from the House. Emmanuelle was in her own office, a small drawing room by the side of the library that no one had much use for, filled with banyan roots and tottering piles of un-catalogued books. The party was still going on, and Selene wouldn't be with her for a while.

The good news was, Morningstar probably wouldn't intrude, either. Emmanuelle breathed in the aroma of her cup of coffee—mouldy, tasting of spices more than actual coffee. It was old, the box dating back to before the war, but it tasted like memories—of first meeting Selene, of their slow and intoxicating courtship, until she'd finally moved her things into Selene's private quarters.

"I was told we'd find you here," Asmodeus said. He looked around him, and got two chairs for him and Darrias, effortlessly pulling them through the maze of books. He sounded as amused as ever, though Emmanuelle, who'd seen too much of him entirely, could see that his mind was already on larger things. Darrias was pale, but otherwise calm.

There was a silence, while Emmanuelle brewed them another two cups—had to, for politeness's sake. Asmodeus, true to form, was the one who broke it. "I'm not sure if we should thank you."

"You did start it," Emmanuelle pointed out, though she'd goaded him into…taking sides? Giving help? Not things she wanted to remind him of, currently.

"The warning about minor Houses?" Asmodeus sipped his cup, thoughtfully. "Fair point."

It was so surprising that Emmanuelle almost fell out of her own chair. "Are you actually admitting you've been wrong?"

"Don't push it." Asmodeus straightened his gloves. "I just thought you might want reassurance that things were going to work out well."

"Will they?"

"It depends for whom, doesn't it?" His smile was dazzling. "Darrias will be safe in Hawthorn while I sort things out with Guy. She's a dead weight to him anyway."

"One he won't be keen to have you keep," Emmanuelle said, in spite of herself.

Asmodeus shrugged. "I've got several swords hanging over him. More than enough means of pressure to bring to bear, should I need it." His tone was utterly relaxed. He enjoyed this, didn't he.

And, meanwhile, House Silverspires owed Hawthorn a debt, and he knew very well they would neither have the will nor the means to interfere with him.

"Are you all right?" Emmanuelle asked Darrias. She hesitated, then said, "I didn't even thank you for—"

"Doing the right thing?" Darrias ran a hand on her shaved head, tracing the contours of a tattoo on her cheek.

"I don't think there was any right thing," Emmanuelle said. "Just… kind ones."

"Ha," Darrias said. "Maybe, though you'll find kindness is a thing in short supply those days."

By Asmodeus's ironic expression and his continued silence, Emmanuelle could guess that he was quite happy with not being a big source of kindness in the world.

"I should thank you as well," she said, as much because she had to as to goad him into speaking. "You didn't have to follow Darrias in supporting us."

He shrugged, an expansive movement that seemed, for a split second, to drag black wings into existence once more. "Once Darrias had made up her mind it was all in the open. It changed little for me."

Except give him an opportunity for more theatrics, a chance he certainly wouldn't pass on.

"I guess it's goodbye, then," Emmanuelle said.

"For now." Asmodeus shrugged. He set his cup on the desk and rose, straightening his swallowtail jacket; turning, graceful and elegant. "I'm sure you'll have other occasions to see us."

And wasn't she looking forward to that.

SHE WAS wrong about another thing: late, late in the night, when the darkness of the House gave way to the grey and uncertain light before dawn, Morningstar came to her office.

"Emmanuelle." He looked odd, the light streaming from his broad frame out of place on the mouldy books and banyan roots, absorbed by them rather than providing illumination.

Emmanuelle put down the book she was reading, and stared at him for a while. "Long night?"

He smiled, slow and casual and utterly unchanged. So much for her hopes he'd learnt a lesson. "The envoys seem satisfied. Impressed, even." His face grew grave again. "And we're pulling the entire parquet of the ballroom out."

Emmanuelle raised an eyebrow.

"It turned out the roots and the mushrooms were just a small, small part of that fungus. There are white strands everywhere. I just hope it's confined to the ballroom, and not spreading elsewhere in the House."

Which meant he'd have to oversee dependents tearing parquet from the entire wing, for days and weeks, if not months—which would serve him right, but Emmanuelle no longer had the heart to say it aloud. "You didn't come here to tell me about the fungus," she said.

Morningstar watched her for a while. Light played in the depths of his blue eyes, the same gaze he'd laid on her when he'd told her to stay away from Selene. Then he grimaced, an utterly unexpected expression. "You're not making this easy."

"No," Emmanuelle said. She kept her voice steady, but it cost her. She stared at her cup. She hadn't even offered him coffee. Did she think him worse than Asmodeus? They were supposed to be on the same side.

"I..." Morningstar was silent, for a heartbeat. "I may have overreached."

It felt very much as though the world had overturned. "You what?"

"I'm not going to say it again," Morningstar said, stiffly. And, a touch more plaintively, "I believed the House would stand no matter what happened."

"You were wrong," Emmanuelle said, softly, carefully. "Even Selene knew that we were fragile."

Silence. He leant against the doorjamb, watching her, his breath coming slowly, evenly. "We're the first House. The oldest. Not that fragile."

"I know," Emmanuelle said. She rose, to get another cup from the shelf, filled it with tea leaves and hot water. "I have faith."

"I imagine not in me." He winced; hesitated again, and said, "You'd be quite justified."

She *had* trusted him, in the end. "I do trust you to help the House." She set the cup on the table, towards him. "And to have changed."

Morningstar didn't answer for a while. He walked into her office, sat down on the chair that Darrias had occupied, cradling the cup in his hands as though it weren't burning hot. Show off. "I haven't changed," he said.

Emmanuelle stared at him for a while, forcing herself to see beyond memories, beyond grievances. "I think you have," she said. And perhaps, in time, she'd learn to take it in stride.

"I'M SORRY," Emmanuelle said, to Selene, in the privacy of their bedroom. "It was a rubbish birthday party."

"Mmm." Selene ran a finger on Emmanuelle's face from forehead to lips, gently, slowly. "I've had worse, trust me. At least the other Houses were happy."

"Apart from Harrier, I guess."

"Don't worry about Harrier," Selene said. She pushed Emmanuelle against the pillow, straddled her. "That's my job."

"Mmm," Emmanuelle said. "You're distracting me, aren't you."

"Also my job." Selene smiled, an expression that seemed to light up the room. Emmanuelle reached for the buttons on Selene's shirt, undid them one by one. "Did you scream at Morningstar?"

"We had a chat," Emmanuelle said, thinking of her office, and subdued light on books. "I can work with him. I doubt I'll ever stop wanting to strangle him."

"True of a lot of us," Selene said. She shrugged off her shirt—underneath she wore a semi-transparent silk sleeveless top, outlining her slim form—and started hunting around for the buttons on Emmanuelle's dress. "This is rather fiddly."

"Party dresses," Emmanuelle said. "Always like that."

"I'd noticed." Her fingers danced on Emmanuelle's back, every touch igniting a trembling fire. Emmanuelle's breathing was coming faster and faster. "He does mean well, you know."

And some people didn't. Kindness, she'd told Darrias. Well, that was something. "I know. And I guess you'll still have the gifts, come tomorrow."

"They're not all tawdry," Selene said. She laughed, shortly. "The wine was actually excellent. You should try it, if you can bear to think of Hawthorn."

Who knew, she actually might. But for now... She drew Selene to her, breathing in the scent of patchouli, the warmth of her presence. "Here and now. Happy birthday, my love."

Story Notes

MANY OF THESE STORIES ARE SET IN THE UNIVERSE OF XUYA, WHICH is a recurring background to my fiction: the basic premise is that China discovered the Americas before the West, which led to a space age dominated by Asian powers. Xuya is the name of the Chinese colony on the West Coast, and later of the galactic empire that seeds off into space. Another major player, which gradually takes centre stage, is the Đại Việt empire, based on Imperial Vietnam (Đại Việt was the name of Vietnam at different stages of its history, most notably immediately before the advent of the Nguyễn dynasty in the nineteenth century). The Galactics or Outsiders are a loose federation based on western powers and western culture.

"The Shipmaker"

This is the first mindship story I wrote: I had the idea of having women give birth to artificial intelligences because I wanted to make pregnancy centre-stage. In particular, I wanted these pregnancies to have drastic consequences, which meant they couldn't be human pregnancies (I am firmly of the opinion that we will sort out the risks of childbirth and maternal mortality completely in the near future, and I side-eye the surprising number of galactic empires that continue to have high maternal mortality and no pregnancy care). So I made my births be those of Minds, constructed blends of organic and electronic elements that were destined to fit into a spaceship. And, just as the mother had to carry the Mind to term, I imagine that there would be someone responsible for making sure the ship's body was ready to welcome its Mind: the work of a team of engineers that needed to be managed and delivered on time.

It's set in Xuya, a Chinese galactic empire, but it concerns itself with the people in the margins of that empire: the birth mother Zoquitl seeks status through her pregnancy, and Dac Kien—an outsider in a slightly less precarious position than Zoquitl—wants this through her art, and the ship she'll create. In the end, the walk that they take together, looking at the ruins of what could have been, is symbolic of how little actually separates them.

This story is part of the Xuya universe: it won the British Science Fiction Association Award.

"The Jaguar House, in Shadow"

This story is set against the background of a totalitarian dictatorship, and it looks at the lives of three girls who make very different choices on how to resist: Xochitl founds a resistance cell within her own order, Onalli doesn't believe in the resistance but chooses to risk everything to rescue her friend, and Tecipiani prioritises saving the lives of the people given into her care over everything else. I wanted to present these three side by side as questions rather than answers, juxtaposing the way that they all arrived to those conclusions through being very different persons with different histories and points of view—Tecipiani clear-eyed, Xochitl idealistic and unsuited to compromise, and Onalli desperately wanting to hold on to her comrades.

I chose that unusual structure of not revealing the point of view character of the initial and final sections to flip the narrative: the reader's immediate sympathy is not going to lie with Tecipiani, to whom fall the ugly choices, so I wanted to have those sections be mistakenly attributed to Xochitl—so that, by the end of it, when Onalli achieves a grudging degree of understanding of what Tecipiani did and what it cost her, the reader has gotten to the same place as her.

This story is part of the Xuya universe: it was a finalist for the Hugo award.

"Scattered Along the River of Heaven"

As I mention in the introduction, this is one of the hardest stories I ever wrote. It was deeply and consciously personal in a way that none of the other stuff I'd written previously had been: I felt very much exposed after producing it. It's articulated around poetry, which has a very strong cultural importance: Vietnamese scholars would produce both literature and reflective poems, and there is a long tradition of disgraced scholars writing mournful poetry about being exiled from court.

This is also a story about exile and diaspora, and the way that cultures diverge, both through time and through different choices: Xu Wen's experiences of being lost on San-Tay Prime and the way she considers the bots as an abomination are both examples of this. It's also, obviously, about the aftermath of a revolution and what this means for the factions who won and the factions who lost—and what the bitter choices this entails within the same family.

The division between languages (High Mheng and Low Mheng) is loosely based on the history of Vietnamese, both during French colonial times and the earlier Chinese colonisation: Classical Chinese was used at the court and in formal writing, but a growing body of Vietnamese scholars started using Chữ Nôm (the Southern characters), Chinese characters repurposed to write Vietnamese. This ended when Chữ Nôm was replaced with the alphabet with diacritics designed by de Rhodes (for a variety of reasons including a push from the French colonisers to cut off Vietnam's ties to China).

This story is part of the Xuya universe: it was a finalist for the Sturgeon award.

"Immersion"

This is one of the few stories I wrote from a place of anger, which I don't much like as a source of stories because I find it very draining. It followed the first time I went to Vietnam with my husband (I'd previously gone, but with my family), and it gathers many things I was struck by, in particular the insidious way that western culture continued to eat away at Vietnamese culture, and the matter-of-fact way it was judged superior, and the way that globalisation was another, more subtle form of colonisation.

The immerser is based on guidebooks. We brought a bunch of them to Vietnam with us, and I was struck when reading them on how subtly or largely wrong they were: they were trying to explain a foreign country and culture to a tourist but they couldn't quite seem to understand that the base assumptions they were making got in the way of their explanations. I reprised them into a futuristic version: the immerser, which is meant to help adapt to a foreign culture. They start as a tourist guidebook, but don't remain that way: because the Galactic culture is dominant, the Rong put them on to better understand what the Galactics expect.

I have a fondness for second-person present tense narration, although it can feel alienating and distancing. In this particular case, it was exactly the right decision for Agnes's character, to create that feeling of distance and unease in the reader.

This story is part of the Xuya universe: it was a finalist for the Hugo, and it won the Nebula and the Locus award.

"The Waiting Stars"

This is a mirror story, a structure which I find very appealing because it allows for contrast between two different strands of narrative: it's on the one hand a tense rescue story of a mindship by her descendants, and on the other a more intimate, claustrophobic story of how Catherine grows up as a foundling dependent on Galactic charity. The Catherine sections show the Dai Viet culture as something horrific: the birth segment shown to the students plays out on the horrifying nature of birth. I didn't have to research most of this: I just drew on the courses of preparation to birth I was given when I was pregnant—I'm sure they don't mean to sound like a horror show, but it's quite easy to see how a slight twist to them would change the focus. The condescending charity with strings which leads Johanna to take her life and Catherine to feel so ill at ease with hers is unfortunately an all too real and all too common attitude.

Jason was a bit of a tightrope: he was originally much less sympathetic, but after a discussion with Ken Liu I decided to change him to make him well-meaning and kind—except that he refuses, consistently, to understand where Catherine is coming from, which to me felt like the epitome of barbed kindness.

This story is part of the Xuya universe: it was a Locus Award finalist and won the Nebula award.

"Memorials"

"Memorials" was a very difficult story for me to write: it deals with the way that history changes depending on who writes it, and specifically with how none of the western accounts of Saigon that I read ever seemed to match my own family stories of the city. This isn't surprising as westerners could have very different experiences of the city compared to my family, but it is something that I wanted to write on. I specifically wanted to address the issue of simulated spaces, and how that gap in perception would translate: the Memorial of the story is an alien place to Cam's people, and contrasted with the places memorialised by her family; but it is also the place that the aunts make theirs. That patch of alleyways deeper into the simulation where everything is made right feels very significant to me: as a possibility of changing the simulation, but obviously as a symbol of how Cam's own life shifts away from selling memories and into a different relationship with her own people and with her dead.

The three-colour dessert the aunts are having is chè ba màu, "three-colour che" (chè is a category of desserts which are liquid or semi-liquid: the three colours are red adzuki beans, green pandanus filaments and mung beans for yellow, served in coconut milk thickened by tapioca flour (but there are many variations to get the yellow colour!))

This story is part of the Xuya universe: it was a finalist for the Locus Award.

"The Breath of War"

Like "A Salvaging of Ghosts", "The Breath of War" was commissioned by Scott H. Andrews of *Beneath Ceaseless Skies* for their Science Fantasy month. It is, first and foremost, a story about giving birth and different ways of giving birth, though its roots are in Vietnamese and Chinese legends of jade carving. In particular, the idea that a piece of jade is whittled down until the living core of it is revealed is prevalent in several legends (and master jade carvers can see what kind of thing is within the jade). I flipped the legend slightly, so that the jade carving became the stone-sibling, without which no babies would quicken: a first act of carving and giving birth that conditions all the future births.

Like many of my stories, this is concerned with war, and the effect it has on people: Rechan carves the ship as a way to escape the restrictions of her life and her war-torn planet, but the ship itself is unsuited to planet-life (and to peace!).

I wrote this story not long after giving birth myself, so I still had a fairly good memory of what it had meant to move in the last trimester, and the way that things that used to be obvious suddenly became very difficult with a baby in the womb and regular contractions—all of which is mirrored in what Rechan's character experiences.

This story is part of the Xuya universe, and was a Nebula Award finalist.

"The Days of the War, as Dark as Blood, as Red as Bile"

This was commissioned by Yanni Kuznia for *Subterranean Magazine*, and I wrote it ten days after giving birth to my eldest—I've always had a fond spot for it, but the depths of darkness it probes probably come from not enough sleep and general state of frazzling!

It's a story that was inspired by Tứ Linh, the Four Guardians of the cardinal directions in Vietnamese belief: I thought the galactic empire in the story would have built four ships and named them after the four directions—except that things went tragically wrong during a civil war…

I'd always intended this to go where it ended, but it was hard to bring myself to the ending where everybody died, as I'm not fundamentally nihilist: the entire sequence from Lady Oanh's death to Mother's death was particularly difficult to write. The idea that a child and a rogue weapon would understand each other echoes the sculpting of the stone spaceship in "The Breath of War"—that, in times where everybody dies, it's children who can turn out to be the most ruthless, because they don't always have the inhibitions that adults take for granted, and they have grown in a world where life is fragile and felt the full brunt of this unfairness. I put echoes of "The Ones Who Walk Away from Omelas" in this story as well: that a child is the one making the sacrifices necessary for peace and prosperity—though in the story both of these are rather tentative.

Lady Oanh is a returning character from my novella *On a Red Station, Drifting*, though here she's seen rather older.

"The Dust Queen"

This is a story about memories and what they mean to different people. It's part of a set of very few stories I've written about the near future: it's set on Fire Watch, an orbital around Mars that watches over the slow terraforming of the planet (in Vietnamese, Mars is Sao Hỏa, the Star of Fire, hence the name of the orbital). In the future it's set in, the Mekong Delta sank under the sea following climate change, and was later reclaimed by its people: the model I took for that reclamation was the Netherlands with a hefty helping of science fiction (though there are also major projects in Asia). It's very much background to the main story, but I wanted a future where people were doing their best to turn around the mistakes of the past, and where Bao Lan and the others were given a choice on whether to continue fleeing into space, or to try and heal the destroyed earth.

It's concerned with pain and art, and how that art can in turn be a comfort to other people; though the opposite argument to that runs through the story: in the end, it's insensitivity to pain that allows Tuyet to rewrite Bao Lan the way she has to be—which is also a work of art, though Tuyet won't allow herself to see it that way.

This story was a Locus award finalist.

"Three Cups of Grief, by Starlight"

Neil Clarke commissioned me to write this story for the 100th anniversary of *Clarkesworld Magazine*. I'd always wanted to do something around tea, which is one of my passions: the idea was linking different kinds of teas to different flavours of something else. Due to personal circumstances, this ended up being grief and the different ways people mourn, except with a science fiction twist! As the story progresses, the reader gets progressively further away from the familiar: Quang Tu is human and resentful; Tuyet Hoa is also human but possessed of the barbed legacy of the mem-implants, a way that makes the dead person manifest for her. And *The Tiger in the Banyan* is a mindship: an artificial intelligence vastly more long-lived than humans and as such, doesn't envision the passage of time in quite the same way—and especially doesn't envision memories the same way.

The teas mirror the grief: we move from the lightly steamed green teas, which are lightly steamed and have the most delicate taste, to dark tea (pu ehr), which are fermented teas brewed for a long time. We also move through the legacy of Duy Uyên, from the personal (Quang Tu), to the professional (Tuyet Hoa, though she is also the professor's student, a highly charged relationship in Vietnamese culture), and to a union of the two through *The Tiger in the Banyan*, who sees both the work left behind by her mother but also the moments they spent together away from this work.

This story is part of the Xuya universe: it was a Locus award finalist and won the British Science Fiction Association Award for Best Short Fiction.

"A Salvaging of Ghosts"

This is a companion story to "Three Cups of Grief", which deals with the loss of a child (just as "Three Cups" deals with the death of a parent). When I was writing this story, I wanted to write something in which the dead had become commodities: there's some of that arc in "Memorials", where there is a mention of Perpetuates being taken apart for their memories, but here it's given centre-stage. The original image I had was of a pearl being dissolved in vinegared tea, which is what I reused in many places in the story: the dead themselves being fragmented into gems (I used "gem" to translate the Vietnamese word "ngọc", "precious stone", a term that includes both jade and pearls), the gems sold to people who get drunk on the essence of the dead, and of course that last image of the story, the ghost finally dissolving into darkness. The name of the mindship, *The Boat Sent by the Bell*, is a reference to Buddhist thought: the bell (and frequently the drum) are a call to prayer and enlightenment. The worship of Thuy's mothers has its root in Vietnamese customs as well: many deities are mortals who are raised to immortality through meritorious acts.

This story is part of the Xuya universe: it was a finalist for the Locus Award.

"Pearl"

This story is part of the Xuya universe: it was a Locus Award finalist.

It's a retelling of the legend of Dã Tràng and the pearl, itself an origin story of the sand digger crab (which bears his name in Vietnamese). Dã Tràng is a hunter who is gifted a pearl that enables him to understand all the animals, and which earns him the favour of the king: however, he lost the pearl in the sea, and died exhausting himself to recover it. After death, he was transformed into a tiny crab, which keeps making balls of sand to fill the sea—which the tide catches and disintegrates.

In this retelling, I made Pearl a remora, a low-level artificial intelligence—except that this one isn't built by a man, but rather by other remoras—because they've always spent their time remaking and modifying themselves as necessity dictates, and Pearl feels like the end goal of this. Dã Tràng uses it to catch the eye of the empress, but without understanding what Pearl truly wants...

This was originally half the length it was: I wrote the parts about Dã Tràng's rise to power and the loss of Pearl but felt they didn't add enough to the story and cut them. Navah Wolfe and Dominik Parisien, my editors, felt that the story was terrific space opera but had lost the fairy tale theme they'd been looking for—so I put those bits back in, and the funny thing is that the story ended up working much better for it.

"Children of Thorns, Children of Water"

I wrote "Children of Thorns, Children of Water" as a reward for people who preordered my novel *The House of Binding Thorns*: it's a prequel standalone story which introduces the character of Thuan, the bi dragon prince who is a character in the novel. The crux of this was meant to be a competition to enter House Hawthorn: originally I meant to have my characters kill someone or have some kind of obstacle competition on the Paris rooftops, and I realised that I could do better than what had become a bit of a genre cliché. Hence, the cooking competition (I loved the cake baking competition episode in *My-Hime* and in other animes, and I always thought we needed more stories about The Great Bake Off), which is crucially in teams rather than individually.

I had entirely too much fun looking up recipes which could be adapted to a "cooking under pressure" scenario: though many cake recipes I know would have fitted the bill of "doable", I thought my team of would-be cooks would be more likely to try something a little more challenging: éclairs are iconic but definitely not for the faint of heart, and seldom made at home by amateur cooks. They do, as Leila says, look rather great though!

"Of Birthdays, and Fungus, and Kindness" (original novella)

I wrote this one for fun: it's set in the universe of my alternate Paris, same as "Children of Thorns, Children of Water", except in a different location. I wanted to have something where the main characters from my novel series would find themselves facing something particularly low-stakes, namely the success or failure of a birthday party (though in this case, the political ramifications are a little larger than people being unsatisfied with the quality of the wine), and where things would keep escalating in a semi-comical manner until all-out disaster broke.

It had a lot of difficulties coming together: part of this was that I couldn't nail down the character of Morningstar, until my friend Fran Wilde made me realise that he'd essentially be a large puppy—eager to please, always making things larger and larger, and never understanding that they'd got well past the point where they could be controlled.

The other part was the fungus, which required deeper research: I turned up a lot of cool details that I sadly wasn't able to use, and part of the difficulty was making sure that the fungus could, in the end, be controlled (because it turns out the darned things are rather resilient!)

The character of Darrias features in other stories in the series, and plays a key role in the last novel, *The House of Sundering Flames.*

Copyright